Albert Murray

THE MAGIC KEYS

Albert Murray is the author of *The Omni-Americans, Stomping the Blues, The Hero and the Blues, South to a Very Old Place, Conjugations and Reiterations,* and *From the Briarpatch File.* He is the coauthor of *Good Morning Blues: The Autobiography of Count Basie* and the coeditor of *Trading Twelves: The Selected Letters of Ralph Ellison and Albert Murray.* He lives in New York City.

INTERNATIONAL

THE MAGIC KEYS

Albert Murray

———◆———

THE MAGIC KEYS

VINTAGE INTERNATIONAL
Vintage Books
A Division of Random House, Inc.
New York

FIRST VINTAGE INTERNATIONAL EDITION, JULY 2006

Copyright © 2005 by Albert L. Murray

All rights reserved. Published in the United States by Vintage Books,
a division of Random House, Inc., New York, and in
Canada by Random House of Canada Limited, Toronto.
Originally published in hardcover by Pantheon Books,
a division of Random House, Inc., New York, in 2005.

Vintage is a registered trademark and Vintage International and
colophon are trademarks of Random House, Inc.

The Library of Congress has cataloged the Pantheon edition
as follows:
Murray, Albert.
The magic keys / Albert Murray.
p. cm.
1. African American men—Fiction. 2. Graduate students—Fiction.
3. New York (N.Y.)—Fiction. 4. Married people—Fiction.
5. Young men—Fiction. I. Title.
PS3563.U764M34 2005
813'.54—dc22
2004060128

Vintage ISBN-10: 1-4000-9553-0
Vintage ISBN-13: 978-1-4000-9553-7

Book design by M. Kristen Bearse

www.vintagebooks.com

Printed in the United States of America
10 9 8 7 6 5 4 3 2 1

FOR MOZELLE AND OUR MICHELE

THE MAGIC KEYS

I

The early-morning walls and windows of the fourth-floor apartment were there once more even before you opened your eyes. And outside, the nightlong mid-September drizzle had finally stopped. So you already knew how the neighborhood streets of your part of Greenwich Village and what you would be able to see of the Manhattan skyline would look later on when you came along the sidewalk to the Sixth Avenue bus stop. With your eyes still closed you were also already aware of how the recently rented three-room apartment looked in the dim early-morning daylight.

But before any of that you were already also very much aware of the also and also of who was no longer in bed beside you because you could hear her moving about in the bathroom, and then there was the sound of the shower, which is why I crossed my fingers for good luck once more, thinking, *This many miles from Gasoline Point, this many miles along the way.*

(You do not wake up every morning actually saying or even consciously thinking: and one and two and three and four and one two three four/one two three four plus the also and also of the specific day of the week, month, and year once more. Not as a deliberate or even conscious routine. But the also and also

3

continuity of the pulse of the conventional actuality of the workaday world of clocks and calendars and maps and mileage charts is there even so. As is also the awareness of local landmarks, and thus destinations and aspirations, however obscure, without which chronology itself may well be not only pointless but perhaps also even inconceivable.)

When I heard the softly padding footsteps heading back through the living room to the kitchenette, I still didn't open my eyes. So what was said was not good morning. What was said was seven o'clock. Which was also the way Mama used to say what she used to say to let you know that it was time to rise and wash up and brush up and shine up before breakfast and the first bell of school bell time. *September, September, and this time in New York. The Philamayork of the old Mother Goose mantelpiece clock fireside tell-me-tale times of the long-gone boyhood nights on the outskirts of Mobile, the Alabama Bay city gateway to the Spanish Main and the Seven Seas.*

And also the New York City during the time of the central Alabama college campus clock tower chimes as you heard them through the shrubbery outside the ground-floor periodicals room of the library and beyond the tip-tops of the poplar saplings outside the long second-floor main reading room during study periods; and also as you visualized it in the after-hours darkness of the dormitory lounge when the radio announcers said it the way they used to say it along with the sound of the station signal.

Nor was there anything more evocative of New York as beanstalk castle town of skyscrapers and patent-leather avenues and taxicab horns and motors and subway trains than the Street Scene *score that so many sound tracks for drawing-room comedies used to begin with, the camera panning the skyline from the air and then zooming in on the midtown traffic and people along the sidewalks with the shopping district showcase*

windows sparkling in the background, before settling on the
swanky hotel, apartment building, or town house where you
picked up the story line.

September, September in New York City once more, and this
time also the also and also of Eunice née Townsend now become
Mrs. Me plus the also and also of my graduate school course of
study at New York University off Washington Square and of hers
at Teachers College, Columbia University, up on Morningside
Heights. Eunice Townsend, Eunice erstwhile Townsend who was
there because she was the one above all others ever considered
all the way back to the crepe myrtle yard blossom and dog fennel
meadow days of Charlene Wingate, who said, Not now, Scooter,
and said, I'll tell you when, Scooter, and finally did. But not for
always.

Eunice Townsend, Eunice née but now erstwhile Townsend.
(And also no longer the Nona that she had been nicknamed during her freshman year at State Normal Junior College.) She did
not say anything else to keep me from dozing back off to sleep,
because we had been married and living together for many
weeks then, and she knew that I was already sitting up. Because
she was also very much aware of the fact that I was the way I
was about never being late for anything, and also that with me it
had already become a matter of not being tardy for school bell
time long before it also became the basic principle of road band
bus departure schedules and being dressed up and tuned up and
onstage before curtain time.

Before I opened my eyes I was also aware of the sounds and
aromas of breakfast preparations in the kitchen then. But then,
as also used to happen during school bell days of the week when
it was Mama in the kitchen, and the stove was a wood burner
and the light was from an oil lamp, it was almost as if you were
all alone. Because you had to prove to Eunice as you used to

feel that you had to prove to Mama that you could go out and do whatever you were supposed to do. *Because then I was remembering what book I had been reading the night before and what references I was using and where I stopped and put in the page marker and turned off the light. Which is why I also already knew how the desk would look in the morning light before I opened my eyes and stood up and headed for the bathroom.*

Which is why what I began to think about then were the specific research materials needed for the term paper I was working on. And about how much I preferred looking things up in the New York Public Library up at Fifth Avenue and Forty-second Street to trying to use the crowded university campus library. *New York, New York.* So far the public library was never overcrowded in the mornings and as you worked on your academic exercises you were also aware of being in the midst of the comings and goings of professional scholars, authors, and journalists, many of whom you recognized at first sight. *New York, New York.*

When I stepped out of the shower and began getting dressed, there was the static blurred chatter that was the portable radio chatter that in those days was the equivalent of the New York tabloid newsprint, from which you could foretell the headlines and flash photos that you would see along with the bright covers of the weekly and monthly magazines on the sidewalk stalls on your way across Sheridan Square to the uptown Sixth Avenue bus stop.

We ate breakfast sitting on the high stool at the barlike sideboard shelf attached to the ledge of the wide window that overlooked the backyard patio four flights below and from which you could also see out across the rooftops of many of the old Federal period buildings in that part of town, which had turned out to be less than a ten-minute walk from the University Place and Washington Square corner of the campus.

All of the graduate school sessions for my course of study in the humanities were conducted in the evening in those days. And the special advanced seminars and laboratory sessions in Education for which Eunice had enrolled at Teachers College met in the afternoons. So there was no rush to be in place for morning roll checks, but we kept ourselves on a strict morning timetable anyway, precisely because of all the local attractions in New York City that were not there for you in any conventional university town, where campus activities were the main local attraction. Not that we passed up very many of the not-to-be-missed feature attractions that we could afford from time to time, but otherwise we followed our regular self-imposed Monday through Friday study schedule, even on the mornings we spent studying in the apartment and taking care of domestic chores.

Me and you, I said as I kissed her at the door on my way to the elevator, me and you, which she knew was a jive line that I had picked up from Joe States, the all-star drummer who was also from Alabama and who had become my self-elected mentor the day after I joined the band of the Bossman Himself as a temporary replacement bass player in Cincinnati the week after I graduated from college, because I had told her about him in the first letter I sent back to Alabama, and I began using it as a complimentary close before my initials on all of my letters and tourist postcards to her from then on. And her response when I finally came back south and said it in person was always a play-ful mock pucker as she kissed me back—as if to say, One jive gesture deserves another.

What she said this time was, See you back here for dinner at eight-thirty sharp, Rover Boy. Or for warmed overs if not too long thereafter. After which it's leftovers—but of course there's always the phone. And I said, Hey me, I did time helping to keep time for the Bossman Himself.

Which is why when I came on outside and headed for the bus that morning I was thinking about Joe States again. Good old Joe States from the 'Ham in the 'Bam. *Who was to say what he was to say when the band came back into Manhattan several weeks later, and I took her backstage that first time. Hey, here he is, he said, coming toward us. What did I tell you about this schoolboy statemate of mine! Check it out for yourself, fellows.*

And as I told her he would, the Bossman Himself said, He said you were most beautiful, but he didn't say that you were this beautiful. And she smiled as he gave me an ever-so-father-caliber avuncular wink as he spoke and then he gave her the one for each cheek routine, and Joe States hooking his arm in hers took her in tow to introduce her to everybody else while I talked to the Bossman and then Old Pro, the chief arranger and straw boss in charge of rehearsals. Then there was Milo the road manager, also known as Milo the Navigator, who gave me the rehearsal schedule and address of the hall that they would be using before moving into the recording studio that next week.

Eunice Townsend, Eunice Townsend, Eunice Townsend, Joe States said again at the stage door leading back out into the audience as he had said when he first heard her name when I mentioned her to him shortly after I joined the band in Ohio that June after graduation, which is when he also said, Eunice

Townsend. Sounds like it goes with somebody come from a family that stands for something very special, Schoolboy.

And when I dropped in on them by myself two afternoons later he said, Hey, she's down home all right, Schoolboy. And Aladambama people to boot. How 'bout it, Bloop! And Herman Kemble the big-toned tenor saxophone player from Texas said, Hey, Schoolboy, when you come up with somebody like that, man, you make us all look good and feel good, too. Just like when one of us hits that right note that sounds like something we were all waiting to hear without realizing it before we hear it.

Which ought not to be no big surprise to anybody in this outfit, Osceola Menefee the trumpet player who sometimes doubled as vocalist said. I mean after all, it was just like he was raised to be one of us as soon as he came on board when Shag Phillips had to split. So now he can't help being one of us for the rest of his life, don't care where else he goes or what else he might end up doing for a living. talking about keeping the right time with the right people, Schoolboy. That's the thing about life, just like it's the thing about music.

And that was when Joe States said, Hey yeah, man, but let me tell you something else. About what I'm talking about when I say what I say about being down-home people. I'm talking about somebody got all them knockout cover girl good looks and all that college girl class about her, who I bet you a hundred to one can also step into the kitchen and stir up a batch of some of them old-time Mobile tea cakes. Just like the ones that come from the old Rumford Baking Powder recipe, the ones your mama used to roll out like biscuit dough and cut out with a top of a baking powder can. Man, what I'm talking about is somebody that can do what your mama or your favorite aunt or even your grandma can do, because she's them

*kind of people along with everything else. Hey, and with them
same honey brown fingers that make you realize what all that
diamond and gold stuff in Tiffany's is really made for. One
hundred to one, first come, first served, and I know my bet is
safe because I know my main man here.*

On the bus rolling uptown from Fourth Street along Sixth Avenue I began thinking about how Miss Lexine Metcalf would be
most likely to feel when she found out that I was back in school
again; and I was pretty certain that I knew what she would tell
her present group of students at Mobile County Training School
about me and I hoped that they felt the way I always felt about
her because she was the one who made me realize that the also
and also of school bell time was not as different from the also and
also of Miss Tee's storybook times in Mama's rocking chair
and yarn-spinning time in Papa Gumbo Willie McWorthy's
barbershop as I and perhaps the majority of people had taken for
granted because of the stern sound of period bells and harsh
actuality of passing and failing grades.

As the bus rolled on toward Herald Square I was thinking
about how Miss Lexine Metcalf was also the one who made it a
point to keep reminding me every now and then even when I
was still in junior high school that I should never forget that I
just might be one of the very special ones who would have to
travel far and wide to find out what it is that I may have been
put here on earth to make of myself.

Which is why as we came on through the intersection of
Broadway and Sixth Avenue at Thirty-fourth Street, I was also
thinking about my old roguish-eyed freshman and sophomore
roommate again who, when I told him about what Miss Lexine
Metcalf used to say about faring forth, said, hithering, thithering,

and yondering, picaresquely but not quixotically, one hopes. Because in quest and maybe even conquest rather than serendipity. Because such a quest is for clues, my good man. That Miss Lexine Metcalf of yours is right on target.

And so was my Miss Jewel Templeton of Hollywood, when she said what she said in the south of France about magic keys (some sharp, some flat, some natural; some solid gold, some sterling silver, some perhaps even platinum, or in fact of any other alloy, whether already in existence or yet to come).

And so also was my good old roommate himself with his yea, verily as he scribbled each entry in the notebook in which he recorded evidence that he called the goods that added up to his personal estimate of the situation for the time being. So was he on target, who was the one who said what he said about necessity being the mother of the invention of fathers and who was also to say what he said about the function of father figures as symbols of direction and thus also of detours.

At the Forty-second Street stop I used the rear exit, and as I came along the sidewalk past Bryant Park and up the steps to the side entrance to the library I was still thinking of my old roommate and I wondered how long it would take his next letter from wherever he was to get to me from the last forwarding address that I had sent to his last forwarding address, and I couldn't help guessing what he would say about my being back in school and about my new roommate.

I took the elevator up to the third floor and came around the corner and along the hall and turned into the old card index area. Then from the checkpoint for the south wing of the main reading room I could see that I had arrived in time to get the table and seat that I had already become used to settling into as if into my own private cubicle.

II

By the first week in October I began to feel that I was getting used to being back on an academic schedule once again without really missing a beat and that I was also beginning to be used to staying on in New York City longer than the three- to fourteen-day periods that I had spent working there from time to time when I was with the band. Because back then sometimes it would be on a three-day stopover for a dance and maybe a two-day recording session, or maybe one or two days for working over new material followed by one solid day of takes with very few retakes as insurance against studio equipment flaws. Or sometimes we would spend all three days in the studio because the Bossman and Old Pro would begin recording as soon as we got set up the first morning and keep on adding unscheduled old numbers because the new items had taken less time than they had estimated, and sometimes also because they both wanted to take advantage of the mood the band was in that day.

You could always count on that outfit rising to the occasion in response to an enthusiastic audience in a dance hall, in a first-run movie showcase theater or at an outdoor festival or picnic. But there were also times when they sounded extra special not in response to an extra-special reception but to show their supporters that they didn't take them for granted, indeed that they would come on just as strong for a midweek audience at a one-night stand in some obscure down-home roadside joint as they had been heard doing on records and live coast-to-coast radio broadcasts. But sometimes they would also hit a very special groove just because they were having such a good time listening to themselves. *You hear these thugs, Joe States would say to me at such times. Can you believe that this bunch of granny dodgers can really team up and get to you like this? Boy, this so-called Bossman of ours is a goddamn genius. Man, what can I tell you. Man, who else can take a bunch of splibs as mixed up as this crew we got and get them each to enjoy hearing themselves and then turn around and have everybody else do the same thing one by one. Man, my money says very few people have ever seen anything like these splibs this man has making his kind of music.*

All of which is to say that I had been to New York as many times as I had been there while I was with the band but never long enough for me to feel that it was home base, as I had thought it would be when I left Alabama to join the tour in Cincinnati. It was not a New York band as the Earl Hines band was a Chicago band and as Benny Moten and Andy Kirk had been Kansas City and Southwest Territory bands along with Troy Floyd and Alphonso Trent, or as King Oliver's bands would always be remembered as New Orleans bands. It was not a regional band but a cosmopolitan band, and its home base was a city that was cosmopolitan rather than regional. As Paris and Rome and London were cosmopolitan rather than regional. You could feel it as soon as you arrived, just as you had anticipated you would. But before there was time to begin to really get with it, as you had gradually become used to being a college freshman and then sophomore and eventually an upperclassman on the campus down in central Alabama, you were back out on the road again, getting used to not being used to being somewhere else.

Not that I had ever actually decided that I was going to make New York City the place of my permanent and official residence one day. I had thought of being at home there as I had also come to think of the possibility of getting to feel at home in Los Angeles and Hollywood and then perhaps in Paris and on the Côte d'Azur and also in Rome and in London. But that was not at all the same as choosing the place where you would eventually settle down for good, which many, maybe most, people do years before their thirtieth birthday.

As a matter of fact, even as I used to listen and realize that the Philamayork of the blue steel, rawhide, and patent-leather yarns being unspooled once again during fireside and swing porch tell-me-tale-time sessions, I also realized that it was also yet another homespun version for the fairy-tale castles I already knew about from rocking-chair storybook times. And it now seems to me that on some subconscious level of awareness I also knew even then that sometimes a fairy-tale castle was no less a point of departure than a point of arrival. Which is precisely what I had found New York City to be when I was a member of the band, *the castle town from which the Bossman and his merrymakers like the dukes of derring-do of yestertimes were forever sallying forth to encounter and contend with the invisible and indestructible dragons of gloom and doom once again and again.*

I knew all that very well. And yet getting to feel like a New Yorker among other New Yorkers (a very significant number of whom had as I was also very much aware grown up elsewhere not only across the nation but also around the globe) was the main reason I had decided to come to do my graduate work in

New York City and not in New England, the Midwest, or any-where in the Far West or out on the Pacific coast.

And it was also why I did most of my library research for assignments at the public library rather than on the campus at Washington Square. In fact, I used the excellent university library only when certain references that professors had put on special reserve status were not also available in the public collection at Forty-second Street, which was not very often, the point not being that it was as if the New York Public Library was really a part of NYU but rather that it was not. Not to me, at any rate. To me it was to big-league research technicians and world-class scholars and intellectuals what Yankee Stadium and Madison Square Garden were to championship-caliber athletes.

There was, as I not only realize and acknowledge now but also as my old roommate and I were completely and admittedly aware from the outset and at every turn even then, an entirely obvious element of make-believe in a considerable amount in everything we did as undergraduate students. And we were also very much aware of the fact that our playing around with notions of medieval scholarship and the Renaissance workshops of the likes of Benvenuto Cellini, Michelangelo, and Leonardo da Vinci, the polymath, led other students to respect our sincerity and dedication. To them it was an act, a jive tune, a put-on.

And as for our identification with life in the grimy garrets of bohemian Paris, not with berets and goatees but with plain gray extra-large sweatshirts symbolizing smocks that made being in college on scholarship merit awards (but in my case mostly without pocket change or even bus fare for a two-hundred-mile trip to Mobile for Christmas) more a matter of bohemian glamour and vagabond adventure and romance than of the grinding poverty that it undeniably was.

But when I arrived in New York that September, being a graduate student was another matter altogether. So much so that the fact that I was now actually living in Greenwich Village, the legendary center for bohemian life in the United States, had much less to do with what I had read by and about the generation of Edna St. Vincent Millay, Maxwell Bodenheim, E. E. Cummings, Max Eastman, and the like than with New York friendships I had made backstage or in nightclubs when I was in town as a member of the band. And besides, along with the time that I had spent doing what I had been doing since leaving the campus in central Alabama, there was also the fact that I had now become a man with a wife.

Perhaps for some of those who go directly from the bachelor's degree to the master and sometimes the doctorate programs, often on the same campus and sometimes with some of the same professors, the break was not as obvious as it was for those who took time out to teach for a while or did something else, as I did before enrolling as a graduate student. In any case, I had decided that graduate-level academic work was really a special form of adult education, and as such there was something part-time about it even when you were enrolled in a full-time course of study that you were expected to complete in a scheduled (even though not strictly required) time frame.

What I really had in mind when I decided that the time had come for me to register for a graduate course of study that year was not a specific profession, but what Miss Lexine Metcalf had kept repeating to me when I reached senior high school because that was when you really began competing not only for college eligibility ranking, but also for scholarship grants, some special few of which were not only for tuition but also for room and board. And it was also at this point in the Mobile County Training School program for upward-bound early birds that vocational guidance sessions began to focus on individual career choices, which in due course also became a matter of the choice of your first, second, and third preference as to the college you hoped to attend, given your final grade-point average and your financial means. Which in my case was a matter of a high grade-point-average eligibility and high faculty recommendation and hardly any financial means whatsoever. As she well knew but only regarded as a challenge to my ingenuity and no great one at that. Certainly not for the sort of splendid young man that she herself always led me to believe that she thought I was, or that she was still counting on me to become, as she had begun doing when she became my homeroom teacher when I reached the third grade. Which was the beginning of geography books and maps and the globe and the sand table projects and windows on the world bulletin board displays of peoples and customs of many lands. That was where and when it had begun between her and me. And she was the one who even so early on as that had already earmarked me as a likely prospect for Mr. B. Franklin Fisher's early bird list of candidates for the Mobile County Training School extracurricular program for the talented tenth, who according to his doctrine of uplift and ancestral imperative were the hope and glory of the nation. It was the early birds from whom he expected the most immediate and consummate response to his exhortation to so conduct, *nay, acquit yourselves in all of your undertakings that generations yet unborn will rise at mention of your name and call you blesséd.*

Incidentally, it was Mr. B. Franklin Fisher, the principal and thus the *man* as in the *big man* and *bossman,* but who looked like a boy evangelist, who was the one who spoke of ancestral imperatives in national and also in ethnic terms, such as our nation and our people and our people in this nation, whereas

Miss Lexine Metcalf never said who else among our people if not you, but who else in the whole wide world if not you. Which is why hers was the school bell time voice that I always found myself responding to even as I had always that of Miss Tee's rocking-chair storybook time voice and as I had also already been responding to the baby talk voice of Mama herself calling me her little mister scootabout man *out there among them!* Which is why Miss Tee also called me little mister man and then my mister. *Hello, my mister. You, too, my mister. You can, too, my mister.*

But it was when Mr. B. Franklin Fisher, whose pulpit eloquence with its reverberations of Henry Ward Beecher and Abraham Lincoln, Frederick Douglass, Booker T. Washington, and W. E. B. Du Bois and ranging from down-to-earth aphorism to silver-tongued oratory as the occasion required, delivered another one of his ancestral imperative pep talks that you heard the school bell time equivalent to the ethnic and political concerns that you had come to know about and identify with from all the talk and signifying that also went with all the tales, tall and otherwise, from the fireside, porch swing, and even on the front stoop and around the hot stove near the cracker barrel in Stranahan's General Merchandise Store on Buckshaw Mill Road.

All of that was what Mr. B. Franklin Fisher was best known and celebrated for. Whereas with Miss Lexine Metcalf, as with Miss Tee and with Mama, you did what you had to do because that was what growing up into full manhood was all about. And yet even when she insisted that you had to go on beyond high school as she did when you were in the ninth grade, she never was to say which college or what for. Nor did Mr. B. Franklin Fisher himself, who after all was not only the ultimate approval authority on college eligibility and scholarship grants at Mobile County Training School, but also had a record as an expert on vocational guidance that was unchallenged. When he referred to himself as a fisher of humankind, a spotter of prospects, and a molder of heroes and nation-builders, nobody ever took issue, not even in private. In public, the response was always applause, which became a standing ovation.

Still, not even he, with whom my status as an early bird was second to none and who was forever predicting to the student body at large that I would become one who would accomplish something that would make me a credit to my people and the nation, acknowledged or not during my lifetime, but would enjoy the high regard of generations yet unborn even so. *All I ask of this one, he said on commencement day, as if keeping a promise to Miss Lexine Metcalf, is that he always do his best. Not even he ever gave the slightest hint of a suggestion as to what my career field would be.*

Meanwhile, Miss Lexine Metcalf was the one who never stopped reminding me that I might just be one of those whose destiny was to travel far and wide in order to find out what it was that I should try to make of myself in the first place. Which she had begun to do when I reached the third grade and the first-year geography book that you had to have for the homework to go along with the maps on the wall rack with the globe and the displays on the bulletin board better known as windows on the world, and also the sand-table cutout mock-up projects that made her classroom seem like a department store toyland from time to time.

That was where she began, and it was as if she were my own private Mobile County Training School guardian from then on, because all of my subsequent homeroom teachers and officially designated class sponsors deferred to her on all matters concerning me. As did Mr. B. Franklin Fisher himself. Or so it still seems to me. Because I still cannot remember any special project that he ever assigned me to be responsible for or any award that he recommended me for that had not already been discussed with her beforehand. But then I had been *her* special candidate for his early bird initiatives program in the first place.

Whatever she said to him, to me she always said, Who if not you? Who if not you, my splendid young man, who if not you? Who if not you may have to go where you will go and find out what you will find out, whatever you will find out? To me she also said, You will know you are where you should be by the way you feel, where you should be for the time being; at any rate she also said because such was the also and also of whatever you do wherever you are.

All of which is also why she had also come so immediately to mind along with Mama and Miss Tee when my old roommate read to me the passage from *Remembrance of Things Past* that he was recording in his notebook, the passage in which Marcel Proust has an artist tell the narrator that *we do not receive wisdom, we must discover it for ourselves, after a journey through the wilderness that no one else can make for us, that no one else can spare us, for our wisdom is the point of view from which we come at last to view the world.*

Which I also find to be entirely consistent with the behavior of Miss Tee toward me, especially as it struck me after I found out the secret about how she came to be in Gasoline Point that I didn't know about until the night I awoke on the front porch in Stranahan's Lane during Mr. Ike Meadow's wake and kept my head in Mama's lap as if I were still asleep.

So yes, on the outskirts of Mobile, Alabama, where I come from, you were indeed weaned from the home to be bottle-fed by teachers, but from these same teachers you also learned that you had to prepare and also condition yourself to assume total responsibility for yourself, *because once you graduated and went out into the world, you were on your own.* And who if not Mr. B. Franklin Fisher himself for all of his community uplift and vocational guidance expertise always ended his annual commencement address by reminding the graduating class that it was going out into the real world equipped with what really amounted to a compass, a knapsack, and a notebook or chapbook *(for what my old best of all possible college roommates was to call the goods).*

III

So you decided to get yourself back on some school bell time for a while, hey statemate, Joe States said as we waited for our orders to be served that afternoon of the day before the band headed back out west by way of upstate New York and a swing over into Canada to Montreal, Ottawa, and Toronto after its second trip back into town that fall.

I had come up from the Forty-second Street library and he had come across and down Sixth Avenue from the recording studio the band was using on Forty-eighth Street about halfway to Seventh Avenue and Times Square, and which was also only a few doors from the music store from which he had always bought most of his drum equipment over the years.

I can dig it, he said. And so can the boss and Old Pro and everybody else I spoke to. But what the hell, I don't have to enumerate and elaborate and all that because I'm satisfied that you really know more about them than they actually know about you. Because you came in with us already checked out on us all the way back to our first records and broadcasts. I just want you to know there's not just only me and the man and Old Pro.

Because hey, man, these cats know a special thing when they see it and they pegged you special from day one. And the thing about how you laid that bass in there with us right from the get-go. That let everybody know that you had your own personal way of listening. Everybody in every section felt like you heard every note they were playing. Because you see, now, me, sometimes my job is to make them get to *me*. And the way you laid your thing in there helped them stay with the man and me. Man, you could have had that job for as long as you wanted it. I mean, even if Shag Phillips had wanted to come back we'd have had two basses. And if you'd wanted to come back we would have had two, you and Scratchy.

Hey, but the thing I'm really getting at, he said as the waiter served our orders, is not just how you fit in the band. I'm talking about how much these guys respect your judgment. Believe me, these cats will lay money on anything you decide to try. And of course that also means if you need some bills, get to us first. Don't hesitate. Get to us first. *Get to us fast.*

We were in a restaurant that he had first taken me to one night between shows back during the first week of the run we had had in that showcase theater in Times Square with Earlene Copeland as our featured vocalist. He used it when he wanted to get away from the showbiz crowd he ran into in the snack bars in or near Times Square and along Broadway up to Columbus Circle. We both had ordered oxtail soup and a mixed green salad and pumpernickel bread, which was still something of a New York City novelty for me in those days.

But now what I'm also to make sure you understand is that every cat in this crew knows exactly what the Bossman and Old Pro were talking about when they said what they said when you stayed behind in Hollywood. As we pulled on out to the end of the freeway and headed into the open country again I went up to talk to them and feel them out. And guess what? The goddamn Bossman sounded like he was more concerned about how much I was going to miss having you to be clucking at and carrying on over than the effect on the music. But finally he also said, You know something, Joe? As much as we all liked having him in here doing his special little thing with us, he just might turn out to be somebody that can do us even more good out there doing his thing on his own. And Old Pro said, Whatever his thing turns out to be, I'm sure that what we're trying to do in this outfit is going to be an important part of it. That's been my idea about him ever since he decided to put off going right on into graduate school at the end of that first summer. Mark my words.

Now me myself, Joe States said as we buttered our bread and started in on the thick, meaty oxtail soup, as far as I can figure it out I myself was put on this earth to make music. This music we play. So what else can I tell you, my man? I'm lucky. Hell, when you come right down to the facts of life, I really owe this band. And the only way I can pay my debt is by always giving the Bossman my best, and I'm also going to do what I can to have somebody else ready to fill my shoes when the time comes.

That was also the afternoon that he told me what he told me because he wanted to remind me of several other details of his special slant on the facts of life that he had begun clueing me in on as the band bus circled down into Kentucky and back up into Ohio, rolled on across to West Virginia, and Pennsylvania on the meandering route to the one-night dance stands we were booked for beginning the weeks following the June morning on which I arrived in Cincinnati.

One thing is for damn certain, Schoolboy, he had already gone on to say during one of those early-on open-road sessions, as far as I am concerned, I for one was definitely not put here on this planet among all these possibilities just to spend my time and whatever little talent I might have going around bellyaching because some paleface somich don't like me as much as I might think he ought to. Hell, me? If somebody don't like me, I don't like him right back, and if we tangle and the somich don't do me in for good, I'm sworn to get him back if it's the last thing I do. Me, I don't look for no trouble. And I don't run from it either, once I'm in it.

But what I'm really getting at, he had also made sure to remind me, is doing your thing. Look, here's what I'm really trying to tell you, my man. You're not out here to prove that some used-to-be little snotty-nosed kid from the outskirts of Mobile, Alabama, can impress some puffed-up somiches just on some old principles from back during slavery time and Reconstruction. You're out here to find out what you can make of yourself in this day and age. So don't give up until you make sure you're on the wrong track. And on the other hand, don't get faked out by a lot of applause too early on, either.

He let me think about that for a while as we went on enjoying our soup and salad. Then he said, So how you making out with these up here splibs, homeboy? You remember what I told you during those rookie sessions I made it my personal obligation to put you through?

And I said, Never is to forget any part of any days like that, Papa Joe. You being a statemate to boot and all. And even as I spoke I found myself remembering exactly how he had looked when he pushed his bus seat all the way back in reclining position. *Because it made him look exactly like a not-quite-middle-aged general merchandise storefront bench Uncle Bud, Doc, Mose, or Remus who might well have been taking a snooze in Mr. Slim Jim Perkins's vacant barber's chair number three in Papa Gumbo Willie McWorthy's Tonsorial Parlor*

up on *Buckshaw Mill Road across the lane from Stranahan's General Merchandise Store on Mr. Slim Jim Perkins's
day off.*

*And as he went on saying what he was saying, I was aware
once again of that ever so subtle wisp of his Yardley's English
Lavender brilliantine and of the fact that he, like Jo Jones
of Count Basie's band and Sonny Greer of Duke Ellington's,
was an expert twenty-mule-team skinner who never seemed to
work up a heavy sweat, which also reminded me of how redo-
lent of bay rum and the aftershave talcum brush mist along
with the cigar smoke and shoe polish the atmosphere in Papa
Gumbo Willie McWorthy's used to be. Then by the time I was
on my way through the last year of junior high school, there
was the precollegiate atmosphere of Shade's up on Green Avenue across from Boom Men's Union Hall Ballroom, where the
hair and skin preparations came from the same downtown
Mobile haberdasheries that carried the latest fashions you saw
in* Esquire *magazine, which by then had become the sartorial
bible of the man about town.*

Man, these up here splibs, he had said one morning on the
road. Man, them and us, and us and them. Man, especially when
it comes to these up here jaspers. My experience is that as soon
as they hear that you're from somewhere down home they're
subject to come on like the fact that they're from somewhere
up here automatically gives them some kind of status over you,
especially if you ask them something about something, and
I'm not talking about asking them *for* something. Boy, but as
soon as they find out that there's a bunch of jaspers carrying on
about you, man, that's another tune. Man, you go from cotton-
chopping pickaninny to street-corner hangout buddy buddy just

like that! But now, on the other hand, it looks like some of *their* jaspers might want to get next to *you*, watch out!

Because, you see, he had also said during another of one of our early-on sessions, speaking of these up here jaspers, man, the problem with *them folks* is how many of them can't tell one of us from the other after all. And these up here splibs figure we're bound to spot how easy it is for almost any old dog-ass splib to take them in like netting mullets in a goddamn barrel. That's the big secret. Ain't nothing a bigger mullethead than a benevolent up here jasper. Man, the hype they lay on these people is a sin and a shame. But the scandal of it is that it's mostly just about some chicken feed, or some goofy broad that don't even wear no drawers.

I dropped some pretty heavy stuff on you, right from the get-go, my man, he said as I chuckled to myself, remembering. You being a college boy and all, he said, and you listened like a bass player is supposed to listen. And I told the Bossman, I can see why we can hang this whole thing on a kid like him. I said he's not only a quick study, he's somebody that's been on his way to getting on our kind of time even before he was old enough to know that he could tell the difference between us and somebody else. Which was a hell of a long time before you realized that for us this stuff is not just a job but a calling. Which is another thing that makes for the great big difference between this man's band and all the others.

That was also when he began saying what he was to say about another thing that he along with a number of others, none of them schoolteachers as such, incidentally, used to remind you of in one way or another from time to time back in the days when I was coming of age but also stretching all the way back to as far as I can remember. Sometimes they called it quality. And sometimes they called it class.

What he had said about that back when he filled me in on "the character of the cast of characters in this man's lineup" was that it was something more than education, and not a matter of birth and family background and how much money you could live on or get to back you up. All of that might give you some clout of one kind or another. But class don't need clout. Class is its own clout, young fellow, and it's pretty much the same with hustle. Because you see the thing of it is that class and hustle don't really go together. It's a matter of being on the ball, on the money, on the minute without coming on like an eager beaver. Man, what I'm talking about is also being able to miss the cue, miss the mark, and still hold your own and not lose anybody's respect and faith in you. In school you've been thinking mostly in terms of passing or failing, but out here, in the everyday here and now, it's also very much a matter of whether you can also lose or fail and still have people betting on you on the next go-round.

Which reminds me that it was also during those initiation sessions he used to continue between naps as the bus zoomed on and on through the open country that he began telling about what he told me about the big con, which was his word for the confidence games that certain hustlers play. There were two main kinds of con artists or slickers, he said. Most people knew about the first kind. Now that somich is an acknowledged criminal and a cold pro. And when he takes risks, the odds are always in his favor, no blind bets, no coin flipping. The deck is always stacked. But now there is also that other kind of con man. Now this somich begins by conning himself into believing that he can con everybody else. All he's got to do is get up enough nerve to give it a try with a straight face. He's like a gate-crasher. In fact, he really *is* a gate-crasher and a self-effacing flatterer at the same time, and I mean to the point of begging and groveling.

And the thing about a somich like that is that he really forgets that he's conned himself. That he's a lying phony. Because once he gets his lie started he gets so deep into it that he believes it himself. Which is why he can get all tangled up in contradictions. A cold-blooded somich never forgets he's lying. This cat just might.

Along with all of the bus sessions out on the open road during those first months, there had also been all of those backstage tips, and after-hours and off-day rounds of pop calls, introductions, and briefings for future personal as well as professional reference. Not to mention all of the ongoing fill-in data not only on each section, but also on each sideman's approach to every tune in the book for the current tour. There was also Old Pro's preliminary technical breakdowns, but once the number was kicked off onstage, he (Joe States), being the mule skinner, was no less responsible for locking things in as the Bossman wanted than the Bossman Himself. You know that old jive about his nose itching and me sneezing, well, you better believe it, Schoolboy, because when I sneeze from now on, you poot—not just by the numbers, my man, but by *my* numbers.

Ever so often when he was passing on another personal background clue for somebody's part on a tricky passage, he would wink and say, Of course you already know what every last one of these cats in this lineup is about speaking in just musical terms. But what we don't ever let any newcomer to this outfit forget is that we don't just play music in this man's band, we play life. L-I-F-E, as in flesh and blood. And me and you and old Spodeody and the man make the difference between metronome time and pulse. Like I told you. Metronome time is mathematics, Schoolboy. Pulse is *soul.* Talking about the rhythm and tempo of life as *the folks* came to know it and live it in *downhome* U.S. of A. Talking about stuff them other folks at first thought was just some more old countrified stuff like talking flat because you cain't spell and articulate and cain't write!

As we came back outside the restaurant and headed along the sidewalk to Sixth Avenue that autumn afternoon in New York, he said, So, now tell me how things are going with them fine people you're camping with, my man. And when I gave him the old OK fingers crossed sign, he said, The unanimous impression back on the old Greyhound is that she just might have what it takes to make a real man out of our schoolboy. Not that any of us think you don't know what you're doing. Man, we're just backing your solo like jamming on a tune you called. Because we figure it'll do you good to hear some amen corner backup every now and then. Especially coming from that bunch of thugs we got in that crew.

Then as we clasped shoulders and stepped back before he turned to head up along Sixth Avenue to Forty-eighth Street, he raised his hands as if about to whisper a last word in the italics of the ride cymbal and said, Daddy Royal, homeboy. Remember Daddy Royal. He's there for you, homeboy. Get to him fast. Get to him fast. Express time, Schoolboy.

IV

O n my way up Fifth Avenue from the library to the Gotham Book Mart at 41 West 47th Street about a week and a half after the band had hit the road out of New York that mostly bright blue and mildly breezy autumn, I overtook somebody I had not seen since my freshman year in college. I had not really gotten to know him back then, because he was an upperclassman, two years ahead of me, and had not come back to complete his senior year, by which time I had come to be on fairly casual speaking terms with most of the more advanced students that I was most curious about. I did know that he was enrolled in the school of music and that he often served as the student concertmaster who conducted the band when it backed up the cheerleaders during athletic events in the campus bowl and field house. But I recognized his walk as soon as I saw him moving along up the sidewalk about ten yards ahead of me.

He was doing his own individual sporty-almost-limp variation of the marching band trumpet player's parade ground strut. I still don't remember having thought or wondered about him after I myself left the campus, but suddenly there he was again, posture correct but shoulders a little less rigid than an eager beaver infantry cadet, right leg with an ever so slightly but unmistakable hint of a drag, which added up to not quite the prance and not quite the lope that anticipate ponies posting on the right diagonal, so that in mufti the effect was that of a civilian musician rather than a military band man.

As I picked up my stride to overtake him I realized that I remembered his name from that long ago although I had never used it to address him person to person. Because the only verbal encounters I ever had with him were when he was on duty as a student assistant checking books in and out at the circulation desk in the main reading room of the library.

Each time, he looked at my name and stamped my slip and filed the card and pushed the book gently toward me and said, Handle with care. And all I said was, Thanks. Now as I came up close enough behind him on Fifth Avenue that many school terms later, I still didn't call him by name. What I said in my old roommate's mock conspiratorial stage sotto voce was, *Hey, let that goddamn bucket down right there where you at, old pardner. You know what the man said!*

And as if we were rehearsing the sequence in a theater piece he turned and looked at me, not in recognition, but as if more amused than surprised and said, What say, man! How are things down the way? And I said, Still in process, man, still in process, and told him my name and my class years, and that was when I said, Edison, Taft Edison. Taft Woodrow Edison. And he shook his head and said, What can I tell you, man. What can I tell you. My folks were big on newsworthy names. All I can do is try to make mine mean what I want it to mean so that when somebody drops it in there on me it sounds as if it belongs as much to me as to that son of a bitch Wilson, if you know what I mean.

And I said, I think so. And then, looking at the attaché case he was carrying, I said, Hey, but man, that don't really look like no bucket I ever did see either on land or at sea, and no trumpet case, either. Is that some sheet music and your batons or something in there?

And he said, Man, that trumpet stays in the same case I had back on the campus. Same trumpet, same case. And when I said, So what's up, man? He said, Man, I really don't think of myself as a musician anymore. My big thing now is trying to find out what my interest in composition and orchestration can do for me as an apprentice writer, man.

Which didn't really surprise me, since I for one had always seen him most often not in the music area of the campus but either in the library or on his way to or from Professor Carlton Poindexter's survey course in the novel. He had not been a member of either of the two student dance orchestras, but I did remember seeing him and hearing him from time to time in the brass section of the chapel orchestra. So not only was I not surprised but even before he said what he said I realized that he had been an upperclassman who had always come to mind above all others when I thought about advanced reading courses, even after he had left campus.

What did surprise me somewhat was the way he was dressed. I had also remembered him as one of the upperclassmen who, not unlike my roommate, dressed in the collegiate style that I most admired in the fashion magazines: three-button tweed jacket with patch pockets and welt-seamed lapels, usually with contrasting tan twill or gray flannel pleated slacks and no hat. You stopped wearing hats and caps at Mobile County Training School in those days by the time you became a junior, knowing, however, that if you went to college you were going to have to wear a beanie or "crab" cap during your freshman year.

Now on Fifth Avenue he was wearing a snap brim brown felt hat, a three-piece Brooks Brothers business suit, wing-tipped shoes (which brought back to mind the two-toned moccasins and plain-toed brown crepe sole shoes back on the campus), tattersall shirt with a solid tie. All of which along with the fine leather attaché case he was carrying gave him the look that I thought of as being post–Ivy League Madison Avenue and/or Wall Street. Not that there wasn't also an unmistakable touch of uptown hipness about the way he wore it all even so.

I said, Damn, man, that just might turn out to be old BTW's freshwater bucket after all. And that was when he said, Man, if I could bring this stuff off that I hope I've got coming along in this briefcase, it just might turn out to be not just a bucket of whatever it is but a whole keg of it. Maybe some dynamite, among other things. He chuckled as if to himself and I smiled and waited and then he said, Man, when them people find out what I think they're up to down there on that campus I just might have to carry myself some kind of automatic weapon around in this thing to protect myself from their network of fund-raisers.

I didn't say anything about that, because at that time I had never really concerned myself about the overall educational policies of any given college. Once I realized that Harvard, Yale, and Princeton were out of the question so far as my undergraduate student days were concerned, the main thing that mattered to me was what range of liberal arts courses would be available wherever I was able to go. My alternative undergraduate choices had been Morehouse, Talladega, and Fisk in that order, but once I was all signed up and beginning class sessions, especially with Mr. Carlton Poindexter, and settling in with my polymath of a roommate, I had been operating on the principle that everything was up to me and I was on my way.

He (Taft Edison) chuckled to himself again and then he said, But man, that's not really what this stuff in this bag is really about. Not really and certainly not only. In fact, only incidentally. When I cut out from down there that spring, I really intended to go back and finish. But by the end of that summer I had changed my mind not only about music but also about my whole outlook on life. And while I was trying to figure out what I really wanted to do with myself I fell back on a few things I used to play around with, beginning all the way back in my first classes in the general science laboratory. I guess you could say that I became a jack-legged gadgeteer who became good enough tinkering around with photography, radio and sound system repair to keep enough coming in for room and board and decent changes of clothes. And I've also shipped out with the merchant marine from time to time.

Meanwhile, he said after nodding to somebody waving to him from across the street, I've also been doing a little journalism, mostly freelance, that doesn't add up to enough to live on, but as of now I'm managing by hook or crook to bring in enough to allow me to spend more and more time playing around with notes and sketches I'm lugging around in this thing.

And as I looked at it again I decided that it was the same type of expensive attaché case that was used by globe-trotting diplomats and that it made him seem even farther ahead of me as an advanced Manhattanite than he had been as an upperclassman back on the campus down in central Alabama.

Then it seemed to me that when he said what he said next, it was as if he had decided to change the subject because what had suddenly come back to mind was a matter that he had been concerned with time and again and that was no less personal than it was intellectual. People, man, he said. They don't really see you. There you are, right there in front of them, or beside them and you think they're looking at you and they don't see you, close up, full view, multiple takes.

I was not sure that I knew what his point was, so all I said was, And they don't always hear you either, man. Then I said,

Sometimes they do at least recognize you by name on sight. But let them repeat something you're supposed to have told them about something and you just might not recognize anything that you ever told anybody about anything at any time in your whole life.

I let it go at that because I decided that he was really only musing about some note he had made or was planning to make on one of the scratch pads that I assumed he always carried either in his jacket pocket or along with the other papers in his briefcase. I remember thinking that maybe it was somewhat like people translating what they think they are hearing when they listen to a foreign language. Their vocabulary reveals the limitations of their conception of things. *(Which suddenly reminded me of old Joe States looking at somebody out on the dance floor and whispering, Man, don't tell that cat he ain't swinging, He really feels like he's swinging his old butt off, and he can't even stay in time with most of them other folks out there. It's all in his own head, man, he said. And then when he said, You got a textbook word for that kind of psychological jive, Schoolboy, and I said, I don't know, maybe solipsism, he said, No better for him.)*

We were standing at the northwest corner of Fifth Avenue and Forty-seventh Street. And when I stuck out my hand before heading for the bookstore, and he said, So what about yourself?, I assumed he was asking more out of the good manners of his down-home upbringing than out of any genuinely personal curiosity, So all I said was that I was checked into graduate classes in the humanities at New York University after two plus years of knocking around to accumulate a little graduate scholarship supplement, among other things.

At that time I didn't mention anything at all about the time I had spent with the Bossman Himself. It crossed my mind, but

I decided against saying anything about it, not only because I didn't remember him as having any special interest in that kind of music back on the campus, but also because there was no reason to expect him to have any special curiosity about any particular details of my background. When I had mentioned that I was from the outskirts of Mobile, for instance, he didn't say anything about the marching bands of the Mardi Gras parades or about jook joint piano players or about itinerant guitar players. Which didn't surprise me because when I thought about him and music I really thought of conservatory musicians who tended to regard road band and nightspot musicians as being inadequately trained entertainers.

As he turned to continue his way on up along Fifth Avenue, he said, Well, welcome to the city of the fables and the flesh-pots, man. Then he said, Maybe we can get together and swap some lies long and short about the old country. I'm in the phone book.

And when I said I just might take you up on that, he said, Some down-home lies in and out of school, foul mouth or fancy tongue, about all this stuff. And I said, I'm for it, man.

On my way on along Forty-seventh Street, I suddenly realized what I could have said about my roommate whom Taft Edison probably would have remembered from the band cottage during my freshman year, because from time to time my roommate would rejoin the French horn section of the marching band because it was being expanded for some special upcoming event, such as a trip up to Chicago for the halftime show during the annual football game with Wilberforce at Soldier Field.

Which, however, was only partly the reason I arrived at 41 West 47th Street thinking of the one and only self-styled Jeronimo as in Geronimo and also Hieronymus as in Bosch whose real name was T. (for Thomas) Jerome Jefferson, also known on campus as The Snake, as in snake doctor and snake oil salesman, because a tent show magician claiming a diabolical contract is what Herr Dr. Faustus came across as in a bull session in which I referred to him as the best of all possible roommates that first September. Of course, "best of all possible" was a phrase I got from him, who got it from Voltaire's "best of all possible worlds" in *Candide* and by which he assumed Voltaire meant things good and bad as they actually are because such is life in our time, but by which I meant and still mean that you couldn't have dreamed of having a better roommate if you had gone to Harvard, Yale, Princeton, Cambridge, or Oxford.

The brief encounter with Taft Edison was reason enough for my train of thought, but even so who else if not my old roommate back in Atelier 359 would pop into mind as you stepped down from the sidewalk and into the entrance of Gotham Book Mart? Not even Miss Lexine Metcalf, who in this instance would come after Mr. Carlton Poindexter.

V

One late morning about a week after I overtook Taft Edison on the way up Fifth Avenue that afternoon, I looked up from my usual place in the south reading room in the library and saw him standing at the checkpoint on his way in. I stood up and raised my hand and he nodded and headed toward me, and when we met in the center aisle he said he had stopped in to double-check a few details in the Americana section, which was at the south end of the reading room in those days, and also to invite me out for a midday snack and chat if I could spare the time. And I said I could and ended up spending most of the afternoon with him.

That was when I found out that when we had parted at the corner of Forty-seventh Street the other time he had continued on up Fifth Avenue only as far as Forty-ninth Street. Because at that time that was where he did what he did from 9:00 a.m. to 6:00 p.m. every week Mondays through Fridays; because what he was using as his writing studio at that time was a book-lined back room of an exclusive jeweler's showroom on the eighth floor of the Swiss Building on the southwest corner of Forty-ninth Street.

I said, Hey, man, I said, Hey, *goddamn*, man! I said, This is some little cubbyhole you've got yourself up here, man. And he said, Man if I ever get enough of this stuff ready to start publishing it nobody's ever going to want to believe that I was up here cooking it up in a place like this. If they don't try to put me in the nuthouse.

And that was when he also said what he said about trying some of it out on me before long. Me being not only a downhome boy but also a graduate student in liberal arts by way of becoming a literary type myself.

And I said, Let me know and I'll find the time, and he said, Maybe during some weekend, and I said, Just let me know.

As I stood looking down through the window onto the low roof of the southeast corner building of Rockefeller Center, I saw that we were diagonally across Fifth Avenue and Forty-ninth Street from Saks and in the next block north was St. Patrick's Cathedral and as far as you could see in that direction in the hazy midafternoon light there were more yellow cabs than any other vehicles weaving in and out of the traffic southward from Fifty-ninth Street, and there was also a steady flow of city Transit Authority buses pulling over to the curb every several blocks.

He said, Man, I come down here on schedule every morning just like everybody else working in this part of town. I check in here just like punching the clock, he said. And I said that I had been surprised to find that he had given up the trumpet and music composition but was not at all surprised that he was working on a book, because I had kept coming across his name on the checkout slip in so many of the books I borrowed from the library, not only while he was there during my freshman year but also during the rest of the time I was in college.

That was when I said what I said about the morning my roommate and I had circled over to the library on our way to our early English class period and found him already there sitting on the steps with his trumpet case between his legs and with an open book on his knees. And when I said I remember the book and it was *The Autobiography of Benvenuto Cellini,* he said he remembered the book but not the encounter. And I said it was not a verbal encounter. I said I just happen to be the kind of freshman who was very curious about what kind of reading other than textbooks and reference assignments upperclassmen were doing. And so was my roommate, I said, and he knew who you were by name because he had already started going over to the band cottage to practice with the French horn section because he wanted to make the free trip home with the band when it went along with the football team for the annual game against Wilberforce in Chicago. I knew that you were waiting on steps for the doors to open because I knew you worked in the library, I said. Because I had seen you working at the main circulation desk.

That's all I said about that at that time and that was when he told me what he told me about how he had come to have use of the Fifth Avenue workshop we were in. It was not really his, he said. It had been leased from the jewelry company by one of his very well-to-do friends, a writer who spent long periods away in Europe doing research for scholarly and critical books and articles on French, Italian, and German writers and artists.

It turned out to be just what I needed to make me buckle down and really try to find out what I could do with some of this stuff I've been playing around with from time to time, he said. And then he said, Man, if I can get enough of this stuff to come off the way I think it should I just might be able to cause a few people to reconsider a few things they take too much for granted. It's not just a matter of saying this is my way of coming to terms with this stuff, it's more like saying Hey, this is another way that might be even better or at least a pretty good alternative. It really is a matter of trying to test the validity of one's own sense of things.

And, of course, you know I know that there are going to be some people out there who are going to think I'm out of my mind. Or wonder if I *have* a mind. But what the hell, man, that's a chance I'm willing to take. After all, trying to do what I'm trying to do with this stuff is exactly what I put the horn aside for. I didn't give up on that horn, man, he said. Hell, I can still make a living with it, but I'd rather be trying to do what I'm trying to do with this stuff, some of which I must admit sometimes sounds pretty wild, even to me. *But I'm afraid it really does represent my sense of what life in these United States is like.*

Then, while I was looking at titles on the bookshelves and thinking of what I was going to say about some of the books of contemporary poetry and fiction I knew he had read in college, he stepped back out into the showroom and said something to somebody there, and when he came back and said what he said about what I had told him in the snack bar about the courses I was taking, that was when he also said, Man, I sure hope your class work is not going to keep you so tied down that you won't have enough free time for us to get together from time to time when I get this stuff up to the point where I'm going to need to start running it by somebody.

Somebody not only from down the way but also somebody who spent even more time in that neck of the woods than I did. And you might just be the one I suddenly realized that I should have been looking for. Somebody from down the way who's also interested in what books are really about. Man, most of the grad students I run into up here seem to think of poetry and fiction mainly as raw material for research projects that will enhance their academic status.

I said, I know what you mean, I really do. I said, Man, I think that was the first big thing I realized when I got to college. Some courses were about grade-point averages, but some were about the nature of things, and I don't mean just geology, physics, and chemistry classes. All of that was obvious. I mean the way some of the liberal arts courses were taught. Man, I used to go to the library to work out academic assignments, but what I really did was get the class work out of the way so I would have more time free to get on with trying to find out what literary books were really all about, *without being concerned about answering test questions about them.*

Then I said, Hey, speaking about research and homework assignments, as things down in Washington Square are going now, I'm pretty sure I can find time to listen to whatever you decide you'd like to run by me from time to time some weekends. Just let me know ahead of time. Not that I can promise any editorial expertise, but that's not what you're looking for at this point, is it? Anyway, you're on.

And he said, The main thing is that you're not only somebody from down the way and was actually in that place part of the time I was there and even saw me there and actually knew about some of the books I was reading on my own along with all that music theory and all those required practice sessions, it's not just that. Man, what I'm hoping is that just the experience of hearing myself reading some of this crazy stuff I'm playing around with to somebody like you, just might be all I need to keep me going in the outrageous direction I'm going.

And that was when I also told him about how my roommate and I had started reading books on the reading list for the special elective course on the novel for upperclassmen because it was being taught by Carlton Poindexter, who also taught our section of freshman English. Then I said, As things turned out neither of us actually took that class in the novel because my roommate

transferred to the Yale School of Architecture after his sophomore year and the course was not available during my junior
year, because Mr. Poindexter was away in graduate school on a
special fellowship grant, because he was going to be the new
librarian.

And anyway, man, by that time the main thing for me was
that other reading list that my old roommate and I had tacked
on the wall of Atelier 359 by the end of our freshman year. And
there was also all of those follow-up references in those wide-
ranging anthologies and follow-up stuff to articles in current
magazines.

And then I also said what I said about spending all three of my
college summers on the campus working as a hospital kitchen
helper the first summer, as a power plant engineer's unskilled
assistant the second summer, and in the stacks of the library
itself during the summer before my senior year.

And he said, You, too? Because it turned out that he had also
spent the two summers of his three college years working on
the campus, first as a baker's helper in the campus dining hall,
and in the library, not only the next summer but also that next
regular school year. Which is why I had not really been surprised when he said that he was trying to write a book, not
a symphony or an oratorio. I had seen him with the band and
sometimes he also wore his band uniform to work when he
had to report to the library directly after playing for an early-
morning cadet parade formation practice, and I also knew that
he was an advanced student in the School of Music because
sometimes he used to come to the library to do his copywork
assignments with the sheets spread out before him at a table all
by himself. But even so, I had remembered seeing him carrying
library books across the campus far more often than I saw him
with his trumpet case.

Man, I said, I couldn't even spare bus fare to Mobile, and the summer jobs that you could get on the campus were so much better than anything available to me down there, anyway. Man, those summers I spent working on the campus were just as important as the regular school term. Hey, come to think of it, those three summers now seem like the equivalent of three full terms. Man, with no formal class assignments between me and all those library books, and with new ones coming in all the time. Man, talking about the rabbit in the briar patch. And he said, I know what you mean, man. I know exactly what you mean. Then he said, They had some very good people in that School of Music down there, but as I look at things now, the best thing down there for me turned out to be the library along with the kind of informal sessions I used to have with Carlton Poindexter. Man, I still think of that library as something special. When you consider the fact that the main emphasis in that school was not that of a liberal arts college like Fisk, Talladega, and Morehouse—but when you remember how many of those younger profs were still doing advanced graduate work, maybe that had something to do with it. Anyway, that library collection suggests that there may well have been at least a few others down there like Carlton Poindexter who had a much richer background in liberal arts than was required by the courses they taught. And come to think of it, that was also true of the School of Music.

Which reminded me that my old roommate and I had thought of Taft Edison as an upperclassman worthy of our special attention and some deference. Not only because his name was on the library checkout card for so many books that were not required for any course of study offered by the college program at that time, but also because on so many that were current and recent publications or were referred to in current and back issues of weekly, monthly literary magazines and quarterly journals.

Man, he said, as he walked with me to the elevator when I told him that I had to be getting on back to the library to finish an assignment for an early-evening class, speaking of the rabbit in the briar patch, did you ever get around to checking out *Of Time and the River*? And I said, I did, remembering that I had put it on my list because I had seen it on Mr. Carlton Poindexter's desk after class one morning along with several other books by contemporary Southern authors.

And when he said, Remember the section that he calls "Young Faustus"? and I said I did and that sometimes I also used to refer to my old roommate as Dr. Faustus after Christopher Marlowe's *The Tragical History of Doctor Faustus*, which only led to his being given the dormitory nickname of the Snake as in snake doctor or snake oil medicine doctor of the tent shows. Because what the bargain that Dr. Faustus with Mephistopheles reminded the guys in that dormitory of was not the Marlowe, Goethe, and Gounod character that I had in mind, but the old satanic-looking tent show magicians who used to claim that they had pawned their souls to the devil in exchange for knowledge of secrets about the nature of things forbidden to other human beings no matter how gifted.

That's the way it got started, I said, but then later on, when they had to realize that for all of his straight A records, his conduct in class sessions was not at all that of an irrepressible academic eager beaver, but that of somebody who always sat in the back row and never volunteered to answer any question or join in any discussion and only answered only nonchalantly when called upon, the Snake nickname no longer referred to snake oil trickster but snake in the grass.

Which gave him a reputation that did him no harm whatsoever when he went cruising among the upperclass coeds during social events, I said, and when the elevator door opened, Taft Edison had said what he said about hearing talk in the band cottage about a freshman known as the Snake because he had a very special recipe for chem lab cocktails that some of the musicians in both student dance bands liked to sneak into the parties they played for on campus back in those Prohibition era days.

And before the door closed I said, Hey, but as for old high butt Thomas Wolfe, man, I don't remember all that time I spent and still spend in the library as any goddamn hunger to devour the whole goddamn earth at all. I can go along with the part about being somebody who reads whole libraries or at any rate whole collections as other people read books. Because, man, I don't think I ever thought of reading as acquisition as such, but rather as preparation. *Preparation for unknown, I thought, as the bus headed down Fifth Avenue toward Forty-second Street. Preparation by reducing the unknown. Be prepared. The Boy Scouts of America had already said that.*

VI

As the fall term moved on into November of that first
school year in New York, I began to feel that I had the
preparation of all of my seminar discussion assignments and
research reports well enough ahead of schedule so I could spend
more and more time doing nonacademic things that made you
feel that you were at last beginning to become another inhabi-
tant of Manhattan at large as well as a student at the Washington Square campus.

*Not that Manhattan or anywhere else could ever become
another benchmark in the same sense as Gasoline Point on the
outskirts of Mobile, Alabama, on the bay of the Gulf Coast had
always been and indeed in the very nature of things, would
also always be. As not even the campus in central Alabama for
all its archival treasures could also be, being, after all, only a
four-year stopover en route to other perhaps temporary destinations as yet as undecided upon as Hollywood had turned out to
be (although California, which was that many miles and travel
days and nights west from Mobile by way of the L & N to the
Southern Pacific from New Orleans and left on the wall map in
Miss Lexine Metcalf's third-grade classroom, had once been a*

boy blue future point of arrival and at least somewhat like Philamayork itself).

Because as benchmark, Gasoline Point, Alabama, would always be that original of all fixed geographical spots (and temporal locations as well) from which (properly instructed as to its functional and thus tentative absoluteness) you measure distances, determine directions, and define destinations, all of which are never any less metaphorical than actual. And, of course, there is also the irradicable matter of the benchmarks of your original perception and conception of horizons and hence aspirations in terms of which everything else makes whatever sense it makes.

The also and also of all of which is, incidentally, why it is also in the very nature of things that even as you finally began to realize that you are beginning to feel about Manhattan as you had imagined you would as you began looking forward to your next return there back during your first year on the road with the band, you also realize that it would nevertheless remain the metaphorical Philamayork of the blue steel, rawhide, and patent-leather preschoolboy fireside aspirations you would always remember whenever you remembered the thin blue horizon skies fading away north by east beyond Chickasabogue Creek Bridge as you saw them from the chinaberry tree, south of which beyond the river and the bay and the old Spanish Main of buccaneer bayou times were the seven seas.

(Along with all of that, to be sure, there was also always that ever so indelible twelve-bar matter of old sporty limp-walking Luzana Cholly picking and plucking and knuckle knocking and strumming and drumming on his ultradeluxe twelve-string guitar singsongsaying, Anywhere I hang my hat, anywhere I prop my feet.)

Which is also why what it all really came down to was a matter of settling in for the time being whether for the duration of the courses at the university or for the duration plus whenever, whatever, wherever. In either case, beyond the immediately functional details of basic household and neighborhood routines that incidentally were no less directly geared to the academic schedule than was campus dormitory life, there was also the also and also of all of the daily, weekly, monthly, and seasonal metropolitan attractions of greater Manhattan and vicinity, which, after all, were why New York University had been the graduate school of choice at the outset.

One of the very first things I almost always remember is how keenly aware I was of the way the northeastern weather changed from late summer to back-to-school autumn plus Indian summer and then to early midwinter as time moved on into my first year-round stay in New York at long last. Not that I hadn't already had to adjust to temperature changes that were every bit as different from the range of variations (mostly above zero and seldom more than ninety plus or minus degrees) that I had grown up getting used to responding to down south. But a difference was that when I was on the road with the band, adjustment had never been a matter of the coming of seasonal changes in temperature, humidity, barometric pressure, and visibility, but rather a matter of traveling into different geographical regions where the climate was different whether you arrived in winter, spring, summer, or autumn. So I already knew from personal experience what the weather of the different seasons was like in areas from border to border and coast to coast, from New England and along the Great Lakes through all of the Midwest and across the Great Plains and beyond the mountain range country to the Pacific Northwest and then down the continental shoreline to the desert and Rio Grande country sometimes before zigzagging back down-homeward across the Southwest Territory before heading back northward again, sometimes as if barnstorming off the old L & N Railroad route from New Orleans by way of Mobile up to Chicago or as if off the Mississippi River by way of Memphis to St. Louis. And sometimes also as if off the old Atlantic Coast line or Seaboard Airline up from Florida.

But the only time between graduating from college and settling into the furnished apartment in Manhattan that I had remained in one place long enough to find out how it felt to have the seasonal changes come and go had been the more than a year of months that I had spent in Hollywood, where seasonal changes were not really very noticeable.

Incidentally, along with all of the other special New York attractions, there were also the famous men's clothing stores that in those days included Abercrombie & Fitch, Rogers Peet, John Davidson, and Triplers as well as Brooks Brothers, J. Press, Chips, Herzfeld, and the men's shops in such high-fashion department stores as Saks Fifth Avenue, Bonwit Teller, and Bergdorf Goodman, but the all-purpose wardrobe I had already gotten together on the circuit included everything I needed for the time being. So it was not me but the first-time arrival from the mostly milder and shorter winter weather down home, whose seasonal initiation also of necessity included Lord & Taylor and B. Altman. Not that I did not also make the rounds with her, nor have I ever cut back on seasonal window shopping. Not in New York, Boston, Chicago, San Francisco, and Beverly Hills, and never in London. On the other hand, I have never had any strong urge to do very much if any in Paris, Madrid, or Rome in the first place. Men's clothing has never been among the things I liked about France. Once I got beyond the beret stage in Paris, that was as far as my personal interest in French men's clothing went until the arrival of bikini swim trunks.

————

You knew that the northeastern winter weather would be there very soon when the roasted-chestnut vendors began to take their places near the warm pretzel stands and pushcarts along the sidewalks. Leaves in Washington Square had already begun to change from deep summer green to an early autumn yellow here and there by the middle of October that year. So we scheduled an outing in Central Park for the second week in November to catch the colors at their peak against the blue and white brightness overhead framed by the smoky gray haze of the Manhattan skyline as we remembered it all from Technicolor movies, travel brochures, and color spreads in the slick paper magazines over the years. And you couldn't have picked a better day to spend doing what we did that Saturday.

On our first visit during the early part of that September, we had gone in at the entrance off Columbus Circle. So this time we began at Grand Army Plaza, at Fifty-ninth Street and Fifth Avenue and came on down by the pond and the skating rink and made our way across to Sheep Meadow and then back through the Mall and by noon we had come along the lake and past the fountain to the boathouse area, where we stopped for a snack before rambling on through part of the birdwatchers' sanctuary before continuing on north beyond the Great Lawn and the Metropolitan Museum of Art area to the reservoir, beyond which by late afternoon we had also come on between East and North Meadows to Harlem Mews, and finally there was 110th Street, which was also Cathedral Parkway in those days.

We came back downtown along Fifth Avenue on one of the open double-decker buses that used to be so much fun for New Yorkers and tourists back then. So on our left were the mansions and ultradeluxe apartment buildings facing out onto and over the east side of the park, and from time to time you could also see through open spaces all the way across the malls and meadows to the towers along and beyond Central Park West.

Then as you rolled on down below Seventy-second Street, there was the Central Park South skyline in the offing, and when you pulled on into the vicinity of the Hotel Pierre, Sherry Netherland, and the Plaza with Fifty-seventh Street and the great midtown Fifth Avenue shopping district coming up you were suddenly aware once more of being in the most cosmopolitan area in the entire Western Hemisphere. *New York, New York, I whispered, thinking, Philamayork indeed: to all intents and purposes the lodestone center of the twentieth-century universe and perhaps beyond. Philamayork, ultima Thule, capital of the world!*

As we crossed Fifty-seventh Street and came on beyond Tiffany's nudging each other and nodding at the glittering stretches of cosmopolitan shop windows, I was thinking what I was thinking about how this part of midtown Manhattan always made you feel and about how when you were in some neighborhoods, sections, and districts you forgot all about the fact that Manhattan was actually an island, even when you were overlooking the Hudson or the East River or even the Battery. And, of course, it was almost always as if the tunnels and bridges had nothing to do with going onto or going away from an island.

But as the bus moved on along in the canyonlike flow of the Fifth Avenue traffic toward Forty-second Street and the Empire State Building at Thirty-fourth Street, everything you saw, including the ever so obvious variety of people of different nationalities, most of whom seemed to be going about their daily routine activities, reminded you of how directly this part of

Manhattan was related not only to Wall Street, the banks, and rail and air terminals and not only to all of the neighborhoods in all the boroughs, but also to the world at large.

Capital of the world I thought again, remembering Ernest Hemingway's short story about what happened to a young Spanish country boy's fantasies in a Madrid that was never the capital of the world as Rome had been and Paris and London became. Then there were also Balzac's young men from the provinces in Paris of the nineteenth century. Philamayork, Philamayork, remembering how the old L & N Railroad porters used to call out stations and say here it is, been long hear tell of it, and now here it is. Take everything you brought with you, you'll need it!

After Thirty-fourth Street there was mostly the sound of the lower midtown Manhattan traffic of that late part of the day, and as we snuggled closer and I kissed her cheek ever so softly as she nodded off, the old sweet heartthrob pop song lyric that I suddenly found myself trying to remember after all those years stretching all the way back to how I was already beginning to feel about pretty girls and crepe myrtle blossoms even before Charlene Wingate told me what she told me that spring now long since once a upon a time was *if you go north or south if you go east or west.* Because the refrain was *then I'll be happy,* which was the title, and the first words of the chorus were *then I'll be happy.* There may or may not have been a verse, but the only thing that ever mattered to me was the chorus. *I want to go where you go, do what you do, then I'll be happy, sigh when you sigh, cry when you cry . . .*

The next big cross street coming up was Twenty-third, which was still that many blocks away so what you would see first in the distance would be the triangular Flatiron Building in the point where Fifth Avenue crossed over to the west side of Broadway, which came in diagonally from Herald Square and continued on down beyond Union Square and on through Greenwich Village and across Houston Street and Canal Street on its way to City Hall, Wall Street, and the South Ferry.

After Twenty-third Street, Fifth Avenue would continue on across Fourteenth Street and end at the Washington Arch entrance to Washington Square and the New York University campus area. But the bus turned east on Eighth Street, so we got off and came west to Sixth Avenue and then down to Fourth and headed toward Sheridan Square and home that way.

It was not until we came back from our bus excursion to see the fall foliage up along the Hudson River countryside that following Saturday that we finally got around to tasting the roasted chestnuts from one of the sidewalk vendors between Eighth and Waverly on Sixth Avenue. And I said, OK, but I'll take chinquapins over these and she said, Me, too, and when we got home and looked up chinquapin in the dictionary and found out that the shrub we remembered from Alabama chinquapin thickets as we remembered huckleberry bushes from Alabama huckleberry thickets was actually a species of chestnut, and I said, bush nut rather than tree nut. And that's also when I said that the only taste of chestnuts I could remember was in a sauce for venison that I had at a big spread for the band one night in Beverly Hills.

I said, Me and you. I said, Me and you this many miles north by east from the chinquapin thickets off the blue poplar trail to Mobile County Training School, and she said, And the huckleberry thickets in the part of Alabama I come from. And I said, And the pecan orchards as you come out of Montgomery heading east on Route 80. And then there was the old crepe myrtle blossom pop tune again, but I didn't whistle it and I didn't hum it, but I did cross my fingers as I kissed her again.

VII

The next time Taft Edison and I got together again was when he came back by the library one late morning about two weeks following that afternoon in his workshop, and that was when he said what he said about getting together from time to time beginning even before he was ready to start reading parts of his manuscript to me. Just to keep in touch, he said. Because he had decided that being two book-loving down-home boys he and I had a lot to talk about, especially about the literary possibilities of the down-home idiom. Something beyond the same old overworked sociopolitical clichés about race and injustice that had long since become so usual that they were also the expected and tolerated and indulged. Neither one of us said anything at all about the down-home music of the blues and jazz at that time, but when I got around to saying what I said about it sometime later on, he said I was on to something basic and that I should consider some sort of graduate school paper on it just for a start. No telling what else would turn up, he said. Just remember the old Hemingway principle and stick to what it has really meant to you over the years and not what somebody else thinks it should have meant. Hell, they were not there, you were.

I said I was all for his suggestion about getting together. And then I also said that I would also be ready for my noon break in about thirty minutes, and he said in that case he would wait in the periodicals room, which was downstairs on the first floor, if I had time to have a snack with him. And I said I would and when I came downstairs he was just putting a magazine back on the rack. And we came outside and east along Forty-second Street to Vanderbilt Avenue and the Oyster Bar downstairs in Grand Central Station and ordered New England clam chowder, and what we talked about that time was what we both remembered about some of the students and members of the staff and faculty on the campus down in central Alabama. He began by asking about some of the old campus slickers who used to hang out in and around the main entrance to the very same upper-classmen's dormitory to which my roommate and I were assigned, in a somewhat atticlike fire-escape room on the third floor as freshmen and where I remained for all four years, two by myself after my roommate left for Yale.

Old Daddy Shakehouse, he began by saying. And I said, the Lord High Chancellor of the Outlying Regions of the after-hours juke joints. And he said, Did that old bear chaser finish whatever it was he was supposed to be taking down there in the trades school area? Hell, he must have already been down there on that campus at least three or four years before I got there. Man, he was a notorious campus operator of long standing when I was trying to get used to being a freshman. And I said, He was there on one of the work-your-way programs and he finally did get his certificate in industrial arts at the same time that I got my degree in a course of study that amounted to liberal arts. And that he then got a job in the maintenance department and was probably still there. We were both aware that we were talking about a place with a standard of living that was much higher than what most of the student population was used to in those days and perhaps most would settle for as graduates, as most faculty and staff members obviously had.

Old Daddy Shakehouse, he said chuckling to himself as he ate several more spoonfuls of the Oyster Bar New England clam chowder that he had not only recommended over the Manhattan recipe but also as being unsurpassed by any other around town, including Gage and Tollner's over on Fulton Street over in Brooklyn. Old Daddy Shakehouse, he said again.

Then he said, What about old Jay Gould, old Jay Gould Weddington? Man, you had to know who old Jay Gould Weddington was. Everybody who was down there when I was there knew about him. And I said, old Jay Gould, old Jay P., John D. Weddington, the wolf of Wall Street. Business school. Man, when I graduated he was still running them floating card games and crap shoots, and was still the number one campus loan shark and pawnbroker. I think he must have hit that campus about the same number of years ahead of me as you did, but he was another one of those special work-plan students on a part-time academic schedule because his background in clerical work was such that he already could take care of several kinds of office jobs well enough so that sometimes he worked full-time during the day and took classes during the early-evening sessions and at other times he took a full class load during the day and did part-time office hours at the end of the day or for a few hours at night.

I didn't really know him, I said, but during my junior and senior years he did hire me to help him tidy up a term report and also to look up something in the library for him from time to time. And, of course, with him it was always cash on delivery. But as for borrowing money from him, man, not me. Man, that was for the ones who were getting those monthly or quarterly checks or money orders from home. Which old Jay was promptly collecting on because he had somebody in the campus post office keeping tabs on when each one of his debtors' letters from home arrived.

Which was when Taft Edison said, Well, I knew him well enough to bet that he wasn't going to finish all of his courses and end his student status until he had accumulated enough capital to go directly from college into business on his own. Because I did know that he already had enough money to take a regular four-year course of study and that he wasn't dependent upon any support from whatever family he had. Anyway, I wouldn't be surprised to find out that he's running his own business by now or even his own bank of some kind. Or that he actually is up here with something going on for him down on Wall Street.

And when I said, Where the hell was he from?, he said, Florida, boy, and then he said, Somebody else that everybody probably remembers from those old bull sessions is old Freeman Clark. And then I said, Better known as the ghost of Marcus Garvey. And old Marcus Garvey himself wasn't even dead yet, he said. And I said, Which is to say ghost as in Holy Ghost, man. Then I said, Zebra jockeys, man, zebra jockeys. I said, Man, Mr. B. Franklin Fisher had inoculated me and most of my classmates against all of that old zebra jockey hocky jive by the time we reached the ninth grade at Mobile County Training School.

That was when Taft Edison said what he said about not having much time to spend on the stem and in the stem lounge, what with working in the library and living in the band cottage, and with all the hours he was required to spend down in those old rehearsal cubicles in the basement of Harrison Hall plus the sheet music copy work and also the endless reading time involved in preparing for Mr. Carlton Poindexter's junior-year course in the novel.

But I did have one part-time buddy that I used to run with every now and then, he said. Old sleepy-eyed Sid Palmer. You must have known him. We were the same year but he was in the School of Education, majoring in science with a minor in math. He used to make it down to old Jay Gould's floating concerns pretty regularly. But when he'd get the urge to hit a few spots in the outlying regions he always checked to see if I could go along, and whenever I could I would, beginning back during that first summer that I spent down there. Man, I stuck pretty close to prescribed campus routine during my freshman year. So by that next summer I was beginning to figure that I knew enough about who was who and what was what and where on campus to do a little extracurricular exploration and by that time I also knew enough about old Sid Palmer to take him up on his invitation to come along on a few rounds in the outlying districts.

He went on eating his clam chowder, smiling to himself as he remembered his days on the campus again. And then he said, Old Sid Palmer, down there from Richmond, Virginia. Man, being a loner that I guess I've always tended to be, old Sid was about the nearest I ever came to having a running mate down there, not that the two of us actually had any common career objectives. He didn't seem to have any trouble getting passing grades in those School of Education courses he was taking, but my guess is that he was really interested in becoming some kind of school administrator, not a classroom teacher. Anyway, the only books he read were the ones required by his assignments, mostly chapter by chapter as assigned. But come to think of it, he was pretty keen on the statistics of tests and measurements, which he was taking during our junior year.

He shook his head still remembering, and then smiling he said, We did have fun hitting those joints together though, but that was about it. We liked the same joints, but we never really talked very much about barrelhouse, honky-tonk, and gut-bucket music as such, except to mention the local guys that we liked or didn't really think very much of. Anyway, when I think about old Sid and all of that now, I give us both credit for realizing that it was something that we should stay in touch with in spite of the fact that most of our teachers seem to regard it as something beneath the taste of the kind of respectable people college-educated people were supposed to be.

I said I knew what he meant because I had gone to college not only from the Mobile County Training School of Miss Lexine Metcalf and Mr. B. Franklin Fisher, but also from the Gasoline Point of old Luzana Cholly and Stagolee Dupas fils and old Claiborne Williams of Joe Lockett's-in-the-Bottoms. And that is also when I went on to say what I said about the one and only Mrs. Abbie Langford, the legendary housemother of the upperclassmen's dormitories on the upper end of the campus who was actually employed as the supervisor of housekeeping and maintenance by the Buildings and Grounds Department but acted as if her authority came from the Dean of Men's Office and the Disciplinary Committee.

Man, I said, not that I have any plans to be heading back down in that direction anytime soon, but boy, just wait till I tell her that old Taft Woodrow Edison is up here in New York City and is still as quietly studious and as dapper as ever, but is carrying a Madison Avenue briefcase instead of a trumpet case.

And when he said, Man, how is that old battle-ax, I said, Still there as far as I know, still exactly the same, and still outraged at the slightest mention of your name.

Oh, boy, he said, shaking his head, and we both laughed and he said, Man, she had me all figured out and sized up on her own and she wouldn't let me tell her anything.

Everybody down there at that time knew the story about Taft Edison and Mrs. Abbie Langford. When he arrived on campus for his freshman year he was not only ten days early, but all he had with him was a state scholarship voucher and one extra shirt and a change of underwear and his toilet articles all folded up inside a twill topcoat, which he rolled so that he could carry it slung over his shoulder with a belt like a knapsack.

He had hoboed and hitchhiked all the way from Oklahoma City and had arrived so far ahead of time that he decided to look for a temporary job to pay for interim room and board until official check-in and registration day. And when the grand old gal heard this story from somebody she not only hired him for the time being, but she also started talking about how if he passed the promptness and precision work test on his temporary tasks as the indigent young Booker T. Washington had done so well to enter Hampton she might sponsor him; and for the next week and a half he had bunked in a basement room and helped the janitors and listened to her praise him for being another young Booker T. letting down his bucket and getting ready to be the next one to keep one foot on the trail between the farmland and shop or factory while he stretched the other all the way to tea in the White House and board meetings on Wall Street.

But behold! Outrage! Scandal! Flimflam!!!

His trunk arrived and it turned out that he not only had a trumpet that was more expensive than any brass instrument owned by anybody else on the campus, music school instructors included; but he also had a wardrobe that was as up-to-date as anything in the September issue of *Esquire,* the number one men's fashion magazine of the day. The twill topcoat that he had used as a knapsack and bedroll turned out to be the latest thing in what my roommate (who also had one) and I called cloak-and-dagger trench coats.

She was so outraged that she threatened to have him kicked off the campus as an impostor who had come not because he was seeking higher learning and the uplift of his people, but to take advantage of inexperienced younger students and well-meaning but unsuspecting staff and faculty members. She didn't follow through with her threat when he explained that he was there all on his own and with no family support whatsoever and that he had spent a whole year between finishing high school and his arrival on campus working in a haberdashery shop earning enough money to supplement his scholarship grant and also outfit himself (at employees' discount rate) in the attire of a self-respecting collegian.

Man, he said, I wasn't about to let anybody treat me like a charity case because I had to have a job to supplement my scholarship grant. Not that I had anything against that Booker T. Washington and Horatio Alger true uplift grit that they were forever evangelizing as the salvation of the masses, but it was just not for me. My mother had to help me to get that far and when I finished high school I was on my own because she had my younger brother to take care of and she said she was very confident that I could not only look out for myself from then on but would also find a way to make myself somebody special.

And that was also when he said what he said about finding his own way, which reminded me of what Miss Lexine Metcalf would say to me about how I was one who would have to go wherever I would go and do whatever I would do in order to find out for myself whatever I should try to make of myself. Miss Lexine Metcalf, who also said, Who if not you? and then always also called me her splendid young man. Who if not you?, my splendid young man. Which is also what Miss Tee, who almost always spoke as if for Mama herself, implied when she called me her mister. My mister. Here comes my mister. *Hello, my mister.* Because what Mama had always said from as early on as I ever remembered was, *Mamma's little scootabout man, that's what him is.*

But I didn't say anything about that at that time. I said what I said about Miss Abbie Langford. I said, Man, you know how some of these old house mothers are about some students that they always remember for one reason or another. Man, ten, fifteen, twenty, thirty years later, when certain ones come back for class reunion, old Abbie Langford is right there expecting them to come by to see her and be reminded of something she reprimanded them for doing however many years ago.

And before he said what he was going to say I said, Hey, but reunion or no reunion, man, you are still one of the ones she remembered every time she heard somebody mention your name while I was down there: *You all talking about Taft Edison? That old Taft Woodrow Edison could blow that horn like John Philip Sousa himself when he wanted to and he also could have become another R. Nathaniel Dett. So they used to say over in that music school. But with all them quiet manners and bow ties, and special tailor-made clothes, he was still tangled up with all that old low-life music, too, him and that old Nighthawk Palmer.*

As we came on outside again and headed back along Forty-second Street he shook his head chuckling and said, Well, the next time you're down that way and see that old battle-ax you can tell her you saw old Taft Edison up in New York City still messing around some more of that old back-alley stuff that she didn't report me and old Sid Palmer for. And tell her I'm not blowing any trumpet like John Philip Sousa or anybody else. Tell her I'm playing my riffs on a typewriter these days.

When we came to the corner of Fifth Avenue, he said what he said about being almost ready to start reading sequences of his manuscript to me, and then just before he turned to head back up to Forty-ninth Street he reached into his right hip pocket and pulled out a set of brass knuckles and said, That old battle-ax never suspected that I was packing these, but man, you never know when you might have to take emergency action on some incoherent fool.

VIII

It was not until the night that I went up to his apartment at 749 St. Nicholas Avenue that I found out that Taft Edison was a longtime friend of Roland Beasley, the painter I had met in Paris before coming back to Alabama after the time I spent on the Côte d'Azur with Jewel Templeton.

I had come uptown that evening because Taft Edison was finally ready for me to listen to him read a few scenes and sequences from the manuscript of the novel I knew he had been working on for some time but that he had not yet discussed in terms of any overall narrative context. So I was looking forward to finding out what the basic story line was. My guess was that the scene of at least some of the action would be a college campus based on the one where I first saw him when I was a freshman and he was a junior. The only hint, however, was what he had said that first afternoon as we came along Fifth Avenue up to Forty-seventh Street, and I said what I said about his briefcase not being the trumpet case that he had in college.

When he called that morning and asked when I would have time to come by and listen to a few passages that he was thinking about selecting to fulfill requests for magazine publication, I got the impression that what he wanted first of all was my response to a narrator's voice on a page, his angle of observation and context of recollection. Then he would want my immediate opinion of the literary quality and orientation that the verbal texture suggested.

But when he opened the door for me to step down into the vestibule of his studio apartment, the first objects I noticed on the wall before following him through the door on the right were two watercolor abstractions mounted on pale blue mats and matching, rimlike maple frames. And when I said they reminded me of the matted tear sheets of abstract paintings with which my roommate had lined the wall from the head to the foot of his bed by the end of the fall term, he said they were the work of a friend of his.

I also said it was my old roommate who told me about what books to check out of the library if I wanted to find out what modern art was about. And when I said, The first book I checked out was *A Primer of Modern Art* by Sheldon Cheney, Taft Edison said that it had to be the same copy he had checked out when he was a freshman because he worked in the library and there was only one copy of it in the collection.

That was when I said what I said about my roommate growing up going to exhibitions at the Art Institute of Chicago because Chicago was his hometown and also said that he was enrolled in the Department of Architecture, but he had a richer background in the humanities than all the students in the liberal arts courses that we took together. And Taft Edison said that the watercolor abstractions that I saw as I came in were the work of a friend of his who had gone to college to study mathematics but had become the painter whose work impressed him more than any other that he had seen by anybody else in Harlem.

Then when he said who the painter was I said what I said about meeting him in Paris and as I did I also realized that I had not called him since coming to New York and also that I had not told Royal Highness about how I had gone over and introduced myself to Roland Beasley at the Metropole in Paris that afternoon because I overheard him telling his companion about seeing the great Royal Highness onstage back during the heyday of the old Lafayette and Alhambra Theaters.

Old Rolly, Taft Edison said as we came on into the one-room plus bath plus stove and refrigerator nook apartment, and I saw the floor-to-ceiling bookshelves and other paintings, watercolors, drawing, and silk-screen reproductions. The furniture included his convertible couch and a coffee table that could be unfolded to become a six-place dining table.

Look him up, man, Taft Edison said, giving me time to glance around. I'm sure he was right at home over there trying to come to personal terms with all of that heritage of articulate mankind. So you already know that he's not just another one of these uptown provincials who have so few if any connections with the very things we went through what we went through to get up here to get next to. Look him up and go by and see some of his really ambitious pieces. I think he just might be the one to do for American painting what old Louie Armstrong and the Bossman are doing for American music.

And that was also what he went on to say what he said about how local or idiomatic variations sometimes become not only widespread but also nationwide, just as a local joke, saying, tall tale or legend may come to be regarded as everybody's common property. And then he also said, Look, as far as I'm concerned, if it's supposed to be American art and it doesn't have enough of our idiomatic stuff, by which I mean mostly down-home idiom, in there it may be some kind of artistic exercise or enterprise but it ain't really American.

I was ready for him to take my hat and trench coat then and

when he hung them in the closet and came back saying what he said about what our old down-home stuff had done for church music not to mention pop tunes and ballroom music, I thought about Eric Threadcraft and the Marquis de Chaumienne but I did not mention them because I did not want to use too much of the time that he may have hoped that I would be able to spend listening and responding to what he had planned to read. Which is also why when he asked me if I wanted to sip something I said, Maybe later.

So, here we go, he said, pointing me to an overstuffed lounge chair as he turned and went over and sat in the swivel chair at his writing desk and began turning the pages of his manuscript, humming quietly to himself until he found the sequence he was looking for. Then he said, Let's see how this comes across without any introduction.

But then as he put on his reading glasses he smiled shaking his head and said, Look, I have just one restriction. I really want to know what you make of all this stuff. So I'm open to cross-examination. Except for one point. Man, don't ask me why I'm trying to do whatever this stuff is about. With a pencil and a typewriter and not with valves and keys.

Stipulated, my good fellow, I said, remembering my old roommate again, Stipulated. Then I said, But I must say this. What I remember about you down there on the campus I am surprised that you seem to have put that horn down altogether, but I'm not at all surprised that you are this serious about writing. After all, I was always more impressed with your interest in literature than with your special status as a scholarship student in the School of Music.

Then I went on to point out that I had always remembered seeing him in the library more often than I could recall seeing him go to and from the School of Music or the band cottage. I also knew that he was an outstanding enough member of the band to be the student assistant who tuned the band for the bandmaster and who led the band when they played for the cheerleaders during football games in Alumni Bowl. But I didn't mention that I couldn't remember how he actually sounded on the trumpet. Nor could I remember whether he was a regular member of either of the two student dance bands. However, I did remember that he played with the chapel orchestra.

On the other hand, however, I could also have pointed out that I had always thought of him as being more involved with becoming a composer and conductor than with becoming an instrumental performer as such. Because that was what had always come to mind when I had remembered seeing him in the main reading room of the library when he was not on duty at the circulation desk. Because he would always be sitting at a table all by himself doing copy work of sheets of music.

When he began reading that night, it was very much as if I were back down on the campus in central Alabama with my old roommate again. Because it was during that first autumn term that he said what he said about tune in the head and voice on the page. He was not talking to me, he was talking to himself, and he said it twice. We were sitting across the room at our individual desks with our backs to each and we were working on our first assignment in English Composition 101. You could supply your own title, but the theme was first-person singular. And the objective was to introduce yourself to your classmates. So we did not discuss what we were going to write about ourselves, and I did not ask him what he was chuckling to himself about from time to time.

But when his paper turned out to be the one Mr. Carlton

Poindexter chose to read aloud to the class as the best example of what the assignment was supposed to do, I was not surprised. And I could still hear my roommate's voice on the page even as Mr. Carlton Poindexter was reading it in his own voice. And when I said what I said about it when we were back in the dormitory that night, my roommate said, Tune in the head, voice on the page applied even when the narration was in the third person. Because even when it was in the first person or even the second person it was not really your ordinary, everyday voice. It was your yarn-spinning, lie-swapping, tell-me tale and so your storybook-time voice.

And so, while I sat listening for his tune in the head as Taft Edison went on reading, I also found myself remembering how I became aware of the narrative voices on the pages of the list of novels I began reading on my own during that first fall term, starting with the voice of Henry Fielding, the author of *The History of Tom Jones, the Foundling,* among the academic classics and that of Ernest Hemingway among the serious contemporaries because part of his current novel in progress was being published in current issues of the leading fashion magazine for men in those days.

Before that fall I could identify some authors with books and short stories but only because I remembered what and/or who they wrote about, not how they wrote, although I was very much aware of the fact that some were considered to be serious and important, and some were popular but not important, although sometimes sophisticated and dismissed as pulp cheap trash. But beginning with my roommate's paper for Mr. Carlton Poindexter's first assignment I became aware of the function of literary craftsmanship as never before.

So as I sat back in the deep, overstuffed armchair that night that many years later listening to Taft Edison read from the typescript of what was to become his first novel, it was as if my old roommate and I were in Atelier 359 once more. And when Taft Edison paused at the end of his first excerpt, took off his glasses, and I said what I said about how it already sounded and about tune in the head and voice on the page, he said, The problem as I see it with this stuff is how to get our old down-home kind of lying and signifying to function as literature.

Then he said what he said about documentation and implication. Look, man, he said as he stood up and moved over to the table where the drinks were, obviously you want the readers to be wherever whatever the action is. Because you want them to witness whatever you want them to witness from a specific physical point of view and listening post. But as important as that is, basically what you are really working for is not just precise or realistic documentation but implication. Man, the very act of writing a story is always a matter of a certain amount of lying and signifying. Think of camera angles, microphones, and the sound track in movies. You don't just describe the people, the places, the weather, and least of all the actions exactly as they were. You reshape whatever has to be reshaped to make the point you try to get across to the reader.

He interrupted the reading only long enough to make one bar-sized shaker of what amounted to one and a half martinis each, and then he spent the rest of the time reading one passage after another without comment, skipping forward, but not in strict chronological order with some sequences being flashbacks to incidents that he had intentionally skipped over and others that suggested a larger context but could stand alone as short stories (which always exist in a larger continuing frame anyway).

When he finished the last selection I still did not know what the central story line was, but I did not ask him about it because I knew that the main thing he wanted from me was my opinion of the relative suitability of each section for magazine publication. So I said what I said about him being into something special both as subject matter and in terms of tone and rhythm. I said, The only problem that the editors would have would be the choice between titillating sequences and self-contained short-story-like episodes. I said, Man, you might have given up the trumpet, but damn, if you gave up composition.

And he said, Well, we shall see. There are two publications involved. One is a slick paper monthly and the other is a literary quarterly. I'm not naming names, but I'll let you know how it turns out.

Then while he was jotting down notes as he put the manuscript pages back in place, I took another quick survey of his bookshelf and when he brought my hat and coat and opened the door, he said, Don't forget to give old Rolly a call and let him know you're up here at least for the time being. And I said I would, and the very next day I did, and I also called Daddy Royal.

IX

So here she is at last, Royal Highness said, as Eunice and I stepped out of the elevator and headed toward where he stood waiting outside the open door to his apartment that evening. I had told him about us when I had called him on the phone shortly after we arrived in New York back in September. And I had also called him from time to time just to keep in touch, but this was our first trip up to Sugar Hill together.

Yeah, here she is at last. So this is the one that's really the one, hey, young soldier, he said, putting his left arm around her shoulder as he slapped right palms with me and said, Miss Lady. Hey, what you talkin' 'bout, young fellow? Yes, indeed. But now look here, Miss Lady. They all told me you were good-looking but ain't none of them said a word about your being *this* good-looking. And with the class to go with it. Well, I guess they did mention something about class. But I guess you had them all tongue-tied.

Then he said, Now see there, that's exactly what I'm talking about. Just look at that brush-off she just gave me disguised as a blush. You're something else, Miss Lady. Because, you see, I know good and well you heard this old jive line before, but this is the first time you've heard it from the *source*. And that goes for this, too, he then said, and put both hands on her shoulder and gave her four mock ceremonial kisses, and still holding her shoulders at arm's length said, A smack for all four cheeks, Miss Lady—if you get the implication of my latter clause.

Man, he then said as he hooked arms and guided us into his living room, you got yourself some fine people here, young soldier. So you all come on in this house and make yourself at home. The rest of us will be out in a little while. I told them to go on and finish what they were doing back there and let me have you all to myself for a little while.

Then when we helped ourselves at the bar and took our seats at the end of the couch nearest his favorite overstuffed chair, he said, You know something, young soldier? I'm still getting great reports about how you handled yourself out there when you were on the road with the band.

It just keeps coming up, he said. Time and again. Even the Silent Partner dropped in a good word about you. Hell, I forget what the hell we were talking about, but at some point there he was asking me when I had heard from you and saying what he said about how everybody was betting on the schoolboy without even knowing or even speculating about any profession or line of work in particular. He just struck everybody in that crew as somebody special, Miss Lady, a young fellow with a very high-class education that didn't put on no airs at all and could pick up on new things like he was born knowing.

Hell, they were not talking about getting along with him as a very young newcomer on his very first professional gig. There wouldn't be any problem with that at all, because the man wouldn't put you in there with all them thugs in the first place if that was going to be a problem. And then in the second place when he picks somebody they all know he already has plans for him because he represents something that he wants to fiddle (hey, dig that) fiddle around with at least for a while and ain't nobody in there ever question the Bossman on anything like that to my knowledge. Not in that band. Hell, in that band they never know what they themselves are going to have to adjust to next.

No, he said, looking at me while still talking to her but signifying at me even so. No, the way we all see this young soldier here is that he's one of the ones that was gifted and lucky enough to go to college. And serious enough to make the most of it. Now he has all kinds of options to pick and choose from.

So you see what you got yourself into, Miss Lady, he said as Stewart Anderson came in from the hallway that led to the dining room and kitchen. Eunice already knew that when Royal Highness had said what he said about the rest of us he was referring to Stewart Anderson, formerly of the old vaudeville comedy team known as Stewmeat and Small Change and his wife, Cherry Lee, née Cherie Bontemps, who were not only his business partners who ran a restaurant for him but also shared and took care of his extensive four-bedroom apartment.

Looka here, looka here, Stewmeat Anderson said, heading straight to Eunice, who stood up to great him. Yes, indeed, he said. And then he said, I'm Uncle Stew, and I just want to say don't be no stranger up this way, and you don't have to wait for him to bring you back. And as for you, young fellow, what can I tell you? I'm not surprised.

His wife, Cherry Lee, had come in then and poured herself a glass of muscatel and she said what she said about us all being from down home and gave me a peck on the cheek on the way to lock arms with Eunice and take her outside to show her the twilight view of Manhattan from the terrace. It was as if she actually had known that it was something Eunice was expected to be shown because I had written to her about it after my first visit.

As I was saying, Stewmeat Anderson said, I'm not a bit surprised that you turned up with a solid stone fox that is also one more fine and I mean certified fine lady like this one, my man. Not after what everybody was saying about how impressed they were with the way you handled yourself in that department all across the country. But now let me tell you this. Man, every last one of them thugs would bet hard money on anything you decide to have a go at. Like when you decided to stay out in Hollywood for a while, for instance. So far as I know, not a single one of them accused you of being dazzled by all that hyped-up glamour and glitter out there. It was something you wanted to stick around and study for a while and that was that, and here you are to prove that they were right.

And as I said what I said about how in my case you had to learn how to tell the difference between good looks and well-stacked availability (even if coy-seeming) on the one hand and a truly certified stone fox on the other in order to make it out of Mobile County Training School let alone out of Mobile and into college, I was also remembering that nobody in the band knew anything at all about me and Jewel Templeton, not even Joe States. The only one I ever told anything about that was Gaynelle Whitlow.

The band had not swung back to the coast while I was out there on my own, but I wouldn't have ever mentioned Jewel Templeton if it had. Not even to Joe States. If somebody in the band had found out about us, that was another matter. But any mention of it by yourself would raise questions about whether you were taking all the make-believe in stride for what it is. After all, how could you ever forget what happened when you said what you said to Ross Peterkin about what happened with Fay Morgan after the Beverly Hills party following the opening night at the Palladium. I hadn't been taken in and exploited by Fay Morgan and I still think that Joe States knew as much but he still let Ross Peterkin lecture me as if I had allowed myself to be used, as if I were a horny greenhorn just to make sure and also to see if I would take the reprimand in my stride.

Now me myself now, Stewmeat Anderson said as we stood up but finished our drinks before following his wife out into the hall and into the dining room, I lucked out. But now, you see, showbiz was my biz in the first place, so what the audiences paid to come to see as something ever so glamorous, I knew damn well was always also a matter of greasepaint. I'm not going to try to tell you that what I saw across the footlights didn't have much to do with it, because it had a hell of a lot to do with me taking notice of her in the first place. But the girl I married is the one I met and got to know backstage.

The main course that night turned out to be possum with sweet potatoes plus side dishes of mustard greens and stir-fried medallions of okra with bits of steak of lean, which they decided would be a nice little down-home surprise for us after that many months of being primarily concerned with picking and choosing New York food markets as well as snack bars and restaurants, and they were right. And there was also corn bread that was crackling bread. Then, since sweet potatoes came with the gamy taste of the possum, there was pecan pie with dasher turned ice cream instead of sweet potato pie. We went on talking about down-home menus and recipes as we ate, and that was when they told us about the truck merchants who came up to Harlem, some from Virginia and the Carolinas and some from as far down the coast as Florida and could be found parked on certain corners and certain blocks displaying and selling whatever was in season, straight from the gardens, fields, orchards, and woods of their down-home localities.

Which is why I was not surprised when Stewmeat Anderson told us that their larder was also stocked with such other special down-home game meat as rabbit and squirrel and raccoon and even venison. But that was the first time I'd ever heard of down-home folks keeping a supply of frozen catfish fillet on hand for an occasion not unlike this one, when fish, not game, would be the pièce de résistance.

And guess what else besides?, Royal Highness said, when I said that I assumed that venison was no problem to come by in New York. He said, You're right. And then he said, I'm talking about turtle meat, underground turtle meat. Not the sea turtles, that's what they have down in them islands in the Gulf. But now talking about some meat that's kind of special down that way but ain't no problem in New York. There's goat meat. As I remember it, the main time for goat meat where I come from was when there was some kind of barbecue, especially a big holiday picnic barbecue or a church barbecue. But now up here some of these splibs from the islands are very big on goat meat with curry and fresh-grated coconut and stuff. And another thing some of those other island folks up here go for much more than I was ever used to down home is a whole pig pit roasted on a spit.

And those Cubans know what to do with chicken and rice, Stewmeat Anderson said. But speaking of them street-corner truck vendors from down home, when it's the right time of year I also know where to find some that bring up stalks of sugarcane and ever so often they might also bring along a few pecks of scuppernongs. Now that's something that really takes me back, Miss Lady, he said.

And I said, Me, too. I said, Not as far back as you're talking about. But not just back to the outskirts of Mobile as a place as such, either. But still back as long ago as those old unpaved streets with horse droppings along with those automobile tire ruts. Then I said what I said about remembering scuppernongs as yard arbor muscadine grapes and also about remembering fig trees as fruit-bearing yard trees. And about never having seen any orchards of fig trees anywhere in or near Gasoline Point.

Which is also when I said what I said about how during muscadine season we used to roam the woods on the slopes above the L & N Railroad bottom at Three-Mile Creek Swamp and sometimes also the slopes and woodlands above Chickasabogue Swamp and even as far as all the way up the AT & N Railroad to Bay Poplar woods. Which also led to what I said about how muscadine season being tree-climbing time because the muscadine vines I knew about entwined themselves around tree branches much the same as scuppernongs entangled themselves in the latticework of yard arbors.

As for vineyard grapes, in Gasoline Point in those days before the fully stocked supermarket chains replaced the old neighborhood grocery and general merchandise stores, like orchard fruits and other street-vendor produce, they came from elsewhere (which for oranges, grapefruit, and pineapples was as nearby as Florida; and for okra, butterbeans, scallions, lettuce, tomatoes, strawberries, cucumbers, new potatoes, and so on was only as far away as the truck gardens across Mobile Bay).

That brought us to what the two of us remembered about canning, pickling, jam, jelly, and winemaking season in our two sections of Alabama; and that was when Royal Highness said, What did I tell you? and nodded at Stewmeat Anderson, who got up and went through the door to the kitchen area and when he came back he was carrying two quart-size bell jars, one of green tomato chowchow relish and one of peach jam and two pint-sized glasses, one of blackberry jelly and one of pear preserves.

Folks down the way don't never let us run out of these kinds of good old goodies, Royal Highness said as Stewmeat Anderson put the jars and glasses in front of Eunice's place and gave me a playful jab and a mock conspiratorial wink on his way back to the kitchen to help Cherry Lee bring in the pecan pie and dasher turned ice cream that he himself had frozen and packed that afternoon.

Well now, seeing as how y'all already been through Christmas and New Year's up in this part of the country, Royal Highness said as Cherry Lee went back to the kitchen to bring in the coffee to go with the dessert, I'm satisfied that you got everything squared away in the chitlins, hogmaw, and trotters department, including all the trimmings. After all, young soldier, you were in that band long enough to pick and choose chitlin joints and barbecue pits from border to border and coast to coast. So I'm sure that old Joe States personally saw to it that you got checked out on the choice of trimmings in New York.

And when I said, Including a little ceremonial taste of moonshine as well as the big uptown, up north thing of champagne, he said, Hey, what you talking about, young soldier, whatyoutalkingabout?

It was a very fine old-time down-home dinner table get-together like some of the very special ones for very special out-of-town company that you remember from childhood. And as Royal Highness and Stewmeat Anderson and I headed back to the drawing room to settle down and puff on the extra-special Cuban cigars that Royal Highness would choose for us from his antique buccaneer humidor while Cherry Lee took Eunice on a tour of the apartment, the topic was the band again. And when Cherry Lee and Eunice rejoined us, I had been brought up-to-date on the band's current tour, and Royal Highness went on to say again what he had said early on about how pleased he was over the fact that I had decided to spend the time I had spent with the band between graduating from college and going on to graduate school.

That's something you'll never regret you decided to do, young soldier, he said. Then as he turned to Eunice he said what he said about having very special high hopes for me not because he thought I had all of the earmarks of a young man on his way to fame and fortune in the usual everyday sense of becoming a widely publicized celebrity with a big income and lots of expensive possessions, but because my earmarks were those of a young man who just might someday be able to fulfill the ambition I finally settled on. Whatever it was, he said. *And that was when he also said what he said about how it was perfectly normal for some people to make up their minds about their line of work way back in early childhood and about how some can remember exactly when, where, and why they did and others can't remember when they had not already done so. And then he said what he said about how it was also perfectly normal for some others, some very special ones, to spend a lot of time still trying to get themselves together and on to some definite course even after their formal schooling was well into the postgraduate level because they were the ones who saw themselves as having so many possibilities to pick and choose among.*

Anyway, he said, as he stroked Eunice's hand, what I'm talking about is what I saw when this one turned up here holding down old Shag Phillips's job like that, *mainly just because he needed a temporary gig for the summer after graduation from college.* When the Bossman brought him up here, the earmarks I saw belonged to a young fellow with as wide a range of eligibility and potential as I've ever come across. And I've covered some territory, Miss Lady.

Which was the very point he came back to at the end of the visit as we stood up to shake hands and head for the door. As he gave her his ceremonial four, one for each cheek, kisses, he said, I hope I didn't say anything to give you any notion that I think you didn't already know what you were letting yourself in for when you hooked up with my young soldier here. I just want to let you know what kind of impression he made on me and the Bossman and all them old thugs in the band, too. So I'll just say this. All of us think that maybe what he's still trying to figure out is how to do something that none of us even know we need him to try to be the one to try to do for us.

Then as we headed for the clevator he said, Now that you've been up here and seen us for yourself, don't be no stranger.

X

Taft Edison was the one who made sure that I was alert to the so-called revolutionary political recruitment operating procedures that you were likely to encounter in New York City in those days. But it was through Roland Beasley that I became more sensitive to New York City variations on old confidence games that he pointed out as having been a universal element of city life ever since the first trading and business settlements came into being and the first bargains and markdown sales were offered and special escort and guide services part-time or full-time became available for hire or for free.

Not that Roland Beasley thought that I needed any of the usual fundamental orientation to big-city life as such. After all, when he met me in Paris I was on my own after having been in most of the biggest cities in the United States. And as for my being a down-home boy, the fact that I was also a college boy who had worked with the band that I had worked with in order to go on to graduate school was not likely to be lost on him either, not to mention the fact that not a few of the most notorious big-city slickers in just about every region of the nation were once down-home boys.

I think Taft Edison may have assumed that the time I had

spent in the band with Joe States looking after me had pretty much taken care of the big-city initiation part of my postgraduate orientation. But I also think that he may have felt that I probably did not know very much about political recruitment because the band never stayed in any one town long enough for any revolutionary political recruiters to make any effective follow-up on whatever may have been set up by any initial contact. And I also think that Taft Edison may have felt that I was a more attractive possibility to political recruiters because I was a graduate student than I had been when I was a musician who was not a headliner with a lot of worshipful fans. As a graduate student I was a potential revolutionary intellectual technician who could be especially useful in recruiting and/or indoctrinating the so-called masses in preparation for the rebellion that would overthrow the status quo.

But he actually told me what he told me when he told me to be me on immediate alert mainly because of what was happening to him, and which he thought might involve me simply because I was beginning to be in regular contact with him. Yet the way he said it also let you know that he did not expect you to be alarmed. It was as if he took it for granted that you would take it as yet another kind of thistle in the briar patch.

Which in effect was also what Roland Beasley expected of me when he explained what he explained to me about confidence games of the local city slickers as a routine part of my orientation as a newcomer settling down in New York for an extended or maybe permanent residency. But unlike Taft Edison, who was outraged by what struck him as the self-righteous gamesmanship of what he called revolutionary recruiters out to kidnap your mind, Roland Beasley almost always sounded as if he were sharing his curiosity about something rather than warning you about it.

He never sounded as if he thought you needed to be warned. It was always as if what he said about some example of the confidence game as he knew it was something that amused him and also something that you could probably match with some anecdote of your own. And whenever you did, he would say, Hey, old buddy, that's my good buddy. Man, you're as up with this stuff as old Rolo.

Even when he started breaking it all down in terms of variations on basic game patterns, it was still as if he were primarily concerned with your appreciation of his anecdotes, and it all came across as if it were more of a hobby, like cowboy and gangster movies and sea stories, than as a matter of serious concern.

But as is often the case with many people and their hobbies, his insights on procedures were no less precise or comprehensive for not being professional, and one day after we had been going to museums and galleries and bookstores together for several weeks after my first visit to his studio, we stopped in at Gotham Book Mart, and while I was browsing the shelves labeled We Moderns, he bought a book the clerk had been holding for him, and when we came back outside he handed it to me and said, Hey, man, I know you already have a good grip on this jive because you had some basic anthropology in college, so you know this stuff is not just a matter of classic pattern and variation, this stuff probably goes all the way back to primitive rituals of those early days when people first started using words to make deals with. Because I'm pretty damn sure that jiving and conniving are just about as old as language itself. Hell, even older. After all, there was a lot of bullshit gesticulating and face-making before they got around to using words.

And that was when he said, Anyway, this is something you might find very interesting when you can spare the time away from your academic assignments. I think you just might find this kind of journalistic writing amounts to something pretty close to anthropology.

It turned out to be as evocative of certain aspects of American city life during the first forty years of the twentieth century as such old Herbert Asbury books as *Gangs of New York, Ye Old Fire Laddies, The Barbary Coast, The French Quarter,* and *The Gem of the Prairie* (Chicago). But its specific focus was on the dynamics of the swindling racket known as the confidence game or the big con, which it described as being operated by one or more *grifters,* who choose and set up the prospective victim or *mark,* who is led to the *store,* which is operated by the often informally recruited but expertly coordinated *mob,* who set him up for the *kill* by allowing him to make an impressive amount of money by some means the *mark* knows is crooked. This gives *the mark* confidence and sets him up for *the kill,* which is the amount of money *the mark* is willing to risk on a sure but illegal bet or investment. *The grifter* then plays *the mark* against *the store,* which is immediatcly raided by the other members of *the mob* disguised as law-enforcement officers. This allows *the grifter* to *brush off the mark* by spiriting him away by pretending to be as vulnerable to the arrest as he is. The objective of the confidence game is not simply to take money from *the mark* but also to do so without allowing him to catch on to the fact that he has been taken.

Indeed, the book also makes much of the fact that *the mark* is not supposed to realize that he has been duped and thus lose confidence in himself. The very fact that his confidence remains high is what leaves him vulnerable for other grifters! Much is also made of the fact that many people become ideal marks who are roped, taken, and brushed off time and again because they have come to believe that the high social status they enjoy because of the money they inherited or married into is a result of some inherent special superiority. His unshakable confidence in his own keen business judgment is precisely what leads him to get roped into one con game after another.

I started reading it on the way home, and when we got together about ten days later I had checked back through *Suckers Progress* and *The Gem of the Prairie*, which was one of Joe States's favorite books on the subject. He had given me a copy of it that he had picked up in the Pickwick Bookstore in Hollywood several days after the visit to Ross Peterkin's apartment after I said what I said about the night I spent with Fay Morgan in Bel Air following the first Beverly Hills party I went to with them after the band opened at the Palladium. And the first thing I said was, Hey, man, anthropological is what it adds up to, all right. But come on now, man, this stuff is not only loaded with ritual patterns and variations. It is also just as full of visual patterns and variations. So don't tell me you haven't been noodling and doodling and vamping and riffing at least some sketches for some uptown takes and takeoffs on not only the likes of Daumier, Goya, and Hogarth. But what about Brueghel's *Revelers* and some uptown takeoffs on Hieronymus Bosch's *Garden of Delights*?

I said, Man, ain't no telling what some Beasley riffs could add up to. I said, Man, how about a series or sequence of *From Down-Home to Uptown Sketches, the Natural History of a Hipster*, or, say, *The Shady Side of the Stem* (as in mainstem), or *Slapping Seventh Avenue with the Sole of My Shoe*, or *The Rounder*, or *The Sidewalk Pounder*? Man, I could go on and on and so could you. Me, I'm just running on and on about something I just thought of.

And he said, Hey, but you're on to something, man. And then he said, Did old Taft tell you that I took classes with George Grosz at the Art Students' League? And I said, *Ecce homo*. And he said, The same. And then said, I was very much into political and social cartoons at that time. But when I went to study with him, he turned out to be the one who really put me on to the fundamentals of serious craftsmanship, and he inspired me to study the world history of art and learn from the great masterpieces.

So like I said, he said, You're on to something, my man. Then he threw a playful left jab and clinched me and on the break he said, So didn't you tell me that old Joe States and the Bossman's wrecking crew called you Schoolboy? Well, that means that they really appreciated what you are really about, and just to show you that I do, too, I'm herewith designating you Chief Literary Consultant. But no kidding, my man, as soon as we got together in Paris, I realized that there were a million things I'd like to talk to you about.

In Paris he had told me that his studio was on 125th Street in Harlem, in the same building as the Apollo Theatre. But when he had answered the phone number that Taft Edison had given me, he said he had moved all the way down to Canal Street near Sixth Avenue, on the way to Chinatown. He had invited me to come down as soon as I could spare the time. But my first and only visit so far had been a very brief pop-in call one afternoon.

Not long after that was the first of the three times that he had stopped by the library to treat me to a snack on the way to the Museum of Modern Art, the Metropolitan Museum, and the galleries on Fifty-seventh Street and along Madison Avenue. This was before the Guggenheim was built, and the Whitney at that time was still down on Eighth Street between MacDougal and Fifth Avenue in Greenwich Village, near where most of the small galleries and studios were located in those days.

On my first trip down to the studio on Canal Street there had been only enough time for me to see the framed paintings, drawings, and sketches of his that were hanging on the walls, along with the framed works of other New York painters who were mostly close personal friends of his. And there were also a few of his framed and unframed and perhaps not quite finished canvases on the floor leaning against the wall, against a chair here and there and the worktable near the easel.

But when I went back the second time, he had brought out a number of framed and unframed but finished pieces from his storage area, and there were also several sketchbooks and folders of drawings and watercolors on the worktable. And when he said what he said about giving me some idea and concrete evidence of what he had been up to and what he was about, I said, It does, man, it does.

And I was impressed but not really surprised because by that time, his responses to what I had gone with him to see in the galleries and museums had given me what turned out to be a very reliable impression of his general aesthetic and intellectual orientation and also what his special individual emphasis was and how it fit into the comprehensive context of the role of art in human consciousness. In fact, at the time of that second visit I had already begun to think of him as someone who just might become my very special visual arts cut-buddy, as Taft Edison was becoming my literary cut-buddy, as my now faraway best of all possible roommates had become during my freshman and sophomore years in college.

Which is why when he said what he said about wanting me to give him my literary response to what he had done, was doing, and would be doing, I said, If you say so, man. Because by that time I also realized that he was as enthusiastic about popping into bookstores and browsing through the literary section with me as I always was about going to exhibitions with him whenever I could spare the time away from my academic assignments.

Man, he said, when I looked at my watch and stood up because it was time to go, I can't tell you how much I'm looking forward to what we are going to be doing about all this stuff. Man, I can't get over it. Man, see now that's that goddamn Paris for you and this goddamn New York. Where the hell else am I going to find just the right kind of down-home cat I didn't even know I was supposed to be looking for?

And that is when I said what I said about being like the man in the frame shop. And he said, The literary man matting and framing for the exhibition. That's it, man, that's it. You already got it. The man in the frame shop is the one who is most immediately involved with how I want this stuff seen. The man in the frame shop. Hey, that's pretty good. That's damn good. Context, man. But I said, Not just in the literary sense of mythological or historical context. I said, That, too, but we're also talking about a frame that functions like the stage proscenium when the curtain opens. It makes the make-believe believable and at the same time it reminds you that it is all also a matter of artifice.

You got it, man, he said, you got it. Then he said, Man, that goddamn Paris. Man, this goddamn New York. This goddamn United States. We got to get with it, man. What does it all mean? What are we going to do? He said, Get with it, man. Me, I'm all about the figure in the fabric, and I think of you as being about the angle of vision, the relativity and ambiguity of it all. My man with the four dimensions of space which include Proust's dimension of time. Plus *metaphor and syncopation*!

XI

Two nights before the band came back into town that next time, Joe States called from Richmond to give me the name and address of the rehearsal studio they were going to be using until they moved into the recording studio I remembered from the last time. He sounded as fine as usual, and when I said so he said what he always said, and I could see his eyes and his lips and the tilt of his head and the angle of his neck, and the sound of his voice made me feel the way it always made me feel.

Me and you, Schoolboy, me and you. Get to me fast. And this time I'm also speaking for the Bossman, too. I just told him I was on my way to make this call when I waved to him over that crowd around him in his dressing room, and he said for me to tell you that he hoped the two of you could work out a little one-on-one checkup this time around. Like I keep telling you, Schoolboy, you got yourself another alma mater, of which he's the papa.

So there you go, statemate, he said, as if using the cymbals to bring you to the solo microphone. And then as if adding a light roll as segue, he said, And speaking of the Bam, give all of our best to them fine people you went and got yourself all married up with. And tell her we also hope that she can also make it by to give us another little peek. Tell her I know how busy she is with both of you all taking classes, but tell I say all she got to do is just pop by the recording studio for a couple of takes and I guarantee that our permanent acknowledgment will be right there on everything else we do for the rest of the session. But now you, he said then, you get to me fast and I know I don't have to tell you that the Bossman ain't shucking about something like this.

The first rehearsal session was from 2:00 p.m. to 6:00 p.m. that Tuesday. When I came into the studio he was all set up, adjusted and tuned, and so was everybody else. But there was time to make the rounds to each section and greet everybody one by onc because the Bossman and Old Pro were still at the copy table deciding on the sequence of what they were going to run through.

Then shortly after I made it back to Joe States, I saw Old Pro begin to gather up the scores, and I moved on over to the copy table and said what I said to the Bossman first, and he waited while Old Pro and I said what we said to each other and I promised to call and find out about his free time.

Then I followed the Bossman on over to the piano, and as Scratchy McFatrick and I were slap-snatching palms again, the Bossman had already started playing around with a series of runs even before he sat down and adjusted his seat to the keyboard. Then as I came on over to him he moved over so that I could sit on the seat beside him and went on vamping what he was vamping at the same time that he was saying what he was saying about letting me know when he would be free so that I could meet him somewhere for an update while the band was in town this time.

Not that we need to lose any sleep over the likes of you, he said, still running variations on the notion he had either made up or picked up. Sometimes it might begin as any old sound at all, just something he heard and decided to turn into music, or sometimes it would be a phrase he heard somebody using as a part of a warm-up exercise and when he decided which way he wanted it to go, he would say, Hey, Bloop, or Hey, Jomo, or Hey, Mobe, how about this, and perhaps more often than not whoever he had picked it up from would not recognize it. But from time to time somebody might also say, Yeah, that's a little run I picked up from old so-and-so back when I first started going to rehearsals trying to get in the high school dance band from the marching band. Or sometimes whoever it was would say, I still got the record that was on and I still remember all of it note for note, but that was the part I had to work on the hardest, so every now and then I use it to check up on myself.

Now you, he said, still doodling and noodling, I just don't want you to forget that my best wishes are just the same old conventional down-home ones handed down from generation to generation, beginning as far back as the time of the abolitionists and the Underground Railroad. All that is a part of it, too, as I'm sure you know, but what I want you to keep in mind is that with me it is also personal. Which means that I'm all for touching base in person from time to time, however briefly.

He went on noodling and doodling on the keyboard, pausing from time to time to make another notation on the fresh copy sheets on the top of the piano. The fact that he could say what he wanted to say to me while going on with what he was doodling on the piano (and with his pencil) was something I had become aware of the very first time I went to hear the band in person that night out at the Dolomite. I cut classes to go out there that day to watch and listen to them rehearse some new material for an upcoming recording session when they hit New York a few weeks later. So when I went back out to the dance that they were in town to play that night, I was already in a state of fairyland euphoria.

But not to such a degree that I would miss what happened when the band came back onstage for the second set. Hortense Hightower came up to say something to him from the dance floor, and he had her come on up to the bandstand and sit beside him. And since they were playing a dance and not a concert, he didn't announce the selections, he just vamped the signal for each number, sometimes bringing sections of the whole ensemble in on the first chorus as written or in any case as I remembered it from the recording; but at times he might segue to another chorus, even the out chorus as if it were the first chorus. And if you were out on the dance floor you would be so involved with what the music was stimulating you to do that you probably wouldn't have time to notice very closely what any individual musician's posture and gestures were as he played what you were responding to.

What you had to get out there and do from time to time, because how could you resist that part of being right there with them playing "live and in person"? But at the beginning of the second set that night out at the Dolomite I was as close to the bandstand as you could get, and that was where I was when I saw what I saw and realized that the Bossman could carry on what was obviously a serious, extended conversation while not only leading the band from the keyboard, but also keeping track of what everybody in each section was doing at the same time.

They were playing a number that was one of my favorite recordings, and I was keeping an eye on the trumpet section because I knew that there was a chorus coming up in which I wanted to see how the three horn men looked doing what they were about to do. So I was watching them and I saw old Osceola Menefee making signifying head gestures to Jomo Wilkins and Scully Pittman about how preoccupied the Bossman was with the conversation he had going with Hortense Hightower.

Then when they came to the part I was waiting for, the three of them stood up to hit one sharply percussive note in unison. But when they raised their sparkling silver horns to do so, old Osceola Menefee didn't put his mouthpiece to his lips, and the instant the rim shot–like note went *spat!*, the Bossman's head jerked up and he wagged his finger at Osceola Menefee, who grinned as if to say, Just checking, maestro, just checking, and saluted as the three of them sat back down.

And now, he said as we took the first sip of our wine after giving our waiter our short order that afternoon on which I had been able to make it up to the recording studio at Sixth Avenue and Forty-fourth Street in time to spend his snack break recess with him as I had promised through Milo the Navigator on the phone the night before.

The two-hour break for the rest of the band amounted to about an hour and a half for him. So he had taken me to a cozy little place two and a half blocks up Sixth Avenue where there was a table waiting for him. And when he gave the waiter his order I said I'd have the same, which is also what I had done when they brought him a glass of the wine that they already knew he wanted.

So now, he said as we put our glasses back on the table before taking a second sip, let's get personal. How are things going for my fine young all-purpose timekeeper? And I said, Still trying to keep it swinging, maestro. Still trying to keep as much of it together as I can, still trying to find out how much else I should be trying to get together. And he said, They get into some pretty tricky stuff in outfits like the one you're hooked up to these days, but of course you already knew all about that part of it before you made your move. I'm satisfied on that score. So I'm not asking because I have any doubts. I'm just keeping in touch.

And that was when he went on to tell me what he told me about what Hortense Hightower had told him about why she had given me the bass fiddle. She told me that it was the one basic instrument that even as a beginner you could play almost the same way you just naturally did whatever you just naturally did when you were just listening and responding to whatever you were hearing when you were listening and responding with nobody else around. Just think how different it would be if you were playing the same notes on a tuba.

That, he said, was a pet notion of hers, and I said it made a lot of sense to me, because it did. But when I called to tell her that I was thinking about sending for you as the stopgap replacement for Shag Phillips, she was all for it, but she still immediately reminded me of what she had told me about not mistaking your all too obvious love for music and close identification with musicians with any personal desire on your part to become a professional musician as such. Not as your life's work. Even though you hadn't yet settled on what you wanted to try to make of yourself.

Which I could also understand, he said, and I promised her, and I kept my word as you well know I did. And by the way in case you haven't already figured out why I picked an inexperienced youngster like yourself to fill in for Shag Phillips, what impressed me was how natural your sense of time seemed to be. *Because what it all added up to was pulse, which is not just metronomic precision but a matter of personal feeling, gut feeling. Technique is fine, but it doesn't always add up to music, not the kind of music I'm always trying to play. Not that you or anybody else were born with it, for Christ sake but you were conditioned to it early on.*

We were well into our snack by that time and he looked at his watch and said, I don't pick my musicians like anybody else anyway. With me it's not their expertise but their potential. So what happened with you was the way you locked in with old Joe and Otis and me was not just surprising, it was downright incredible. And so far as I was concerned it had to do with a lot more than execution. It had to do with feeling. Look, we could always improve your execution with practice. That's what the hell rehearsal is always about, but feeling is something else, and the texture of my music is always all tangled up with the blues.

Which I could have said was essentially a matter of idiomatic sensibility. But I didn't, because I didn't want to sound that much like a graduate school academic. So what I actually said was that I knew exactly what he meant. And even as I said it I was remembering those old long-ago summer twilight times on the steps of the swing porch, with the antimosquito smoke wafting and curling across the chinaberry yard, when old Luzana Cholly used to come sporty limping up along Dodge Mill Road from the L & N Railroad bottom, strumming his twelve-string guitar on his way to whichever honky-tonk or jook joint he was going to play in that night.

Not that it wasn't as if church music was also always there. But church music was about church service, which was about heaven and hell. Whereas the blues was about everyday good times as well as holiday good times. I don't really know which I heard first, but I do remember that Luzana Cholly with his guitar and sporty limp walk was there quite a while before old patent-leather-tipping, flashy-fingered-piano-playing Stagolee Dupas fils first came to town.

So I said what I said because suddenly all of that had come to mind. But what he was saying then was that as far as he was concerned, musicians should never become so preoccupied with what they were doing technically or theoretically—and certainly not with how their technique is impressing other musicians—that they forget that the truth of the matter is that the people in the real audience respond to what you make them *feel*.

So, he said, when we returned to that part of the conversation as we finished our dessert and stood up to leave, so what good is impressing other musicians with your virtuosity if nobody out there in the ballroom, the auditorium, and the record store is responding? *Which sometimes people do in spite of themselves.* In other words, describing and explaining how the sounds are made is elementary for musicians themselves, but all of that is only a matter of craft. But when my band plays something, I want the craft to add up to what good music is supposed to do for people who come to hear it and dance to it. Not because they understand it but because they feel it.

Then as we came on back along Sixth Avenue toward the studio, he said what he said about Hortense Hightower and that was when I said what I said about Luzana Cholly and Stagolee Dupas fils. That was when he went on to say what he said about what great but undefined expectations Hortense Hightower had told him she had for me. And I said what I said then because that was when he had gone on to say, As you already know I'm with her. And so is everybody in the band. And that was when he smiled his very pleased Bossman Himself smile and then raised one eyebrow and said, But I still can't help being curious about what you yourself think about how you happened to come by such an intimate identification and involvement with music without becoming a musician.

So that was when I said what I said about that and I don't

remember having ever said it or even thought about like that before. *I said that there never was a time when I wanted to become a musician per se. I said as much as I always wanted to do things like Luzana Cholly, who was my very first legendary hero in the flesh, I don't remember ever wanting to become a guitar player, not to mention a twelve-string guitar player. I said old Luzana Cholly's sporty limp walk was in itself a downright epical statement but whenever I did it, the imaginary object that I would be pretending to be holding so expertly would not be a make-believe guitar but old Gator Gus's baseball pitching glove. I said, even when little Buddy Marshall and I tried to skip city by hopping a northbound freight train to follow him that time and he himself caught us and brought us back to Three-Mile Creek bridge, neither one of us had thought of ourselves as hitting the troubadour trail as an itinerant guitar player.*

And the same was true of old Stagolee Dupas fils, the flashy-fingered jook joint and honky-tonk piano player from down in New Orleans, the Creole and voodoo and steamboat city beyond the Gulf Coast Mississippi canebrakes and bayous where the L & N Railroad made its junction with the California-bound Southern Pacific and the Santa Fe. I used to spend hours just listening to him practicing, sometimes on the piano at home and sometimes all by himself some mornings in old Sodawater's empty honky-tonk, just practicing and playing for himself or making up new numbers or new twists to use on old numbers. But I didn't ever really want to become a piano player either. I just wanted to do whatever I decided to try to do like he did what he did playing the way he played the piano.

I said, With old Luzana Cholly what I heard was blue steel routes and destinations and what they required was rawhide-tough flexibility. I said, With old Stagolee Dupas fils and his custom-tailored big-city clothes and jewelry, it was the sights and sounds along patent-leather avenue canyons. I said, I told you that time about Papa Gladstone's band. But I must say, maestro, as many of those rehearsals as I used to go to and as many of his dance dates as I began listening to from outside the dance halls even before I was old enough to buy a ticket even if I had been able to afford one, I don't remember ever having any urge to play any instrument for him someday, even though I memorized and could hum and whistle just about every part of most of the numbers in his book and could spot any phrase that any newcomer didn't get right.

And that was when he said what he said about having not only the knowledge but also the feeling about how it all goes together and if the feeling comes first, so much the better. He said, Our friend Hortense knew exactly what she was doing when she gave you that bass. She knew good and well that a special scholarship college sharpie like you could and would pick up on the basic technical facilities in no time at all and that whatever skill you were capable of just naturally followed.

We came on across Forty-fourth Street and into the building where the studio was, and as the elevator started upward he said, So with that kind of background you actually came into our band knowing why I sometimes kept the fluffed notes in. And I said, Because if you like how it sounds, it becomes the right note. And that was when he said what he said about sheet music versus ear music. So far as his band was concerned, sheet music was there to remind you of ear music.

When we came on back into the studio where Old Pro was waiting for him at the piano, he gave me the old mock French military one for each cheek farewell for now routine and said, And incidentally for whatever it's worth, I also want you to know how pleased I am that you're still touching base with old

Daddy Royal. Ain't but the one. As I'm sure you already know, and as I'm also sure you already know what it means to have somebody like that expecting something special from you, even before you yourself have settled on what you would really like to do with yourself.

When I went back to the studio at the end of the week for my this-time-around get-together with Joe States, the very first thing he said as we came on out onto the sidewalk en route to Sam's Musical Supply Shop on Forty-ninth Street between Sixth Avenue and Times Square was also about something that Royal Highness had said about me.

Well now, just let me say this, my man. Old Daddy Royal has got your number. So if the impression you're making on them profs down there at that university is anything like your hitting it off with him, you got this grad school gig off and popping like these old thugs in this outfit hitting when the Bossman sics them on with one of our old surefire getaway jump tunes. Man, talking about a bunch of jackrabbits! Man, when the Bossman sics them splibs in that outfit on a Broadway audience they hit like they got the lowdown on the mainstem of every metropolis there ever was.

XII

When I finally told Taft Edison about the time I had spent on the road with the band, I said, Man, it began as an incredible summer transition job that I needed because I had to get enough cash from somewhere to supplement the graduate school fellowship grant that I had been awarded along with my B.A. degree at commencement that spring. I said, Man, nothing like that had ever crossed my mind before. I said, Man, when I left home for college my main musical involvement beyond listening and dancing to it was humming and whistling it.

That was my second visit to the writers' work space on Fifth Avenue at Fiftieth Street that he was still using five days a week, Monday through Friday, because the owner was still away on a biographical research project in France and Italy. He was sitting at the long heavy oak conference table that he used as a writing desk, and I was sitting across from him in a chair near the window through which I could look north beyond St. Patrick's Cathedral toward Fifty-seventh Street and Central Park South, and from that many floors up, the sound of the traffic was all a part of the midtown Manhattan hum and buzz as I already remembered it from movie sound tracks when I heard it on my other visit.

I said, Man, when Hortense Hightower told me what she told me about suggesting me as a stopgap replacement when the Bossman Himself called and just happened to mention in passing that Shag Phillips had given notice, I couldn't believe it. But she said, Don't worry about it because he doesn't go around looking for superstars. He makes his own. Not because it's a game or some kind of challenge to prove anything about his ingenuity as some kind of mentor either. She said, He hires his musicians because he has decided that he wants to find out what he can do with something he's heard them playing. And that is when she also said, Believe me when I tell you that the very fact that he remembered you as soon as I mentioned you is what counts, because that means that you did something that caught his ear—not necessarily something musically technical either, something that goes with something he's got filed away in that steel-trap mind of his. You've heard about those big-time college profs talking about those legendary linguistic experts that can listen to half a sentence and tell you where you come from? Well, that's him when it comes to music. And then she also said, One thing is for sure, you can't find a better way to spend a summer after four solid no-letup years on a college campus down here in central Alabama than hitting all those towns all across the country with those guys in that outfit. You just wait.

I said, Man, the thing about it is that I don't remember ever really touching, let alone trying to fool around with, the bass fiddle before Hortense Hightower gave me that one in the spring of my junior year. Man, or any other instrument, except for the toy snare drum I once got for Christmas because I wanted Santa Claus to bring me one like the ones in the Mardi Gras parade bands that I used to imitate on a tin bucket during my preschool days—and come to think of it, there was also a time when some of us, in spite of the fact that our main interests were cowboys and baseball and boxing, used to make ukuleles out of wooden Cuban cigar boxes, but I don't remember that as something that I still had very much interest in doing by the time I reached junior high school. By that time it was track and field events and the Boy Scouts.

I said, Man, the one who took me through my rudimentary exercises on that present from Hortense Hightower was a sophomore string major and chapel orchestra cellist from St. Augustine, Florida, named Willis Tucker and called what else but Pluck Tucker because he also played the string bass in one of the campus dance bands, whose fingers were even more nimble than those of old Tricky Lou Cartwright, the fanciest bull fiddle thumper I ever heard during all the time I was growing up on the outskirts of Mobile. I said, Now I'm pretty sure that old Tricky Lou started out on the tuba like the one I first heard him tooting in Papa Gladstone's marching band in the Mardi Gras parades long before I found out that old Papa Gladstone also had the number one (and sometimes also the number two) dance band in town.

Then I said, Which reminds me that Tricky Lou sometimes also used to play the tuba in the dance band, because I can still remember him tooting what I used to call the circus elephant parade tuba part in old Jelly Roll Morton's "Kansas City Stomp" when the dance band used to set up in the front rows of the grandstand at the baseball field and play a few numbers to advertise the eight-o'clock dance that would follow the game after supper that evening.

I said, But man, old Pluck Tucker was strictly a string man. I said, He was in the freshman class that checked in for the fall term of the year that you cut out. So my guess is that he's at least about a year younger than I am, so he just might have started out on a cigar box ukulele, the four strings of which you tuned from top to bottom by playing the right tones for "My Dog Has Fleas."

That was when Taft Edison said what he said about how popular Hawaiian and Latin American music became for a while back during the early days of radio when I was just getting up to junior high school level and he was on his way out of it. And he said that was probably also when Spanish guitars, which had been becoming more and more popular ever since the Spanish-American War back in 1898 (and the Panama Canal project), became more widely used in dance bands than banjos. And when I asked him if he had ever played around with any of the south of the border high-note fiesta trumpet stuff, which sometimes we also used to think of as being bullring trumpet stuff, and also peanut vendor trumpet stuff, he shook his head, chuckling to himself .

Then he said, Man, well do I remember when young trumpet players around my hometown used to find that stuff just about irresistible. But man, some of the strictest musical teachers around my hometown were also the very ones who had been directors and instrumentalists in military bands down in Cuba during the Spanish-American War and in the cavalry on the Mexican border in the teens.

I had never thought of him as having ever had any serious personal professional interest in dance bands as such. As far as I knew, none of the music school courses of study had anything whatsoever to do with becoming bandleaders and arrangers/composers like the Bossman Himself. There was no school of music as such at Alabama State Teachers College in Montgomery, but if you were mainly interested in becoming a dance band musician, that was your best bet so far as college was concerned in those days.

My impression of Taft Edison from the very outset was that his ambition was to create compositions based on down-home sacred and secular music, including workaday chants and hollers, that would be performed in concert halls by concert hall–type instrumental and vocal groups and philharmonic orchestras. Because when I arrived on the campus as a freshman that fall, he was a junior who impressed me more than anybody else in the School of Music because he was the student who conducted the school's widely popular college marching band when it took its place in the grandstand in Alumni Bowl to play for the cheerleaders during football games, and he also was the one who supervised the tune-up before the faculty bandmaster took over to direct the concerts in the bandstand on the promenade lawn across which the weather-green copper tower of the chime clock faced the rust red dome and the white Doric antebellum columns and eaves of the brick red dining hall, in the basement of which the student social center was located in those days.

I can still remember how special the musical insignia on his nattily tailored ROTC cadet uniform looked compared with the plainness of those worn by most other cadets who were infantry privates without cadet NCO stripes or the Sam Browne belts and rank insignia that cadet officers used to wear. So he was obviously a very outstanding student musician.

But although there were also two student-led dance bands on the campus at that time, I can't remember having ever seen him playing with either of them. Not that I ever got the impression that he disliked or had no interest in that kind of music, or that his attitude was one of condescension, as was the case of many conservatory-oriented students at the time. Not at all. Because when you saw him at seasonal and fraternity and sorority socials and at benefit dances, he was not only very much in circulation, as we used to say, but was also always up-to-date on all the latest steps. And also when he stopped by the Mainstem Lounge, where you used to listen to the late-night radio broadcasts from such then famous nightspots as the Savoy Ballroom and the Cotton Club in Harlem and the Grand Terrace on the South Side of Chicago in those days, he could identify as many bands and sidemen as instantaneously as any of the dance band musicians, record collectors, and patent-leather avenue sharpies as happened to be there at the time.

So when I told him what I told him about my stopgap gig with the band, I didn't know what his response would be, but I did so because I had decided that I had better mention it myself rather than running the risk of having him find about it just incidentally somehow and wonder why I hadn't mentioned it on my own and why I hadn't yet said anything at all about ever having played any musical instrument, not even in junior high school. Not that I thought that he would think I was trying to impress him; however, I felt I was in an awkward position either way. And also what if he already knew about it?

But as I should have remembered from his completely unsurprised and ever so casual response when I introduced myself to him on Fifth Avenue that day, he didn't register any surprise at all. Not to avoid any embarrassing questions about my qualifications but because he also seemed to know almost as much about how the Bossman Himself picked musicians as Hortense Hightower did. Anyway, all he said was that he hadn't heard the band during the period between Shag Phillips and Scratchy McFatrick.

But, he said, I do remember hearing something about some college boy filling in for a while. So that was you! Which just goes to show you. If whoever it was that I heard it from had mentioned the name of the college boy's school, I probably would have asked you if you happened to know him when we met that day down in the Forties. I must say that must have been something. Man, as definite as I was about moving out of music as a profession by that time, I myself would have had a hard time turning down the chance to hit the trail with that fabulous crew of thugs for a while. Man, I can just imagine it. Man, when I woke up every morning and realized why I was wherever I was I would have had to pinch myself.

I didn't say anything about me crossing my fingers, because then he changed the subject to what he had been planning to talk about when he called me the night before and invited me to come by that afternoon, and that was when he said what he said about how much talk about political issues, movements, organizations, involvements, and affiliations you heard among the people in the academic and literary circles he had begun to move into shortly after he decided to settle in New York for at least a while instead of going back down to the campus for his senior year.

Look, man, he went on to say, I don't know how politically active you are, or what your political affiliations, if any, may happen to be, but I was wondering about how much of that sort of thing you might have run into by now. Because, man, one of the first things that struck me about this town when I arrived and first started making the rounds was all the political recruitment I was forever running into. Somebody was forever trying to get me to join some political group or other, all of them calling themselves either liberal, left-wing, or downright radical if not outright revolutionary.

Man, you'd see some very fly fay chippie and catch her eye or the sparkle that she's aiming at you and you move in on her or she might move in on you and take her to your place or perhaps more often to hers, and the next morning you'd find out what the game is. She was the one that had you in her sights as soon as you hit the scene. Not because of all that ever ready automatically syncopated action she says you inherited from your stud horse male ancestors she was thanking you all night for laying on her. Man, all of that hair-trigger ecstatic response is subject to be the standard prelude to a bunch of political pamphlets that she's going to lay on you. And if she doesn't quiz you about them on the next tête-à-tête she's definitely going to check you out on the third. Then if you become a recruit she might keep you in her stable for a while before passing you on to somebody closer to the inner circle.

SOP, man, he said, chuckling again. Standard operating procedure. *Standing revolutionary recruitment procedure for the ostracized minorities!* Man, you've got to watch that stuff, or you'll be well on you way to becoming a statistic on somebody's revolutionary agenda. Man, that stuff used to be downright evangelical. But of course I don't have to tell you that most down-home cats drop those pamphlets in the first trash can they came to en route to the subway. Man, you know as well as I do that what them down-home boots were out for was not some abstract political program but some unsegregated easily accessible living and breathing hot-to-trot body action for free, or at least for not more than a drink or two.

He said, Man, a few jive artists might have tried to fake and cross talk their way through some of that stuff if reading it was what you had to do to get to the sack in the first place. But my guess is that not many were likely to work their way through that kind of stuff to get back to the sack for a second go-round.

Because all they were out for was a one-night pickup in the first place. Man, as far as they were concerned, it was not a matter of how many times with the same chicks but how many chicks.

But on the other hand, though, as you also know, there were and are also some splibs who figure that they have to read that stuff to prove that their formal education qualifies them to move in such exclusive, articulate and up-to-date company as they assume their present company represents—just in case there's any question of basic intellectual eligibility. *Hey, don't play me cheap, Miss Lady Blueblood playgirl. Some of us may be from across the tracks, but here's one who can dig this dialectic jive, too!* Now, man, that's a sitting duck.

Which brings me around to why I've been meaning to get around to this topic in the first place: so here comes old Taft Woodrow Edison with his high grade-point average flashing like stop-look-and-listen at an express crossing. Not to mention three years of college earned through meritorious scholarship! So what does he on whom little in the weekly, monthly, and quarterly journals and critical reviews in the periodicals room of the campus library was lost—man, what does he do with those evangelical pamphlets? *He reads them! Man, he reads them to satisfy his endemic Oklahoma suspicion that they are not worth reading. They are not worth the cornbread paper they are printed on. And then does he dump them in the nearest garbage drop? Absolutely not! Because he's made so many marginal notes that he wants to argue about that he calls up his recruiter for another date! And man, that call led me into some stuff that is a part of what I'm still trying to come to terms with on my own as a writer.*

Then he said, Of course when I think back on it now I see it as something that turned out to be a sort of catalytic agent. Or let's put it this way: I would not be going about this thing of being a writer in the way I'm going about it as of now if that encounter hadn't turned out to be one of those encounters.

That was why it was on the same afternoon that I told him about my time on the road with the band that I also told him what I told him about what happened when my roommate and I read André Malraux's *Man's Fate* during my sophomore year. I said, Man, the first thing I ever really heard about what that kind of recruitment was like was what my roommate told me about what he had already found out about the movement (meaning the underground movement) in Chicago by the time he finished junior high school. Before that the only kind of political recruitment I can remember hearing about was labor union- ism, mainly the longshoremen's union strikes and picket lines and scabs down on the Mobile, Alabama, waterfront, where Uncle Jerome worked for the United Fruit Company. Man, what my roommate told me about the movement in Chicago made it all sound like joining a very strict church whose members were always on the lookout for transgressors.

I said, Incidentally, we also read Malraux's *The Conquerors*, but he had transferred before I read *Man's Hope*, and I didn't get around to Karl Marx until my senior year, and by that time not only did dialectic materialism sound as much like the gospel as something you were reading in a political bible, but man, that was also when I realized *that all political systems were run by politicians, just as all religions were run by preachers and preachers and deacons elected or self-designated.*

I said, Man, when I was a senior in high school, what I was mainly concerned with was getting to college. I said, Man, my preoccupation was not with changing the world. Man, I was still trying to find out what all this stuff was all about. And what I was eligible for. I said, Man, in the third grade there was geography along with all of those maps and the globe and the bulletin board windows on the world and peoples of many lands.

I said, Then when I got to senior high school and started spending more and more time in the library I discovered world history and anthropology. And that was when I began to realize that I was going to have to be a schoolboy for some time to come. So man, I guess that's where whatever immunity to political recruitment I've developed began. I said, Anyway, by the time I was halfway through college I was too wrapped up in doing what I was doing on my own to be recruited for any political movement. I said, Man, none of that theoretical stuff I was also reading in those current political journals in the periodicals room added up to the magic keys I was looking for (*mentioning Miss Lexine Metcalf, who said some golden, some silver, some platinum, and maybe some of some as yet undiscovered alloy. But not mentioning Jewel Templeton, who said some sharp, some flat, and some natural*).

Then I said, But to answer your question, as yet I haven't run into the kind of recruitment you're talking about. Not since I've been here and not anywhere on the road with the band. Not even in Hollywood. I said, Man, now that you bring up the subject, come to think of it, I don't remember anybody in the band ever bringing up the subject of political recruitment at all. Maybe they thought that being a college boy I was already hip to all of that *theoretical* jive. But none of the fans I got to know in any of our stopping places ever asked me very much about anything except myself and my relationship to the band.

But I didn't go on to mention anything about people like the Marquis de Chaumienne and Jewel Templeton, and that was when he said what he said about down-home church folks and hypocrisy. There was all that Sunday church meeting singing and shouting and amen corner moaning and clapping. And for those who wished to express a more comprehensive devotion, there were midweek prayer meetings with hymn singing. But as often as not, when things came down to the nuts-and-bolts actualities of everyday goings-on and the situation added up to put up or shut up, you couldn't tell a spoonful of difference between the most righteous church members and just plain old everyday looking-out-for-number-one folks. So man, you get my point about the folks. Down home it's religious hypocrisy. Up here it's political hypocrisy, which just might turn out to be a very crucial saving grace indeed, given the political temper of the times.

XIII

At the end of the spring term I had completed all of the requirements for the Master of Arts degree except the thesis, on which (in addition to the other research reports) I had begun working during the Christmas holiday break and which I finished and submitted by the late-summer deadline. So I was eligible to enter the Ph.D. program that next September. But when I went to register and work out my course of study and request my choice of professors, I had already decided that I was going to spend only this consecutive year attending formal classroom lectures and seminars and doing academic research reports in preparation for the dissertation required for the doctorate in the field of humanities in those days.

One more consecutive year of academic gumshoe, I told Taft Edison the day after I was notified that my thesis had been approved. And when he asked what about the year after that, I told him about Eunice's plans and also about the letter back in June from the English Department down in central Alabama offering me a temporary position as an instructor of freshman and sophomore composition and introduction to literature.

You didn't have to explain that the offer did not imply that anybody down there assumed that I had decided to be a college professor and that it had been made only as a suggested option in the event I needed more cash to supplement my fellowship grant. Taft Edison already knew that because he already knew that the head of the English Department making the offer was Carlton Poindexter, whose junior-year class in the English novel he was enrolled in and who also was his informal extracurricular reading consultant when I was a freshman.

By that time Taft Edison also knew that I had not yet decided *not* to become a college teacher, because he knew that I had not yet finally made up my mind not to complete the Ph.D. program. But he did know that I was beginning to question the relevance of the Ph.D. degree to achievement in the arts. Because he was the one to whom I had said what I said about the difference between formal training in the arts and in the sciences and mathematics. I said if my main intellectual orientation had led me into science and mathematics I probably would have been aiming at a Ph.D. since junior high school. Because you had to work your way up to that academic level just to become involved with what had now become an indispensable part of the most elementary terminology, equipment, and procedure.

In the arts and the humanities, on the other hand, I said, you could actually come by all of the fundamentals by the time you could function on a senior level of an accredited high school. Because by then you would have been initiated into the realm of the great world masterpieces of literature, music, and history, and the ones you had not read as class assignments on your own initiative were part of the same universal context as the ones assigned. After all, it was not as if you had to go on beyond high school and then college and then graduate in order to read other masterworks by the same Homer, Virgil, Shakespeare, Balzac, or George Eliot, a sample of whose works you had already come to terms with in high school or even as a high school dropout.

Eunice, who had fulfilled all of the requirements for the M.S. degree in education at Teachers College, was looking forward to spending the next year in New York working as a part-time substitute elementary school teacher. But I knew that she felt that after that she should spend at least several terms working as a teacher, administrator, or supervisor down in central Alabama. She knew very well that the hometown benefactors who had provided the four-year college scholarship to earn her B.S. degree, without which she would not have been in position to win the fellowship for graduate study for the master's degree at Teachers College, would not feel that she had deserted them.

She knew as well as I did that their reaction would be exactly the same as when down-home folks have always celebrated local people who succeed elsewhere, especially up north in Philamayork. Who knows? Such down-home celebration of locals who make good elsewhere may have begun all the way back in the era of the fugitive slave, of whom those still down on the plantation most often said not that he or she ran away and left us, but rather *if he or she could do that, other folks down here can do it, too.*

I could already hear all sorts of variations on remarks like: Y'all remember little ol' frizzly-headed Eunice Whatshername that use to pass by here going to and from school? And went on through high school and got that big send-off to college? Well, they say when she finished up her college course she got another big send-off to New York. And when she passed some courses up there they hired her. Everybody always did say that girl was going places. I always liked the way she carried herself on the way to and from school and anywhere else. Always neat as a pin whatever she was wearing and never one to cash in on being that good-looking. You can ask anybody and they'll tell you. Didn't go around with her nose in the air neither. That child had her nose in them books every chance she got. I always did say she could make it anywhere doing anything she put her mind to.

She was as aware of all that as any other scholarship student I ever met. So she also knew that her hometown folks, like mine down in Gasoline Point and Mobile County Training School, wanted her to go wherever her quest for further development led her. And she also knew that their trust of her judgment was such that none of her down-home benefactors had assumed that she had given up on her own professional objectives to get married. After all, it was as if she had gotten married and gone straight off to graduate school as if on an extended honeymoon.

In any case, if I had said nothing about going back down to central Alabama because I had decided to stay at New York University for a third consecutive year as I had originally anticipated, she would not have said what she said about going back when she did since she already knew that I had begun to question the relevance of my academic research assignments to the way I was beginning to want to come to my own terms with things. When I showed her the letter with the offer from central Alabama she said, Why not? She said, Meanwhile, I have some unfinished business of my own down in those parts.

You didn't have to explain any of that to Taft Edison, and when he said, Speaking of roommates, I've been making a few cautious moves in that direction myself, and there is somebody you'll be meeting soon, I knew that he was changing the subject. And I said, Whenever you say.

I knew that he had been married for a short time during his

second year in New York, and I also knew that former wife's name and that she was a nightclub entertainer, but he never discussed their relationship except to say that it was a mistake that was soon corrected and that there were no lingering after-effects. That was all he said and I did not ask him anything else about her.

He said, Her name is Janice and we've been seeing each other for a few months now and have just about decided that we've got something going that should be continued at a closer range of involvement. So we're looking for a place. I must say, and as you probably guessed, this was not something I was looking for at this time. It just happened and I must tell you, man, as much as she has going for her, no small part of it is the fact she knows how I feel about this thing I'm tangled up with, this goddamn albatross of a manuscript of a homemade novel—*man, talking about mammy made!*

And that was when he also said what he said about what he was trying to do and also said that if he came anywhere close to what he had in mind he did not expect the sales to add up to enough to put it on the bestseller list and that if there were enough sales to encourage the publisher to offer him a contract for another book, he would consider himself as having been successfully launched on a career as a literary professional.

Man, he said, she knows that I have to try to see if I can do what I think I should be doing with a book.

And I said, She sounds like she's the one, all right. And he said, Could be and he said, So far, so good, I must say. So now we're going to find out if she can put up with the likes of me on a daily basis.

When he called again several weeks later, he said, Hey, man, looks like we have a change of address on our hands over here, and yes, that means that I've given you obvious reason to as-

sume it implies. We've jumped the broom, tied the knot, and are about to give up my place on St. Nicholas and her place on Convent for a larger place over at 730 Riverside Drive, an eighth-floor place from which you can see directly across the Hudson River to Palisades Park and also a partial view of the George Washington Bridge! So, man, we're hoping to get it all presentable enough during the next few weeks to have you all and a few other friends over for an old down up plus "up here" New Year's Eve celebration. With pigs' feet, black-eyed peas, collard greens, okra, and corn bread, plus down-home bootleg white lightnin' as well as up-here champagne, and for dessert gingerbread muffins and/or sweet potato pie.

XIV

As for the one who was to be the one for the likes of me, when I got to college the main thing during those first two years was the necessity to maintain the grade-point average required for the renewal of my scholarship grant. Then there was also the no less urgent matter of coping with how my roommate was taking all of those college-level course requirements in stride as if they were as routine as current newspaper and magazine articles.

I was the one who was enrolled in the Department of Liberal Arts. He was in the Department of Architecture. But it was as if the main thing for him was the wide selection of the great books of world history, literature, philosophy, and science that he could check out of the library and read on his own.

Elementary, my dear Watson, he said when we came back from our first exploration of the card index in the main reading room and the racks and shelves of the periodicals room. Elementary. Name me *any* human concern that your qualified architect is not expected to know where to find the goods on. Context, my dear fellow, nor do I speak only of material surroundings and time frames.

Jerome Jefferson, polymath. T. Jerome Jefferson. Better known on campus as Geronimo from Chicago, and also as the Snake, as in snake in the grass, and as snake doctor as in snake-oil doctor. But only partly because the snake oil was actually the chemistry laboratory alcohol cocktail he used to concoct and bootleg from time to time, especially when there were campus socials.

Taft Edison, who was there only during that first year, now remembered him not only because his chem lab concoction had predance customers in the band cottage, but also because as a freshman he had joined the augmented French horn section that the band took to Chicago along with the football team for the annual game with Wilberforce University at Soldier Field.

Neither of us became involved in an ongoing relationship with a special on-campus girlfriend during those first two years. With me it was a matter of avoiding encounters that were not mutually casual, because I couldn't spare the extra money you had to have for regular dates, treats, and ceremonial gifts. But for him, it was a matter of choice. He could afford the extra spending change, but he preferred "freelancing" because it was consistent with the bohemian nature of college life that he had in mind for us when he labeled our room Atelier 359.

When classes began on the first day of my third fall day on campus, my roommate was no longer there, because he had transferred to the School of Architecture at Yale. And as much as I missed him, I was also pleased that, so far, nobody had been assigned to replace him because I was then twenty-one years old and I had never had a room all to myself before. Now I was twenty-one and also an upperclassman.

Then it was the first week of that third October, and there she was. I was on my way up the steps of the main entrance of the library and I overtook someone I had not seen on campus before and stopped to hold the door open for her to step past me into the lobby. And in that time frame of less than one bar of music it was as if I had stepped into that enchanted boy blue zone of crepe myrtle yard blossoms and dog fennel meadows again. And I had to say something more than just hello or good morning. So I said, How is freshman orientation coming along this year? And that is how I came to know that she was a sophomore who had transferred after spending her freshman year at State Normal. And I said, I hope you will be glad you did.

We came up the wide staircase side by side and step by step, but I didn't say anything else until we stepped onto the second-floor landing and then all I said before she turned left to go into the main reading room was, Well, good luck, and I hope you like it here enough to stick around.

And she said she already liked it very much and when I said, So we'll be seeing you around, meanwhile, best wishes, she said, Thank you again. So far everybody has been very understanding and very helpful, especially when they find out that I'm not a freshman.

That was all that happened. And I came on into the reference room and checked out the books I wanted from the special reserve list shelf and it was not until I sat down to open the first book that I realized that I had not asked her name and I had not given her mine. That was how it all began for me, because even as I realized that I could go into the main reading room and find her, I also realized that all I could do was just sit there with my fingers crossed and hope that she had not been on her way to join somebody. Maybe even somebody she had transferred from State Normal to join—or even more probably, someone she had met since arriving on the campus.

Which is why for the next week every time I went into the dining hall I crossed my fingers hoping that I would not see what I did not want to see. I came through the same side entrance that I always used because it was the one you came to first when you came along Campus Avenue from the dormitories on the upper end of the campus or across from the quadrangle, which included the library, the main academic building in those days, and the gymnasium, which included the main entertainment auditorium, beyond which were the tennis courts and the campus bowl. But instead of scanning the tables to locate who was already there and sitting with whom and where, I headed straight to and through the serving line and onto an empty table all the way at the back of the hall near a window through which you could look down the slope to the campus power plant and campus laundry area. And when I finished I left through the exit nearest that part of the building, which was also the shortest route back to Atelier 359.

So I didn't see what I didn't want to see and after four days I realized I hadn't seen what I really wanted to see either. And then I also realized that I was crossing my fingers again, not only because I wanted to see her all by herself again, but also because I was hoping that she had not decided to go back to State Normal or had transferred to Talladega or Fisk or Spelman. Or maybe she didn't eat in the cafeteria because she didn't live on campus. Maybe she had relatives or family friends with whom she was boarding on or off campus. *Or maybe she was living off campus because she was married to somebody who already lived off campus and that was why she had transferred from State Normal in the first place!*

Not that I was any more able to begin a steady on-campus relationship than I had been during my freshman or sophomore years. I could spare enough cash for an off-campus caper now and then, and I could also manage to keep enough petty cash on hand to go out to listen to the best of the topflight dance and variety orchestras when they included a one-night stand at the

Dolomite on their annual coast-to-coast and border-to-border bus tour schedules.

So far this had happened only several times each year. But it was something I didn't intend to miss. Because although I never had any urge to become a musician myself, old Luzana Cholly and his twelve-string guitar, and old Stagolee Dupas fils and his honky-tonk gut bucket and patent leather avenue stride time piano and the sound of Bessie, Mamie, and Trixie Smith and also old Jelly Roll Morton and King Oliver and Louis Armstrong on Miss Blue Eula Bacoat's gramophone over in Gin's Alley were already indispensable parts of what having a good time was all about that many years before I was to become the school-boy that Miss Lexine Metcalf and Mr. B. Franklin Fisher wanted me to be.

So I felt the way I felt about the Dolomite because out there not only could you finally hear the actual bands playing the music they had made famous on recordings and radio, you could also get into personal contact with the musicians themselves.

So far, so good, I remember thinking as I moved along in the registration line for junior-year students that third September. So far, so very good. So far, so very, very good. I had not been able to go back home since I arrived on campus, but by taking a full-time on-campus job during the Christmas holidays and the summer vacation months I had been able to supplement my scholarship grant budget and provide myself with basic incidentals with just enough left over to get by on if you pinch pennies.

Indeed so far, better than ever because not only was I halfway to graduation but I was also enjoying the highest standard of living I had ever had access to. Nothing was hand-me-down or makeshift. On the contrary, dormitories were inspected daily and there were also summer entertainment features and campus recreational facilities plus the library and all that freedom from class assignment time for the extracurricular reading I had come to realize I needed to do. And besides, what would I do back in Gasoline Point, anyway? I had never had a job in Gasoline Point or in downtown Mobile either, and unskilled jobs were as scarce as ever.

So far, so good, yea verily. And after all, when I got on that Greyhound bus with my new gladstone bag and my scholarship award voucher and my one-way ticket, my intention was to be long gone and farther, and when I arrived on campus my question was not When do I return to Gasoline Point and Mobile? but Where do I go on to from here? Philamayork, Philamayork, the also and also of Philamayork, to be sure, which even before junior high school was already a fireside, tell-me-tale code name for the best of all possible places.

But even that early on you had also already come to realize that even if your Philamayork turned out to be Philadelphia or Pittsburgh, Pennsylvania, or New York City, New York, or Chicago, Illinois, or Detroit, Michigan, or Los Angeles or San Francisco, California, once you headed out from Gasoline Point toward the ever so Marco Polo blue horizon mists beyond Chickasabogue Bridge it would be as if your destination were wherever east of the sun and west of the moon was.

So far, so good. But what now? Because there I was with my fingers also crossed because this time I was wishing what I was wishing as if the crisp autumn green campus, lawn grass, and shrubbery and the bright blue silk and cotton white autumn sky made my circumstances no less fancy free than they had ever been back during the springtime elementary school bell days of honeysuckle thickets and dog fennel playhouse games. All I had to go on was that ever so polite exchange in the library. I didn't even know her name and was not even certain that she was still there. But by the middle of the next week, the very thought of her being on the campus had become as much a part of my speculations about what my junior year was going to be like as about any of the new electives on my academic course of study.

Then after that many days, there she was in person again, coming up the steps and into the library again all by herself again. And as I opened the door for her and said, Nice to see you're still here, she smiled but I couldn't really tell if she remembered me or was just being a nice, well-brought-up young lady who was not cynical and didn't consider herself vulnerable. So when I said what I said about becoming used to not being used to being at State Normal, she smiled again. And when she said what she said about becoming used to being a sophomore and that she had originally expected to be a freshman on this campus in the first place, all I could say was, Is that so? Because I couldn't say how glad I was that she had not arrived before now, not to mention my freshman year.

We stepped onto the second-floor landing again, then and to keep her from realizing how excited I was to see her again and how eagerly I was looking forward to seeing her as often as possible, I stepped in the direction of the reference room before turning to say, So nice to see that you're still here, and that was also when I finally said my name and where I was from and that I was getting used to not being used to being a junior in liberal arts.

And when she smiled and said her name and what part of central Alabama she was from, all I could say was, Well, hello again, statemate. And all I could do was tighten my fingers because they were already crossed.

That was how it all began with the one that I decided was the one for me, because, as luck would have it, when it was deep purple wisteria time on the campus again that next spring we had become as close as we had become because our self-imposed restrictions were as compatible as they were because it turned out that we both were there on renewable scholarship awards that had to be supplemented with what you could earn in cash or credit from jobs available through the student employment office.

So I had not seen her in the dining hall because she did not eat in the dining hall. She lived in the sophomore women's dormitory, but she ate all her meals in the visitors' guesthouse, where she worked when not in class or at the library and from the early-evening meal until seven-thirty, after which if she did not have to go back to the library, she did what she had to do back in the dormitory. As for nonacademic activities, she had decided to restrict herself to an occasional choice from the schedule of athletic events, movies, stage productions, and concerts covered by the prepaid incidental-fee admission coupon.

I didn't make my first obvious move until the fall dance gala on the night following the homecoming football game in November, the biggest social event of the fall term. During my freshman and sophomore years my old freelancing roommate and I went to such shindigs unattached and made our forays on targets of opportunity as we spotted them from the stag line (or "Murderers' Row") near the table of refreshments. But this time I was glad he was not there anymore, because I still had not seen what I had not wanted to see in the dining hall or anywhere else. And because I was still hoping what I could not keep myself from hoping since that midmorning when I first saw her on our way up the steps and into the library.

When I arrived, the band was already halfway into the first

set, and the dance floor was already more than half full of couples, with a steady stream of others joining in, some directly from the coat-check windows. My old roommate and I had always stopped at the refreshment table for a waxed paper tumbler of student punch-bowl punch, which he always spiked—his, not mine—with his own chem lab cocktail concoction from his pewter hip pocket flask. But this time I took mine and sipped it as I slowly mcandered my way toward the bandstand, because I still had no way of knowing whether I was going to see what I hoped I wouldn't see.

So she may have seen me before I saw her this time, because when I came within eight yards of the bandstand, there she was sitting at a front-row table in the waist-high spectators' gallery on my right. And with her were two other sophomore coeds whom I remembered from the year before but had not met. And when I was as sure as I could guess that I was in her line of sight, I waved and she waved back and when I held out my hand, she stood up and came down onto the dance floor. And when I said her name, she said mine.

XV

Hi ya, fellow, the voice on the phone said. And I said, Eric von Threadcraft. And he said, Got you. He said, Got you in two rings. And I said, Hey, man, I said, What say, Mice? I said, Goddamn, man. How you been and what you been up to? And he said, A little of this and some of that plus the same old ongoing, but always on the afterbeat, man. You know me, fellow. And then he said, Hey, what this is about is that I caught the band in person out here tonight for the first time since you cut out, and naturally I went backstage to check with Papa Joe and he gave me your number and told me what you were up to and into these days. So how is school and how is family life?

And I said, Man, the thing about graduate school is that the more advanced the courses of study, the more basic the material and the more obvious the assumptions and the more relative and tentative the conclusions. So it's the also and also all over again, my man, the also and also and also, perhaps even as the also and also of arithmetic becomes the also and also of algebra, calculus, and trigonometry.

Then before he could say anything about that, I said, As for family life, affirmative by me, man. What can I tell you, man? *Je suis tout à fait en train d'être dans le vrai*, if you remember that old Flaubert riff you tried to sneak in there on me that time. Or should I say *heureusement en train*?

And that was when he said what he said about me spending the time I spent keeping the time as a bass player, and about how lucky I was to have come across that particular instrument of all musical instruments the way I did. Then he also said, Speaking of fundamentals, my man, that fabulous Miss Hortense Hightower you used to tell me about, had your number, fellow. Just think about it, Schoolboy, if you will pardon the expression. There you were up there in college because your Miss Lexine fairy-tale aunt Metcalf had earmarked you as early on as the third grade for some undefined something special requiring higher education. So there you are up there on the campus flat broke except for what little was left over from the fellowship grants, but determined to pass the academic equivalent of every obstacle that Jason the argonaut was supposed to pass to qualify himself for the ultimate boon of a golden fleece and here you come out of there on commencement day having earned yourself not only the magic sheepskin but also the bull fiddle, of all things. A goddamn completely unacademic jazz-anchoring bull fiddle!

That's something else, fellow, he said. That's something to think about. Because, man, are you sure that your Miss Hortense Hightower was not your Miss Lexine Metcalf in the disguise of an after-hours nightclub diva? And what about that roommate of yours that turned up down there from Chicago and stayed around just long enough to become in some ways even more and certainly no less indelible than your Mr. B. Franklin Fisher himself, without whom, after all, there would have been no Miss Lexine Metcalf in the first place? No him without her, but hey, no *her* without him to bring her there as if specifically to find the likes of you. Fairy-tale stuff U.S.A., fellow.

Just look at how it all hooks up, he said. It was Hortense Hightower who got you that incredible quantum leap of a break that didn't just land you a gig with the greatest band that ever was, but also meant that your *elementary*, repeat elementary, as in beginner's school music, faculty was made up of none other than Joe States, Old Pro, and the Bossman *Himself*! Incredible, fellow! *Incroyable!* Think about it, fellow, think about it.

And I said, I hear you, man. I really do hear you. But you feel like that because of what music means to you as a musician. But man, I was doing what I was doing because that was what came up for me that summer, and I've always done the best I could and once more it was good enough to get me by. Because they were not looking for an expert. You know the Bossman, Mice. Sometimes he just likes to find out what he can make of whatever turns up. You and I have been over that, I said, reminding him of references he and I had made from time to time to how visual artists sometimes used unaltered and somewhat altered found objects!

I said, man, they weren't even looking for an expert when they picked up Scratchy McFatrick. They were looking for a replacement for Jameson McLemore, who was only a temporary—no, interim—replacement for me. Because Jamie had no intention of staying away from L.A. and his family for more than a short period. So when old Scratchy Mac turned up with all of that virtuosity he also fell right into the Bossman's old utilization approach, but this time there was so much more there than anybody on that instrument had ever come in with from anywhere. Man, I like to think of old Scratchy as the Bossman's reward for the good deed he did for me.

I said, Man, as for me getting with cutting them dots, that was Old Pro's department and sometimes he used to call me up to sit with him on the bus as he checked through the score sheets and made sure that all of the Bossman's latest revisions were in place. That was something he used to do, especially during those long stretches when the landscape was the same old stuff mile after mile after mile and everybody else was nodding and I was awake and happened not to be reading.

And he said, See what I mean, man, that's precisely the kind of priceless stuff I'm talking about. But hey, look, I better cut this off so you can get back to your homework. Speaking of which, I must tell you this. Man, when Papa Joe States clued me in on your whereabouts these days I could just see you relaxing back in one of those comfortable, heavy-gauged oak New York University classroom chairs with your invisible bass fiddle sound box between your legs like a cello with your pizzicato fingers here and your fretting fingers up here and the ornate tuning pegs and scroll protruding above your head like some kind of regal decoration.

And then he said, Anyway, I just want you to know that I've missed you, fellow. As tied up as I've been since I came back from that deal in Europe not long after you cut out and also disconnected your answering service. I still kept expecting you to turn up any day. But hell, I guess you can tell I've been thinking about you. And oh, by the way, before I hang up I also want you to know that Felix has some loot for you. That movie thing didn't go through because something so much better turned up for me. But there was something up front for the preliminary work that we did and part of it is yours and we kept expecting to hear from you. So it will be on the way to you tomorrow.

So I really better get off the line now, he said then, but I just had to call and let you know how much I'd like for us to get together the next time I'm in New York. And naturally I'm just dying to meet that fine stone fox of a roommate of yours that Joe States was carrying on so about. He calls her some fine people, which just knocks me out, fellow. Because just leave it to old Papa Joe. Because I don't know whether he's riffing on our man James Joyce's Annalivia or not, but calling her some fine *people* brings back to this schoolboy's mind is *Plurabelle,* which I distinctly remember you yourself using in a conversation we were having about "Sweet Georgia Brown" on the way back to Hollywood from a Central Avenue jam session one night. I kept talking about how those battling tenors kept leapfrogging each other and you said what you said as if any parody of James Joyce or Williams and Walker, or was it Miller and Lyles in a vaudeville skit? *Man talking about Annalivia, man, I could tell you something about Annalivia, about the plurabilities of Annalivia Plurabelle! Yeah, man, but what about this? Man, I know that, but let me tell you about the time when. Hey, yeah, man, but listen to this . . .* with the rhythm flowing like old James Joyce's river running all the way back to Eve and Adam.

I often think about how you used to come up with stuff like that, my man, he said then. Who knows? Old Joe States has a set of ears second to none. And a mind like a steel trap. If you ever started signifying about that tune like that anywhere near him he's subject to pick up on that Plurabelle part right away, and riff it back at you so fast you won't even recognize that you're the source. His source, in any case.

Then just before he actually did finally hang up he said, But hey, look. Speaking of Plurabelles and plurabilities, I must confess that there are perhaps some possibly significant reorientations in progress chez your old scene cruising friend Mice these days. But which I'm not going to tell you about until I get to New York before long or maybe even sooner. But definitely as soon as I can make it and that means the next time I call I just might already be there on my next as of now inevitable trip back east.

XVI

Man, what can I say? Roland Beasley said as we crossed Madison Avenue on our way along Fifty-seventh Street to Fifth Avenue and Rizzoli's Bookstore. We had spent the first part of the afternoon at an exhibition of Jacques Callot drawings, sketches, and etchings that Roland had invited me to come along and see at an upstairs gallery near Park Avenue.

I had told him what I had told him about how I had begun reading about the Commedia dell'Arte during the fall of my freshman year in college. And when he called he had also reminded me that I also said what I had said about Jacques Callot the first time we talked about the reproductions of the Harlequins and Saltimbancs in a book from the Museum of Modern Art about the first fifty years of the paintings of Pablo Picasso.

I had become aware of the origin and existence of medieval miracle, morality, and passion plays by the time I finished junior high school at Mobile County Training School, where nobody who ever heard Mr. B. Franklin Fisher talk about how citizens of the German town of Oberammergau traditionally spent ten years developing the roles of the biblical characters they had been chosen to represent that many years ahead of the next periodic production, were ever likely to forget what a

Passion play was about. And of course, that story was also related to what you already knew about Christmas and Easter pageants, not to mention class work that became a part of the history pageants presented as part of general assembly programs and graduation exercises. Not to mention the fact that Mobile being not only the pre–New Orleans French Gulf Coast settlement town that it was, I had grown up knowing about riverboat entertainers along with traveling tent shows and vaudeville acts as well as annual carnival costume masks and parades.

But before the fall term of my freshman year in college I had never become aware of anything at all about the Commedia dell'Arte as such, although I did know what Harlequin and Pantalone costumes looked like and that both represented stock characters like the stock characters in newspaper comic strips and also like Punchinello in the Punch and Judy puppet shows and like Charlie Chaplin and Buster Keaton of silent moving pictures.

As we stopped at the corner of Tiffany's and waited for the light to change so we could cross over to the west side of Fifth Avenue, Roland Beasley shook his head and clenched and rubbed his palms, saying, What can I say, my man? What can I tell you? I really do think that we just might be on our way to getting next to something that we can riff on for days, man, and I mean day and night.

And I said, You said it, old partner. I said, All you've got to do is start vamping and riffing around stuff like "Drop Me Off in Harlem" or "Echoes of Harlem" or "Slapping Seventh Avenue with the Sole of My Shoe," and what about stuff like "Harlem Airshaft" and stuff like that. And just watch how variations on old Jacques Callot's and all that jiveass crew will start turning up stomping at the Savoy and jumping at the Woodside and cooling it at Connie's Inn just like they did in Picasso's Belle Epoque Montmartre, and just look at all of those theater and nightlife characters already there in Toulouse Lautrec. And don't forget Degas and all those dancing girls and scenes.

There we go, he said as we turned into the entrance to Rizzoli's, no doubt about it. Degas and Toulouse Lautrec and Picasso at Connie's Inn and Small's Paradise, at the Lafayette and at the Savoy, *the Home of Happy Feet*. You know what I mean? Not them, me. Old Rollo! *Old Rollo's visual echoes of Harlem*. Old Rollo. Not Miguel Covarrubias and all that old-trouble-I-seen-eyed blubber-lipped, blubber-butt, blubber-foot refugees from the goddamn cotton field out barrelhousing on Saturday night in their Montgomery Ward and Sears, Roebuck Sunday best. Man, talk about square. Man, even the goddamned drummers looked square in that goddamn Covarrubias stuff. I know better. Man, I was right up there. Man, I'm from North Carolina, but I grew up right around the corner from Connie's Inn and the old Lafayette Theater. Man, remember to remind me to tell you about Big John's, where they used to serve that Big John Special that Fletcher Henderson's band made that Big John Special record about. Boy, we used to live right off Seventh Avenue on 131st Street, and the Old Rhythm Club, where most of the uptown hoofers and keyboard ticklers used to hold those legendary cutting contests while waiting for gigs in between tours, was on 132nd Street, right down the block from the Lafayette going toward Lenox Avenue. Boy, if old Covarrubias was ever in there, he must have been blind as a bat and had plugs in his ears.

You got him, I said. And then I also said, He was OK on that stuff in the Balinese islands and the southern part of Mexico, because he was looking at it as something ceremonial, ritualistic, and anthropological. But his down-home, across-the-tracks stuff and uptown stuff is only ethnic caricature that gets swinging all mixed up with being wild and gets being cool all confused with being melancholy.

Then I said, OK, so we know very well that Callot's Commedia dell'Arte stuff is very much the same stock character stuff as our old minstrels used to be based on. But hell, man, for my money even old Roark Bradford understood the farcical and satirical dimensions and implications of that stuff far better than Covarrubias, who gets it all tangled up with the grotesque. Man, as that tongue-in-cheek director and cast of *Green Pastures* knew, Old Roark was out to swing that stuff no less elegantly than Old Rabelais.

We didn't spend the amount of time that we usually spent browsing in Rizzoli's whenever we were in that part of town, because it was already as late as it was when we got there that afternoon, and I wanted to get on back down to Forty-second Street to the library and the assignment I had planned to finish before going down to Washington Square. And also even as he went on talking about what we were talking about as we came back outside and along Fifth Avenue, I knew that when we came to Rockefeller Center he was going over to Sixth Avenue to take the D train down to Canal Street because he wanted to get back down to his studio and sketch pads as soon as possible.

So when the phone rang as if on cue just as I was finishing my homework that evening I knew exactly who was calling and I picked up the receiver and said, Rollo, old Rollo. How about that stuff, Rollo? And he said, Man, what can I tell you, man,

I'm off and running like a striped-assed ape. Man, I just had to stop and buzz you before you got to bed.

And when I said, I was expecting this call, man, he said, I'm not going to keep you but a minute, but this stuff is coming at me so fast that all of a sudden I was beginning to feel like the man in that story about mounting a horse and dashing off in all directions. So I'm calling this late because I wanted to make sure to clue you to remind me to tell you about a bunch of fellow teenagers I used to hang out and make the scene in the after-hours rounds with, and how we used to sneak out after bedtime because our turf also included eavesdropping which-ever any of those old rent party piano ticklers cutting contests and all-night jam sessions you could get close enough to. And man, sometimes we also used to just trail along, just following our favorite stage show entertainers to their all-night hole-in-the-wall joints. Then we would have to sneak back home to bed before daybreak. But guess what we called our crew? The Dawn Patrol. You remember that silent movie, etc.?

When he came by the library to take me out to lunch that next Thursday, he was carrying a five-by-eight sketch pad in each of the two bottom pockets of his safari jacket. And as soon as he saw me spotting them, he smiled and patted the assortment of colored felt-tipped marking pens in the jacket's left chest pocket and said, What can I tell you, Hawk? I'm hooked. Like I told you. All directions, coming and going. Man, I don't dare get fif-teen feet away from pen and paper. Man, I have to keep this stuff in reach, even in the bathroom.

So you and your after-hours cut buddies used to call your-selves the Dawn Patrol, I said as we came outside and down the steps to Fifth Avenue and headed south to Forty-first Street on the way over to a French bistro on Madison Avenue that he wanted me to check out. And he said, Making the rounds, man. Talking about making the rounds, and we also used to call ourselves the Rounders. Here come the old rounders, bounders, and sidewalk pounders, which meant that you had to be slick enough not to get spotted by the cops walking the beats and tapping the lampposts and curbs with their billy clubs in those days.

Then he went on to remember that the main avenues were Lenox and Seventh, and the cross streets were 125th, 135th, and 145th, with 125th Street just hitting its stride as he reached his mid-teenage years. And the Apollo was becoming as famous for having the music of the great bands onstage as the Savoy Ballroom up on Lenox was for dance dates and swing band battles. Down the block from the Apollo there was the Hotel Theresa, on the corner of 125th Street and Seventh Avenue. It was also during this time that the Hotel Theresa bar was just becoming the mainstem where most musicians, actors, entertainers, sportswriters, entertainment page columnists, politicians, pimps, gamblers, and racketeers popped in almost every day to keep current.

There was also the Woodside Hotel, up on Seventh Avenue and 142nd Street. It's a long block over from the Savoy on the east side of Lenox Avenue, stretching from 140th Street to 142nd Street. By the time I left town for my freshman year in college, the Theresa was the cornerstone of the mainstem and there were joints jumping in just about every block east to Park Avenue and west to Broadway and the Hudson River.

At the cozy little French restaurant, we were seated immediately, and as the waiter left with our orders, I said, Believe it or not, Rollo, but down in that sawmill and L & N section gang quarters settlement on the outskirts of Mobile that I come from, my running buddy and I began eavesdropping outside the old piano and/or guitar jook joints and honky-tonks and at about the same time that we were considered big enough to go to and from school on our own.

I said, We called ourselves the Rover Boys because we were also explorers and trailblazers. And then there was a classmate I started running around with as I moved on from junior to senior high school. We were the ones who eavesdropped on the admission fee dance hall dances, where the bands from downtown Mobile and New Orleans and other towns in the southeast territory used to play from time to time. We called ourselves the Night Owls. But actually we had to be home and in bed by midnight, because we were underage! And then we didn't have the price of admission anyway.

The latest thing we got a chance to stay up for back then was the radio, with those coast-to-coast network hookups. Back in those days they used to sign off at midnight, so eleven to midnight in New York was only ten to eleven in Mobile. So we knew about the Cotton Club in New York, the Grand Terrace in Chicago, and old Louis at Frank Sebastian's Cotton Club all the way out in California.

That was when we said what we said about listening to the sports announcers broadcasting the Rose Bowl games, the World Series, and the championship prizefights on radio. And he said, Look, man, we had a radio right there at home, but I'm sure you already know that the Dawn Patrol always had to get together somewhere for stuff like that even if it was in our own living room. Some things you might just take in on your own, but not stuff like that.

He had taken his work pads from the pockets of his safari jacket and I had just started looking at his sketches and doodles he had pushed across to me when I saw the waiter coming back with our orders. And I said, I can already see what you mean by all directions. You also mean panorama. So now you've got to look out for old Goya. Old Goya zooming in. Old Goya's microscope. Old Goya's X-ray. All become old Rollo's vamps, riffs, takeoffs, and getaways on Jacques Callot plus the Belle Epoque. We started in on our lunch as I was saying what I was saying, but before we were half finished, he opened the other work pad and started doodling and sketching again, moving back and forth from plate and fork to pen and pad as smoothly as if he were taking dictation on the phone while eating and talking about what we were talking about.

Then, when it was time for me to be on my way back across to Fifth Avenue and the library, I said, Man, you and old Taft Edison. You and the Bossman Himself, and Old Pro and old Joe States. I said, Here I am, doing what I'm doing on this goddamn schedule and there you guys are, doing what you're doing on your own. Because you want to and even as you're doing it for yourself, you're also doing it for others. Others here, there, and elsewhere. I said, One of these days, man. One of these days. But as of now I've got to be going back to the salt mines at Forty-second and Fifth.

XVII

The next time I had a midafternoon snack with Taft Edison our table was the same one at which I remembered finding Old Pro having breakfast and checking through the final morning editions of the newspapers as the two-way traffic outside along 125th Street rolled east and west between Seventh and St. Nicholas Avenues on that first day in New York. I was on my way with my guidebook to see as much of midtown Manhattan as I could find my way around to alone before coming back uptown by check-in time for rehearsal. So I had come in to have a very quick snack, but when I saw him there by himself I remembered what Joe States had said about getting to the one closest to the Bossman Himself as soon as I could catch him off-duty and alone, I cut back on my sightseeing plans and asked him if I could join him.

I didn't mention anything about any of this to Taft Edison as we settled into our seats and gave our orders to the waiter that afternoon. Because when he called me that night before about joining him to check out the matinee performance of the band being featured at the Apollo Theatre that week, he had also sounded urgent when he said that there was a personal matter that he wanted to tell me about, and I was still waiting for him to bring up whatever it was, because he had not yet given me any clue to what it was about. Not even during the set changes between the variety acts.

He hadn't brought it up on our way to the restaurant and as we waited for the drinks he began talking about the music we had just heard, and about the band, which had begun as one of those now-legendary "territory bands" like the old Oklahoma City Blue Devils that he had grown up hanging around, as I used to listen to Papa Gladstone's Dance and Mardi Gras Marching Band in Mobile and at the Boom Men's Union Hall Ballroom up on Green's Avenue in Plateau. The territory bands operated mainly out of Kansas City, which was where the Blue Devils became a part of the nucleus of the world famous Count Basie Band.

Those guys. That music, Taft Edison said as we finished our drinks and started on our snack. That's something I always have to keep in touch with. Hearing and seeing those guys riffing that stuff like that reinforces my connection with a lot of idiomatic fundamentals that I am not only trying to work in terms of as a writer, but also that I don't ever want to get too far away from as a person. Man, that stuff plus all of that old church stuff was my raw material even when the music I was trying to learn to compose was concert hall music. Which is why I was all the way down there in Alabama and not at Juilliard or the Boston Conservatory or even Oberlin in the first place.

And that is when he also said, Man, just the opposite of those folks taking owls to Athens, or coals to Newcastle, I'm trying to take chitlins to the Waldorf. And I suspect you're also up to the same caper. Otherwise why would a liberal arts major with a fellowship to graduate school spend as long as you spent on the road with a band that keeps dipping as deep down into that old gut bucket no matter what else he's up to. Anyway, the more I

think about it the more I look forward to running some of my
prose sequences by you even while I'm still fiddling around
with them.

Look, he also said, I know quite a few literary experts up here
who think they know where I'm trying to go. But I'm counting
on you to spot where I'm coming from. After all, since you and I
took going to college as seriously as the best of them did we
don't need them to tell us what we're trying to do. We just want
them to be un-condescending enough to acknowledge what we
are doing when we do it.

It was not until we were almost through eating and ready to
order coffee that he finally got around to bringing up the personal matter that he had mentioned on the phone the night
before. And it turned out to be personal not in the sense that
it was a very intimate private matter, but only in the fact that it
concerned him as an individual. Which did not make it any less
important or urgent, but it did make it less delicate and not
embarrassing to talk about. But no less confidential—or maybe
even more confidential because it was also potentially if not
already a matter of personal security.

Because it was about politics. By which it immediately became clear that he meant political indoctrination and recruitment for international revolution, any involvement with which
required a degree of loyalty that exceeded the strictest religious devotion known to most Americans, if you were not for
the organization you couldn't possibly be neutral or politically
uninvolved, you were against it and might even be a special
espionage agent whose purpose was to collect names for some
sort of blacklist for investigation by some wing of the federal
government.

You remember me telling you about those party girls and those pamphlets? he said. And about how I got myself mistaken for a likely prospect, because instead of throwing that crap in the trash can en route to the subway the next morning, I read it?! I told you about that. Well man, I'm not sure that that crew don't have me tagged as an active enemy of the goddamn cause. I do think I have reason to believe that they are checking me out for some reason. Now it could be to find out whether or not I'm worth intensifying their drive to recruit me since I've published several little pieces of attempts at few basic definitions, nothing polemical, no clear cut position taken or specific political alignment, just attempts at elementary clarification. But you never know what they might make of it. They might see it for what it is and write me off for an academic which I'm not. Or they might decide that it is some sort of cover device for my underground mission. Anyway I'm pretty damn sure they're checking me out, and I don't know what the hell they're up to.

Man, he said, if this sounds paranoid, hell, maybe I am paranoid. But damn if I'm hallucinating—as I think I'm going to be able to show you before you head back downtown. Maybe I'm exaggerating but not out of thin air I assure you. I'm a suspicious son of a bitch I admit, but I'm not that suspicious.

And that was when he said what he said about being more of a loner than anything else and reminded me that if I remembered anything about him from that year when we were on the campus down in Alabama at the same time, I couldn't possibly have missed noticing that he kept to himself most of the time when he was not with the band or in class. And I agreed. Not that he ever struck me as being out of touch with what the hip crowd was up to.

I made a reasonable share of the dance parties and the seasonal balls, he said. But I never was a joiner of any kind. Not even back in Oklahoma City. I had my contacts, but I didn't belong to any gang. My only club on campus was really a scholarship club that also had its own socials from time to time.

Then he got the waiter's attention, and as we were waiting for the tab he nudged me and nodded toward a pedestrian strolling along the sidewalk outside the plate glass window and said, Whether you noticed it or not he's been passing back and forth and looking in here ever since we came in. Sometimes on this side of the street and sometimes on the other, and I'm pretty sure that he's not going any further east than Seventh Avenue and no further west than St. Nicholas.

And I said, Now that you mention it. But after all I am not familiar enough with this part of town to make anything of what he might be up to. What do you make of it?

And that's when he said, Well now he could be a pimp keeping tab on his chippie or chippies. Or he could be in the numbers racket. Maybe. But I don't think so, unless they're just breaking him in, and I doubt that the numbers wheels would put a novice in this area. You earn your way up to territory like this. And of course he could be a greenhorn out on his own trying to peddle some cheap light stuff. But I don't think so. No, this just might be something else. I have my suspicions. The question is whether this guy is as obvious as I think he is because he's supposed to be obvious.

So let's find out, he said as we came outside and headed for the subway stop at 125th and St. Nicholas Avenue. He didn't look back to see if we were being followed but he steered me to the uptown entrance instead of the downtown side. He still didn't look back to see if we were being followed. But when we pulled into the 145th Street and St. Nicholas Avenue station, we crossed over to the downtown platform and took the express to Columbus Circle, from where he said he was taking the bus back uptown, and I continued on downtown on the express to West Fourth Street and Sixth Avenue.

Well, that was that, he said on the phone when he called after I came home from class that night. I think he may have given up on it when we switched over on 145th. Anyway, my guess as of now is that the organization is spot-checking me. They evidently think that this writing involvement makes me somewhat special. On the one hand it's something they can utilize in a number of ways in propaganda operations, not just as a journalist or a theorist working on one of their own publications, but as one of their agents working as a regular staffer on some establishment publications.

But the problem as he saw it was not a simple matter of saying yes or no. The problem was that they knew that he spent Mondays through Fridays writing whatever he was writing in an office on Fifth Avenue at Forty-ninth Street as if on an official schedule for which he was paid by the hour. So, as far as they were concerned, he could very well be an undercover agent of some kind on official payroll and yet as he explained it, it was not necessarily as simple as that either. Because in addition to having to be on the alert for counterrevolutionary agents they also had to be able to spot agents from their own internal security system.

I just called to fill you in, he said. That's what I had in mind when I called about meeting to catch the show, and then there it was. So now I just want you to know that I don't think it has anything to do with you personally. But if you notice anything like what happened today, let me know. I have my ways of dealing with invasions of my privacy. After all—or really first of all—I'm trying to write a goddamn novel, man, and, besides, I absolutely have no patience at all with any outfit that operates on the assumption that it has to enslave me in order to free me.

Hell, I know something about military and also maritime discipline and these characters don't allow furlows or shore leave.

Later, he was also to begin filling me in on what he had been thinking about such matters beginning all the way back during his senior year in high school, when what it amounted to was applied civics. But for now he just wanted me to be on the alert to what you could be getting yourself involved with if you showed any sign of inclination to become affiliated with or even curious about a certain kind of political ideology.

As for myself, he said before hanging up, Man one of the very first things that I began to realize when I checked in on that campus down there in central Alabama was that I have to learn how to be a good man on my own, because I was the one and the only one who had to decide what kind of person I wanted to be. Which was exactly the same as choosing what I wanted to do with my life. The profs were there and the books and so were the laboratories and practice facilities, but as soon as I got there and began finding my way around the campus, I began to realize that for all the legitimate pride that the administration faculty and trustees took in the achievements of their alumni, I had not come down there to be turned into another one of any kind of any of the graduates that I knew anything about. That's when it hit me that you might think that you're already on your own in senior high school, but for me being away from home made all the difference in the world. Anyway that was when I actually began to realize that the one I had to answer to from then on was myself. Hell, I didn't even have to be down there in the first place if I didn't want to be. I had felt that I had to come, but once I got down there I realized that I did not have to *stay* if I didn't *want* to. Hell, *I had forgotten all about truant officers after the ninth grade!*

But look man, he said as if suddenly realizing again how late the phone call was, I know you've got school work to get back to. I just wanted to give you a quick follow-up on what happened today. Not because I'm worried about you but just to let you know that I'm not. Man, I'm pretty sure that you're already as aware as I am that we're already one up on anybody that thinks that because we come from down the way and are impressed with New York City we are also impressed with them!

Man, I said just before hanging up, Most of the uptown splibs I've met so far couldn't care less about the New York I came up here to get next to.

XVIII

When I picked up the phone and heard Eric Threadcraft's voice again, I said, What say, Mice? I said, So you're in town. I said, So can you look out and see old Sherman heading south even as we speak? And he said, Howya, fella? How'd you know? I mean, not only that I'm here but also where I'm calling from? And I said, Gotcha. But it was a dead giveaway, man. Damn, you sounded like you're already heading this way, very soon if not sooner, even as you hung up. And where else would a certified Hollywood maestro popping into New York be calling from if not the Plaza or the Sherry Netherland? Because we are talking about romance, aren't we? And I don't figure you for a Waldorf man. Anyway, if you hadn't sounded so much like you had your fingers crossed when you said what you said and didn't say what you didn't say I would have guessed that you were popping into the Algonquin on film score business as the saying goes, if I remember correctly.

And he said, Touché, fellow, touché. It's like our man Joe States clued me in on you at the outset. Bass fiddle time is your thing whatever the gig. Context, fellow. That's the Joe States thing about you. But listen, I'm calling you because I've been looking forward to this trip ever since old Joe gave me your number and told me about what you're into these days. But just a couple of days before I was to pull out, something came up that changed the whole nature of the trip, something that I've got to check into right away.

Then he said, Hey, fella, you said I sounded like I had my fingers crossed just before I hung up that last time. Man, that was humility before an incredible possibility of good fortune. What I'm into now is anxiety.

And when I said, Hey, man, next time around. After all, I plan to be here for at least two years, he said, Hey, but that's not what I really mean, fellow. This is something confidential that I really want to talk to you about as soon as we can find a corner to whisper in. Man, I'm calling to find out how fast I can get to you. This morning, if possible. I don't know what you can do about this new situation. But since I was already looking forward to touching base with you, I decided that you're the very one I should run this by. Even before I let anybody else know that I'm already in town.

So I said, Since I'm going to be up at the Forty-second Street library by midmorning, why not the Algonquin lounge at say ten-thirty? Not later than eleven.

And when I asked for a hint, he said, Hey come on, fellow. Why would I have my fingers crossed if it didn't have anything to do with a woman? We're talking heartthrobs here, fellow. Man, I don't think I ever crossed my fingers in a boardroom full of wheelers and dealers, or even out at the track, win, lose, or place, or else. But when it comes to what I'm into now, it's wishful thinking from the get-go.

Which was about as much of a hint as you could expect to get on the phone from somebody you already promised to meet as soon as you could get up to Forty-fourth Street from Eighth

Street and Sixth Avenue by bus or subway. So I said, See you there, man.

And when I came in and spotted him in the lounge, before looking into the bar, he was at a table for two, being served coffee. He saw me and stood up and we slapped palms and bumped shoulders, and he said, Man, this is not quite the New York junket I had in mind when I said I'd probably already be in town when I called the next time.

So when I said, So what's up? he began at the beginning. Her name was Celeste Delauny (as in Sonia and Charles Delauny, but of another family), a French fashion designer from New York, and he had met her at a party in Beverly Hills while she was in Hollywood on special assignment as a costume designer and consultant for a production that was in its early planning phase and for which he had also been offered a position as a special music consultant, arranger, composer, and combo leader. What was being planned was a high-budget comedy of manners showcasing clever dialogue, state-of-the-art furnishings, and high fashions that would also include after-hours combo music as well as hotel ballroom production numbers.

And guess what, fellow? A high-fashion expert turns out to be not only a Parisian but she's also a jazz buff! Man, the very first thing she says when I'm taken over to be introduced was that she hopes that it won't be too much of a bother for a professional like me to suggest some truly authentic spots for her to check out during the ten days that she was scheduled to be in town during this preliminary stage of the film. *Which incidentally also just happens to be the biggest thing ever to come my way. I've been doing all right, but man, this is about as big as they come for this kind of slick flick.*

But the production as such and the big breakthrough it

represented for his career as an arranger/conductor was only incidental to what he had come to the Algonquin to tell me about as soon as possible that morning. Because, as he went on to say, as important as all of that was, the minute the producer who was taking him around the room introduced him to the French fashion designer from New York and he saw how she responded when she was told that his main interest as an arranger/conductor was jazz, he could hardly wait to get through the rest of the introductions and figure out a casual way to get back to her before some big-time glamour boy zeroed in on her.

And what happened was absolutely the biggest surprise he had ever been taken by. He made his way to the bar, and as he turned to sip his margarita and figure out an excuse to go back and say something to her in French, if only *aimez-vous le* jazz hot? the very first person he saw less than twelve feet away was her, obviously heading directly toward him. And before he could get his tourist guide French together she was apologizing in British English for intruding and was asking him if he could spare a few minutes and give her the list she had mentioned.

Man, what can I tell you? he said taking another sip of his tea. I told her in English that out of my longtime awareness of and respect that I had for French taste in jazz, I would not only supply her with a list of the best spots in and around town but would also be only too happy to serve as her personal tour guide. And when I saw that she was going for it, I said, Beginning as soon as you think it's discreet to check out of the present festivities. To which she said, Fifteen minutes. So we separated to take leave of our host and acquaintances and then when we came outside, she said, My limousine or yours? I heard myself saying mine because that way I get to take you home.

Then he said, Now you know damn well that I don't have to tell you which way I told my driver to head. I'll just say that

Jameson McLemore and all the rest of the cats really came through for me, inviting me to sit in for a couple of numbers that they knew very well would give me the opportunity to not only show off a few of my favorite licks, but also would vouch for my authenticity. As for old Papa Ford Shelby, he treated me like a member of the family, and to my classy-looking French stone fox he said, Hello there, Miss Lady. Come on in this house and make yourself at home. You've gotta be somebody special to come out here to this scene from Paris by way of New York and latch on to somebody as with it as my boy here on the first go-round. So just make yourself comfortable and familiar, because if you dig the music, like most folks who come in here from Paris, we'll be seeing you again and again.

Man, Eric Threadcraft said as the Algonquin waiter brought more tea, I never felt so lucky in all my life, and when I took her to her hotel just before dawn the next morning, all I could think of was that I was going to be with her again that very night, which, by the way, turned out to be no letdown whatsoever from the night before, and I was on cloud nine for the rest of her stay in Hollywood. And when she went back to New York that next week, I had just about decided that we were made for each other, although, by that time, she had mentioned the fact that she had been married some time ago. Man, all that mattered to me was her future availability, which I was hoping, really fantasizing, would be exclusive. And actually I had already followed up with a brief visit here as if on urgent music business just before Joe States gave me your number. Which is why I dropped that crack in there about some anticipated changes chez Mice, just before hanging up. And you picked right up on it, fellow, because I sure as hell did have my fingers, toes, and everything else crossed.

So anyway, he went on, when old Joe States gave me your

number, the renewal of our friendship on purely personal, or in any case, nonbusiness or transactional terms, gave me another perfect means of making another pseudo-urgent visit to New York to see her seem somewhat incidental withal, if you get what I mean. Man, I was really looking forward to seeing you again, but I was absolutely dying to see that fantastic and unbelievably receptive woman again, and also as often as possible without seeming overeager.

Then he went on to explain why she was not making any return trips to California. First of all, his trips were not to be taken by her as visits, but pop-ins incidental to other very urgent matters, which, as luck would have it, coincided with his admitted desire to see her as often as possible, circumstances being what they were. Which was the fact that the big Hollywood production was already very much under way, as he very well knew. But she didn't have to leave her exclusive fashion enterprise in New York to come back out to California until time for the in-person cast fittings for the actual wardrobes.

Hey, man, Old Mice has been in there doing what he can to keep any possibility from fading—as coolly as possible, you understand. Which just about brings us up to why I am here talking to you about why I am here talking to you. Man, there I was with my hotel reservations all set and my airline ticket all laid out along with my all-purpose Manhattan-bound travel gear, and when I go out to the studio two days before I'm booked to leave, there are whispers about a security check on all new foreigners under contract, and on the list to be investigated is French high-fashion designer Celeste Delauny, known in the trade as Celeste. Man, I don't know what the hell any of this has to do with designing a chic wardrobe for a super-sleek drawing room comedy. But a routine background check seems to have turned up evidence that she's being blackmailed and they're going to be digging in to find out if there's any connection with any questionable political affiliation past or ongoing.

Man, he said, shaking his head, I never felt so much like I was one of those frail-looking kids wearing thick glasses and carrying a violin case. Man, I never felt so unhip and unwith-it since way back in my preteen days when I was a conservatory-bound piano prodigy and a scholarship shoo-in and heard my first jazz records on radio and snuck off to my first chitlin circuit theater to hear some musicians playing it in person in one of those matinee vaudeville variety shows. Man, I don't remember ever being so unwith-it about anything in my life before.

And when I said what I said about that kind of idiomatic initiation adding up to the maestro that Joe States put me in touch with in Hollywood, he said, Man, that was the music scene. Man, this stuff sounds like some international intrigue involvement that I never thought of as being related to me on any personal level. Man, the only personal concerns I ever really had about international relations have been with keeping my passport up to date and getting my stuff through customs, duty-free or not, it's all the same to me.

So here he was back in New York to see her again, but now the cover story about being in town to reestablish his special schoolboy-to-schoolboy relationship with me also covered the fact that he was also in town to get some expert advice from some of his old local show business contacts about hiring a reliable private investigator to fill him in on the political past of Celeste Delauny of the very exclusive Celeste haute couture line and boutique.

Look, fellow, I know you know damn well that I know how uncool this sounds, he said. But man, I'm also counting on you to realize that all of this is still very much in vamping phase. Which is why it's absolutely impossible for me to even hint that

I question anything of any sort whatever about her. Man, I'm just trying to vamp this infatuation thing until she comes back out to the coast. What all this has been about all along is me vamping this thing until she comes back when the producers start pulling all the logistics together and now I've got to find out if it's worth it or if it's all going to go up in smoke.

XIX

When he finally called me from Hollywood to bring me up-to-date on the situation a week and a half later, as soon as I heard his voice I knew that whatever had happened during the rest of his trip to New York or after his return to the coast had changed his mood from shock and anxiety to an enthusiastic anticipation that I remembered always being there whenever we were doing whatever we had been doing in California.

So what can I tell you, my man? he said, before I could even say Hello. You already know that Hollywood is seventy-five percent if not ninety percent pop song romance, Sunset Boulevard and blue horizons indeed. So what can I tell you, fellow? Old Mice got it bad and gotta try to make it good. So I got over that attack of cornballitis.

Man, he went on, I realize what had hit me right after we came outside and you headed across the street to the arcade to Forty-third Street. Suddenly there was this irrepressible need to hear her voice again as soon as possible. So that I could be sure that I hadn't made the whole goddamn thing up. So I decided to call her up and ask if I could pop by the boutique.

Which he had done from the phone in the lobby of the bank at the corner of Fifth Avenue, and she had said yes and as he hung up he suddenly realized that the relationship he was trying to develop with her was only incidentally and at most only temporarily connected with the film production that neither of them had ever mentioned to each other. After all, her profession was high fashion as such, not costumes for show business, and she had come out to Hollywood only to look around, mainly because the producer had sent for her, hoping that the visit would change the "maybe" she had given them to a "yes."

Look, man, he said, I think I made it pretty clear that I got to meet her in the first place because she was more excited about the music she might be able to check out while out there than she was about the technical details in the production of what to her was only a sweet drawing room comedy that she was out there to decide whether she wanted to work on.

I grunted to let him know that I thought he was making his point, and that was when he went on to say, Now hey, fellow, you know as well as I do that a job as composer/consultant on a high-budget production like that was a pretty big break for Old Mice's status as a sound stage studio pop pro in this town, as far as that sort of thing goes around here. But although it was my new status that got me to that Beverly Hills production party where I met her, it was because of the music that I'm most serious about that I got to take her out that very first night.

You've got to believe me, fellow, he said, neither one of us mentioned anything at all about that goddamn sleek-ass production. Not even a word about when or if she might have to come back out for final fittings and the shooting. My guess was that she would take the script and do all the designs and sketches in New York and send them out for approval and suggestions and make whatever adjustments and revisions they requested and sew everything up in New York and come back out west to check things out when the actual shooting began.

Anyway, as he had come on along Forty-fourth Street and turned up Madison Avenue, the only thing that mattered was that she was waiting for him and he would be there in less than ten minutes and would see how her head tilted and her hair fell as her eyes sparkled when her Parisian lips moved as she said whatever she would say.

He had not taken a taxi because he needed that much walking distance to get himself back together after what he had put himself through. But every time he had to stop at a traffic light he realized he was struggling to keep himself from springing forward before the yellow light changed to green again.

Hey, man, when I stepped into that *endroit* of ultimate chic while the fragrance matched the background like music and a design on display seemed almost as much a part of nature as the flower arrangement and here's this stone fox of a Parisian high-fashion designer looking like she's one of her own models. Man, not just waiting for me to pop by for a brief arrival chat but also ready to turn me right around and head for a cozy, nearby bistro because it's lunchtime.

He then went on to say that by that time it was as if he had never ever heard of a private investigator or ever even seen the ones he grew up going to see in the movies. Then he also went on to tell me that even as I had disappeared into the arcade that it hit him. He was not going to hire a private investigator because he was not going to let this incredible prospect of a relationship that would fulfill so many of his adolescent and undergraduate fantasies get away whether she stayed on that movie production or not.

We're talking infatuation here, my man, he said. That's why it's taking me this long to call up and report. I was in bad shape when I called you that morning and I'm glad I did, but afterward I was so embarrassed because I must have sounded so unhip.

But then I finally said what the hell, my man has got to meet this trillie. He's got to see for himself what made Old Mice hit the panic button like that.

Man, every time I think about how I must have sounded to you. All ready to plunge into class B movie international intrigue because a goddamn Hollywood studio that's running a routine background check on a classy Paris fashion designer who is already established in New York and who has no special interest in working on flicks in the first goddamn place.

Look pal, he said, the more I thought about that, the more embarrassed I became until this morning, when I finally said, Goddamn, here I go again. And that's when I said, What the hell is all this? I've gotta call him. That's my man and all I did after not seeing him for that long was to lay that on him. So here's Old Mice, pal. What can I tell you?

That's when I said, Ah, come on, Mice. You're the professional musician, not me. I'm just the schoolboy. You're not only an arranger, you also love to jam, catching as catch can. And when you hit a goddamn clinker, which everybody, including the Bossman Himself, does from time to time, you don't stop playing. You riff right on beyond it.

Hey, yes, he said, and I visualized him looking down at the keyboard because I already assumed that he was calling from the phone he kept on the piano, when you're rehearsing you can stop and hack at it until you make it something you feel you can live with, but when you're out there with a mike and footlights on, it's the real thing and the metronome is still clicking and clocking you. You've got to get with it.

And besides, I said, don't nobody know anything about this but you and me, man. The main person has no idea what you put yourself through. So come on, man.

And he said, Hey, fellow, you said it, man. That's exactly

what this is all about. So look, the main reason I'm finally making this call is to get us back to what I thought my other trip to New York was going to be about. *I've got to get the four of us together.* Man, you've got to meet this lady, and my stock-in-trade with her will go up when she meets you. As for your fine people, as Joe States calls her, tell her how sorry I am that I got too tangled up to meet her on my last trip to town. But don't tell her why, as of course you wouldn't anyway. See you soon, fellow, real soon. As soon as I can get this recording studio backlog out of the way of that movie thing. So expect me, fellow. Any minute.

XX

Guess who? Eric Threadcraft said as soon as he heard my voice answering the phone. And when I said, Maestro, what say, Mice? You back in town, Mice? He said, Just checked back in across Fifth from old you know who southbound. Haven't even unpacked yet. First item being your earliest availability for that too-long-overdue foursome for lunch or preferably dinner and music. Music afterward, that is. And then I said, Hey, sounds absolutely top-notch to me, Mice, and I myself happen to be fairly flexible this week, but I can't speak for the family. So call me back for the official estimate of the situation—say, round about midnight. Which he did and when he gave the date, time, and place he said, Celeste chose the restaurant and you and I will decide whose group to check out afterward.

Hey, man, he said then. This is great, fellow, just great. Not only am I finally going to meet Miss-All-Them-Fine-People rolled into one that old Papa Joe has made me so curious about. And not only are you going to see what the goddamn French hit Old Mice with right out there in the world's most over populated briar patch of starlets trying to become movie queens. And man, you yourself are just going to enhance the idiomatic authenticity of Old Mice's musicianship. Man, you know how the French are about the natural history of this stuff. Remember what I told you about taking her over to West L.A. that first night? Elementary, as your Sherlockian roommate used to say, elementary.

We saw them as soon as we came into the four-star midtown French restaurant that mild midspring Friday night. We were not quite ten minutes early, but they were already there waiting for us near the short line to the coat-check counter, and when he saw us coming he waved, and as we joined them he said, So here at long last is her fantastic self in person. And this is Celeste, also in person. But also a part of Old Mice's world of fantasy even so.

And I said, Who else, maestro, who else but, my man? Man, my confidence in your piano vamping applies to these matters, too.

From the very first time he mentioned her, he had been so busy telling me how he felt about her that he had never got around to describing any of her physical features at all, not even the color of her eyes and hair. But she looked just about like I expected her to look. Because she looked more like French women look in French movies and paintings and as you visualize them when you read about them in French novels than like pictures in the fashion magazines.

We checked our New York early-spring wraps and as we fell in behind the two of them following the maître d' leading us to our table, I was thinking that I also assumed that the way her eyes and lips moved as she spoke English with a throaty British-tinged Parisian accent would have a very similar effect on his U.S.A. schoolboy sensibility as it would have on mine.

So I nudged him and whispered, Hey, man, the way she gasps *oui!* is worth the whole price of the goddamn admission. To which he said, What can I tell you, fellow, what can I tell you?

He put his arm around my shoulder then and said, Look, I'm well aware that this thing of mine is only a matter of months, but even as ongoing as the excitement of the newness of it all, at this very moment I still have the feeling that this pas de quatre is long overdue. Which probably just goes to show what I've been putting myself through these last months.

Then when we were seated and Celeste had suggested choices from the menu, he turned to Eunice again and then turned to me and said, Incurable schoolboy as I myself also am I must point out a little academic detail that you and old Papa Joe left out: Nefertiti, fellow, Queen Nefertiti, sans the Egyptian head-gear, of course.

Sans Egyptian headgear, to be sure, I said. And then I said, Because as my old roommate, who cut out before Miss You-Know-Who arrived, but who was the one who was reading the volume on art history in which I first saw a color photo of that famous bust, said, Who knows but the head beneath that ever so regal crown or whatever it is may be as hairless as a cue ball. So I concede the teacake tan skin, quibble the neck as artistic license, but no deal if Nefertiti's hair is not Creole or Latino frizzly.

And he said, Deal, fellow. I never would have guessed central Alabama if you hadn't already told me out in Hollywood when you first mentioned her. I would have guessed she was the one from Mobile and the Gulf Coast area and you were the one from central Alabama. But then your flesh-and-blood parents are from central Alabama, aren't they? See, I remember you telling me about that, too. But anyway, fellow, old Papa Joe got it right. She is fine people. Extra-fine people. Extra-superfine people.

He turned to get her attention then, but I didn't hear what he said because that was when Celeste asked me if a teacake was an American madeleine. And I said not really because it was really a very plain, not very sweet soft cookie, whereas a madeleine was very sweet like a down-home muffin and was baked in a muffin pan. You could bake teacakes on a cookie sheet, but since they were made from rolled dough like biscuits, a bread pan was better, but teacakes were not as spongy as biscuits.

When I paused I could follow what Eric was asking Eunice about campus life in central Alabama, but before he turned to me, our waiters arrived with our orders, and we all turned to Celeste, and Eric said having her as hostess was absolutely the next best thing to being in the region of France where each recipe came from.

When Eric asked me to tell Celeste about my trip to the Côte d'Azur and Paris and I mentioned Marquis de Chaumienne, she said she knew who he was but she had not become aware of his special interest in American music until she returned to Paris after her first trip to New York.

I was here on business, she said, an ambitious young upstart that I already was, I had spent all of my time in midtown on Fifth and Madison Avenues and down in the garment district. And at night there were the midtown restaurants, including this one. And also the Broadway and Times Square movie houses, which I'm afraid I had very little time for. But when I came back to Paris and said no when asked if I had been taken up to Harlem to hear American music not to mention dancing at its best and in unmatched variety, I was made to feel that I was deficient in an indispensable dimension of the spirit of the times. They were shocked. It was almost as if a supposedly sophisticated Englishman had come to Paris and remained oblivious to what Montmartre, Montparnasse, and St. Germain des Près were all about!

Or so I felt, at any rate, she went on to say. And that was what led her to find out that the Hot Club of France was neither just another Parisian fad or cult, but included truly cosmopolitan people like the Marquis de Chaumienne, who regarded many of the jazz musicians they heard on recordings and in person, on tours that included Paris and other European capitals, as representative contemporary artists who transcended the context of popular show business entertainment that they most often worked in.

I've never met the marquis, she said, but I'm told that in addition to recordings, he also collects other American artifacts, especially of ranch life and the western frontier, which I'm told also includes paintings and bronzes by Frederic Remington.

To which I said I had also been told included a very special interest in quarter horse racing and rodeos, sporting events that required skills basic to cattle-herding. The quarter horse was a sporting version of the sprint-oriented, ever-so-maneuverable cow pony. And the rodeo also included such cowpuncher skills as roping, throwing, and binding calves for branding, as well as demonstrating the cowpuncher's ability to hang on to a wildly bucking untamed horse, the first step in taming his own mount.

I told her that it was said that there had been a time when he came over for the quarter horse racing season every year, but that he also had no special interest in western music beyond its use in Hollywood movies about cowboys—nonsinging cowboys. And Eric pointed out that back during the days of silent films, cowboy movies used to be called *horse operas*, because the incidental music played along with them in the theaters on an organ consisted of excerpts of classical compositions by European composers.

That was, I also told her, what I had heard about when he came over for the Thoroughbred races, his trips to the Kentucky Derby also included visits to hear music in New Orleans, Memphis, and Chicago. And when Eric said, And New York was his home base for the Preakness and the Belmont Stakes, right? I said, So I've been told, but I've also been told that there was a time when he used to spend the night before or after the Preakness in Baltimore because it was the hometown of so many eastern ragtime piano players, especially Eubie Blake and also Joe Turner, who was to spend a number of years touring in Europe, settling in Paris from time to time.

That was when Eric Threadcraft said what he said about his trips to Paris, so I didn't say anything else about the Marquis de Chaumienne and he went on to say what he said about not having had a chance to see Paris and France with Celeste yet, because she had not gone back since the two of them had met, which, after all, had been a matter of several weeks rather than months.

When the waiter cleared the table and left with our orders for desserts, I asked how their production assignments were coming along, and Celeste said that her designs had been approved and were in production and that she was not needed in Hollywood until time for the fittings for the actual filming.

And Eric said, Man, as you were out there long enough and close enough to that operation to know, you're not through with a film score and the final cutting operation until after the previews or even after the official opening—while they're holding up distribution. But as of now, I'm feeling pretty good about how things are coming along so far, and at least nobody is squawking yet.

The cab ride downtown to the nightclub took less than fifteen minutes, and we arrived in time to get seated and to order our after-dinner liqueurs and brandies before the second set began. And it began on time. The group was a five-piece combo led by a piano player and included a drummer, a bass player, trumpet, and tenor saxophone. None of them were famous, but all of them had played and recorded with well-known leaders. Eric was more familiar with all of them than I was. He was also more up-to-date on the latest musical fads and trends—that was an indispensable part of his job as a recording studio technician and conductor.

That was also why I had deferred to his choice of an after-dinner music spot without suggesting any alternative. And he had said, Hey, no big deal. Something OK, but won't get in the way. It's just a thing I have about coming back to New York, however briefly. You know me, fellow, missing out on this music in New York would be like not even getting a glimpse of the plage on a trip to the Côte d'Azur.

And that was also when he went on to say, Like I said, fellow, this pas de quatre has its own sound track. Man, I must confess: if the Bossman and old Papa Joe and that gang were here tonight, it would be *too much,* if you know what I mean. Later for nights like that. Too much for how I feel as of now. You know what I mean.

XXI

I didn't hear very much of what Celeste and Eunice talked to each other about in the restaurant and between numbers at the nightclub that evening. But the last thing Eunice said when the cab let us out at our address before heading up to midtown was that she would call and confirm before Tuesday afternoon.

And Celeste said, *D'accord, merveilleux.*

And Eric and I slapped palms.

And the cab pulled off, and as Eunice and I headed across the sidewalk to our entrance, she said she had promised Celeste that she would let her know which day next week would be most convenient for the two of them to meet for lunch and for a visit to the boutique.

They spent most of that next Friday afternoon together. And it was when Eunice told me what she told that night at dinnertime that I found out what I found out about what her impression of him was when they were introduced to each other at that producer's party in Beverly Hills on her first trip to Hollywood.

Of all the artists and technicians involved in the production being initiated, the ones she had been most curious about were the composer and conductor of the incidental music score. She had already read the script and had already seen sketches and models for the settings. But she had no idea of what the incidental music would be like. The production was not a Hollywood musical, but she was hoping that the score would not be what she thought of as standard American drawing room comedy music featuring a light or semiclassical string orchestra playing the all-too-conventional pipe organ–derived urban soap opera variation of the old Wild West horse opera music.

She knew very well that designing a chic wardrobe for an American sitcom was not to be confused with designing costumes for an opera or ballet. Costumes could be obviously unrealistic, downright symbolic, or even outrageous. Sitcom wardrobes were perhaps not only au courant but perhaps most often dernier cri—indeed, as dernier cri as the current fashion magazines. Certainly that was what this script called for. So what she had been hoping was that her haute couture designs would be obviously consistent with, if not altogether emblematic of, the contemporary American spirit as it was expressed in the music and the dance movements that she had become so fascinated by.

So when she and Eric Threadcraft were introduced to each other and he turned out to be a young American professional recording studio arranger and conductor of jazz-based popular music, she was pleased because she felt that he would be responsive to her conception of how her wardrobe designs and his score would go together.

Not only was he sympathetic, his immediate response was to invite her to come along as he made the rounds, dropping in on several of his after-hours spots, beginning in West Los Angeles and including a cruise along Central Avenue, depending on who was where. After all, in addition to the headliners in the glittering addresses along Sunset Strip, there was always a wider choice of first-rate professionals from every section of the country playing somewhere in or around Los Angeles just about every night, and he kept tabs on most of the best.

That was when I told Eunice what I told her about what he told me when he called from the Plaza that first time, and I met him at the Algonquin that morning. I said that was not the first time he had mentioned Celeste Delauny, it was also the first time he had ever mentioned anything about any date he had ever had with anybody, not only in Hollywood but anywhere else. I said I knew he was single and that my impresson was that he had never been married but had not mentioned having any special girlfriend even when I would say what I would say about Miss You-Know-Who from time to time when he and I made the rounds we used to make to nightspots from time to time. My impression on those occasions was that his interest was not social but musical, not with getting a date, but getting an invitation to sit in on piano during a jam session.

I said I had told him about us when I told him about the campus not long after Joe States had introduced us that night at the Palladium, but it was not until Joe States told him about me showing up with Miss Fine People Herself that he not only mentioned that he had met Celeste but also that he expected to see me soon because he was coming to New York to see her.

I didn't say anything at all to Eunice about how upset he was when he and I met at the Algonquin that morning because just before leaving Hollywood he had found out that the studio's background check report contained evidence that suggested that Celeste was being blackmailed by somebody in Paris.

I hadn't mentioned anything about it to her at the time, and I didn't say anything about it later on because he had not said anything else about it since he said what he said when he called when he got back to Hollywood. I wondered what happened between that call and the next, but I didn't ask and he didn't tell and I acted as if he hadn't told me anything except how much he liked everything about her.

She likes him very much, Eunice said when she came back from the luncheon date in midtown and the afternoon visit to the boutique on Madison Avenue in the Sixties. She kept saying how *très gentil* he is and freshly American, not fresh in the down-home sense, but in the sense of being enthusiastic instead of laid back. But as excited as she seemed about how things have been going for her in New York and now also Hollywood, and as enthusiastic as she seems about dating your friend Eric, not only because he is so nice, but also professionally involved with the movies he's involved with, I must say I don't think she's about to give up Paris for New York and/or Hollywood.

And I said, We shall see what we shall see. But as for him, I can see him giving up what he's doing in Hollywood to take a band out of New York on the road for a while, but I doubt he'll give up what he's into in Hollywood for what he's likely to be doing in Paris. But we shall see what we shall see about that, too, won't we?

XXII

When Joe States called from Chicago that night and told me that the band would be back in New York that next week for a brief stopover en route to Europe, he said, Get to me fast, as he almost always did, but this time he also added, Even if you have to skip a class session or two. Details eye to eye. Just be ready to zip to me at the time and place I'll give you a lead on as soon as I arrive and schedule my pretakeoff errands.

They were due in at twilight that next Wednesday with time off until the night flight to Frankfurt Friday, to open in Berlin that Sunday for a week before going on to Paris, Amsterdam, Copenhagen, Stockholm, and back Stateside by way of Amsterdam and London.

I was to pick him up at Gabe's Barbershop up on Broadway between 151st and 152nd Streets, and when I got there he was in a barber's chair with his back to the entrance, but we saw each other in the mirror at the same time, and he said, Here's that schoolboy ahead of that tardy bell as always. What say, States? Hey, Gabe, this is my young statemate from the Beel I was telling you about.

And as Gabe, who was the barber serving him, turned the chair around and shook my hand, somebody in one of the other chairs near the magazine rack said, Mobile, old Cootie Williams used to play all that signifying trumpet with Duke was from Mobile. And somebody else said, old Satchel Paige. Old Satchel already had all of them fancy strikeout pitches, including the *fadeaway,* before he left Mobile and freelanced and barnstormed his way to the Kansas City Monarchs.

Joe States was standing up then and as Gabe went on to finish brushing and whisking him, he said, And don't forget the one and only Mr. James Reese Europe, the head honcho of the famous Clef Club back in the States when Hotel Marshall down on Seventh Avenue and Fifty-third Street was the main hip brownskin hangout in midtown. I'm talking about where you'd find all them old pioneering show cats like old Will Marion Cook and old Harry T. Burleigh and where Bert Williams and George Walker used to touch base regularly.

Old Jim Europe came to New York from D.C. but he got his start right down there in the Bay-City-on-the-way-to-the-Gulf-Coast-town of Mobile, Alabama. Yeah, old Jim Europe, Gabe said. Man, back during World War I old Jim Europe took a band of syncopating hellfighters from the old Harlem 369th to France and became the rage of Paris! And even before that he was the one that helped that classy ofay dance team of Vernon and Irene Castle establish the fox-trot. Good-bye, cakewalk, and look out, waltz! Here come the shout, the shimmie-she-wobble, the mess around, the stomp down, the Birmingham Breakdown, not to mention the Charleston and all them Lindy-hopping jitterbugs!

Nice to meet you, Mobile, Gabe said as he walked us to the door. Come on back and touch base with us from time to time. This a regular checkpoint for a lot of down-home cats, especially ones in showbiz and sports. Also a few grad students from Columbia. Now old Joe here usually pops in here when the band's in town long enough, but always whenever they're heading across the water. Got to get that fresh touch-up, boy, especially back in the old days when the conks were in. Them Euros dig our music and jive, but they're not quite down with our hair styling yet. Although they like what we do with it. They're coming along, but they ain't quite there yet and so far all them different kind of Africans over there speaking the hell out of all them European languages plus educated British English, don't add up to much help in the barbershop.

As Joe States and I came down along Broadway toward the subway station he said, Hell, let's walk a while. You know me. I've got to keep myself in shape for driving that twenty-mule team. As you well know, the goddamn Bossman expects me to be as ready as he always is, and I mean always is. So let's go see who's at the Y.

And when we came to 145th Street we turned east and headed toward Convent Avenue, which would run on past Hamilton Mews and into the campus of City College to the turnoff path that you could take downhill to St. Nicholas Avenue and 135th Street.

Now look, he said as we stopped for a red light at Amsterdam Avenue, all you've got to do is just say you already have enough plans of your own. This is just something we came up with when I heard what I heard from my man Eric and mentioned it to the Bossman and talked to Old Pro. My man Eric just happened to ask me if you had mentioned anything about getting away from that Ph.D. jive for a while and do some thinking and researching on your own while doing a little part-time college teaching back down on your old stomping ground.

Then as we came down the sloping sidewalk to the Convent Avenue turnoff he said, So the three of us put our heads together and the boss came up with something so fast that we realized that he already thought about it some time ago, and Old Pro and I said, Why not? This is just the thing! And I said, Let me be the one to take it up with him, because if the boss suggests it he'll say yes whether he really wants to do it or not. Because he feels he owes him anything he asks for and the same thing goes for you, Pro.

So here we go, he said, punching me playfully, And I can help you lie your way out of it if you'd just as soon not take it on. We could just say sometime later after you check out the routine down the way.

Then when I said, What's the proposition, Papa Joe? he said, First let me say this. Because this is not just some kind of stop-gap favor. This is foundation stuff, a real fundamental research and writing project and the thing about it is that the man had you pegged from the get-go. And I'm talking about all the way back to when he heard you in that combo with the one and only Miss Hortense Hightower. She wanted him to hear you in that combo in that lounge that night, not because she thought you might be on your way to becoming a musician, but she just wanted him to pick up on how you listen.

Man, he then went on to say, you may not have ever really thought about becoming a musician, but your ears are something else! So who the hell knows? Maybe it's a part of your gift as a storyteller and lie swapper like back in primitive times even before English was English or, hell, even Greek was Greek or the Bible was the Bible. I don't know, but I do know you've got the musical version of a photographic memory. You hear it, you've *got* it. And that includes absolute pitch, and along with all that, you hum everything like a conductor who knows how all the sections hook up.

Hey, but look, he said as we came along Convent Avenue to

the 140th Street entrance to the campus, I know that I don't have to go into all this. You already know that you're as much our own special schoolboy as anybody else's, including who else but the one and only Miss Hortense Hightower, who sold you to the Bossman in the first place and is in on this, too. In case you haven't guessed.

Then he said, So here's the proposition. The Bossman wants you to write up Daddy Royal. When I told him what my boy Eric told me about you thinking about taking a term or so off to do some part-time teaching while deciding what you really want to do with all that big-league education besides teaching it, what he came up with was Daddy Royal and all them prizes and souvenirs and stuff that he's accumulated over all these years.

All I could think to say was, Hey, man, this is some pretty heavy stuff you guys want to lay on me. *But even as I said it I began to smile because it was as if I were all the way back in Miss Lexine Metcalf's third-grade classroom in Mobile County Training School again and she was going to say, "Who if not you, my splendid young man?"*

By which I knew she meant that I, who was only nine, was already her preteenage choice candidate for Mr. B. Franklin Fisher's Principal's Corps of Talented Tenth Early Birds.

So I also said, But after all, this is not the first time you guys would be taking a chance on a novice. And he said, Man, the boss already had your number months before Shag Phillips's emergency came up. Our Miss Hortense Hightower saw to that just out of Alabama pride because she herself was impressed.

Then when I said, What about Daddy Royal himself? he said, The boss is ahead of all of us on that, too. And I mean way out in front of everybody. Didn't he take time out to personally take you up to see him the first break he got on your first trip to New York? As busy as he always is when we're in town, he took time out to personally take you up there and introduce you to him. Not as a new sensational fiddle player, but as a schoolboy who was trying to learn how to fit a whole lot of stuff together.

As we left the CCNY campus to come down the steep slope and across St. Nicholas Avenue to 135th Street, he said, Now get to this: when we brought Scratchy Mac into New York with us that first time, the Bossman and Old Pro couldn't hardly wait to send a limousine up to the Hill so Daddy Royal could put on his light fantastic patent leather boots and come down and pat his feet and wiggle his toes while old Scratchy and me did what we did to Broadway. But he didn't take Scratchy up to Sugar Hill to go one on one with Daddy Royal.

On the way along 135th Street to cross Eighth Avenue all he said was, Of course you know good and well who the Bossman had called all the way down in Alabama, even when he and Old Pro and I were still talking about what my man Eric had told me. And she also thought that working down there was not only a good idea but also a lucky coincidence.

Then there was only the sound of the traffic and our footsteps as he let me think about what I was thinking about for a while. But when we came on to the corner of Seventh Avenue and stood waiting for the green light with the Harlem YMCA poolroom now only half a block away, he said, So, what say, States? What do I tell the man and Old Pro? Check with Miss Fine People and buzz me anytime tonight or before ten in the morning and if I'm not in, I'll be buzzing you from wherever I am, because I'm buzzing the boss around ten, probably about lunch.

And I said, Me and you, Papa Joe.

And he said, Charm Miss Fine People for me, Old Pro, the Bossman Himself, and Daddy Royal. Not that I have my fingers crossed, because I know one when I see one. And she's for real.

XXIII

Well, here's that down-home johnny-right-on-the-dot schoolboy, Royal Highness said as soon as he heard my voice saying hello into the telephone that Wednesday night. Then he said, What say, young soldier? Damn if I wasn't already thinking about you just before the phone rang because I was actually expecting to be hearing from you round about now. So, the Bossman and Old Pro sicced old Joe States on you.

And when I said, You know them, Daddy Royal, you know them better than anybody else I know, including everybody in the band, he said, Hell, I probably do at that. And as I'm sure you already found out before I said this the first time, that band is a family, and I guess I'm something like a godfather and grandfather or granduncle all rolled into one. I told you about me and the Bossman and me and Old Pro. And I'm absolutely certain that old tight-butt, trigger-footed Joe States clued you in on himself and the two of them as well, you coming right in there with him and the boss in the rhythm section plus also being from Alabama and all.

Then when I said what I said about what I would be doing on the campus back down in central Alabama, he said, So before you go down there, why don't you just come on back up here the first chance you get and let's see what the hell we can do about this thing while you're down there. You know you're long over-due on your next visit up here anyway.

And when I went back up to Sugar Hill to see him that next Saturday afternoon, he said, Let me tell you something, young soldier, this proposition don't really come as no big surprise to me at all. Hell, I know something extra special was up from the very get-go. Here you were on your very first trip to New York City and you're going to be here for only a few crowded days with the goddamn time clicking like a goddamn roller coaster, and here he come calling to tell me he's bringing Shag Phillips's *temporary* replacement by here to make my personal acquaintance! Some nice neat kid fresh out of college down in Alabama and on his way to work on his master's and Ph.D. as soon as he can come by enough cash to go with his college commencement grant for advanced study.

I remember, I said, and I see what you mean, but at the time I thought that visit was mainly about rhythm and tempo because he was getting me ready for my first recording session—and also because he probably knew that I grew up knowing about you from placards and also from pictures and articles in the *Chicago Defender* and the *Pittsburgh Courier*.

Yeah, that's a good point, all right, he said. But mark my words. If he had any doubts about you being ready to record you wouldn't have been heading for that studio in the first place. No, he had something else in mind, and this proposition just goes to bear out my hunch about what it was.

And when I said, You really think this goes back that far, Daddy Royal? He said, No doubt in my mind, now that I think about it. But here you come talking about a temporary replace-ment and anybody could see he was already treating you like you were his adopted son or at least some kind of newfound nephew or godchild or something, knowing full well that you are not about to give up going on to graduate school to get yourself at least a master's degree. In literature, not music, even when you stayed on beyond that first summer. I know he knew that because I know him. So I knew he had something else in mind other than keeping you out on the road with the band.

Look, he said, just think about it. This whole thing is as plain as day. All we've got to do now is just continue what we started the very first day he brought you up here and have continued off and on ever since you came back to go to the university.

I'm telling you, young soldier, he said, even when you left the band to stick around out there in Hollywood, he didn't give up on you. He just chalked it up as some more useful experience that went right along with what he had in mind for you when the time came. And he knew what he was doing because you didn't give up on school for them bright lights out there either.

We spent the rest of that afternoon looking at some of the items in his collection of show business memorabilia that he had not gotten around to bringing out for me to see before. But this time he limited his ongoing remarks to identification and chronology, saving all anecdotes for the actual work on the project.

And when I stood up to get ready to move toward the door, because it was time for me to head back downtown, he said, Of course you know good and well by now that all this about me and my story is just the beginning of this thing. What they got in mind for you goes a long way beyond me and this. As a matter of fact, as soon as I just said that, it put me in mind of something, some old professor in Germany or Switzerland or somewhere over there said to me when I was first touring over them countries across the water years ago. It just popped into

my mind again after all these years. He said people started dancing before there was any music to dance to. So dance comes first
and then music. Of course, you know as well as I do them pro-
fessorial cats over there got theories about everything. But I bet
you music follows dance *this* time, if you get my point.

He had come on along the hall to the elevator with me then,
and just before I pushed the button, he put his hand on my
shoulder and said, Of course, you also realize that this whole
thing just might have got started with Hortense Hightower
down there in Alabama in the first place. This could have been
the deal from the very beginning. I wouldn't be a bit surprised if
all of this wasn't the main point of the deal when she got the
boss to let you fill in that summer when Shag Phillips had to
check out. She knew the boss knew damn well she wouldn't be
asking him to take somebody in there that couldn't cut the
mustard. And you know as well as I do that she wouldn't even
think about asking him to do something like that before checking it out with Joe States. No way she would ever go straight to
the boss with something like that without first checking with
old Joe.

XXIV

So there I was once more en route south and into the also and also of a very old place once more. *Me and all of the obligations, expectations, and ever-alluring and expanding horizons of personal aspirations that were already beginning to be part and parcel of those now ever so wee lullaby rocking chair storybook adventure times even before I was yet old enough to stay awake for the long winter night tell-me-tale-time semicircle around the red brick fireplace beneath the Mother Goose chime clock mantelpiece.*

Southbound once more by erstwhile thunderbird become at least for the time being Whisperjet. *Me and the one who was the one for me and would also go north or south and would go east or west and also east of the sun and also west of the moon even as she also fulfilled ancestral hometown expectations along with personal aspirations of her own.*

In those days you took the Delta Airlines Shuttle from La Guardia in New York to Atlanta International. Then you transferred to the southwest-bound commuter flight to Montgomery and central Alabama and so on to Mississippi and Louisiana was only one more hour, departing Eastern Standard Time and arriving the same hour Central Standard Time. *And as our flight entered the landing approach pattern and we brought our seats upright, I said, Here we go, thinking, all the way back to within this many Alabama miles north by east from the outskirts of Mobile and the river and the canebrakes and cypress swamp moss and the state docks and the bay and the Gulf Coast beyond the storybook blue and storm gray horizons of which were the old Spanish Main and also the Seven Seas and the seven storybook wonders of the ancient world.*

As the airport limousine pulled on away from the city limits and settled into the thirty-mile interstate highway drive to the campus exit, we said what we said about the central Alabama preautumn countryside, and when she closed her eyes I went on remembering how uncertain everything had been for me that first September.

But I had said to myself what I had said to myself even so. Because I was there not only from Mobile County Training School and Miss Lexine Metcalf and her windows on the world and Mr. B. Franklin Fisher and the early birds, I was also there from Gasoline Point. So I said what I had already been saying long before school bell time became more urgent than train whistle and sawmill whistle time. I said, Destination Phila-mayork, remembering the comings and goings of old sporty-limp-walking Luzana Cholly with his blue steel .32-.20 in his underarm holster and the delicate touch and locomotive thunder of his rawhide tough twelve-string guitar fingers and what he said that time under the Three-Mile Creek L & N bridge. And there was also old patent-leather-footed, pigeon-toed-tipping Stagolee Dupas fils with his diamond-flashing piano fingers and tailored-to-measure jazz-backed suits, who did what he did that night at Joe Lockett's in the Bottoms and didn't skip city afterward. *Because Philamayork was not somewhere you escaped to. It was somewhere you earned your way to, your hithering and thithering way through, thick and thin and wherever and whatever to.*

I also said what I said when I arrived on campus that first September because my destination was already what it was long before I was aware of anything at all about what actually made Luzana Cholly Luzana Cholly and Stagolee Dupas fils the notorious Stagolee Dupas fils. Because for me it all had actually begun all the way back during the now only vaguely remembered time when Mama began calling me her little old scootabout man, even before I had learned enough about words to know what scooter and scooting about actually meant.

But by the time I had arrived on campus as a college freshman that first September I had learned what I had learned from that many rockabye tale times and all the midwinter fireside times and summer night mosquito smoke times even before the day came when Mama let Miss Tee take me to be enrolled because my school bell time had come. And I was a schoolboy from then on and Mama said, That's Mama's little old Buster Brown scootabout man over there scooting about that schoolyard just like some little old cottontail jackrabbit scooting all over the briar patch.

So I said what I said about myself as I looked out on the part of the campus you could see from my dormitory room, and when my roommate arrived from Chicago, I said what I first said about him because his nickname was Geronimo, which I associated with the escapades of Reynard the Fox. But when class sessions began I said he was like a young Dr. Faustus, which earned him the campuswide nickname of the Snake, as if that made him a devil-ordained tent show and vaudeville magician or snake-oil con man, not to mention an ever so—and ever so lethal snake in the grass.

When the limousine stopped, I opened my eyes and realized I had dozed off and that we had taken our exit from the interstate highway and were waiting to pull into the local route into town. So I said what I said because I knew we would be rolling through the Court House Square area and on out by the old antebellum Strickland Place and into that end of the campus within the next twenty-plus minutes.

We signed in at the campus guesthouse, and when we came back downstairs after I called Mr. Poindexter and helped with the unpacking of what was needed from the luggage for the time being, it was not yet late afternoon. So we decided that there was enough time for a leisurely homecomng alumni stroll before changing clothes to join the Poindexters for dinner and information about a choice of a furnished apartment on or off campus.

Which was why we headed up the incline of Campus Avenue under the overhanging oaks and elms instead of popping across to the off-campus main drag for a drugstore fountain Coca-Cola, for a quick peek around in Red Gilmore's Varsity Threads Haberdashery, and the mandatory back-in-town-from-up-the-country-and-elsewhere round of palm slapsnatching and back patting in Deke Whatley's Barbershop.

So here we are once more, I said, as the upcurving sidewalk leveled off and we came on by the concrete steps leading down to the main campus promenade lawn where the outdoor concert bandstand was and across which the three-story dormitory where the dean of women's office and the campus clock tower faced the white Doric columns and recently repainted dome of the antebellum-style brick red, white-trimmed dining hall. We came on past the main building of the School of Music and came to the turnoff to the dining hall, the building on our right was the one then known as the Office Building because at that time it not only included the president's office and registrar's office and those of the treasurer and the dean of men but also the post office and the bank.

The street you came to from the rear entrance of the office building was the thoroughfare that ran from town and on out past the residential neighborhoods where most faculty, staff, and other campus employees either owned or rented homes. So we had to stop for the fairly steady stream of traffic, and then we crossed over and came on along the hedge-lined walk to the wide quadrangle in which the gymnasium faced the open end and across which the library faced the Science Building.

As we passed the tall shrubbery framing the main entrance to the library we nudged each other without looking or saying anything. Then as we came on to the next open space, you could see the red clay tennis courts beyond the parking space reserved for the buses of visiting athletic teams. And up ahead near the side entrance to the gymnasium there was a traffic circle, beyond which were the ticket booth and entrance to the bowl down the steep hill directly behind the gymnasium.

We followed the curving walk on around past the box office and main entrance to the gymnasium that was not only the headquarters of the Department of Physical Education and the venue for the annual conference basketball tournament in those days, it was also where all of the big campus dances were held, weekly movies were shown, and where touring repertory theater companies and dance and musical groups performed in those days.

Off to our right as we came around the loop to the science building side of the quadrangle was the campus water tower, beyond which was the baseball field, which was up the steep wooded hill and on the other side of trees directly behind the covered student grandstand in the bowl.

When you reached the other end of the science building, you were back at the tree-lined throughway, and as we came on across to Campus Avenue, the dormitory on the right of the quadrangle you faced was the one that Atelier 359 overlooked, and suddenly I missed my old one and only and best of all possible roommates again. But as we came on back along the main stem past the dining hall, the bandstand and the clock tower again, all I said was "seven league boots, indeed."

XXV

The Poindexters lived in the first block of the faculty and staff off-campus housing area that began outside of the Emancipation Memorial Pillars of the main entrance to Campus Avenue. So it was only about a two and a half block stroll from the guesthouse, which also meant that they lived only about seven blocks along the municipal thoroughfare from the academic quadrangle where the office of the English Language and Literature Department was in those days.

When we arrived for dinner, our on-campus apartment assignment, and preliminary registration orientation that first Wednesday night, they both greeted us in the living room and there was now a second child, a boy, born during the term following my graduation. The first was a daughter, whom I remembered as having been in elementary school during my senior year.

I knew that Mrs. Poindexter, whose first name was Estelle, and who was just about the same shade of teacake tan as Eunice, but with freckles that you didn't see until you were close enough to shake hands, had been his hometown sweetheart when they were in high school in Washington and that they had married the year after he came back to Washington with his M.A. degree and then came down to central Alabama that following September. By the time I arrived on the campus he had not only been back to graduate school to finish his residence work toward his Ph.D., he had also become the chairman of the English Department, which always surprised visitors and newcomers to the campus because he could still be mistaken for an upperclassman.

The first time I had seen his wife was during the break between the winter and spring terms of my freshman year, when I was invited to come along to his residence with my roommate and several upperclassmen for an informal extracurricular discussion of current books, magazines, and quarterly literary reviews.

She didn't come in to say hello that time until we were all in the study, which was on the left as you entered the living room. We were still standing and moving around looking at the bookshelves and the diplomas and citations and also at the paintings, sketches, and photographs. She had come in, and he presented each one of us by name in class, and she served us tea and cookies and excused herself to do what she had to do as a young mother.

This time she left us in the living room with her husband and went to turn the children over to a babysitter and finished what she had to do in the kitchen and dining room before calling us in to dinner. So we were led into the study for a glass of dry sherry, and that was when the orientation session began. And the first item on his briefing agenda turned out to be a matter that was more personal than official.

Incidentally, he said, you probably haven't been back on campus long enough to have been cued in on one unmandated change in common student parlance since either one of you was

last here. Your host this evening is no longer addressed or referred to by the official name you and your classmates used. He
is now generally addressed and referred to even by faculty colleagues as Prof Dex.

So it was to be Prof Dex and Prof from then on. I never
addressed him as Dex even when he and I became as casual with
each other as my relationship with my old roommate and with
Taft Edison had become. I would say, Hey, man, and hey, Prof,
but never hey, Dex, and he never did call me Scooter. He called
me Don. Because from our Composition 102 self-portrait paper
he had found out that when my roommate and I were not make-
believe Belle Epoque, Montmartre bohemian offspring the likes
of François Villon, we were the local versions of Oxford and/or
Cambridge dons, which was not only appropriately academic
but also had the titular ring of jazz, kings, dukes, counts, earls,
and barons as well as tongue-in-cheek overtones of Don Juan
and Don Quixote.

As for our on-campus apartment assignment, all he had to do
was name the address and give Eunice the keys. Neither she nor
I had ever been inside that particular faculty residence, which
was near the student nurses' dormitory area and not far from
the campus infirmary, but I was pleased because I liked the
cross-campus walk from there past the clock tower, the bandstand on the campus promenade lawn, and through the post
office to the main academic area.

We had made no special requests other than for an on-campus
apartment for two, but both Eunice and I had hoped that we
would not have to be assigned to one of the duplex or triplex
units on the deans' and administrators' row along the municipal

thoroughfare between the main academic quadrangle and the block where the drugstore, Red Gilmore's Haberdashery, and Deke Whatley's Barbershop were.

Our on-campus quarters assignment turned out to be the only official orientation item on the agenda for the evening, because any detailed clarification of specific academic assignments and standard operation procedures in the orientation material would be addressed during the preclass period departmental meeting that first Monday morning and in one-on-one appointments with the department head.

So I asked what I asked about faculty and staff changes since my graduation, because the only officials I had seen since our arrival that afternoon were the ones on duty at the guesthouse. And that was when I found out which of the people I remembered were away in graduate school completing their time in residence required of Ph.D. candidates. Then as we were taking our last sip of sherry we were called into the dining room and as we settled into our first course I said that I had nothing else to add to what I had said on the phone from New York about the Bossman's Royal Highness proposition. So the main thing we talked about was the work of fiction that Taft Edison was already preoccupied with when I introduced myself to him in New York and told him that I remembered him from my freshman year on campus. Two of the sequences he had read to me sometime later had recently been published in current highly rated magazines, both of which placed more emphasis on literary quality than on social issues and political positions as such.

I've seen a few things he did for the sociopolitical corn-bread paper sheets a year or so ago, Prof Dex said, but these new pieces are impressively different, and I must also say that they represent not only a logical but also an astonishing development of the Taft Edison who was a student in the course in the English novel which, by the way, he was concurrently supplementing on his own initiative with works of Zola, Hugo, Tolstoy, and especially Dostoevsky.

As Jerome Jefferson and I were well aware, I said, and he also knew that he was reading a lot of twentieth-century poetry. You know, Pound, T. S. Eliot, E. E. Cummings, Wallace Stevens, Marianne Moore. Incidentally, I can also remember the copies of Thomas Hardy's *Return of the Native, Jude the Obscure,* and *Mayor of Casterbridge* on your bookshelves in the office of the English Department and also how old Jerome Jefferson, better known as Geronimo, used to sneer whenever he heard somebody saying, Beyond the maddening crowd. It's *madding crowd, my good fellow.* Hardy got it from Thomas Gray's poem, not from some goddamn sports column hack. *Madding,* my good man. You're on a college campus. *Faites attention.*

Then when I said, So you like what old Taft is by way of getting into these days, he said, If he can bring even most of it off as these two excerpts suggest, he just might be capable of doing. We just might have a quantum leap to reckon with.

And I said, Well, I'm ready to tell you that he just might do just that. I can personally vouch for the fact that there is more to come that is even more outrageous. Voltaire, Cervantes, Rabelais, none of that stuff was lost on our boy. I must say, though, that it surprised me because as much as I had come to know about the library books he had checked out, old Jerome Jefferson was the one I had associated with the outrageous adventures and misadventures and absurdities of Candide, Gargantua and Pantagruel, and Don Quixote.

My main concern is that the universality of the picaresque misadventures of Candide and Don Quixote may be mistaken for a fictionalized sociological documentation of yet another black boy being done in by his own incompetence or downright stupidity. Whereas nobody assumes that Candide stands for all Westphalians or Don Quixote represents the nuttiness of, say, Spanish idealism.

He's very much aware of all that I said. So he hopes to make some of it outrageous enough to offset at least some of the ever-ready condescending compassion of survey-addicted do-gooders. He has already concocted a hilarious takeoff on Don Quixote that I think he's really going to bring off. The draft he read me reminded me of some of the sneaky stuff that old Jerome Jefferson used to read to me from his sketch book, which he referred to as the goods as in the goods on.

That's good, he said. The idiomatic particulars should be as evocative as possible, but beware of fictionalized sociological findings. Remember the great allegories about *"everyman"* and *Pilgrim's Progress* is about everyman who—*who would become whatever.* Let us not forget *Rake's Progress.*

Anyway, he continued as we headed for the door, this is all good news, and I don't have to tell you how pleased I am to have had anything whatsoever to do with you two becoming the kind of, what shall I say, collegial friends you have become.

And when Estelle Poindexter, who was walking arm in arm with Eunice, said, Spoken in parchment with the Honors Day enthusiasm of a certified and formally berobed Prof Dex if I ever heard one, he said, So, flip your tassels across your mortarboards.

XXVI

When we came downstairs to the cafeteria for breakfast that next morning, the main item on our agenda was what we were going to have to do to get settled into our on-campus apartment by that next Monday morning. It was now Thursday. Freshman students were already arriving, and general registration would begin Friday and end Saturday.

At that time there were five academic class days per week, with some courses meeting on Mondays, Wednesdays, and Fridays, and others on Tuesdays and Thursdays. My first classroom session would begin at eight o'clock on Monday. But on that first Monday morning there would be a faculty orientation session in the office of the English Department at seven-thirty. That was when you picked up your roster of registration enrollees, your attendance and performance record book, along with your first stack of publishers' promotion copies of new and revised editions of textbooks and anthologies.

Meanwhile, the fall term of the county elementary school in which Eunice was going to be teaching would not begin until Monday of the week after the first week of classes on campus were under way. So according to the instructions she had received in New York along with her contract and other orientation data, all she had to do to arrange for commuter pickup transportation was call the telephone number provided along with the class schedule and give her name, address, and phone number, and the dispatcher would call her back and give the time to be ready to be picked up.

Given the school's widely celebrated emphasis on good housekeeping and also as returning graduates, we were not surprised to find that our on-campus apartment was as suitable and well furnished as it was. All we had to do before that next Monday was to arrange for the books and other items we had shipped from New York to be delivered from local railway express, and shop for provisions for the kitchen and items for the bathroom.

From the window at the end of the living room where the executive-size desk was, you could see the valley and the trees, beyond which were the clock tower, the promenade lawn, and the dome of the dining hall, which you could not see. The other end of the living room could be converted into a dining area by expanding and raising the coffee table. And when you stepped into the hallway from the living room, the bath and bedroom were on your left, and the kitchen with a breakfast nook was on your right.

Before sundown that Thursday we had received all of our deliveries and also completed our shopping, so we checked out of the guesthouse that Friday morning, and by noon we felt that we were ready to take off and have a snack at the drugstore lunch counter on the off-campus main drag. And afterward, while Eunice went to look up some of her old instructors in the Department of Education, I would drop in on Red Gilmore in the Toggery and Deke Whatley in the barbershop to let them know that I was back in town for a year or maybe two.

Red Gilmore was busy with two customers, so all I did was slap palms with him and take a quick look around at his fall term display and point to the barbershop next door as I came back out onto the sidewalk.

Hey, here he is, Deke Whatley said as I came into the doorway and then into the lotion-, talcum-, and tobacco-scented ambience of the barbershop. He did not have a customer at the time, so he was sitting in his jacked-up chair facing the entrance with his legs crossed as he puffed and flourished his cigar exactly as I remembered him doing when I saw him for the first time during my freshman year.

Hey, what say there, young fella, he said, extending his hand. We've been hearing some pretty reliable rumors about you heading back down this way this term. Hey, y'all remember this boy. Came up here on one of them special scholarship deals from that school down around Mobile way. What say, my man? Look at him, y'all. Yeah, here he is.

They were all looking at me then, and when I pointed at Skeeter and said, Hey, I'll be seeing you again at least for a while, he said, Man, you've been to a lot of super hip experts since the last time you were in this chair: Hollywood, Chicago, New York, and even all the way over to Paris, France.

And I said, Man, all I was ever looking for wherever I was, was somebody to keep it looking like you had it looking when I left here.

Of course, Deke Whatley said then, You must know who the main ones keeping me up on your doings and whereabouts was. Giles Cunningham. Y'all know that. Old Giles and Miss Lady took a liking to him. She was the one spotted him out at the Dolomite one night. Not because he was a musician, but because he was such a good listener. She could tell how keen his ear for music was just by the way he listened. So she checked him out and she invited him over to her house and they started listening to her collection of records and she said, Deke, that boy heard everything. She said, He listened like an arranger! And that's what led to her giving him that bass fiddle she had fixed up for him. So he could get some student in the string section of the chapel orchestra to teach him to run scales. Not that she was trying to make a musician out of him or anything like that. She just liked the way he kept time when all he was doing was listening just to be enjoying himself. And I'm not talking about dancing in your seat or something like that. What I'm talking about is that you don't have to be a music mechanic to be musical. That's what she realized right away. Hell, when you come right down to it, a lot of big-time musicians turn out to be more mechanical than musical!

Yeah, yeah, I see your point, Skeeter said as he turned his chair for his next customer to be seated. Just listen to how musical all them church folks always been and most of them can't read no music even if it's in boxcar printing.

Anyway, Deke Whatley went on, I know Miss Tense well enough to know very well that she knew good and well that this boy hadn't come up here to college to learn how to be no musician. No question about that. Because that's just how hip she is. So even when it turned out that along with all that special talent for time that she spotted from the stage that night, he also had that magic gift of whatsitsname, whatchamacallit, absolute whatchamacallit, absolute pitch! That's it—absolute pitch! Tone-perfect. And also that other genius-gifted thing, whatsitsname—*total recall, photographic memory.* One go-around and this cat's got it cold! But you see now, that's the boss lady for you. Even when she decided that he was good enough on that thing to start earning a little emergency change gigging with her combo out at the Dole from time to time, she still wasn't trying to entice him away from whatever it was that he was trying to do with his life.

But hey, he said, interrupting himself as Red Gilmore came in from next door, as I expected him to. Here's old Red boy. He knows almost as much about Hortense and old Giles and all this as I myself do. Tell him about them and this boy, Red.

Then when Red Gilmore shrugged off the compliment and bowed, signaling for him to continue, he said, Like I said, when she got to the big Bossman Himself to let him go fill in that summer while they were looking for a replacement when old Shag had to cut out and go back home. She said she was just trying to help him pick up some summer cash and see some more of the world on his way to graduate school. Right, Red?

Right, Red Gilmore said, and it was the same when he cut out from the band to spend that time doing what he was knocking around doing out there in Hollywood.

And, Deke Whatley said, as Red boy also remembers me telling him, it was old Giles himself that was the one that brought me the word about his girlfriend graduating and him marrying her that same summer in her hometown and taking her straight on off to graduate school with him like it was the same as going on their honeymoon.

Well, Deke, Skeeter said, since they both had them graduate school fellowship awards or grants or whatever you call them, it *was* a kind of honeymoon, a special kind of honeymoon, wasn't it?

That's exactly what I'm saying, Deke Whatley said. Hell, they both come through here on scholarship awards from high school, him four years from that Mobile County school and her three years when she transferred from State as a sophomore when he was a junior.

So now here he is, gentlemen, Red Gilmore said, back down here because they sent for him to come back and join the faculty, even before he finished his Ph.D. Nice going, Mobile.

Like old Giles said, Deke Whatley said, that just goes to show you about this generation we got coming along down here in this neck of the woods these days. And they fanning out and making good in every section of the nation. Check it out. Don't take my word for it. Check it out for yourself.

Well, heyo, there, young Mobile, old Showboat Parker said. He had pulled up out front in his Cadillac taxi and had come in and waved and waited while Deke Whatley and Red Gilmore said what they were saying about Giles Cunningham.

What say, there, Mr. Globe-trotter? We been hearing that you just might be heading back down this way for a while. So when did you get in?

And I said, Number nine, number nine. Old getaway number nine. Yesterday afternoon, number nine. Number nine and old Floorboard whatshisname, or was it Dashboard?

Floorboard, Showboat Parker said. Because he was the one noted for stepping on the gas to get the chippies back on campus before library closing time during the old days of warden-strict deans of women, and herd-riding housemothers. Old Floorboard is taking it easy somewhere down in Florida these days, young . . . excuse me, young prof!

And speaking of Florida, Red Gilmore said, that's where old Giles and Miss Tense ought to be rolling back in here from, just about now, this being registration week and also season opening week out at the Dole. Old Wylie was in to see me yesterday. Everything is all set and ready. All Giles and Tense need to do is to get back in place in time to greet people.

Hey, Skeets, I said as I was about to leave, I think I can promise you that you can expect to see me more regularly than in the old days. And he said, At your service, young prof. At your service. I just want you to know how much I appreciate what you said about remembering me in all them different places. That's nice to know.

Now me, Deke Whatley said, uncrossing his legs and stepping down out of his chair to walk me out onto the sidewalk, I just want to make sure you know that the fact that you made a special stop in here just to let us know you're back in town, says a lot. That's a true down-home boy, Mobile. A true homeboy come back to tag up and get long gone again. And further. Some of these somiches come back through here just to show off like they escaped from something here, forgetting that it was what they took up there from down here that took them up there out there and over there or wherever they got come by whatever. But so much for that. Here's what I just want to say. Not that you don't know it already. Giles and Hortense talk about you like family. That's the kind of folks to have in our corner. But hell, I ain't telling you nothing you don't know already. I'm just saying amen!

But just let me say this. The main thing about education. No matter what kind of course you take, and how many degrees you get, The main thing is *knowing what to want!* You understand what I'm saying? Don't care what courses and how many degrees, the main thing is know what you really want for yourself. I'm not talking about self-indulgence. I'm talking about self-satisfaction. Knowing what to choose. Knowing how to pick and choose.

XXVII

Well, here he is just like you said, Giles Cunningham said, as much to us as to Hortense Hightower, when Eunice and I arrived at the Pit at one-fifteen that next afternoon and headed for the table where the two of them were just pulling out their chairs to sit down for the light midday meal I had guessed they would be having at that time. We stepped down from the entrance level to the dining level and came on over to where they were, and when we all had gone through old Daddy Royal's jive time greeting routine and sat down, he said, Right on the money. Man, the boss lady is still right on your case. When old Deke called last night to see if we were back from Florida and told us you were already back on the scene and making the rounds, you know what she said? She said, Well, most likely he'll be dropping by the Pit to catch us on our lunch break. Man, what can I tell you? Didn't I tell you she don't miss? Here you are and there are those two extra place settings.

I didn't remind him that even before he had given me the part-time job that summer before my senior year I had already heard enough about him to know that he usually spent the first part of Monday through Friday mornings in his headquarters office at the Pit, where he had breakfast and worked until midmorning. Then unless there were appointments elsewhere he usually drove on along the interstate highway to the off-campus settlement area where the Dolomite Club was, and where if he had no other errands he stayed until he came back to the Pit to have lunch and an updating session with Hortense, who usually slept late, had breakfast at home, and spent the rest of the morning working on her own agenda, which was usually domestic, but along with which there were also details involved in the operation of the after-hours lounge at the Dolomite, where she sang with her own pickup combos from time to time.

Sometimes she also went along with him on his afternoon trip out to the Plum to keep in touch with Flee Mosely, but the only time she took her combo out there to play was on special occasions during the mid- and late-summer picnic and barbecue season, mainly for afternoon sessions that did not conflict with her after-hours schedule at the Dolomite.

So here he is, Giles Cunningham said as we settled into our chairs and I picked up the menu. And look who he brought along with him this time. It's just like the Bossman Himself said when he called us from Ohio to let us know that he could use you to fill in for Shag Phillips. He said, This kid may be just a beginner but he's already pretty much free of clinkers both personwise and musicwise.

And when I said, Meet Miss You-Know-Who, Hortense Hightower said, Miss Who-Else-But. Hi, sweetie. I hear you're already beyond the main part of getting settled in on your own. But any more help you need for getting around picking up stuff or whatever, don't hesitate to call me. Don't worry about interrupting my schedule. And don't wait until you need something. After all, I'm always available for another one of those sprees-of-the-moment girlie shopping trips, whether downtown or out of town to Montgomery, Atlanta, or Birmingham.

And when Eunice said, I promise, Giles Cunningham said, There you go. What did I tell you? How the hell the boss lady going to miss out on somebody you pick out for a wife? They got your scholarship record up there on the campus, but she's got your number. And like I say, she don't miss. No doubt about it.

Then she said, old Deke Whatley and Red Gilmore were the ones who knew that you were the one up there on the campus. And whenever this fella's name came up, even when he left the Bossman and the band to stick around out there in Hollywood, they'd always say, He'll be back through here. Mark my words. He's still got some unfinished business that's still in the works right across the throughway and campus avenue.

And that was when Hortense Hightower said what she said about not trying to get in touch with Eunice because they hadn't been introduced by me. And a casual encounter had been just about out of the question because in those days nightspots like the Dolomite were strictly off-limits to young women who lived on the campus.

As for this weekend at the Dole, Hortense Hightower said then, there's nothing special, no big deal. Just this snappy, up-and-coming, Columbus–Phenix City combo for the upperclassmen, with local contacts and incoming hotshots out to survey the off-campus possibilities.

And that was when Giles Cunningham said, Actually, you won't be missing anything special out at the Dole between now and when the fall season road band booking schedule clicks in— say, about the middle of next month.

We came on outside then, and as we stood waiting for Hortense Hightower to come and drive us back to the campus, Eunice said, Who is Speck, and why do they call him that? And

I said, He is the one who runs the Pit. Wiley Payton runs the Dolomite, and Flee Mosely runs the Plum. They call him Speck because he has freckles. Speck is for Speckled Red, as in speckled chicken, and there are also some who just say old Florida Red—as in Tampa Red.

That was that Friday afternoon. I spent the first part of that Saturday morning unpacking and arranging my books and phonograph records on the waist-high shelves under the windows behind the desk in my work area off the living room. Then as I made my way across the campus to find out which work carrel in the stacks behind the circulation counter in the main reading room would be reserved for me, even as the sound of the clock tower chiming above the hum and buzz and honking traffic and the chatter of the students reminded me of my own arrival as a freshman, I crossed my fingers, because I suddenly realized that I was rearriving as a freshman, a freshman with a graduate degree plus further study from New York University, but a beginner once more even so.

XXVIII

As we pulled on away from the campus avenue parking spot where she had told me she would be waiting when I came down the steps from the post office that next Wednesday afternoon, Hortense Hightower said, About this Daddy Royal proposition. Of course, you already know that Giles and I have been in on it all along. So I thought I might as well clue you in on how it all got started and what it's really all about.

So as we came on down along the early-fall tree-shaded mainstem to turn left at the traffic circle and head for the exit to the municipal throughway outbound, she said, The fact of the matter is that I'm really the one that's actually responsible for starting it, although I really had something else in mind when I came up with the idea that led to it.

What I really had in mind, she went on to say as we pulled on off the campus to head along the thoroughfare to the intersection with the interstate highway across which was the street that led to the Dolomite, what I had in mind from the very beginning was something that had to do with the Bossman Himself personally. Something that I had first spoken to him about some time ago, once I got to be close enough friends with him.

And to tell the truth, she said, that's what all this about

Daddy Royal is still about. Because old Daddy Royal is a very important part of the big picture, to be sure. But the Bossman, like old Louis Armstrong, is one of the main ones that somebody is always coming up with when questions turn to achieving a place in the history of music in the United States.

And that was also when she also said, As soon as I felt that my friendship was close enough I started mentioning that it might be a good idea to get somebody to help him start compiling all of the stuff that's been accumulating about him over the years. I would mention it to him every now and then without pushing too hard, and since he didn't dismiss it, I figure he just might have been considering it.

So then, she said, I began to wonder about who was going to be the one or one of the ones from the life this music comes out of that's going to be helping him pull all this stuff together. And I also made a point of mentioning that to him as often as I could without making him feel like he was being rushed because we were worried about you know what. That's why I always made it a point to put the emphasis on volume and kept saying what I kept saying about his *future* output overwhelming the present, with the past getting dimmer and dimmer.

This had been going on for some time. Not that she had ever thought of herself adding her voice to a lot of others, because she knew he respected her opinion and would give some serious consideration to anything she suggested, and that was as far as she was personally involved. She just brought it up from time to time, sometimes jokingly, saying things like, You understand, of course, that I'm not talking about a biography. What I'm talking about is a memoir. That's about as far as it went.

And then you showed up, she said. Then she said, Let me tell you something. The very first time I laid eyes on you sitting back there, just sitting back there on that stool at the bar listening like that, I said to myself, This one ain't just another one of them campus hipsters out looking for the latest do to impress them other hipsters and squares. I said, This one is out here to hear some music to connect with something he came to college to learn about life. You just struck me right off as somebody who came to get a college education. Not just to learn how to make a living doing something above common labor, but also to learn as much as you can about how to appreciate what a full life is really all about.

And that was when she told me that she had been more impressed when I said my course of study was liberal arts than she would have been if I had said it was music. And that that was when she decided to invite me to come by her house and listen to whatever I selected from what turned out to be her very comprehensive collection of recordings. We were at the intersection then, and as we came on across the interstate highway and headed through that settlement to the Dolomite, she looked at me and said, Although I didn't mention anything about it at the time, that was the beginning of what led up to getting you that summer gig with the band was all about. That's why as soon as I heard that Shag Phillips was going to have to go home, I called old Joe and said, See what we can do to get our schoolboy in there as a stopgap for the summer, and Old Pro went along with old Joe on it.

So, she said, that's how I went from making a suggestion to being knee-deep in the whole thing. But anyway, I was pretty certain that he would give me the benefit of the doubt. And when I heard his voice on the phone when he called to tell me when and where to send you up to Cincinnati, I considered my scheme was already under way, even if you had gone on to do that grad school work at the end of that first summer. Because by that time he had you checked out. So even when you decided to stay out in Hollywood that next time around, he was just as confident as I was that you hadn't given up on grad school because you were starstruck or anything like that. On the contrary. And also by that time old Daddy Royal was in on the scheme, so when you made that trip to Europe and came back and got hitched and checked into NYU, everything was falling into place, with old Joe keeping tabs.

Come to think of it—she began, as we came up the incline to the Dolomite and pulled into her parking place at the side entrance. Then she went on, You know something? Everybody in that band knew more about why you were really in there with them than you did. Because I hadn't said a word to you about what that bull fiddle was leading up to until now. And that was when she said, This is not what I had in mind when I had it fixed up and gave it to you, but it sure did come in handy when old Shag had to go home. That's when it hit me. Because I remembered that I had invited the boss to hear you with the combo and right away he spotted you as being from Mobile or somewhere in old Daddy Gladstone's territory. That's when I decided on what I said when I called old Joe.

Then as we came on into her office and dressing room after she said what she said to Wiley Payton in the main entrance lobby and also told him to send in two tall fountain Coca-Colas, she sat at her desk and had me pull up a chair, and as we waited for the Cokes she said, We got a call from the Bossman last night and from Daddy Royal this morning, and I told him that I thought you were pleased with your class schedule and I was expecting to pick you up on the campus this very afternoon.

Then she said, So here we are. Because as soon as old Joe found out that you were thinking about taking a break from grad school studies and had an offer to do some part-time teaching down here, we both said, Hey, this could be the time. And I said, Let me be the one, and when I called the Bossman he said, Why don't we start with Daddy Royal. So that's the proposition old Joe laid on you.

So here we are, she said again holding up her fountain Coke again, and isn't it just like the Bossman to set us up with a vamp? *The deal is on, but we vamp till he's ready.* And you know what old Daddy Royal said? He said, That just goes to show you. He said, Once you bring up something you want him to consider and give him a little time to get around to it, that's exactly what he'll do.

Then he said, Yeah, I'm the vamp. He said, Don't you always start patting your feet before you start the music? Patting your foot and sometimes also snapping your fingers? You're already dancing before the instruments come in. See what I mean? And you can always bet when he comes in with that segue he's ready. He's ready. Jam, scram, or straight-ahead chronogram.

Old Daddy Royal, I said, Old Daddy Royal. *Old Daddy Royal is always on the case, I said, remembering but not mentioning that already before any proposal of any kind had been brought up, he had begun showing me his memorabilia simply because he assumed that I was a special kind of schoolboy who was curious enough and hip enough to appreciate them. And when we came to the scrapbooks that included clippings and other souvenirs of his early tours in Europe he said, Now we're coming into a territory where they have another attitude about all this stuff. It's not just some kind of light entertainment to them. Like that old guy. Some old professor somebody over there told me one time. I can't call him by name right now and he's not in any of these clippings but I'm bound to have it around here stuck in somewhere and maybe a picture, too, and*

I'll recognize it as soon as I come across it. But anyway, he's the one that said dancing came before music as such. He was talking about way back there, if you know what I mean. All the way back in what they call prehistoric times. And he was also the one who also said that the first floor of the theater is called the orchestra because that used to be the word for dancing space. I don't remember exactly what he said about how that word got to be the word for a big band. Maybe because that's where they used to sit before somebody came up with the idea of the pit. But anyway, the main thing for me was that dancing came first. He said, Dancing came first, then music. So that's the boss for you, and that's why he's the emperor.

I tell you what, Hortense Hightower said as we finished our fountain Cokes and stood up. Since this thing has come back around to me, and I'm the one that brought you into it in the first place, why don't you just go on and get your campus stuff in the groove and maybe by, say, Thanksgiving, you will have had enough time to think about how all this can really fit in with what you went on beyond college to graduate school to learn.

Believe me, honey pie, she said, the last thing I want is for you to feel that we are rushing you into this thing. I haven't forgotten and never will forget what you told me more than once about what they taught you and what they absolutely did not try to decide for you down there at that Mobile County Training School under your Mr. B. Franklin Fisher.

But even as she was saying what she was saying and did not say what she did not say, it was as if you were listening to, Miss Lexine Metcalf herself again in her school bell morning enchanted classroom through the wall-length windows of which you could see the Chickasabogue sky beyond Bay Poplar woods even before it was your turn to stand erect and make your way past the bulletin board, the globe stand, and the map rack to the blackboard realm of schoolboy verbal and numerical derring-do.

Miss Lexine Metcalf, Miss Lexine Metcalf, Miss Lexine Metcalf, I said, Mama, Miss Tee and Miss Lexine Metcalf who was the one Miss Tee took me to when Mama let her be the one to take me to the campus to be registered when the first day of my first school bell September morning arrived that year. And Miss Lexine Metcalf took us to Miss Cox in the primer grade room and said, I will be waiting for you when you reach the third grade.

Miss Lexine Metcalf, who would be the one who would say what she said about me to Mr. B. Franklin Fisher himself, who said of himself Fisher—yes, Fisher, as in fisherman. Fisher of men. Fisher of men of special promise. Men worthy of the women who bore them and nursed them. Who said, Many are called but few are chosen. And my question is, Who will be one in that number??

Then on the day he came back to add my name to that year's list of prospects selected for matriculation in the Early Bird Preparatory Program when you reached the ninth grade, she was the one who said, Who if not you, my splendid young man? Who if not you, my splendid young man, from all the way down in Meaher's Hummock on Dodge Shingle Mill Road near the cypress swamp by the bottoms and the L & N Railroad. Who if not also you, indeed.

As Hortense Hightower took me around to see the changes that she and Giles Cunningham had made in the Dolomite since I graduated and left en route to Cincinnati to try out for the summer job with the band before going to graduate school, every time she pointed out and explained another addition or renovation, you could see she was not only pleased with what she and Giles Cunningham were doing but also with where they had decided to do what they were doing.

Which meant she was also pleased with the choice she had made when she decided to leave the band she had gone on the road with when she finished her college courses at Alabama State.

XXIX

Remembering the trip out to the Dolomite as I settled myself at the desk of my carrel in the arts and letters stacks of the library that next afternoon, I suddenly found myself thinking about old Deke Whatley saying what he said as we stood at the curb outside his barbershop after I had popped in to say hello that first Thursday afternoon.

I just wanted to thank you for dropping in on us like this so soon after you got back in town. It tells me a lot. It tells me you still the kind of homeboy I took you for when you just set foot in there as a freshman. So I also just wanted to step out here and tell you how much I appreciate the postcards from some of the different places you got a chance to see for yourself after reading about. That tells me something.

That tells me something about knowing what education is really about, he said, and then he said what he said about education and self-satisfaction, and that was when he went on to say, Man, I been seeing them coming in as freshmen and checking them that come back for their class reunions over the years all this time I've been right here on this block. And you know what I think education is really about? I mean really about adding up to? *Knowing what to want.*

That's the key, he said again. Man, that's the key to the whole thing. Man, you miss that and you miss the main thing about what book learning is all about, don't care which colleges and universities you go to and how many degrees you come back with. Remember them gold watch chains and neck chains and graduation keys graduating classes used to buy to wear once they got their diplomas? What did they fit into? Nothing. No locks that your grade-point average hadn't qualified to open, by that time if you see what I mean. And even as I said I do, I really do, the very first person who had come to mind was Creola Calloway, not because she knew what to want but because she was somebody who knew what she did not want, no matter how many other people agreed with each other about what they thought she should want. The one and only Creola Calloway, who became notorious in Gasoline Point because it was as if she was just about the only one in town who did not think she should go into show business and become rich and famous because she was as good-looking as she was.

Not that she thought that being that good-looking was not supposed to be a special blessing and a God-given blessing at that, and therefore something to be grateful for and modest about. And the fact of the matter was that just about everybody seemed to be so impressed with how good-looking she was that it was also as if they regarded her as public property, and had no choice in the matter of what she should do with her own future.

As I sat musing in the library that afternoon that many years later, I suddenly realized that it had been as if just about everybody in Gasoline Point back during those days had been so dazzled by how she looked that it was as if they never paid any attention at all to how nice and friendly and just like another one of the folks she always was with everybody. Nobody ever accused her of being stuck up. On the contrary, what some people said about her implied that her big problem was that she was not as stuck up as people wanted her to be!

I hadn't mentioned anything about Creola Calloway to Deke Whatley as we stood at the curb outside the barbershop that first Thursday afternoon. All I said at first was what I said about Miss Lexine Metcalf warning me that I might be one of the splendid young men who might have to travel far and wide to find out what mission I was best suited to or called to fill, and that splendid young men were precisely those who qualified for their mission even as they searched for it.

To which he said, See what I mean? So take your time and go step by step and get it right. Right for you yourself, man. I know exactly where she's coming from. Right out of that old one about answered prayers bringing more tears or grief and stuff than unanswered ones. You heard what I said when I said what I said about knowing what to want, didn't you? Well, there it is.

So before starting in on the academic materials that I had come to start collecting in preparation for the winter term for the course I was teaching, I went on thinking about what Deke Whatley had said to how pleased Hortense Hightower was with what she decided to do after she had finished college and spent the time she had spent singing with a road band.

And then I went on remembering how when I graduated with a fellowship for advanced study she got me the job as summer substitute and how that led to the time I spent in California that led to what turned out to be my friendship with Gaynelle Whitlow in West Los Angeles, and my very special relationship with Jewel Templeton of Beverly Hills by way of Minnesota on the upper Mississippi.

To Gaynelle Whitlow, not unlike Joe States, Hollywood was

really pretty much the same as a factory town where production companies made movies, just as Detroit was a motor town
where motor companies made automobiles.

So to her, glamour in Hollywood was really a sales device,
much the same as body and accessory design were in the automobile industry.

As for her current means of livelihood, she described herself
as a freelance projects administrator and office manager. As for
the future, I'm all for it, she liked to say, and then go to point
out that sometimes it brought good luck and sometimes bad
luck but it was always hard on good-looking women whose
beauty was their stock-in-trade. Not that she herself did not
have the kind of good looks you could trade on. She didn't take
your breath away, as Creola Calloway did, but as soon as I saw
her in that booth in the Home Plate I knew she could get along
very well on her looks alone. But as that first evening got under
way I found myself thinking that she was just the kind of bosom
pal Creola Calloway needed when I was the boy becoming the
schoolboy I was becoming in Gasoline Point.

When I met Jewel Templeton, she had just recently met and
become a friend of the Marquis de Chaumienne and some of his
French and Italian friends, and was more concerned with what
to do with the success she had already achieved as featured leading lady and costar than with becoming a superstar.

In any case, I got the impression that what made her friendship with the Marquis de Chaumienne so important to her
was not his rank and social status as such but his cosmopolitan interests and his *taste*, which, as my old roommate would
surely have reminded me anew even if he didn't think I had
forgotten, was not unlike haute cuisine, predicated on a fine
appreciation and respect for the intrinsic quality of the basic

ingredients. Elementary, my dear fellow. Nobody appreciates the elementary like the ones who know what is relevant beyond subsistence.

So, upper Mississippi River pragmatist that she still was indeed and withal, she no doubt thought of the people in his set, beginning that season at St. Moritz, as being *dans le vrai* precisely because they struck her as knowing so much more than she did about what to want.

Dans le vrai, dans le vrai, dans le vrai indeed, I went on thinking as I stood up and headed for the shelves and the books I needed for my winter term lesson plans. Wasn't that what she also had in mind when she said what she said about magic keys when we said good-bye at the autobus station in Nice that afternoon? Some gold, some silver, some platinum. Or how about some sharp, some flat, some natural?

Why not? After all, had I not arrived in Hollywood, the land of lotus eaters, as a neophyte timekeeper in a notorious band of syncopated calypso vagabonds? Why not indeed, since they were not only keys that gave access to enchanted castles but also served as talismen in the pernicious passageways to the chambers with the chests of infinite treasure therein.

Not that the true storybook hero's quest is ever likely to be for material riches as such except to pay off *somebody else's* debt, otherwise his quest is likely to be for some magic means, not unlike the seed that became the beanstalk or the sporty limp stride of the seven league boots.

But old Flaubert was not talking about castles and the treasures and pleasures of court life when he said what he said. He was talking about the pastoral life of peasants, the blisses of the commonplace.

Creola Calloway herself would not have put it that way, I thought as I came along the aisle to the shelves from which

I would select the books to be transferred to the reserve book room for supplemental reading for term papers, but the new friend of the Marquis de Chaumienne would have no problems pointing out that the blisses of the commonplace were precisely what nobody in Gasoline Point seemed to want Creola Calloway to want.

XXX

When I called Taft Edison that next weekend and told him about my arrival and about my dinner and informal but official orientation session out at the Poindexters', he said, Man, as ready as I was to get the hell out of that goddamn place after the three years I spent down there, I have to admit that you make me realize that I do get little twitchings of nostalgia for the old place from time to time. After all, it was a beautiful campus, as I have had no trouble recording in print, and the standard of living in the surrounding neighborhood and even some of the outlying regions was also impressive. And as you know as well as my instructors down there did, I never had anything but enthusiasm for the library.

Me and you, man, I said, mimicking Joe States's old catch-phrase. Me and you. And my old roommate and your old class-mate Treemonisha Bradley. Which is when he also went on to say, Man, the truth of the matter is when I look back on the year-round time I spent down there maneuvering among that nationwide, and I mean coast-to-coast variety of thugs, in that student body in those days, I'm absolutely convinced that I was better prepared to cope with these Manhattan hip opera-tors than I would have been had I come straight up here from my hometown, which, believe me, was no hick town by any measurement.

Then he said, So our very own bespoke Ivy League liberal arts–type professor is still also pulling his share of the mandatory freshman composition and intro lit courses required of ag and tech as well as gym and bowl types down there, is he?

And I said, As of old, and also as of now yclept campuswide as Prof Dex. I don't know, man, maybe all those jocks don't mind flocking to his lit classes because they are sure to be outnumbered by all of these high-grade-point-average females whose help with term papers they can pretend to be in urgent need of, and also because if they earn the kind of money and celebrity status they're aiming at, a little spot of that belles lettres jive might come in handy in the high social circles they might move in. Not to mention jobs on a college coaching staff someday.

Then when I told him what Hortense Hightower had told me about her involvement in the Royal Highness proposal, he said, Man, like I told you when you told me what you told me when Joe States first brought up this thing in New York, bring this thing off and good-bye, academic gumshoe. Incidentally, the Pit and the Dolomite seem to have really come along since I was down there. But gigging in places like that as close to the campus as that was strictly off-limits for music majors in my day. The two campus dance bands used to play off-campus gigs, but that was mostly for high school hops and civic benefit socials. The Dolomite was off-limits for anything representing the school, especially music majors. Come to think of it, rules for members of the chapel orchestra and choir were pretty strict, too, even if you were a local resident. If you were a member of the chapel choir you had to get cleared by the dean of the Music Department to sing in the choir of your family church.

Man, he said, I think I told you about how old Sid and I used to hit those joints in the outlying regions and beyond every now and then. But nothing as close to the campus as the Dolomite, which, from what you tell me, must have really hit its stride during those three years you were down there after I took off. The only big outfits on tour that came through that way when I was there were booked in the gym on the campus by the recreation committee, and they played concerts in the gym, not dances. Of course, the Pit was a restaurant that started out as a barbecue pit stop out on the highway about a mile going west from Court House Square, where the old Confederate monument is.

Old man Johnny Reb, I said. And he said, Old man Johnny Reb Comesaw. Yeah, I can still see the old son of a bitch.

So anyway, like I said, he said then. In my opinion this could be just the thing you didn't realize you should have been hoping and looking for just about now. And, of course, another thing I like about the whole deal is that it means that you'll have to be making trips back up this way far more often as a routine part of the project than you'd get around to doing otherwise at your own personal expense. So I'm all for it, man, after all, as you know very well from firsthand road experience, travel expenses are just about the most routine budget item in the world these cats operate in. So take them up on it, man, and save yourself some round-trip expenses back up here and save me some long-distance phone calls.

So what did I tell you when you told me what you told me when this thing first came up, Roland Beasley said when I called him to bring him up-to-date on how things were getting under way. Didn't I tell you I was not surprised that the boss and Old Pro had spotted my framemaker? Because they know one when they see one. So when one turns up, zap! They got him pegged. They can tell when you know where you're coming from. Man, my guess is that old Joe States has known what this thing was leading up to all along.

And hey, man, he went on to add, from what you say about that Miss Hortense Hightower of yours just about takes the cake. That's them cakewalking babies from home for you. That's down home for you, all right. And there ain't no such thing as up home. There is Philamayork. But it takes a lot of down-home stuff to get you there.

Speaking of expectations, there were also those of Gaynelle Whitlow and Jewel Templeton out in California. And as for the one and only Miss Slick McGinnis, she was the flesh-and-blood dimension of the actuality of the fairy-tale aunt that the real flesh-and-blood Miss Tee could not become, and that the official actuality of Miss Lexine Metcalf made taboo (but that Deljean McRae may well have turned out to be had she still been there as she had been early on).

The next time I saw Jewel Templeton after we said what we said and didn't say what we didn't need to say on the Côte d'Azur was at a party in one of the ballrooms at the Pierre two weeks before I pulled out to come back to Alabama. I was there backstage because two days earlier Joe States had called to give me the date and time that the band would be back in town to play a one-night stand in one of the ballrooms.

Get to me fast, my man, he said with his usual mock conspiratorial urgency. Let's touch base before you split for the 'Bam. This thing we're booked into for just one night is a private shindig, and we expect you backstage as soon as you can get there because we'll be pulling in just in time to set up to hit as scheduled. And we'll be pulling out for Canada as soon as we can repack and hit the trail. So we expect to see you backstage as soon as you can make it after we pull in, if not before. Milo will have someone on the lookout for you.

That's why I happened to be where I was backstage when one of the ushers came calling for me to tell me that one of the guests would be waiting to speak to me at the backstage exit to the ballroom during the first break. I said OK without asking who the guest was because I was talking to Old Pro, and when the time came we were there before I could guess who it could be. Eric Threadcraft came to mind, but I knew if he were in town, not only would he have called me, but also he would have found a way to get backstage on his own.

We were there then, and when I saw who it was, I was surprised, but not as surprised as I would have been if she had called me on the phone or even sent a letter or a postcard. But I was almost as surprised as I had been that Sunday night outside the Keynote Lounge on Sunset Boulevard waiting with my bull fiddle to take a cab back to the Vine Lodge when she pulled to the curb and offered to give me a lift.

So there you are, she said, extending her arms and initiating the old one-for-each-cheek routine that we had never done in public except on the Côte d'Azur. Then holding me at arm's length she said, You look every bit as good as you should.

And I said, Hey, coming from a marquis-certified sparkling daughter, that's enough to make brown sugar bubble.

A waiter came by then and she ordered a spritzer for herself and a vermouth cassis for me. And I said, *Comme d'habitude*. And that was when she said, I must tell you I'm here because ever since we did what we did with the marquis in the south of

France, I come to listen to this band every time our paths cross, and I make a report to the marquis, which pleases him no end and me no less. Because in a way it is as if I've stumbled on my own version of Alexis de Tocqueville.

So this evening's encounter was bound to happen sooner or later, she said, especially in New York. But I must say I didn't expect to see you here tonight, although you do always come to mind whenever the band is mentioned. So you were part of the content of my consciousness all day today, even so. And then all of a sudden there you were.

I just happened to get a glimpse of you in the wings, she said, because the drummer kept winking and flashing his sticks and brushes at someone in the wings during the warm-up number before the great charmer himself came striding out to direct the festivities from the piano. That's when I called the maître d' and gave him your name and told him where I wanted him to ask you to let him come back during the first intermission and take you to where an old friend from California would be waiting to say a brief hello for old times' sake.

That was when I told her that I was getting ready to leave graduate school for a while to take a part-time teaching position at my old alma mater. And she said, Well, good for them. They appreciate their own product. That's a good sign. A very good sign. This is good news that I must pass on to the marquis right away, so he'll know where to find you on his next trip over here. Ever since he met you in person in the south of France he has been looking forward to seeing your part of the U.S.A. with you. So now that he will know where you are going to be, watch out.

So that was when I told her that I also had been asked to help Daddy Royal write his memoirs. And she said, Who else? You are precisely the one I would suggest that people with questions about him go to as I'm sure the marquis would agree. Indeed, the very first thing I'm going to do when I get back over to the Plaza would be to call the marquis and pass your news along to him. And by the way, when you get word on him heading back over here, be prepared for sessions about Norman Rockwell's year-round Fourth of July paintings and images of the U.S.A. in Hollywood musicals.

Then as the band filed back on the stage for the second set, she said, But I must not intrude on your backstage errand any longer, especially in view of the fantastic project you're involved in and that I'm certain that you're going to bring off brilliantly. So says the authority of my muddy water daughter intuition.

We went through the old one for each routine again, then, and I said what I said about her recent movies. And then when I said, And of course you will tell Maurice and Esther that I asked about them, she said, But of course. And when I tell them that you're heading back down to Alabama for a while and what you will be doing in addition to your part-time classroom schedule, they won't even try to hide their satisfaction. To them, education is what you're all about. Knowing what things are about and how they're related to each other. How about that? Remember what we said about the magic keys? Well, they think of you as forging the *skeleton key* that opens up all sorts of treasures.

So there you have it, I said, stepping back through the entrance to the backstage passageway, fairy tales for the likes of me and you, but nuts and bolts for them without the likes of whom not!

Also before I left New York there had been a call from Gaynelle Whitlow, who had recently seen Joe States, who had told her about Miss Fine People and had given her my phone number to have somebody in her office to call me for her, and when whoever it was called and I answered there was a pause and the next voice was hers, saying, So the all-American schoolboy is, as the saying goes, by way of becoming the what shall we say?

And when I said, Journeyman, she said, That's you, all right. Still on your way wherever it is you're headed.

Then when I said, Hey, thanks again for rescuing me even before I needed to be rescued, she said, You know the old saying about an ounce of prevention. A smart boy like you I'm sure you know that first night was a setup. Joe and the man. I'm pretty sure old Joe would have brought you by on his own, but it was on the boss's agenda, and he sent me a bouquet plus that was waiting for me when I got home that next morning—or was it still morning? So anyway, since you said you were definitely going back to school, I figured they had other plans for you other than just plucking on that bass fiddle.

And I said, Hey, that part was all news to me, too.

As I think about it now, she said then, as good as I thought you sounded in there with them that night in the Palladium and also with old Radio Red and on those other things you did with Eric Threadcraft I never really thought of you as an all-out, full-time musician. I said, Hey, he's on it, all right, but there's something else to this cat. So when you stayed in town and got yourself hooked with the all-American Miss Blue Eyes, I kidded you. But you knew I knew you were still on course whatever it was, didn't you?

And I said, Hey, some kidding! And then I said, For which much thanks, and when she said, I just didn't want you to forget your down-home upbringing, I said, Not me. When they used to say if you could make it down there on the outskirts of Alabama you could make it anywhere else in the world, I believed them, especially one very special teacher once I got to the third grade.

Which I could tell as soon as old Joe left you with me, she said. Then she said, So let me let you go now. I just want you to know that I'm looking forward to what you're going to be doing with old Royal Highness. That's old Joe, Old Pro, and the man for you. And I also got a pretty good idea of what you might be following it up with. So if your research brings you back out this way, let me know if you can. And by the way, our Miss Jewel still has most if not quite all of her blue-eyed American sparkle.

XXXI

When I called Royal Highness that Saturday morning he said, Hey, here he is. Hey there, young soldier. What you say, young soldier? Things shaping up on schedule down there? You ready to lay that comp on me yet? And I said so far, so good in the English Department and that I was just about ready to find out if he thought I was ready yet.

And he said, OK. So let's see which way you think this thing should go. You know what I mean? Not just another record of the same old rags-to-riches and fame and fortune and comfort jive. I'm not saying that that's not a part of it. But the main part of it was that I was *dancing*. That's what I'm about. That's what I have always been about, and that's what this book's got to get across. Just like the Bossman's book's got to be about him and his music. With him it's food, clothing, shelter, and music. And with me it's food, clothing, shelter, and dancing, with or without music.

So me and you, young soldier, he said. You're the schoolboy and I'm the subject matter in person, talking about the natural-born flesh and blood. So let's figure out how you're going to get me to tell them in words what I've been *showing* them from up there on the stage in all these different ways over the span of all these years I've been up there in the spotlight. Because, hell, you know how folks are. You draw them a picture or show them an act and an imitation of a picture in the flesh and they want you to explain it with a legend or something. Or if you start out with a legend they're going to want to see it as a picture, and let me tell you something, young prof, being a schoolboy you know even better than I do that pictures were mostly about action long before moving pictures as such came along. Hell, all that was right there for you in primer grade readers and them Sunday school cards, and what about old Santa Claus and them reindeers in the sky? And don't let nobody tell you that them so-called still-life paintings can do without rhythm. I'm a dancer. What about when I hit them with a freeze? It's like a bolt of lightning! Wham! Take the breath out of the whole audience.

But you get my point, he said then. So you tell me what was on your mind about this thing when you decided to pick up the phone and call me this morning.

That was when I said that the theme that I had been playing around with was *the dancing of an attitude,* which I said was like saying dancing is what I'm all about because this is the way I deal with what life is all about, because what I'm doing when I'm dancing, it is like saying this is the way I see it, the way I feel it, and the way I feel about it. And this is the way I say what I have to say about it.

So then I said, What I jotted down was ROYAL HIGHNESS, *The Dancing of an Attitude.*

And he said, Hey, *yeah,* young soldier! You really mean business, don't you. I can already see right down the road you've got me headed along. Boy, you already got me going back to the days when I first found out about this kind of music and this kind of dancing.

Because first there was the church and that kind of group

clapping and strutting and shouting. And then there were also the jook joints, honky-tonks, barrelhouse dives, and all that shuffling and slow dragging and bumping and grinding and then the traveling tent shows and all that fancy solo stuff, and that was for me. And then somewhere along the line I realized that I was doing what I was doing the way I was doing it because the solo was like a sermon, a foot sermon in the spotlight. Like the spotlight was my pulpit.

And that was when I said, Hey, I think you just said it, Daddy Royal. Man, I think you just said it. So how about this?

The Dancing of an Attitude

The

Footnotes

of

the One and Only

ROYAL HIGHNESS

And he said, See there? There you go, right on the afterbeat! Footnotes! Boy, you got it! Boy, you know something! Boy, them thugs in that band mean it when they call you our schoolboy. Notice they don't call you the Professor or young 'Fess or anything like that, because they know that the Bossman and Old Pro wouldn't have had you in that band if that was the case. And hell, they could see for themselves that you as hip to what the band is about as you are deep in all that college and university jive.

Footnotes, he said again, then, footnotes on the afterbeat! That just about sets it up, young soldier. Hey, man, I'm beginning to see this whole thing already, but hell, I'm not surprised. Hell, I know good and well that if there was such a thing as a literary comp artist, the Bossman would spot him if he showed up.

I bet it didn't take no time at all for him to realize that Hortense Hightower had sent him one.

Then he said, You noodle and doodle and jive and connive to my segue *and here I come with my rawhide stride and my sporty, syncopated limp walk just like along any patent-leather avenue mainstem anywhere on the circuit, chitlin or caviar, transcontinental or intercontinental.*

So there you go, young soldier, right on the money. The dancing of an attitude! Now, that's saying something. Talking about not just what you say, but what you do and how you do it. That's who you are. That's your personal fingerprint, no, *footprint*, how about that, *footprint* in the footlights (thanks to Hollywood). After you've gone.

So what's all this got to do with them blues you get in the planetarium? It's what you're stomping with, young soldier. And when you trip the light fantastic at them you really mess with them, because then you're carrying on just like they ain't even there. Hey, then the softer you tip, the faster they fade away! Man, that's worse than thumbing your nose at them, because then you're carrying on like they ain't even there.

Man, when you start riffing on them breaks like they're clause after clause and chapter and verse after chapter and verse of the Emancipation Proclamation, while treating all that border-to-border and coast-to-coast U.S.A. dissonance and cacophony like it's sweet honey in the rock, you're taking care of some business, *and I'm talking about taking care of the nitty-gritty like it's all fun and games and one feast day after another! What you talking about, young soldier, what you talking about?!*

Footnotes, he said again then, that's really pretty slick, young soldier. Footnotes! Right on the button from the get-go. Footnotes on insights and outlook. That's exactly what riffing the blues on the afterbeat is all about. Walking that walk, like talking that talk. Because walking that walk, which ain't straight and narrow, you've got to zig as well as zag. But don't zig when you're supposed to zag. And don't be tapping when you're supposed to be tipping, especially when you're supposed to be tipping on the q.t., which I don't have to tell you has as much to do with politics as poontang. Talking about signifying, young soldier. So let's tell them what I've been showing them lo these many years on the boards here, there, and elsewhere.

So let's roll, young soldier, he said.

Then before I could say what I was going to say about getting back to him as soon as I could spare the time, he said, So now just go on and find your classroom groove, and get back to me and let's see what we can do about your Thanksgiving and Christmas breaks. Hey, how about me getting you all up here for Christmas? Anyway, whatever schedule we come up with, as far as I'm concerned this thing is already under way. As I'm calling to tell the Bossman and Old Pro and old Joe as soon as we hang up.

Hey, now, talking about some terpsichorean riff signification. Man, we got it percolating on the afterbeat already.

XXXII

Castle or city-state, my old long gone and now also long since last heard from but still best of all possible college freshman and sophomore year roommates imaginable used to say, Castle to castle, stone walls with or without moats (or beanstalk with or without keeps) no less than chapels whether perilous or beneficent, the second law of thermodynamics always applies. Entropy, my good man. There you have it. That's the goods, my fine fellow. My estimate of the situation, as any elementary school trip to the planetarium should have long since made all too obvious. Elementary, my dear Watson, elementary indeed. *Your notorious snark by any other terminology is still a bojum!*

Thus if you miss the fun of the safari as such, what with all the standard deluxe equipment and provisions, *sine qua non*, you've missed the point! You've missed the *metaphor!* There is *entropy*, my good fellow, and there is *metaphor*, and if you miss the implications of the metaphor, you're stuck with clichés, which most certainly should not be confused with the *blisses of the commonplace*! Which so often turns out to be precisely what luxury is really about after all—*nay, first of all!*

Moreover, he also used to like to say, arching his ever so

subtly academic brow as he used the transitional device I never heard another freshman or sophomore use before or since. Moreover, as our very own La Bohème of Greenwich Village, NYC, U.S.A., said long before the publication of her ever so fatal interviews, *"Whether or not we find what we are seeking is idle biologically speaking!"*

So heh, heh, haay, roommate, he would go on in his mock penny dreadful villain's voice once more, clasping his archcriminal hands and rubbing his insatiably avaricious pawnbroker's palms, his eyes and nostrils narrowing satanically as if he also had a satanic tail to wag as he pounced!

It was ever thus, roommate, and so it will ever be—not only biologically speaking, but also geologically speaking, not to mention speaking in terms of third-grade geography after that field trip to the planetarium.

Anyway, so much for the all-American pursuit of the all-American melodramatic climax. After all, there is also the no less American soap opera, with its movie star good looks across the board and deluxe fashion and shelter magazine perfect town and country settings and dernier cri haute couture, may be concerned with existential problems that are much more relevant to human actualities as such in the context of the planetarium. After all, they almost always seem to be very well off indeed, biologically speaking. *Their perpetual concern is with the ongoing problem of getting along with each other.*

There is no guaranteed all-American movie-concocted melodramatic resolution out there, my ever so appropriately ambitious and unimpeachably sincere young man from the northbound L & N Railroad outskirts of Mobile, Alabama. Take it from old Geronimo, your newfound fellow trailmate from the South Side of Chicago. There is only the ultimate actuality of the entropy (repeat, entropy) *of the void,* upon which we impose such metaphorical devices as AND, as in (andoneandtwoandthree-andfourand) and one, and two, and three, and four and so forth and so on and on, from which we also get "*and it came to pass and so on it went time after time after time*, as has been recorded here, there, and elsewhere.

Picaresque, my dear fellow journeyman, he also used to like to repeat from time to time. Don Quixote and Candide, each in his own way, equals *farce*, the dynamics of coping with chaos, slapstick for slapdash: Buster Keaton's deadpan, Charlie Chaplin's ever so elegant nonchalance.

In all events, however modest that garden Candide so earnestly promises to cultivate, it had better include an adequate crop of ever more elegantly refined or at any rate resilient pratfalls, if you know what I mean.

So there you go.

XXXIII

So there you go, fellow, Eric Threadcraft said on the phone from Hollywood. Man, old Papa Joe and the crew were in town last night on a stopover on their way up the coast to Monterey, and he gave me the double rundown on what you're up to and also heading into. Fantastic, old buddy. Like I always say, I'm still getting special kicks out of the fact that old Papa Joe was the one who had the idea that the two of us should get to know each other and stay in touch. Anyway, man, I must say that campus gig couldn't have been more timely. And, of course, you know that the Bossman's proposition knocks me out. Man, who else but him would realize how slick it is to begin with Royal Highness. Hey, that's just as slick as it is deep, fellow, and so obvious that you hardly notice it.

Then before I could ask about Celeste, he said, And now comes the update on the situation chez old Mice: *We are just about to do it, fellow. Man, I'm taking the plunge. So there it is, old buddy. You're the first to know.*

Then he said, Man, you remember that studio thing about foreign employee clearance that had me so nervous about political intrigue and extortion and stuff that morning when I got you to meet me at the Algonquin and then didn't bring it up anymore because I was already so far gone on this lady that I just decided to play it as it lays.

And guess what? It turns out that what those studio-foreign background checks came across and mistook for some kind of political extortion and payoff turns out to be a very personal family matter. Man, Celeste is a very young widow with a daughter whose father was what she describes as a café au lait painter from North Carolina, who was killed in a racing car accident. So guess what all the suspicion about political shakedown was about? Celeste didn't want her child to come into this screwed-up racial situation over here until she's gone far enough in school in Paris to have become indelibly French. Anyway, fellow, the suspicious "extortion payoffs" were all for child care. It was as simple as that. No international political intrigue at all. Hell, fellow, not even a case of small-town family illegality.

Then before saying, Buzz you later, he said, Oh, by the way, I've done my etymological homework on your Miss Fine People. So Eunice means happy victory! So what can I tell you? She couldn't have happened to a more deserving person.

XXXIV

My old roommate had already said what he said about whoever turned out to be the one who was the one for me, when he replied to the letter along with the snapshot of me and Eunice that I had sent to him at Yale to tell him about what had happened to me and her between that third September and wisteria blossom time that next spring.

Man, he responded within the same week, you make it all sound like it's those Gulf Coast area boy blue skies above those crepe myrtle yard tree blossoms and dog fennel meadows, not to mention those playhouse times all over again. But man, watch out this time around. We're talking castles and perhaps even chapels perilous again, my man, he wrote. Because this, after all, is about fairy-tale princesses in the first place, is it not—without whom your castle may not be any more than just another earlier version of Fort Apache, if you know what I mean. Man, I know good and well that I don't have to tell you that without a fairy-tale princess your castle is no more relevant than any old ultradeluxe wayside inn.

It is she, my good fellow, who is the embodiment of the quintessential. That fifth essence(!). Without her, there is only air, earth, water, and fire. She is the element, my man, that gets us back outside the soundless fury of the planetarium and into the realm of the blisses of the so-called commonplace!

Nor, as any competent student of architectural design and engineering should be able to testify, does the perception of the so-called blisses of the commonplace have any less to do with the dynamics of enchantment than do nursery rhymes, fables, and Mother Goose tales. After all, to us a multimillion-dollar mansion is no less a stage set for being registered as privately owned real estate!

So here again, it's the metaphor that generates either the bliss or the banality! Thus one person's restriction may be another person's incentive! What one person may perceive as the outer limits of all that really matters (as the Chinese once dismissed whatever was beyond the Great Wall), another group of people may regard as *the come-hither region of ever more promising horizons of aspiration.*

In all events, that certainly strikes me as the snapshot of a fairy-tale princess you sent along with your update, my all too obviously lucky old cut buddy. So cross your fingers and touch your talisman and polish your wiles to their highest sheen. Who ever said that romance was not a game of chance?

Nor should you ever be unmindful of any of those slapdash—slapstick, nay, downright farcical escapades and labyrinthine misadventures old ever so jam-riff-clever Odysseus himself had to maneuver his way out of and back on course to and through the gateway to the remembered hometown boy blue bliss with the one for whom he had forsaken all others not only in Ithaca but everywhere else.

Taming the Wild Child

Excerpts from mothers' writings:

"We tried every type of parenting technique, took him to counseling, and even tried medication.... He was smoking, stealing, huffing, running away, sometimes staying out all night, and constantly lying. Nothing helped."

"We were living a nightmare at home, and because of my son's extremely charming and charismatic personality, people outside our home thought we were the ones with the problems. Even the receptionists at the psychiatric hospital kept telling us how great he was and insinuated that we were the ones who needed help."

"I remember driving home from work, putting the car in the garage, and just sitting there. My home life was miserable. I did not feel I could relax when I entered my home; instead, I felt anxious and fearful of walking in the door. But, eventually, I had to go inside. I couldn't sit in the garage all night."

"I am not exaggerating when I say that the changes I have seen in him after six weeks of treatment with the RAD Consultancy have been more profound and definitive than any I have seen in him cumulatively over the last six years, throughout which time I aggressively pursued remedies for his psychological, emotional, social, and educational difficulties."

"I was desperate and scared. My beloved son was self-destructing before my eyes, and everything I tried to

do to help him backfired.... [My RAD counselor] led us away from the brink. We began a process to regain communication and trust. Today, he's doing better in school and looking ahead to college and the future."

"Our psychiatrist, who treats a lot of kids like my son, said that people like him are never able to hold down full-time jobs or be contributing members of society. I believe that because of the work Aaron Lederer does, there will be a lot more successful, contributing members of society."

"I had felt from the beginning that taking my son to a therapist to work out his issues wasn't the key—that somehow *I* was the key. I just had no idea how. Aaron Lederer works solely through the mother. This matched my instinct."

"For the first time in sixteen years, I am able to divorce myself from the horrible weight of feeling like a total failure as a parent. I no longer own my son's problems, and I am finally giving my daughter the kind of attention she needs and has needed for a long time."

"My daughter is doing well and is sweet to be around. She is doing all the 'favors' I've asked of her. In the past, I've tried having her take care of the animals, but it has never worked out. But because of these new methods, she's been feeding all the animals, walking the dogs, changing the cats' litter box, and cleaning the bird cage, all without once being reminded."

"I have been working with Aaron Lederer for eighteen weeks now. For the most part, my adopted son now functions beautifully in school.... He is still extremely self-centered and insensitive, but on most days, he makes his bed, brushes his teeth, takes a shower, sleeps through the night without disturbing my husband or me, respects my requests for time to myself, and asks permission before he touches me, all without being reminded."

"I was astounded that changing my way of communicating with my son made so much of a difference. I didn't realize how much commenting and directing I had always done until I was not allowed to do any at all."

"This morning, my sixteen-year-old daughter stopped by the family room to say good-bye before she went off to work. We exchanged pleasantries, she talked about her day's schedule, and she blew off a little steam about her boyfriend. It was just a normal, friendly little exchange before she called 'So long!' and flew out the door. And it made my day. Three months ago, such an event would have been totally unthinkable for either one of us."

"Aaron was able to help. In less than four months, I have seen a tremendous change in my daughter. She used to come to me only with problems, and now she finds me to talk about other things, too. She shows real interest in family get-togethers. She handles disappointment without tantrums."

Taming the Wild Child

◆

From Living Hell to Living Well

How Mothers Can Use Corrective Communications to Make Their Out-of-Control Children Easy to Live With

Aaron Lederer

iUniverse, Inc.
New York Bloomington

Taming the Wild Child
From Living Hell to Living Well

iUniverse books may be ordered through booksellers or by contacting:

iUniverse
1663 Liberty Drive
Bloomington, IN 47403
www.iuniverse.com
1-800-Authors (1-800-288-4677)

Because of the dynamic nature of the Internet, any Web addresses or links
contained in this book may have changed since publication and may no
longer be valid. The views expressed in this work are solely those of the
author and do not necessarily reflect the views of the publisher, and the
publisher hereby disclaims any responsibility for them.

ISBN: 978-1-4401-0142-7 (pbk)
ISBN: 978-1-4401-0144-1 (ebk)

Printed in the United States of America

Contents

If you want to change a child, just change the way you communicate with him.

— Aaron Lederer

Foreword

Mothers Can Turn Kids from Bad to Glad

This little book introduces the reader to mothers who have been helping their children to reverse lifelong habits of extreme negativity under the guidance of Aaron Lederer, a pioneering psychotherapist, and his team of counselors. Lederer's approach is unique in that it empowers the mother to be the agent of therapeutic change. Her role makes complete sense: as the child's main caregiver, the mother comes with a ready-made influence on the child. She also has an innate passion for and commitment to helping the child make positive changes. Lederer's approach is also unique in its convenience: there is no need for face-to-face meetings, as the counselors give all their advice in sessions over the phone.

Aaron Lederer's success with difficult children may stem from the devastating traumas in his own early childhood. Because of the insights he gained from his own experiences, it's as if he can project himself into the minds of difficult children and know what help they need. His many years of training and practice as a psychotherapist have been devoted to repairing damaged relationships caused by neglect or abuse in early childhood, and Lederer has developed a treatment that lets him tell mothers what to do moment by moment, day by day. In a relatively short time—generally within the first four to six weeks of

treatment—the child begins to show signs of becoming a lovable and responsible family member, a mother's dream come true.

Aaron Lederer and his team instruct the mothers in weekly phone meetings supplemented by e-mail contact as needed. He instructs each mother to talk to her child only in ways that develop the child's desire to cooperate. He is interested in cooperation driven by a child's inner desire to do the right thing rather than by obedience. The idea is for each child to develop his social compass, his lifelong guide for living a good life, through his relationship with his mother.

The first phase of Lederer's program is intended to give the child a period free from the pressure to change. The purpose is to give the child a chance to rework the traumas he experienced in his early years, the time when his mother was (or should have been) the center of his world. Disruptions during this vulnerable period are often what cause a child to develop attachment disorders or other developmental problems that manifest in a destructive, negative response to the world or in withdrawal from it altogether.

Lederer teaches that threatening, punishing, scolding, and the like often backfire. We might be able to scare a child into doing something if our threat is dire enough, but we would merely get resentful compliance, not cheerful cooperation. Furthermore, rubbing a child's nose in his powerlessness in the face of our threats can contribute to his developing depression, thereby making the problem worse. Lecturing has a similar effect. The child can feel as though he has been called stupid and told that he cannot think for himself.

When the initial period, during which the mother suspends her usual responses to the difficult child, has succeeded, Lederer introduces additional tactics that are aimed at "socializing" the child. Lederer defines a "socialized" child as one who is willing to do what's required even when he doesn't feel like doing so, is willing to expend the necessary effort even if the reward isn't immediate, and is willing to take other people's feelings into account.

Lederer often says, "If you want to change a child, change the way you talk to him," so he introduces what he calls "corrective communications." Each corrective communication targets a specific behavior. For example, he instructs each mother to ask her child to begin doing something or stop doing something regularly as a "favor" to her. Notice that favors are voluntary, not forced. The child is free to be cooperative or not. He can choose. If he refuses or fails to follow through, the mother is then instructed to give the child a scripted communication that resolves the child's resistance without struggle, always without a hint of negativity or an "or else" attitude. The point is to nudge the child gently toward an understanding that in a loving relationship, people do favors for one another.

Another of Lederer's tactics is to have a mother turn her child into a consultant on himself. After all, all of us are the best experts on ourselves; who knows better how to motivate us? The mother asks her child for advice about a problem she has with him, and her questions are worded in such a way that presents the mother as the one with the problem, not the child. These requests are also scripted as corrective communications. Usually, being

given the important role of adviser touches the child. Whatever answer he gives, he is likely to become far more cooperative simply because he is helping his mother, not being controlled by her.

The success of the mother's approach also lies in what she does not do. She learns to give mild reminders instead of orders. For example, a mother might say "It's bedtime" in place of "Go to bed now"; "The garbage is overflowing" can replace "Please take out the garbage"; and "Women are attracted to men who hold down jobs" may produce better results than "You're twenty-eight years old, and you still can't pay your own bills." Through corrective communications, children can become willing to take responsibility for what goes on outside of the home and at school.

Mothers tell Lederer that through working with him or a member of his team, they have learned new ways of communicating with their children. These methods work not only with the designated child suffering from oppositional defiant disorder (ODD) or reactive attachment disorder (RAD) but also with other children, family members, and the world at large. Most human beings do their best when they feel understood and appreciated as opposed to ruled, controlled, or bullied. Lederer's approach fosters mutual respect, interest, and appreciation, the feelings that underlie the best things in civilization.

Sheila Zaretsky, PhD

Dr. Zaretsky, a psychoanalyst, is the founding director and a supervising analyst at the Academy of Clinical and Applied Psychoanalysis and at the New Jersey Center for Modern Psychoanalysis. The author of many well-received clinical papers, Dr. Zaretsky has also been a sought-after speaker at clinical presentations since 1989.

1

The Makings of the Wild Child

Early in his work, Aaron Lederer identified the three most frequent causes of destructive behavior in children. These causes can affect children singly or in combination, but more often than not, all three can be found in the wild child's life. These causes are clearly visible in this book's stories.

Here is his description of these causes:

Failure to attach

The lack of a secure attachment between an infant and his birth mother occurs as a result of a deficiency in or complete absence of contact between the two. The mother might not be emotionally available to her infant if circumstances interfere with the quality of her contact with the baby. Illness, pain, drug addiction, alcoholism, postpartum depression, immaturity, family problems, and financial difficulties are all possible causes of insufficient emotional attachment. The mother is also physically unavailable if she gives the baby up for adoption or goes back to work too soon after giving birth.

There can also be other causes that have nothing to do with the mother. The infant may suffer from colic or another painful condition, be born prematurely and kept in an incubator for too long, or be hospitalized for too long with an illness. Sometimes attachment fails simply because the infant and mother are mismatched temperamentally.

In some cases, the mother's emotional availability is also affected when a pregnancy is unwanted. One such mother writes:

> I have a fourteen-year-old son who is making our lives miserable. He was a "surprise" pregnancy that I really didn't want. However, I thought that since I already had a son, it would be great if I had a daughter! Then the ultrasound revealed another boy. I was crushed! I was so depressed. I don't think I've ever gotten over him being a boy. I tried to warm up to him after a few months, but I never felt about him the way I do about my oldest boy.

The infant with a failed attachment shows clear signs: apathy, a weak cry, sleeping too much, and a lack of interest in his immediate surroundings. Later, these children become increasingly difficult to manage. The mother continues:

> Now my son is moody and argumentative, he lies constantly, he steals from stores and individuals, and he's repeated two grades. But believe it or not, he's absolutely charming to others! Adults love him immediately for his courteous manners and displays of respect. He's a con artist—he knows just what to say to suck adults in. He's always been overly friendly

to strangers and never cried much as a child when he was away from us. We never let him go anywhere without us now. We're afraid to. He's constantly getting kicked out of school for his belligerent behavior or his smart (and sometimes foul) mouth. He has spread fecal material throughout our home more than once. He also did this at a private school at which he was formerly enrolled. He's hurting our entire family, and he doesn't seem to care. He has no remorse for anything he does and can always find someone else to blame for his behavior.

These children who were unable to bond with their mothers often suffer from reactive attachment disorder (RAD). Because the research and academic communities are more familiar with RAD than the therapeutic community and because children with RAD display some behaviors that are typical to other, more familiar disorders, these children are too often misdiagnosed with attention deficit hyperactivity disorder, bipolar disorder, post-traumatic stress disorder, depression, obsessive-compulsive disorder, or anxiety. The symptoms that lead to these diagnoses almost always disappear during Lederer's corrective communication process, sometimes within weeks.

Children with RAD are often prescribed various medications that are readily available for these other, more common disorders. But their parents often find that the drugs' side effects just add to the child's and the family's problems without solving the child's underlying issues. One mother wrote the following about her experience with her thirteen-year-old child's medication regime:

We started him on Ritalin when he was nine. It was ineffective. Then the psychiatrist put him on Effexor, which made him manic, and then concluded that he was bipolar, since Effexor can induce mania in people with bipolar disorder. He went on Depakote for that when he was ten, enduring the requisite weekly, then monthly, then quarterly blood tests. The psychiatrist then added Concerta and Zyprexa to the mix. The Zyprexa made him ravenous, and he ballooned from fifty pounds to ninety-nine before we switched him to Risperdal. Then the Concerta took over, and he lost huge amounts of weight. So then we dumped the Concerta for Adderall, which is very hot on the college circuit—I had to confront one of my sitters when our supplies didn't add up. We also used Clonidine to help him get to sleep at night. Finally, the psychiatrist put him on Klonapin, which is an anti-anxiety medication and is highly addictive. Every time we tried to cut his dose, he got aggressive, so we kept him on that even after school ended.

The RAD Consultancy takes a neutral position on prescribed medication, leaving all decisions about it between the parents and their doctors. But experience shows that there are often no ill effects when the children get off their medications at some point during the second half of the corrective communication process.

Remaining stuck in the "terrible twos"

The quality of a child's early maternal attachment is critical to his view of the world and his place in it. An infant whose attachment is inadequate can suffer devastating consequences, one of which can take place

in the course of the child's next developmental stage: the "terrible twos."

The terrible twos (called "the separation and individuation stage of development" in professional literature) is a phase crucial to a child's becoming "socialized." During this phase, the child is typically unhappy, whiny, pouty, difficult, and hard to control. He wants to be "the boss" and responds to loss of control with temper tantrums. By the end of the terrible twos, the toddler stops seeing himself as the center of the universe and becomes a cooperative, ordinary member of his family, willing to abide by rules, delaying gratification when necessary, and taking others' needs and feelings into account.

Why would the toddler become willing to abdicate his throne and become an ordinary citizen? For one reason only: to please his mother and preserve her love. But that desire exists only for a toddler who has a stake in preserving a strong attachment with his mother. This is not so for toddlers whose attachment has failed. These toddlers have already lost their mothers. They have nothing to gain from giving up their claim to the throne and nothing to lose from doing all they can to preserve it.

The mother of such a child writes:

> My son is five years old. I'm not sure when it started or when I started to notice it, but as far back as I can remember, my son would become furious when he didn't get his way, even over very small things. He'd start to get angry and then explode, screaming and hitting or throwing and destroying things. Even now, he wants what he wants immediately, and if he

doesn't get it, he explodes. I wish I could help him now before it becomes a bigger problem.

Failing to end the terrible twos successfully, these toddlers can't continue their emotional and social development and remain stuck ("fixated," in the professional literature) in this phase while continuing to grow physically and intellectually. They remain unsocialized, self-centered, selfish, uncaring, irresponsible, argumentative, angry, resentful, touchy, spiteful, and vindictive. They refuse to comply with requests or rules and blame others for the consequences of their own behavior.

These children who cannot move on from the terrible twos suffer from oppositional defiant disorder (ODD), and, as with RAD, treating these children with medication is often counterproductive.

A need to be hated

The wild child makes those in charge of him suffer when they try to control him or when they fail to comply with his wishes immediately and perfectly. But he also is compelled to make them "lose it" and attack him angrily, even hatefully, in order to gain a needed sense of belonging. When he succeeds, a little smile often appears on his face, hinting at his satisfaction at the hateful reaction he's just received. Here's why: As social beings, we all have a primitive, biological need for contact. (Its primacy is demonstrated by prisoners who die or go insane when kept for too long in solitary confinement.) When a person goes for too long without contact in his daily routine, he feels compelled to reach out. He may

suddenly remember a phone call that he must make, or he may find himself exchanging a few words with the cashier at the store. The kind of responses the person elicits may be positive or negative, but they tend to reflect the kind of contact to which he became accustomed in his early years. If he grew up in an affectionate and caring home, he'll tend to draw affectionate attention. If he was raised in a hostile, humiliating, or indifferent environment, he'll tend to draw hostile, humiliating, or indifferent responses.

Everyone prefers affectionate responses and hates receiving hostile ones. But the kind of response a person receives may not be the one he *wants* to receive: it will be the one he subconsciously *needs* to receive. The contact that every person *needs* is the type that is reminiscent of his home environment and, in particular, the one that elicits the feeling of his mother's early presence. For a person who was raised in a friendly atmosphere, the most biologically fulfilling contact is positive, and he'll tend to block out negative responses. Conversely, the most biologically fulfilling contact for a person who was raised in a hostile environment is hostile, and he'll reject positive responses.

Children with reactive attachment disorder believe that they are unlovable and unwanted. They therefore can't internalize affection, and they meet any offer of affection with disbelief. Starved for contact, these children make do with the only available alternative—hostility—and they assure a reliable supply of it by regularly provoking others into offering them hostile responses, starting with their mothers.

Even if children with oppositional defiant disorder are not already predisposed to negative responses through failed attachments, they become accustomed to them during the "terrible twos," when their difficult behaviors elicit too many hostile responses from their caretakers. The toddler responds to the hostility with more negativity, to which the caretaker reacts with further hostility. A self-reinforcing loop of hostility, dislike, and revenge ensues and soon becomes a permanent aspect of the child's relationships.

In the professional literature, the tendency to need and provoke negative responses is called "negative attachment behavior." Children with negative attachment behavior induce feelings of hate and rage in their caretakers that make it impossible for them to avoid lashing out, criticizing, yelling, or even hitting. To avoid these responses, some caretakers withdraw; they give their children the silent treatment, send them to their rooms, and often eventually send them away to residential treatment centers or military schools.

Parents who try to deal with these troublesome children as they would with misbehaving, normal children—by setting limits, applying consequences, and rewarding good behavior—find that these methods backfire, causing the children's behavior to get even worse. Parents who send these children to therapy usually find that after two or three years, the children have simply become older and even more troublesome.

These children are not "bad." Their destructive behaviors are not consciously intended to cause harm. They unavoidably become as they are in reaction to their early environment, over which they had no control.

But they do cause a great deal of harm: their siblings get abused while being deprived of needed attention from their unhappy and exhausted parents; the problem child is unloved and becomes the focus of hostility from both his parents and siblings; fathers grow distant from mothers; and mothers feel exhausted, demoralized, and guilty for disliking their child. Everyone suffers.

2

The Unwanted Child

Everyone knew that Sam and Marilyn were deeply in love. When they were blessed with a healthy baby boy, their happiness was complete.

The little boy was bright and good and basked in his parents' care and adoration. He walked at one year of age and spoke in full sentences at two years of age. Not surprisingly, in this wonderfully secure environment, the little boy began to display a loving, open personality, a thirst for knowledge, and a generous character.

Tel-Shalom was a fifty-family settlement in Israel, halfway between Tel Aviv and Haifa, built on land newly purchased from the Arabs living there. A carpenter, Sam built a house for his beloved wife and son there. The family of three lived in it together.

This idyllic life came to an abrupt end when the boy was three years old.

On a clear evening, the small boy and his parents were sitting on the porch outside their home when Arab marauders began shooting at them from a fold in the ground nearby. Marilyn was recuperating from gallbladder surgery, so Sam carried her into the house and then carried in their little boy. As he was closing the door, Sam was shot and died instantly.

Marilyn lost her mind. She was hospitalized for two years, during which time she made a slow—and only partial—recovery. During that time, the little boy, who had been on top of the world, was passed around among strangers and had nobody to attach himself to. His entire world collapsed; he had lost both his father and his mother in one day, all at the age of three.

Marilyn came out of the hospital when her son was five, but she was not fully functional; though he was happy to be living at home and in one place again, the little boy could not appreciate her as a mother. Instead of a happy, secure boy, he became a sad and angry one.

He grew up and—he thought—left it all behind. He served in the Israeli air force, then he became an engineer. He got married. But despite the much-discussed success of his own parents' marriage (which he got tired of hearing about after a while), he was not able to maintain a lasting relationship with his wife, and his marriage failed.

By the time he reached his thirties, the young man had grown certain that somehow his failed marriage was connected with his aborted, tragic childhood. He went into psychoanalysis, determined to understand

why he was not successful in relationships. He soon left engineering and began to study the human mind.

In his forties, he remarried. This time, he was able to attach normally—through positive behavior, not negative—and the marriage was a keeper.

In his fifties, he published a series of papers in the peer- reviewed *Transactional Analysis Journal* under the title *The Unwanted Child*. These papers describe his unique understanding of the effects of early abandonment and abuse on children.

The man began to understand, and to teach others, that a person's maternal attachment (or lack thereof) in early life is the strongest influence on that person's ability to form secure and affectionate attachments (to employers, siblings, and parents—not just to a spouse) throughout life. And when he began treating patients of his own, he began to formulate a strategy to remedy the effects of insufficient or nonexistent maternal attachments in others.

His theories were borne out in his practice when he began to speak with the desperate parents of troubled children. Many of these children had been adopted into loving, secure homes, many in infancy. Why were they so much trouble? Why couldn't they just blossom and grow, basking in all the love that was poured into them? Why were they hell-bent on destroying any love their adoptive parents had for them? His theory provided the answer: they had been abandoned, neglected, and often abused in their early lives. Consequently, they had developed the belief that they were unlovable and unwanted; they felt they had nothing else to lose, as they had already lost their entire worlds, their primary attachment figures.

This wasn't just the case with adopted children or those whose parents had died. As described in the previous chapter, many acted as if they had been abandoned if they had been hospitalized for an extended period of time. Some had arrived at bad times in their mothers' lives and were plainly unwanted when they were born. Although their mothers may have come to love them later, vestiges of the initial rejection remained. Some were put into day care too early or for too long. Others had a sibling born too soon, thereby harming their maternal attachments. One child was placed in his grandmother's care soon after his birth. Another had an alcoholic, detached mother. Yet another was premature and was placed in an incubator for almost two weeks, deprived of the human contact necessary for normal maternal attachment.

Many of these children were diagnosed with oppositional defiant disorder because they were so destructive at home. Entering into the "terrible twos" without the foundation of secure, affectionate attachment, they weren't able to complete this difficult stage and leave it behind. They became stuck in it, unable to mature emotionally. (Other children become oppositional and defiant even though they did attach to their mothers well enough early on.)

After grappling for years with these similarly tragic cases, he developed a successful treatment for these children who had been rejected, abandoned, unloved, or unwanted and for those who were stuck in their terrible twos. He called it the "corrective communication method." He formed the RAD Consultancy, LLC, a company where he and other professionals that he trained provided guidance by phone to parents nationwide, teaching them

to use his corrective communication process. He began to receive e-mails like this one every day:

> I never knew there was a name for my son's problem. I have told more than one professional that I felt a lack of bonding with my son, who was initially an unwanted pregnancy. I was sure that was the source of his antisocial and uncooperative behavior. They all told me that he was just strong-willed and independent. But he was only six months old when they started saying that. He is a very bright and sensitive child but is so difficult to deal with. He is very moody, disruptive, and inflexible with everything, and everything is a struggle. He has problems keeping friends, and he has no interest in school or in learning anything. I need help. I worry about him constantly, and I feel desperate, like I'm running out of time to correct our poor relationship. I try everything to connect with him, but it seems impossible. I love him so much and feel terribly guilty; I cry a lot and am almost obsessed with finding out what he has and what can be done.

Working only through the mother, whom he calls "the change agent," he and his team members are often able to help children like this in a matter of a few months, with significant improvements usually seen in four to six weeks.

And how is our tragedy-stricken child-turned-therapist doing today?

I looked in the mirror this morning, and I looked okay today. Yes, the little boy whose father was killed by Arab marauders, whose mother lost her mind—that was me.

I am Aaron Lederer. Through my years of studying the effects of disturbed maternal attachments in children, I overcame my own past, and so can your child. Welcome to my book. I will now let some of the mothers we have dealt with tell their stories.

3

John, 13

John was adopted when he was three years old. By the time he was seven, he had been diagnosed with reactive attachment disorder, attention deficit disorder, and bipolar disorder (RAD, ADD, and BPD) and was on multiple medications. His adoptive mother complained that he was "out of whack; bedwetting; had violent loss of temper; couldn't do anything independently; made strange noises; played with food; was in and out of bed at night; couldn't be by himself; was annoying; knocked over furniture when couldn't get his way; threatened to hurt [her] and also himself; was immature physically and behaviorally; wanted to control and make the rules; was unable to socialize with peers; missed social cues; and hoarded candy and other things in his pockets, pillows, and drawers."

My son was a mess when I adopted him as a three-year-old. As he grew, he became more scary and violent, and I grew more desperate. I am not exaggerating when I say that the changes I have seen in him after six weeks of treatment with the RAD Consultancy have been more profound and definitive than any I have seen in him cumulatively over the last six years, throughout which

time I aggressively pursued remedies for his psychological, emotional, social, and educational difficulties. These included psychotherapeutic solutions of all shapes and sizes—play therapy, perceptual development therapy, traditional psychiatry and psychopharmacology, family therapy, and group therapy. I consulted and contracted with social workers, learning specialists, psychiatrists, and teams of psychologists and psychotherapists. John was variously diagnosed with attention deficit disorder, attention deficit hyperactivity disorder, oppositional defiant disorder, bipolar disorder, depression, generalized anxiety disorder, obsessive-compulsive disorder, and atypical pervasive developmental disorder. When we started working with Aaron Lederer, my son was taking four different prescription medications: a mood stabilizer, an atypical antipsychotic, a Schedule II amphetamine, and a blood pressure medication to shut off the effects of the amphetamine at night so that he could sleep. All of it helped, yet none of it worked. That's the critical distinction.

I approached the RAD Consultancy with the battle-scarred cynicism that might be expected of someone who was thoroughly frustrated—but ever hopeful. I found the initial consultation both refreshing and chimerical. The investment was low—I didn't even have to show up for appointments or involve my other children or husband in the process or, for that matter, even include John—and the promised payoff was high, so I was willing to try it out. I especially liked the assurance that if after four to six weeks I didn't see any positive changes, I should drop the therapy. Another aspect that appealed to me was that it was a terminal program that would, at some point, end.

So many of the other therapies we had tried had no end in sight.

Aaron Lederer, with whom I spoke, told me that he couldn't predict exactly how long it would take to help John but that it was likely to be less than a year. He also told me he didn't care about my son's meds—that was between me and the psychiatrist who had prescribed them—but that most of the children he treated successfully got off their medications once the therapy took hold. This was an incredible thought to me.

I agreed to try the therapy, calculating that I'd spent as much on summer camp fees as I would in a year of working with the RAD Consultancy and that I might see better results than the previous therapies. I promised myself to stick with it for thirteen months—my son was thirteen at the time, so I gave myself one month per year. I really liked the convenience of the program, as much as the promise of results.

Aaron gave me my first assignment right then and there. (At the time, he was able to work with me himself, and that was the last time I ever saw him in person. All our work since then has taken place over the phone or via e-mail.) The assignment was to stop talking to my son. I was stunned. It was such a bizarre suggestion. How was I supposed to get him to do things? How could I tell him to stop beating up on his brother and sister, come to dinner, brush his teeth, or clean up his room? Aaron just shrugged and told me not to worry about these things for now. Unless my son spoke directly to me, I was not supposed to talk to him at all. I was not to scold him, greet him, or communicate with him in any way. And if

he did talk to me, I was to answer briefly and in a friendly manner without bringing up any ideas of my own.

So in late August of 2004, I stopped talking to my son.

In each weekly phone call, Aaron would ask about the week that had just passed and then give me a single instruction, sometimes based on my report or my complaint of the week (he's not bathing; his room is messy; he's stealing money to buy candy) and sometimes independent of them. He would have me write these instructions down and then say to John what he told me to say, word for word. I complied. I was only supposed to say each thing once; I was not to nag or remind or *ever* repeat something.

The first three weeks of the therapy were challenging. I was a willing student, but I found the initial instructions difficult to execute. Sometimes they brought out the worst in my son. I struggled to reform the way I interacted with him. But even in that short period of time, I saw glimmers of hope. The transition from summertime to the school year, traditionally a time of great disruption and anxiety in our house, was accomplished without mishap, and I was able to successfully discontinue one of John's medications with no discernible effects. Other changes included John's taking full responsibility for his morning routine, which eliminated much conflict in the household, and the startling absence of his violent temper tantrums.

There was a breakthrough moment one Saturday afternoon after four weeks of treatment when John's behaviors literally turned around in a matter of hours, transforming from combative to cooperative. In the weeks

that followed, we started to build on the foundation we had established—slowly, step by step. While he still had a long way to go at that point, his behavior definitely changed for the better, and his most difficult moments grew fewer and farther between.

The RAD method of treatment had tremendous practical appeal for me. The support—both in specific instructions and e-mailed hand-holding, of which I often availed myself when I was confused about how to deal with particular situations—was unparalleled. It was also the first therapy we had undertaken in which my husband and I saw eye to eye; it fit with both his observations about John and mine, which before that time had seemed irreconcilable. For example, for many years, he had maintained that John was a child who could not experience love, and I had maintained that he was a child for whom punishment was meaningless.

The next four months were pretty rough. The way Aaron explained things, my son's "nasty" behavior was driven by his need to elicit negative reactions from me. This was partially retaliatory—payback for not getting his way—and partially a conditioned response: as a baby, the only time he got attention was when he was crying or being bad. In those cases, reactions were generally hostile and dismissive. It was my task to deprive him of these negative reactions and to rebuild his internal desire to seek positive responses by pleasing me rather than provoking me. While others (his teachers, my husband) were very good at motivating my son to behave by threatening him, this was a less desirable and less permanent way of getting my son to behave; it was merely a form of external motivation. Our goal was to try to get my son to behave

because he wanted to please his mother and not because he was scared he was going to get whacked or was angling for a reward.

When the six-week mark came, I had indeed seen results from the therapy and was willing and eager to continue, but we were still far from "graduating." My son's behavior actually got worse for a while, especially when he saw that the things he usually did failed to provoke reactions from me. I, meanwhile, was working on disengaging when provoked, on the language I used with him, and on several little schemes Aaron gave me to bring him into line. The entire therapy was communication-based, as Aaron often said to me that if you want to change the way a child behaves, you must change the way you communicate with him. I was deeply worried in the beginning that the changes in my son might be superficial and that the evil child still lurked in my son, looking for a way to get out. Aaron insisted that my son's tantrums will continue tapering off and his behavior continue to improve.

Meanwhile, a psychopharmacologist was still seeing my son once a month, and she was increasingly against this new therapy; she didn't understand it and didn't like me to do things she didn't understand. I still brought him in to see her—I was too scared to take him off the meds—but dealing with her was becoming a problem.

At Halloween—always a difficult, tempestuous holiday for us, as John could not control himself around candy and would spend hours hoarding it, counting it, eating it, and getting all jazzed up on it—Aaron told me to tell my son that he had to turn all his candy over to me. I had already been instructed not to give him any

money (another weak spot for him), and any money he obtained or found was to be turned over to me. But I was also to hold the candy and dole it out one piece at a time when he'd "give me good feelings." This was a paradigm that Aaron had me set up: I was not to do anything for my son when he didn't do me "the favor of making me feel good, even when he felt bad." This was really interesting to me, since it didn't specify to him what behaviors might give me "good feelings." Since I'd always thought he was an ADHD kid, I had always tried to be as specific as possible with him; this is what the ADHD experts had advised. So I would say, "Please put on your shoes, put on your coat, and meet me at the front door," instead of "Let's get ready to go out," for example. Aaron's instructions were often deliberately vague and ambiguous, so my son was forced to figure things out for himself. Aaron also stopped me from saying "no" to him altogether. Instead, I was told to say "We'll see" or "I'll think about it" or "What a great idea" even to his most absurd requests. But it was part of this whole program of removing opportunities for confrontation.

At Christmas, I was instructed to give John none of the presents I'd bought him. Nada. None. And not to mention it, but to dole these presents, one at a time— as with the candy—whenever he gave me the feeling of wanting to do so. So my son came down Christmas morning to a tiny pile of gifts from my husband and nothing from me. That was difficult for me, but by then Aaron Lederer had earned my trust. John seemed puzzled, but didn't react negatively.

I slipped up a lot and had to spend several months learning how to relate to my son in new ways. The

fact that I had two other children made it both more complicated and in some ways easier. I got frustrated sometimes, or I "cheated"; for example, I might tell the other kids to do something that I wanted my oldest son to do, hoping he'd take the hint. But it helped a lot that Aaron was available to me 24/7 on e-mail, and I took advantage of this often.

There were a couple of positive signs in the early spring. For example, we went to Europe, and my son behaved well—certainly far better than he had the year before, when he'd had a major meltdown on the Underground, forcing me to pull him and the other kids off in the middle of a strange neighborhood of London. He was starting to follow a morning routine, which we'd worked hard to establish; there were several mornings when he left the house disheveled and unbathed or didn't leave the house at all, having missed the bus.

By June, ten months after we began, my son's level of cooperation had improved markedly. His psychopharmacologist noted that she was thinking of moving him onto a new drug regimen that included more mundane drugs—Prozac instead of Depakote, the heavy-duty mood stabilizer he was on; Strattera instead of the Adderall stimulant. She also prescribed an antianxiety compound for him, which worked so well that she said she was starting to believe that anxiety was his underlying issue rather than bipolar disorder. It was, to say the least, disconcerting. My goal was to get him off the meds, so I was torn about just moving him to less powerful drugs. I had been systematically reducing his ADHD drugs—he went from thirty milligrams to ten over the course of the school year. However, I couldn't seem to get him off

of them altogether, or I would get reports from school that he was having a hard time concentrating. He still took Clonidine to counteract the Adderall so he could sleep at night, so as summer started, he was still taking four drugs (Adderall, Depakote, Clonidine, and the antianxiety Klonapin). The psychopharmacologist wrote me prescriptions for the summer, but it turned out that I had no refills for one of them. When I couldn't get hold of the doctor midsummer to phone in the order, I decided to try to just remove him from the meds, one by one, by taking him down to doses of one-half and then one-third of the remaining dose over three-week periods. By the third week of August, a year after we began the program, he took his last pill, and he hasn't had anything at all since then.

It was clear to me that this course of therapy was working, and Aaron cut our phone consultations down to every other week. Each time we talked, there was less and less to report. I stuck with him past the thirteen-month mark, but we were really pretty much done by the end of the summer. I have now "graduated," and it has been most enjoyable to watch my son catch up with his age group emotionally, socially, and academically. He's not quite there yet, but he's come a long way. There is a certain irony in seeing a child undergo such a remarkable turnaround at the start of his teenage years, a time when most kids cut loose, and not always in pleasant ways. He listens, but he expresses emotion. He still gets mad, but it's a controlled anger, and he gets over it and moves on. He understands what to do to make friends and keep them, and he is much, much happier.

Needless to say, so am I.

4

Lisa, 17

*A new convert to the importance of infant-mother bonding,
Lisa's mom, Sandy, quit her job at the end of her pregnancy
to devote herself to the baby, something she had not done
after the births of Lisa's two older siblings. Lisa was breastfed
for two years, a fact of which Sandy is quite proud. And yet,
by the time Lisa reached the age of five or six, something was
clearly "off." Mother and daughter started having fights, and
they continued to fight into Lisa's teens. Lisa would say and
do things that caused Sandy to explode, and Sandy would
lose control and hit Lisa or throw things at her, which was
not typical of Sandy. Sandy wanted to understand what was
going on and how to repair it.*

Lisa was born at a bad time. My husband was in a
deep, clinical depression. We had two older kids, aged
three and five. I stopped working just before Lisa was born
because I knew I wanted to be there for her completely,
but this added to our money pressures. Although I tried
my best to make our home a happy place, it was a struggle
that I sometimes lost.

When I found Aaron Lederer, my older children
were twenty and twenty-two, and Lisa was seventeen.

I described to him my relatively calm and peaceful relationships with my other children, and I had one question: why was Lisa so difficult with me and only me? Why did we have these explosions, as we called them, in which she seemed to know just which buttons to press to get me to lose my temper completely and sometimes even throw things at her?

After every explosion, I would feel terrible and apologize. Our explosions had become so frequent and so bad that at one point I asked her quietly, sadly, "Lisa, what's wrong with us? Why does this happen?" She replied just as quietly and sadly, "I don't know, Mom, but it's really bad." I said, "We have to do something about it." She nodded her head miserably and walked away.

After listening to my story, Aaron Lederer replied that it seems as if Lisa is stuck ("fixated") in the "terrible twos" developmental stage, where the toddler's slogan is, "I want what I want and I want it *right now,*" alternating with, "I won't and you can't make me" and attempts to enforce these through her tantrums. He added that there is no strong evidence that such is the case with Lisa, but that often, when the mother is distracted by serious stresses, her bonding with the infant suffers and the infant enters the "terrible twos" unprepared and is unable to successfully finish it and leave it behind. He said that children who are stuck in their "terrible twos" are often diagnosed as having oppositional-defiant disorder. He then said that there seemed to be something more and asked me whether there was anything unusual about Lisa during her first two years. I then remembered that Lisa had suffered from recurrent earaches as a baby, up until she was about five. We went to the doctor frequently.

Many nights she would cry with pain, and I would give her medicine and then let her sleep with us.

Aaron Lederer said, "This is very significant. She may have learned to associate her maternal attachment with pain because of her earaches. Now she seeks pain to feel attached to you. She achieves the pain of the attachment she craves through causing you to attack her." He called this tendency "negative attachment behavior," which means seeking hurt where others seek love. He added that the negative attachment behavior often induces negative feelings in the mother that are so overwhelming that she can't resist acting on these feelings.

I was fascinated by his explanation and asked many questions. It didn't quite make sense to me, but it had the ring of truth to it. Clearly, Lisa was provoking the explosions, but I had never been able to pinpoint the reason until then. It felt accurate to me that she did it to achieve a sense of attachment.

Outside of her relationship with me, Lisa was a success. She had a responsible position in the student government of her high school, and she was popular, capable, creative, and an honor roll student. She had found a well paying, Saturday-night job playing her guitar at the Y, and she bought herself the clothes she wanted. But the relationship between Lisa and me was not only painful—it was clearly abnormal. Aaron said Lisa could be helped to change her "negative attachment behavior" to a positive one and that the person best equipped to help her accomplish that was me, her mother. He offered to lead me through that process.

When I concluded my conversation with Aaron Lederer, we agreed to talk on the telephone once a week.

He asked me if I minded if one of the therapists he was training joined our conversations, mostly to listen. I didn't. I figured that more feedback might even be helpful to me (and it turned out that it was).

I felt as though a great weight had been lifted from my shoulders after my first conversation with Aaron. I had promised Lisa that we would "do something" about the situation, and now I was.

I followed Aaron Lederer's instructions very carefully. When I felt myself getting close to exploding, I would quietly leave, e-mail him with the details of the situation and get his advice and instructions instead of yelling. It was not easy, but I did what he said. I had to physically walk away from a situation ("without an attitude," he said, if I could manage that), even if Lisa was calling me back. "*Mom!* Where are you *going?* We were talking about my best pants that *you* left on the floor so they got stepped on, and now they're *ruined!*" I tried to just keep walking, even though I was sometimes shaking from the effort it required for me not to reply or react at all.

By following all the instructions—it was hard!—I saw results very quickly. The explosions ceased completely. As of this writing, it has been four months since we began our weekly sessions, and there has not been one explosion. I truly believe they are things of the past. It is a huge relief. I did not enjoy losing control, because I felt abusive. Lisa certainly did not enjoy it either, although on some level she may have needed it and therefore provoked it.

We are going through another difficult time. My mother- in-law is very sick, and the burden has fallen largely on my husband. Guess who is the one child who has shown the most caring and sensitivity toward me and

my husband? Yes—it is Lisa. As Aaron explained to me, "When you remove the negative attachment behavior, the loving, caring, affectionate person underneath can emerge."

For some reason, hearing him say these words made me cry. I was overcome with gratitude, and I was also blown away by how fast it had all happened. The hard, slow part was finding Aaron Lederer; that took us seventeen years. Lisa is a different person. She is much more cooperative, and she is often actually nice to me.

As Aaron says, a person who is just a little bit hungry can afford to be fussy. I'll take the steak, but no potatoes. I hate oatmeal, no thanks. But if someone hasn't been given anything to eat for several days, she will eat anything. Suddenly, even stale bread is delicious. My goal (and I did accomplish it!) was to starve the negative attachment behavior operating in Lisa's brain. Lisa was out to provoke negative, painful, responses in me. But if I refused to give them to her for long enough, she—by then starving for contact—would finally, in desperation, turn to the only alternative: positive behavior to stimulate me to give her positive responses.

When I controlled my negative responses as I had been taught to do, completely eliminating all forms of instruction except for the ones Aaron gave me, Lisa was thrown off balance—this is not the Mommy I know. It was fascinating to hear the changes in her voice. Suddenly, it was "Thanks, Mom, for the ride," and "Sorry about the mess I left, Mom," and "Let me do that," comments I had never, ever heard from her before.

I think that at this point, she is still waiting for the other shoe to drop. She doesn't trust that I am really

finished exploding at her and lecturing her and screaming at her. But I really, really am done with those negative reactions. Now that I understand them, I don't have to play those games anymore.

I am so grateful to have dealt with this now, while Lisa is still in her teens. I understand that people with Lisa's problem tend to act this way with whoever their primary attachment figures are. So long as she was single, it would be me. Once she got married, it would be her husband and children. Had we not dealt with this, Lisa might have had a very stormy marriage, if not a failed one, in which she was always provoking her husband to explode at her. I wonder how many failed marriages could be prevented if parents would study and follow the Aaron Lederer method of dealing with provocative children. A month or two of work, no drugs or surgery, just verbal instructions, and you have saved a child's life and, by extension, generations to come.

I told Aaron Lederer this morning that I feel we are ready to discontinue treatment, and he agreed. Lisa and I have not had an explosion in the entire six months since we started treatment. I have become adept at disengaging in a casual, friendly way when she is trying to provoke me. Her provocative behavior has gone down in strength, on a scale of one to ten, from a ten (irresistible, you *have* to explode) to about a two (extremely easy to disengage, barely worth noticing). She hardly ever tries to provoke explosions anymore, and when she does, they are halfhearted attempts, the way one might scratch an itch that doesn't really itch anymore—just absentmindedly reaching for that spot out of habit.

I asked Aaron Lederer what to do a few weeks ago when Lisa humiliated me in front of my colleague from work. He said to wait until the emotion was spent and then to say to her, "Lisa, I really like the way our relationship has been developing. But there is one thing, and that is that when you snap at me in front of others, I feel hurt and humiliated. Will you do me the favor from now on of always trying to make me feel good, even when you feel bad?"

When I said this to Lisa, she rolled her eyes and indicated through dramatic hand gestures and facial expressions that I was not making sense. But I knew she had heard me. I had learned from Aaron that repetition is not reinforcement; it only makes the impact *lighter* when we repeat ourselves. So I gave a mysterious smile and walked away.

Asking Lisa to make me feel good even when she felt bad was the last request, the "global favor."

It has now been six months since the end of the treatment. Lisa has become a pleasure to live with. Who would recognize this child? She is no longer difficult. She loves when I come to hear her play guitar at her performances and is eager to go out to eat with me afterward. There are no explosions, period. There hasn't been one since day one of implementing Aaron Lederer's plan. Sometimes I think, soberly, of how Lisa might have ended up on drugs to "control her temper" or some other such tragedy. But my changes in behavior alone caused her to grow up and become a calm, happy person who has her needs fulfilled through positive behavior, not negative behavior.

Lisa still subconsciously tries to provoke me sometimes. For example, the other day she said angrily, sarcastically, "Thanks for letting me use the car, but you gave it to me on empty, and you *knew* it was on empty. I had to fill up the tank!" The old me would have taken the bait and would have responded with even more sarcasm, "Let me understand the problem: *you* had to pay for the gas to do *your* errands in *my* car? My, what a tragedy!" Instead, with absolutely no effort on my part, I nodded my head to show her I had heard her, then turned and walked away and got busy in the garden. Out of the corner of my eye, I saw Lisa give a sigh and turn on the TV. I could not help smiling to myself as I pruned my roses. I smiled because walking away from the provocation had been natural and effortless for me. I smiled because Lisa has fully absorbed positive ways to feel the love bond that all human beings need and because she has integrated these ways into her personality. I smiled because I cannot wait to see Lisa live a full, rich, and happy life. I feel lucky that I will be part of it.

5

Mason, 6

Mason was not adopted, and his mother didn't think that he had problems due to insufficient maternal bonding (RAD) because she and Mason had bonded. However, as an infant, Mason had two major surgeries and endured all the separations hospitalization necessarily entails. Since then, he has been developing normally and is extremely intelligent, but he has had behavioral problems in school and at home. His mother has noticed his behavior getting worse. Mason has been diagnosed with ADHD and acts very oppositional. He is demanding and controlling and wants to have all the power. His mother writes, "I have tried everything and am at my wits' end."

My son was born with craniosynostosis, a premature fusion of the bones in the head. He underwent major reconstructive surgery at the age of three months. Mason was always a happy baby and was mentally and physically normal. He has always been an active child and has a very different personality from the personalities of my other two children. Right from the beginning, he was very sociable, confident, and strong-willed.

Our problems began in earnest when Mason was three years old and he entered a day-care setting. Almost every day, I would receive a call from the day-care center concerning different behaviors that Mason was displaying. He was biting the teachers, he wouldn't listen, and he was hitting and biting other children. When told to do something, he would ignore the instruction and do what he wanted to do. Most of the time, they would ask me to come pick him up midday because they had done all they could do, and he was still too much of a disruption.

I had to keep my job, and I was in tears a lot. I knew what the day care was talking about because I had experienced these problems at home, also. I knew none of it was their fault. He was out of control and would not listen to me or anyone else, and I knew it. I couldn't take him anywhere because he would take off at a run. If I tried to get him to stay near me, he would have a tantrum, complete with hitting and screaming.

At home, he tormented his brother and sister. If they were playing with something, he would approach them from behind and then pounce, grab what they were playing with, and proceed to destroy it. No punishment seemed to work. No reward seemed to work. There was constant chaos in the house.

I went to my pediatrician and described Mason's behavior, and he prescribed Adderall, saying that my son had ADHD. I left his office relieved, thinking that I'd finally found an answer to the problem. Well, things only got worse after Mason started taking Adderall. He would have temper tantrums at night because he was coming off the medicine and couldn't fall asleep. He began having night terrors and would be a zombie during the day

due to his lack of sleep. His personality was gone, and he seemed so unhappy. The doctor tried him on several different medications, but none of them seemed to be the answer. I discontinued all ADHD medicines.

Not surprisingly, I was told that Mason could no longer attend day care because of his behavior. I was devastated. I enrolled him in a pre-K class at the public school, but he had major problems there, also. He wouldn't listen to the teacher at all. Instead, he did what he wanted when he wanted. A team of child behavior specialists evaluated Mason and decided that he needed Special Education. I knew that was not the answer, as he was able to learn normally if he could only sit down calmly and focus. In short, crazy as this may sound, I knew that he was totally normal and that if we could just get a grasp on his behavioral problems, his learning would be fine. He did not need Special Ed.

I pulled him out of the pre-K class and began taking him to day care in a woman's home. Again, there were all kinds of problems. He bit, scratched, refused to listen, and could not play with the other children in a normal manner. By now he was almost five, and I knew kindergarten was right around the corner. I was a nervous wreck.

Everyone had advice. Some people told me that something was seriously wrong with him. Others told me that he was just a strong-willed boy who needed more discipline. But everything I tried to do seemed to backfire, and the harder I tried, the worse things got.

I read books, looked on the Internet, went to psychologists, and searched with growing desperation for the answer to his problem. It was a mystery; I could not

help him because I had no idea why he was acting as he was.

Kindergarten started, and again, we dealt with many behavioral problems. He often had after-school detention and detention during school, and he was constantly in trouble. I began searching the Internet again, and that is when I found the Web site for the RAD Consultancy, which described Aaron Lederer's corrective communication method. The descriptions of other children's oppositional defiant behaviors sounded so much like my son's that I decided to give it a try.

I had my first consultation with Aaron Lederer, and he accurately described my son to me and told me that because of his young age, I may be able to turn him around in a matter of a weeks. He attributed Mason's behavior to his surgeries, which caused him to "lose" me several times and to confuse pain for nurturing.

Aaron Lederer thought that his method would work with Mason. Without ever having met him, he seemed to understand my son. His confidence that he would be able to help Mason was music to my ears, as I was completely desperate by this point. Aaron assigned me to a counselor who had been through his training and was under his supervision.

My first instruction was to stop talking to my son. I was supposed to let him initiate contact with me, and I was to respond only to his contact. I had always shown him a lot of affection and tried to be a positive influence, so this was very foreign to me, and I almost felt guilty for doing it.

But I was desperate and also determined, so I tried it. It was amazing. I found that when I did not engage

him in conversation or direct him, he had no reason to begin arguing with me. That first week, I avoided taking him places where I would have no choice but to confront him. The comments that I did make were short, friendly, and to the point, like "Bath time," "Bedtime," and "Time to eat." For some reason, when I stated things like that, he would cooperate. It didn't seem to him like I was telling him what to do, so he could comply without losing his autonomy. He knew he was free not to comply. He had always very much wanted to be in charge, and if he felt that anyone was trying to control him, he would not comply. It was as if he was saying, "Nobody tells me what to do!" Under the new system, if he didn't come to supper, then I left his plate out, and he could eat when he came. I was told to immediately disengage if he argued or began yelling at me. My husband could continue relating with him normally; the program didn't involve him. The mother was the change agent.

There were times when Mason didn't have a bath or when he had to dress in the car because he wouldn't get ready on time. And there were times when I would slip up. But, for the most part, I followed through, and Mason's troubling behaviors began to melt away.

I was astounded that changing my way of communicating with my son made so much of a difference. I didn't realize how much instructing and directing I had done until I was not allowed to do any at all. For instance, right before it was time to get out of the car to go into a store, I used to begin with "Now, stay with me," and "Wait for me to get out of the car," and "Don't get lost in the store." Instantly, this would trigger him to take off without me. When I didn't give those warnings,

guess what? He stayed right with me. Even in the first week of the program, it was absolutely fascinating for me to watch the changes in him.

The next week, we began to eliminate his remaining bad behaviors one by one. I was given one sentence to say to him, and I was to say it only once. Sometimes, Mason became irate because he couldn't manipulate me into doing what he wanted. But soon he began to comply without questioning. For some reason, this was all that my son needed.

I am writing this after six weeks. At this point, my son still has days every now and then when he decides he doesn't want to please me. In those cases, I use the techniques that I have learned.

I have never seen my son respond to anything like he has responded to this program. To other parents suffering as I did, I say this: the program is definitely worth trying, and if it doesn't help, you won't have invested much in time or money, and there is never any obligation to continue it.

I am so thankful to Aaron Lederer and the program that he runs. It has made a vast difference in my family. There is not as much arguing, the household is generally a peaceful and happy one, and we can pick up and go places without worrying that it will end in disaster.

6

Will, 13, and Kevin, 16

Will and Kevin were adopted into a family that had previously also adopted a girl. But then the adoptive father died, leaving Elizabeth, his wife, to raise all three children alone. The adoptive family was a challenge before the father's death; afterward, dealing with everyone was impossible. Will was diagnosed with RAD, ODD, developmental delays and additional unspecified emotional disorders. He was unhappy and very needy, stayed up all night, cruelly teased the family dog, and ran away from home regularly. He did poorly in school and believed that everybody hated him there. His behavior at school was, at different times, labeled as "uncontrollable," "inappropriate," and "verbally aggressive." Kevin was physically threatening toward family members and destructive at home, punching holes in the walls and damaging furniture. He was a gang member, used drugs and alcohol, and sneaked girls into the house for sex. Kevin constantly provoked Will into fights, and between the two of them, the house was in a state of constant chaos.

I remember driving home from work one day, putting the car in the garage, and just sitting there. My home life was miserable. I did not feel I could relax when I entered

my house; instead, I felt anxious and fearful of walking in the door. But eventually I had to go inside. I couldn't sit in the garage all night.

If I was lucky, there would only be a few fights between my children and we would mostly keep to ourselves, like strangers living in the same house. If I was unlucky, some minor infraction would set off my younger son, Will, who was in his early teens. Doors would be slammed, holes punched in walls, tables overturned, and papers strewn about. Just thinking about it made my stomach turn.

When Kevin was challenged, it often resulted in attacks. He pushed, shoved, tripped people, screamed in your face, and threw things. I was often intimidated, overwhelmed, and afraid for myself and my other two children, especially my youngest son. My older daughter, June, and Kevin had physical fights when she tried to control him. Our home life was horrible and out of control.

To make matters worse, my younger son, Will, had serious developmental delays and learning disabilities. His behavior was often bizarre and uncontrollable. Kevin's outbursts would get Will going, and then I would have two obnoxious and scary boys to contend with.

I had no privacy. Phone conversations were impossible. I stopped having visitors over, and we were no longer invited to our friends' homes. My husband had died suddenly several years before, and I was very isolated. Because my friends did not have similar problems with their kids, they had a hard time understanding why my family was so out of control. I was sure that if I tried hard

enough, I could fix the problems, but the harder I tried, the worse everything got.

I went to conferences, I read books, and I consulted with many therapists, but things continued to get worse. The basic message I got from all my sources was that my situation was hopeless. If I had been wealthy enough, I would have sent my sons far away to some boarding school.

I couldn't find joy or comfort in my family life. I dreaded the holidays, family gatherings, and birthdays. When I saw families spending time together harmoniously, enjoying each other, I was filled with sorrow and envy. That was the family life I had planned to have; but instead, I was caught in a nightmare.

A friend must have noticed how my life was falling apart. She invited me to dinner, and we talked. Her support and understanding gave me hope.

She told me about a therapist, Aaron Lederer, who specialized in helping parents with difficult children. I immediately made an appointment and was relieved to find that this person seemed to know what he was talking about. More important, he knew what I was talking about.

The longer we worked together, the more confident I felt about his skills. His recommendations lessened the tension in my family and helped me bring order to the house. Progress was slow, and the steps I had to take were painful for me, but over time, I have regained control of my family and my home life.

Now, at the end of the treatment, Kevin is transitioning out of Special Education classes and has settled down quite a bit. Outbursts are rare, and we are

building a relationship based on trust and respect. Will is in a residential program where they can help him with his emotional problems. I am hoping he can learn to be independent.

As for me, I am looking with excitement toward a future in which I hope to build a life filled with satisfaction, love, and peace. That seemed impossible a few years ago.

Two years later, Will, now sixteen, is able to control his behavior, can carry on conversations normally, and is respectful of others, though he's still somewhat depressed and is still convinced that nobody loves him.

Kevin, nineteen and living at home, is self-sufficient, cooperative, and more respectful and is mostly likeable, caring, and helpful toward me. I couldn't have lived with him any longer if he hadn't changed. He holds down a full-time job that he likes and at which he's liked and appreciated. He goes to a local college in the evenings.

As both my sons have improved, I have paid closer attention to my own life. I quit my low-paying job at a nonprofit organization and accepted a much better paying job as a school counselor, which I love. I have more time for myself in which I can pursue my interests, and life is immeasurably better than it was three years ago.

Thank you, Aaron Lederer.

7

Margaret, 16

Margaret has had problems all her life. At sixteen, she has no friends and is inconsiderate, temperamental, emotionally distant, negative, and promiscuous. Margaret smokes, drinks, can't accept rules of any kind, and constantly provokes her sister into fights. Margaret's birth mother was diagnosed with borderline personality disorder and is manipulative, provocative, and dishonest. She is in prison and is scheduled for release when Margaret is eighteen. Margaret lives with her father and stepmother and has a horrible relationship with both. Her stepmother hates coming home in the evenings. She says she "can't stand" Margaret, who "ruins everything at home."

This morning, my sixteen-year-old stepdaughter stopped by the family room to say good-bye before she went off to work. We exchanged pleasantries, she talked about her day's schedule, and she blew off a little steam about her boyfriend. It was just a normal, friendly little exchange before she called "So long!" and flew out the door. And it made my day.

Three months ago, such an event would have been totally unthinkable for either one of us.

For years, Margaret and I have gone out of our ways to avoid any unnecessary contact with each other because it could only go badly. There were no "good mornings," and we exchanged no words at all on a good day. Most days, there were harsh, angry exchanges. I saw her as a selfish, self-centered, lazy, manipulating liar, and her behavior bore out my interpretation. She argued bitterly about anything she was asked to do; any rule we set down was intentionally and repeatedly broken; she went out of her way to humiliate and provoke her brother, who is ten years younger than she is; and she was accusatory and nasty to my husband and me. The house was a war zone of her making. She sucked the joy out of our existence.

Outside the house, she was scraping the bottom of the barrel for friends; she had sex with a boyfriend three years her senior, and she smoked, drank, and let her grades slip. This girl, who had always been in the talented and gifted classes, a straight-A student, seemed hell-bent on self-destruction.

Everyone except me saw these behaviors as new, but I had always known there was something seriously wrong with her. Living with her had never been easy. Even as a little child, she was secretive, sneaky, and manipulative. When I'd hear her wake up in the morning, I'd suck in my breath and brace myself, thinking, "Okay, here we go again." Nothing was ever enough; no treat, no matter how much she begged for it, ever made her happy. She was always convinced she wasn't getting fair treatment, never had friends for long, had no allegiance to anyone, and, most tellingly, shared no confidences with anyone— ever. She rarely had female friends, but since she'd grown

very pretty, there were plenty of boys with cars at her disposal. She used them for whatever she needed.

Over the years, we tried art therapy, counseling, rules, incentives, punishments, everything you could think of, and nothing ever worked. Finally, after she ran away this year, we found Aaron Lederer. This has been our turnaround year.

The work Aaron Lederer gave me was simple to do, and when the results came, they were very rewarding. Our house now has a much more relaxed, happy atmosphere. There is no shouting, door-slamming, or hateful language. The pressure is off of me and my husband to try to "change" her or "control" her: the onus has shifted to her, and she must try to modify her own behavior. After following Aaron's instructions, we simply watched and waited for her to fall in line. The responsibility was mostly hers. We've learned to view her behaviors as symptoms of a condition rather than mere hatefulness and provocation.

We still have a lot of work to do. While things are generally fine and are even sometimes great for me and the rest of the family, my stepdaughter is still hurting inside. Aaron Lederer thinks that if we keep up with our work, we can ease her way in life so that perhaps she can learn to have meaningful relationships and a more fulfilling life. With the kind of results we've seen so far, we have every reason to trust his instincts.

It has been nine months now since the end of treatment. As I sit here at my computer typing this letter, my children, Margaret and David, are upstairs having a pleasant conversation, calling to each other from their bedrooms. The three of us have just shared a nice dinner

(my husband is away with the army again), after which, without a word, we all got up and began cleaning up together. Margaret was the one who got up first.

During the meal, David offered to give up his bed to allow Joe, Margaret's new boyfriend, to spend the night tomorrow. Margaret and Joe met this past semester at college, where they both are freshmen. He is a very nice young man. After their first semesters, Joe has a 3.5 GPA, and Margaret is a little disappointed with her 2.7. She wishes she could take the courses over because she feels she knows where she went wrong and could do better. She says she knows she'll do much better this semester.

Before she went to college, we asked Margaret to keep the lines of communication with us open, take college seriously, and pass all her classes in order for us to continue paying for her education. If she failed to meet any of those stipulations, she would need to get a job and be on her own financially. She has called me or her father every other day, on average. As she has encountered problems with her classes, she kept us informed. She sought tutoring on her own. And she passed everything, getting mostly Bs. She thinks she may be interested in studying sociology.

A girl from her high school who goes to college with her recently got heavily into drugs. This concerned Margaret, and she confided this to me. I offered a listening ear, empathy, and no advice unless she specifically requested it. She told the girl that she was worried, and the girl attacked her cruelly. She called me in tears after that. I know it helped her to talk to me. She ends most calls with, "I love you, Mom." When I was hospitalized in October, she got a friend to drive her to visit me and

brought me a little gift. She spent what little money she had on Christmas gifts for all of us.

It's hard to say which development is most important, but to have them all come together during the course of one fall semester seems amazing. I still had a fair amount of animosity toward her when she left in August. Pete, the old loser of a boyfriend, broke up with her within the first week she was away. I thought the whole semester was shot. But she held on and made it work beautifully. I am so proud of her and happy for her. I really think she is going to be okay now.

Aaron, thank you so much for teaching me how to be a mother to her. We never could have achieved this without your help. You know where we were when we started. In all of my dealings with her, in each conversation we have, I recall the basics of communicating with her properly. I hardly ever offer advice or come on strong. I wait to be asked. I never react in anger. I provide any form of help that she requests, as long as I feel good about her. As David gets older, these practices work well with him, too. He is really a pleasure. And thanks to you, so is Margaret.

8

Jenny, 2 1/2

Jenny was adopted when she was nine months old. Later, her parents thought she was merely a "very terrible two-year-old"; but, after reading some articles about attachment disorder, they realized she was actually suffering from those issues. When she was adopted, Jenny refused to accept love and wouldn't make eye contact. Eye contact seemed to be painful to her. When told, "We love you and will take care of you," she'd walk away. Jenny tried to control everything. She talked incessantly. She pushed her adoptive parents to the edge. She kept doing whatever it was that she was asked not to do. When her mother took something away from her, Jenny hit her. She also hit her older sister, other children, and the other children's parents, as well.

We were all so excited to welcome Jenny into our family that we never thought there could be any problems associated with adopting a nine-month-old child. At first, we just thought she was trying to adjust to us. Then we thought she was jealous of our five-year-old daughter, Kelly. Then we thought she was just a *very* "terrible two." It wasn't until my husband and I both realized that we

didn't want this child living with us that we came to understand that something was very wrong.

Jenny seemed to thrive on our anger and knew at a young age how to push us to our limits. Our friends thought we were crazy, of course, because she saved this behavior only for us. One day she was so bad that I told my husband I was leaving and that when I got back, I wanted Jenny to be out of the house.

We were almost at the point of calling the adoption agency and saying it just wasn't going to work out when a friend asked if we had read about attachment disorder. We immediately started reading everything we could find on the subject and quickly realized that this was what was troubling Jenny. From our first phone conversation with Aaron Lederer of the RAD Consultancy, we knew that he and his team would be able to help. He knew exactly how we were feeling and assured us that because of Jenny's young age, it wouldn't take long before we would see a change in her behavior.

We were anxious to get started but were also afraid of the impact it would have on Kelly and our family life as we knew it. Aaron assured us that our family life would only get better—and it did. The first few weeks were trying, but now I believe that those were the most critical. The assignments the RAD counselor gave us each week were simple, but the results were phenomenal. After several weeks, Jenny began to regress, as the counselor had predicted she would. She acted like a much younger baby. She wanted to be wrapped up tightly in her blankets at bedtime and became attached to a stuffed animal that she still sleeps with. We felt that this was a turning point

because every night prior to that time, she had thrown everything out of her crib and cried herself to sleep.

We continued with the weekly phone calls and assignments, and it *did* get easier. When we switched to biweekly phone calls after only ten weeks, I missed the counselor's encouragement and found it hard to stick with the basics, but e-mail was the next best thing.

Alltogether, it has been just over three months, which is a very short period of time when you consider the impact this will have on Jenny's entire life. Jenny has become easy to love. I know now that I can deal with her, I completely understand her, and I have the tools that I will need down the road.

We have had some ups and downs, but the good times far outweigh the bad now. When we look back at photos of the first year that Jenny was with us, it makes us so sad that we didn't realize what was wrong with her sooner. She was crying in most photos, and when she wasn't crying, she had a vacant look in her eyes and rarely looked straight at the camera. Now she is a happy girl most of the time, and a neighbor recently told me, "Jenny has a new sparkle in her eye!" She had no idea how much this meant to me!

Jenny no longer tries to push the limits because she no longer gets the attention she used to get for her negative behavior. She still cannot tolerate too much closeness, but that is getting better as well. She now likes to cuddle, especially at bedtime, and just the other night she fell asleep in Troy's arms, something that had never happened before. There is nothing better than holding a peaceful, sleeping baby!

It has been nearly six months since my work with Aaron Lederer ended. Since then, we have e-mailed a few times and had one follow-up conversation. Things are going extremely well. Jenny's behavior is now typical of her three-and-a-half- year-old age group. She has become a very affectionate little girl and seeks out my physical touch many times every day. She likes to cuddle and even lets me hold her "like a baby" sometimes. This was never possible before. She would not allow us to hold her facing us and would cry and yell, "Ouch, you're hurting me," if we even tried. The gleam in her eye now tells us that she enjoys this closeness and the special time we spend together.

Jenny and her older sister, Kelly, now get along as well as siblings can be expected to get along. At this time last year, they could hardly stand to be in the same room. Now they play together, and it's obvious that Jenny actually looks up to Kelly and tries to be like her. Likewise, Kelly adores Jenny, and she sometimes protects her and rarely makes negative remarks about her behavior like we all used to do. Another major milestone is that Jenny likes to play by herself and often does so for what I would consider long periods of time for a child her age. She is very animated when she plays with her dolls and stuffed animals, and I have even heard her use the "favor formula" (one of Aaron Lederer's "corrective communications") with them at times!

The biggest change over the last year has been in my feelings toward Jenny. I never thought I would even like this child, let alone love her. This whole process has made me realize that I do have room in my heart for her and that I do have enough love for both her and Kelly. It has

been tough, and at times I wondered if it was even worth it, but now I can't imagine life without Jenny. I believe that the things you work hardest at are the things that end up meaning the most. That doesn't mean that I love Jenny more than Kelly, but it is a different kind of love. Kelly was my first baby, my easy baby, and it was love at first sight. Jenny, on the other hand, has a special place in my heart because I had to work so hard to love her and to get her to love me.

From the first time we spoke with Aaron Lederer, we truly believed he could help. He made us feel comfortable and completely understood what we were going through. Had we never spoken with him, I am afraid to imagine where we would be now. Now we have the family we always dreamed of having.

9

David, 16

David was diagnosed with major depression, for which he was medicated. He was also oppositional and defiant toward authority figures, was short-tempered, and had bursts of violent rage. He was addicted to cigarettes and alcohol, had used marijuana, and was in trouble with the law for drug use and for fleeing the scene of an accident. He once attempted suicide. David was treated by a succession of counselors, psychiatrists, and outpatient programs, all to no avail. He was emotionally distant from his parents and was an outcast at school.

I was desperate and scared. My beloved son was self- destructing before my eyes, and everything I tried to do to help him backfired. In fifth grade, when he started middle school, he became self-conscious and was bullied. He hated to go to school and would feel sick every morning. I sought counseling and told the school authorities. Then there was a change: David became frighteningly alienated and constantly got into trouble— he always got caught when he did something bad. These may have been calls for help, but whatever I tried to do—family therapy, youth group therapy, an intensive

outpatient program, and antidepressant drugs—seemed only to make him hate me, himself, and the world more. We were in a downward spiral.

There were some tender moments with glimpses of communication, but they were always followed by more catastrophes. He got into trouble with the police for marijuana, he got suspended from school, he punched holes in the walls, and he drew pictures of him harming himself. I was so paralyzed with fear, shock, and grief that I did not know how to love him properly.

One day, I saw the mother of one of his friends in the grocery store. She asked me how I was. Instead of nodding and saying I was fine, I told her how worried I was about my son. She told me about Aaron Lederer and the RAD Consultancy.

I was afraid to call. I did not know what to expect, and I felt hopeless.

On my first phone contact, I told Aaron Lederer about a long litany of events. Aaron led us away from the brink. We began a process to regain communication and trust with my son. He would tell me how to talk to David, and I would take notes. The advice made sense. For example, in certain tough situations, I was told to ask David for suggestions. These were things I could do, even in my anxious state. Then things began to change for the better!

Now that we are near the end of treatment, I still have the typical worries of a parent with a normal teenager, but I don't fear that he will go into uncontrollable rages against himself or authority figures. Today he is doing better in school, looking ahead to college and the future. He sometimes calls me at work and tells me about

something that has gotten him "pissed off." I get upset that he is angry, but I am relieved that he calls me; he is communicating, and he has chosen me. A few days ago, I told him I was going out and asked if he wanted anything. He said, "Why don't we just go together?" Privately, I cried tears of joy.

During the three years since the end of the treatment, David has graduated from high school and is now finishing his second year of college. He goes to a university in a city about a hundred miles from home. When I started to work with Aaron, when David was in middle school and had already accumulated a long list of psychological diagnoses, school suspensions, and police arrests, this outcome did not seem possible.

It has not been a straight path. David only slowly became more communicative and responsible. But now we enjoy each other's company—we especially enjoyed the college campus tours.

There were setbacks. We had some good times together on his home leaves, but he also seemed to get in trouble on some of these occasions. During his first year of college, he was arrested hours after Thanksgiving dinner. He wrecked his car on Christmas morning at about 2 a.m. and I felt like I was back in hell. Then, over the summer, he was arrested for DUI. I felt sick and afraid—were we in another downward spiral? While awaiting trial, he went to the beach with friends and was arrested for disturbing the peace. I realized that being home was toxic to him. I must admit that I love to see him, but I dread school vacations. When he is home, I am awake and on guard, hoping he doesn't backslide into his old patterns.

In spite of these mishaps, we have shared many good times. I am still almost afraid to be too optimistic, but I realize that my fear does not help the situation for either of us.

With all that, his smile warms my heart, and I really think the feeling is mutual. There is hope for both of us.

10

Carla, 19

Ever since her parents separated when she was eight, Carla has had problems. She now has no contact with her father except through e-mails, which usually end in arguments. At age nine, Carla was caught stealing at school and was given counseling for six months. At age thirteen, she made a suicide pact with another girl. She was put in a hospital outpatient program and was medicated, but to no avail. Carla is oppositional and defiant. She responds with tantrums when she doesn't get her way: she yells, screams, curses, knocks things off counters, and physically prevents her mother from leaving the room. The following is Carla's mother's report after the first fourteen weekly telephone sessions with Aaron Lederer.

I was working from home one day when my nineteen-year- old daughter had one of her tantrums. She stood very close to me and yelled threats and obscenities in my face. She seemed out of control, and that made me afraid. In an effort to get her to stop, I did not respond. She stormed out of my study and began calling me from her cell phone. Every time I picked up the phone, she hung up and redialed. If I ignored the phone, I had to listen

to it ring. I felt incredibly harassed, and it seemed like it would never end.

When she finally retreated to her bedroom, I sat at my computer and cried. I didn't know where to turn. We had already been through counseling, and she was taking Prozac. Nothing seemed to work. I didn't want to live with her anymore, but I knew she would not be able to survive on her own. I can't explain the hurt I felt inside at being a mother yet not being able to reach my own child.

I frantically searched the Internet. I found some programs for troubled teens, but none of them seemed like it was the right fit for Carla. Then I came across the RAD Consultancy's Web site. I read the description of oppositional defiant disorder. I was so surprised: I was reading a description of my child. I sent an e-mail to Aaron Lederer to see whether he could help.

Aaron was able to help. In less than four months, I have seen a tremendous change in my daughter. She used to come to me only with problems, and now she finds me to talk about other things, too. She shows real interest in family get-togethers. She handles disappointment without tantrums. In fact, she has not had one tantrum since I started working with Aaron. She is starting to take responsibility for her actions.

We still have a long way to go, but I feel like I have my daughter back. Aaron Lederer worked with me to change the way I was communicating with her. How amazing it has been to watch Carla change and mature in response to my new way of communicating.

Thank you, Aaron, for giving me my daughter back.

11

Robbie, 16

Soon after adopting Robbie, his parents sensed that there was something fundamentally "wrong" with him; he seemed to refuse all emotional contact, and he was an "emotional loner." In time, Robbie was diagnosed with Asperger's syndrome, a high-functioning form of autism. He was reclusive, hostile, uncooperative, rude, and inconsiderate, but he was also highly intelligent and extremely gifted musically. Something about the way Robbie functioned impressed Aaron Lederer as being both attachment-based and oppositional, and he offered to work with Robbie's mother as if Robbie suffered from RAD and ODD, separately from Asperger's.

The Biblical definition of hope is "desire plus expectation." Almost six months ago, I certainly desired to "find" my son (age sixteen, adopted at the age of sixteen months), but I had little expectation that I could do so. I sent frustrated, despairing SOS messages out into cyberspace, praying that someone would answer and offer help before the window of opportunity to establish a normal parent-child relationship closed. My husband and I believe the answer to that prayer was Aaron Lederer.

It has been four months since we began working with Aaron Lederer, and our work is not finished. But now I have a son who does not pull away when I put my arm around his shoulders, who does not leave the room when I enter, and who seems to want to be near me at times, to walk side by side. Are these little things? Are they insignificant? Not to a mother who knows how precious and important these little things are and who knows how disheartening their absence can be. I now have a son who stands straight rather than slouching and slithering around corners after-hours, like a "creature of the night," as we formerly described him, trying to find humor in a humorless situation. I am developing a sense of trust and confidence in the young man he is, and I am getting glimpses of the adult he has the potential to become.

Our journey is not complete, but I believe we are on the right road. With prayer, confidence in the expertise and methods of Aaron Lederer, and willingness to sacrifice, to work, and to do whatever is right and within our means, we will finish the course. Ultimately, we rely on God to bless all our efforts. The result of the process, we hope, will be a productive human being and a caring, compassionate soul. What more could any parent desire and expect?

About a year ago, I wrote, "Our journey is not complete, but I believe we are on the right road." Well, the time has now arrived when I may say "Our journey's end is near," and it promises to be a welcoming, comfortable place. During our last communication, Aaron Lederer listened patiently as I bubbled over with a positive report on the progress we had made in recent weeks. When he took the opportunity to speak and told me that we were

coming to the end of our work and that our son was "as normal as he can be," I wept tears of joy. (It doesn't matter to me whether he meant "normal" for our son or "normal" for any teenage boy.)

My husband and I realize that our son will always have a reclusive nature—he will always need time to recuperate and refresh his spirit after socializing and being in stressful situations, but we have a better understanding and appreciation of him, and he of us. He knows he is loved and seems to appreciate that fact. He is cooperative and patient with his old "out of touch" parents—perhaps more so than your average teenager. He wants his privacy and independence, of course, but he seems to find security in knowing we are his safety net, ready to catch him until he is truly ready to be on his own.

He has also revealed some compassion, which in times past seemed nonexistent. For example, yesterday he wanted to make an extra stop on the way home. My husband said, "Your mother really isn't feeling very well—maybe that can wait until later." Our son said, "Oh! Okay." One might ask, "Well, how revealing can those two words be?" But it was the tone of his voice that touched me. There was a sound of surprise and concern that Mom might not feel well. Perhaps the fact that I could feel ill was something that he had never thought of, or if he had, it had never mattered to him before.

And surprisingly, our son's memory seems to have improved. Several days ago, I told him that some real estate agents were coming to look at our house on Wednesday morning and that I needed him to do me the favor of being up and ready by 8:45. Nothing more was said about it, but on Wednesday morning at the time

I had indicated, our night owl was up, showered, and dressed, and his room was straightened (except for the unmade bed, of course—he still doesn't do beds!).

We have now joined the ranks of "parents of a teenage boy"—yes, one who is somewhat of a turtle and who still seems to find the world somewhat mysterious and threatening, but one who is venturing out more and more and who also finds the world to be alive with potential and possibilities.

Where would we be if we had not found Aaron Lederer? I don't know, but now, at the very least, I do know that we have done the best we could possibly do for all of us. The knowledge and training Aaron Lederer has given us has changed our lives so much for the better.

It has now been two years since we ended the treatment. All three of us are working with the TV network, and Robbie is doing a good job. Right now, he is training a new editor to assist with the growing production demands. He seems to get better consistently, gradually, and steadily as he matures, and our lives are good right now. Of course, there are still the times when Robbie recluses himself, but there are also many good moments that make it all okay.

Our holiday activities have stretched out over an extended period since Thanksgiving, when our married daughter and her family visited. We had a great time. Robbie was an integral part of the fun—except, of course, when he was out with Kitty, his mystery girlfriend. One day he even took his sister's family, except the youngest, out to play paintball. Our daughter videotaped the event, and we so enjoyed watching the good time they had. They are all amazed at the changes in how social

Robbie is, and I believe we have Kitty to thank for many of those changes. Also, Robbie seems to get taller, more muscular, and stronger all the time—more comfortable and confident in himself, and it's not just a lot of pretense and bravado.

Stephanie, our other married daughter, came to visit with her family. They arrived later than expected the night we were to exchange gifts, so we postponed our exchange until the next morning. Robbie had already used his days off work to go to Texas with his paintball buddies the previous week, so he had to go to work the next morning. So we gave him his gifts that night before he and Kitty went out for dinner. After receiving his gifts and giving his nieces and nephew their gifts (bought by me, though he reimbursed me at his suggestion!), he went upstairs and returned with a gift and a card that said "To Dan and Denise, from Robbie and Kit."

For the first time in his life, Robbie gave his dad and me a Christmas gift!

He said, "This is from Kitty and me—well, mainly from Kitty."

I had mentioned to him at some point that I thought the Dance Revolution game looked like fun and good exercise; I had seen some boys playing it at an arcade in Houston. Well, that's what we got, and though I look rather silly trying to do it, I am determined to master it just because I value that gift so much! Robbie even let me hug him and give him a kiss on the check. That had definitely not happened in a long time!

I thought that the nieces would be real little nuisances to Robbie in their efforts to meet Kitty, but he has been playful and patient with them, teasing and tormenting

them in return and acting very normal. Robbie also continues to attend worship services with us. He still doesn't drive, but he apparently has a girlfriend and friends willing to transport him wherever he wants to go. Of course, our communication still has to be casual, indirect, and nonintrusive, or we risk his withdrawal.

Now we have been finished with treatment for three years. Robbie has been talking about getting a car for many months now, but he has only discussed it, never really making any actual moves toward it. I thought he only wanted to satisfy the expectations of his friends, who have their own vehicles and are driving. But today, he walked to the driver's license testing station and passed the test to get a learner's permit. I think he may be on the way to completing this project!

Robbie is still a pain many days, though perhaps just a typical teenage pain, although he is now twenty years old. He still gets himself up every morning for work and completes a full day at his assignments, but he usually spends his paycheck as fast as he gets it. He is always ready for every church service, but he is not always as neat in appearance as I would like him to be. Then again, that may be a normal teenager/parent kind of issue. He has some friends with whom he plays games on Friday or Saturday nights. Sometimes he camps out in their apartment, but he always comes home on Saturday nights, turns out our signal light so I know he's in, and is ready to go to Sunday worship with us on time.

At times, I need to snap him into shape. Today, when I saw the disgusting appearance of his newly renovated room, I remembered Aaron Lederer's permission to occasionally express myself freely and give him a tongue-

lashing, as we call it here in the South. His attitude always seems to be improved after such an event.

Thank you, Aaron Lederer, and may every parent you help ultimately feel the gratitude for you that Dan and I do.

12

Dennis, 16

Dennis exhibited many of the symptoms of RAD and ODD. He was in a therapeutic school for three years, where he received group and individual therapy, but he became increasingly violent and disruptive, necessitating frequent visits from local and county police. He provoked his teachers intentionally, as if he enjoyed making teachers "lose it" and frequently refused to work. At home he threatened and intimidated his younger sister, repeatedly attacked his mother and father, and destroyed property. His parents had to hire an ex-policeman to take him to residential treatment. There he behaved like a model citizen and never got into trouble. After a month, the facility sent him home. He was well behaved for a week or so, then resumed his provocative behavior. He has been home for the past month, neither attending school nor working. He blows up when asked to do the simplest of tasks. Sometimes he cooperates, but for the most part, he trashes the house and hangs out with other kids who are often in trouble.

For five years, my husband and I tried to have a child, aggressively pursuing fertility treatments. Finally, we decided to consider adoption. I talked to my immediate

family about adopting a child from Asia. Because my uncle had been killed in the Pacific Theater during WWII and my brother had been wounded in Vietnam, I wanted to be sure that a child of Asian descent would be welcomed into the family. Everyone encouraged me to begin the process.

While I was on a business trip with my husband, we received word that a newborn boy was available. While my husband worked, I rushed out and bought a car seat, linens, clothes, and baby books. I even looked into information about nursing adopted children. That night, we opened a bottle of champagne and read our baby-naming book in the hotel's outdoor Jacuzzi, where we were joined by a gentleman who had also recently adopted a child. We simply could not believe our good fortune.

When he was one week old, Dennis came to us, and he was perfect: dark hair, intense blue eyes, never crying unless he needed something. We fell in love with him immediately. Because I was a psychotherapist, I couldn't just stop working without warning. I closed with my clients over a five-week period, but my husband, Brad, was able to work from home and care for Dennis. We loved having him near us—if anything, we spent too much time holding him and interacting with him. When my mom met him, she looked at him and said, "He notices everything; his road won't be an easy one." Her comment really irritated me. I thought, "The child is less than two weeks old, and already you're predicting trouble." Little did I know that this sixty-eight-year-old, former teacher was a prophet.

Dennis brought joy to the entire extended family. He walked at eight months and reacted with obvious intelligence to everything around him. Brad spent lots of time teaching Dennis to be gentle with the cat; he would stroke the cat, then stroke Dennis's cheek, softly spelling out G ... E ... N ... T ... L ... E.

At ten months, Dennis hit me for the first time.

We continued fertility treatments because I didn't want Dennis to be an only child. (Most of my friends were onlies, and they hated it!) I have always had wonderful relationships with both of my siblings, and I wanted to provide that for Dennis. When he was nineteen months old, I finally conceived. I was thrilled about the pregnancy and was so excited that we would soon have a real family with *two* children! A few days before I gave birth, I looked at the sleeping Dennis and wondered if I could ever love another child as much as I loved this one. I worried about our relationship changing, and I hoped that there would be room in my heart for the new baby.

Jill was born, and I could not imagine being happier. After fifteen years of trying, my family felt complete: I had "one of each."

One day when Dennis was two and Jill was six months old, we were sitting around the table, enjoying a simple meal, when Jill let out a bloodcurdling scream. "What happened, little girl?" I asked anxiously. Dennis looked at me proudly with his forefinger extended and said, "I poka baby eye." That was the defining moment of their relationship, and it would continue to be that way for the next sixteen years.

Dennis was also often hostile to his best friend, our next- door neighbor's little boy. Dennis would play with

him at first but would then push and hit him until he left.

At age four, Dennis began to have asthma attacks. I completely redid our house, had Dennis tested for allergies, and avoided any substance that might provoke an attack, but nothing helped. I suggested that there might be an emotional cause because I'd noticed that Dennis often had attacks on holidays and special occasions. The allergist didn't want to go there!

At the ages of three, four, and five, Dennis was a perfect, very bright student. But at age six, I was told that Dennis needed a special reading program. I knew this did not make sense; something was off, but I could not identify the problem.

When he was in first grade, I was informed by his teacher, who was also a friend of mine, that Dennis had been sent to the principal's office that day for telling a boy to "have sex" with one of the little girls in the class. At first I thought that he hadn't known what he was saying and had just repeated something he had heard, but upon further investigation, we discovered that he was quite aware of the sexual act. I had to go through a whole apology session with Brad, the teacher, and the little boy's parents. I told Brad, "I'm not doing this for the next twelve years!"—a prophecy that did not come true.

By the time Dennis reached sixth grade, school crises, including suspensions and expulsions, were the norm. Brian, a boy Dennis's age, lived across the street, and they began to hang out. When they were thirteen, Brian (who is now in jail for manufacturing methadone) introduced Dennis to sex and drugs, and we put Dennis in therapy. We had difficulty setting limits and enforcing rules, and

our family life continued to deteriorate. I looked for a private school for Dennis, but none seemed to be right for him. The closest one was fifty miles away. And anyway, Brian was right across the street.

What had happened to my perfect family? Dennis and Jill hated each other's guts, and Brad and I were wiped out from trying to keep them from killing each other. Jill was clearly suffering, and Dennis was spinning out of control.

I slipped into a major depression and was hospitalized over Christmas. I was barely able to function as a parent. I started serving grilled cheese sandwiches and canned soup for dinner. (I used to serve organically grown vegetables and homemade everything!)

We continued with Dennis's therapy, but we continued to have great difficulty setting limits and enforcing any household standards at all. Dennis and Jill fought constantly, both verbally and physically. During their violent fights, they broke household item after household item: double-mirrored doors, walls in the living room, wooden bedroom doors, French doors, porch windows. Dennis began writing on himself constantly, and the dark ink looked almost like self-mutilation. He drew excessively violent pictures: Nazi symbols, skulls, bleeding heads, flames, and gang symbols. He also carved them into doorframes, walls, desks, and boxes.

I had three more major depressive episodes, though I was not hospitalized for any of them. I was finally diagnosed as bipolar in 2001, and the right medication has kept me on an even keel since then.

Things peaked when Dennis threatened to stab a classmate. The classmate's mother pressed charges.

Dennis threatened suicide, and I stayed in his room all night. Eventually the boy's mother dropped the charges at her son's urging.

At the end of seventh grade, we learned that Dennis was failing all of his classes. He entered a special program but often fought us in the mornings, not wanting to go.

Dennis managed to pull his scores together enough to get into high school. He played soccer, basketball, and baseball for his high school teams. He lettered in soccer and baseball and was always a starting player. He began to mess with his coach occasionally, but by some miracle— maybe because the coach was our friend, maybe because Dennis won games—the coach still wanted him on the teams.

By sophomore year, Dennis had become increasingly aggressive with both his classmates and teachers. When a teacher tried to break up a fight between Dennis and a classmate, the teacher wound up in the hospital. The school told us that something had to be done. They suggested residential treatment for a time. Dennis refused to go, so we had to arrange for an ex-Marine, ex-parole officer to shackle him and drive him to Boys' Town. This man had to receive medical treatment when we arrived: Dennis had injured him while he was being shackled.

For twenty-eight days, Dennis was perfect. When we visited, he told us he loved us and missed us. At the end of the month, his evaluation read, "Dennis does all his household chores; he never fights with anyone. He has become a favorite of both staff and clients." We had family therapy, and he was sent home. We had renewed hope.

Within a few days, it was hell again. Dennis swore at everyone, broke doors and walls, verbally abused his sister, came and went as he pleased, and caused trouble at school. We got a new parent group therapist, and she wondered aloud if Dennis might have reactive attachment disorder because he was adopted. I tried to find the woman she recommended for treatment, but I had no luck. She had gone on maternity leave, and I didn't try to contact her again. Dennis completed his sophomore year of high school, but not before provoking his coach so much that he caused his resignation. We were the coach's friends, and Dennis's great pride in having made him leave was matched only by our great shame.

I looked up RAD on the Internet and found the RAD Consultancy and Aaron Lederer, who said he could help me. The first session was free, so I figured I had nothing to lose. After our first session, I realized that after seven years of family therapy, five therapists, three psychiatrists, and two homeopaths, I had finally found someone who understood Dennis's problems.

Aaron explained to me that Dennis could not relate to people in a positive way; that he had a compelling need to provoke people to react hatefully toward him, a trait common in many adopted children. Then he gave me an entirely new way to talk to Dennis and interact with him, one that seemed counterintuitive. We were told that instead of telling him what to do and reinforcing him when he did it, we should respond neutrally. We should let him make his own decisions; we were not supposed to praise him if he did well, and we were not to bail him out if he got in trouble. If I couldn't control my anger, I was to leave Dennis's presence *before* I lost my temper.

The change in Dennis was almost immediate. He took Driver's Ed and got a B without having one run-in with the teacher. (This man had been Dennis's teacher before, and they had not gotten along.) He also began to address me in a more acceptable manner.

However, he was still bent on self-destruction. Dennis got a job and then made sure to lose it. He got a car, then lost it for not keeping up the payments. He needed only two more credits to achieve a 2006 high school graduation, but he fell short and could not graduate.

He still hung around with kids who had no supervision and no goals and who did drugs, fought, and stayed out all night. They all began crashing at our house, stealing from us, and stealing from my parents. Aaron Lederer told us how to put a stop to that, and we did, thus infuriating Dennis, who threatened to kill us and to destroy our things. To show he meant business, he kicked a huge dent in our old van and keyed our new one. Both my husband and I had a lot of trouble following Aaron's advice; it was difficult for us to disengage before "losing it," as instructed.

Things went from bad to worse. Dennis stole Jill's car, and after we got it back, we took out the fuses to disable it. He found the fuses and stole it again, and this time he wrecked it. On Aaron's advice, we called the police, but they recommended that we not file charges. "Don't get him into the 'system' with a felony," the kindly sergeant advised.

Under Aaron's guidance, I completely stopped telling Dennis what to do; I only took action. When he drove without a license, I took his keys. When he got tickets, I didn't pay them. When he failed to make his

car payments, I let the dealer repossess the car. When he hit his girlfriend, I called the police. When he was incarcerated, I didn't bail him out. I was very reluctant and scared to try these things, but Aaron assured me that it was what my child needed, and he was absolutely right. It was hard for me, and I could tell I was being a difficult client, having been a psychotherapist myself. Aaron must have been most impatient with me at times, but he never showed any frustration. Frequently, I didn't want to do what he said, and sometimes I totally refused to implement an intervention that he recommended. Fortunately, he didn't give up; he gave me alternatives that eventually worked for both of us.

Dennis began sleeping in other places, but he still came in and out of our house at his whim. He began treating Jill and me better, but he still constantly fought with Brad. Their fights occasionally became physical, and we became good friends with all the policemen in our town. Aaron told us to let Dennis know that he could not stay at home anymore. We hadn't been very good at following Aaron's instructions, and this was no exception. Although Aaron said with certainty that we needed to get a restraining order, I was reluctant to take that step. Instead, we offered Dennis the deposit for an apartment and the first month's rent. Dennis accepted happily and moved out, but his uninvited visits continued.

Soon afterward, Dennis was arrested for missing a court date regarding one of his many illegal acts. We did not bail him out. We left him in jail, and I visited him only once. After five days, he was assigned a public defender and released.

We left for a family reunion, and Dennis stole Jill's car again. I called the police, and they also told me to get a restraining order, which was what Aaron had been suggesting for months. Dennis called Brad, and Brad told him that he could no longer legally enter the house. Dennis called me and asked if he could pick up his things. I put them outside, and his girlfriend and her mother came to pick them up. When his girlfriend's mother asked permission to let Dennis live with her, I agreed.

The more I listened to Aaron's instructions, the better things became. I no longer feel angry, guilty, and distressed all the time. Letting Dennis take care of himself has relieved me of a tremendous burden. It has also improved communication between us. As long as I'm neither judgmental nor compassionate, we enjoy each other's company. Unfortunately, old habits die hard, and I occasionally fall back into old ways of communicating, but I can see that they never work. I only wish that we'd found Aaron when we first noticed that Dennis had serious problems. I wish I had understood the special needs of adopted children, who have, by definition, experienced total abandonment and terrible loss.

Now, Dennis is on his own. (This was our main goal.) He still sometimes calls and asks me to make deals with him concerning a car. When I refuse, he no longer verbally abuses me. He just hangs up or says "okay," and I change the subject. I never thought we could have such a good relationship. I believe that eventually it will be even better. I truly believe that if we had found Aaron earlier, Dennis's life would have been 100 percent better, and I *know* that mine would have been as well.

For the first time in sixteen years, I have been able to divorce myself from the horrible weight of feeling like a total failure as a parent. I no longer own Dennis's problems, and I am finally able to give my daughter some of the attention she needs and has needed for a long time.

Dennis no longer has violent outbursts, and we have begun to allow him to come into the house again. There are no new dents in the car, holes in the wall, broken windows, or broken doors. He now addresses me in an appropriate way most of the time: there is no more "I'll kill you" or "I'll take you to court" or "You'd better watch your back." We sometimes have "couch time" when we just sit and talk about what he is doing. As long as I remember to respond as Aaron taught me, we do fine.

13

Marta, 24

Marta was born less than one year after her brother. Their mother, unaware of what she was doing, rejected the new baby to protect the older one. Twenty-four years later, Marta was the failure in of a family of successes; she could not even do her own laundry or hold down a job. She was on several drugs for obsessive compulsive disorder (OCD) and anxiety, but nothing helped.

My daughter Marta's sad childhood began even before her birth. Our son was only a few months old when I accidentally became pregnant with Marta. I was very attached to my son and resented the intrusion.

When Marta was born, nursing her was emotionally wrenching for me; it made her older brother cry, and I was so attached to him. So even in the hospital, I let the nurses give Marta a bottle, which is something I never allowed with any of my other children born before or after Marta. I did not want to become attached to her.

Of course, I did not realize all this at the time. All I knew then was that Marta did not seem to like me, and I felt indifferent in return.

Marta was the only child for whom I did not have enough milk; we are a Christian family, and I have six children. In retrospect, I know this was because I did not let her nurse long enough, as I was in a rush to get back to my much-preferred oldest. I worried that he would feel neglected and unloved if I spent too much time with Marta.

When Marta was about two years old, I realized something was very wrong with our relationship, and I knew I was responsible. I had made a mess, and now I wanted to clean it up. So one day I picked her up, sat down on the rocking chair with her, and said, "Marta, let's let bygones be bygones. I love you. Would you please forgive me? Come, let's be friends from now on." I held her and rocked her and cried tears of bitter regret at how I had treated her. How terrible to be unwanted before you are even born! She, however, sat there upright and sucked her thumb. She didn't cry. Generally, she hardly ever cried. Why would she? I had not exactly been responsive to her tears. Can you blame her for not liking me, for not trusting me?

The years passed, and while I was always extremely close with our other children, the relationship between Marta and me was almost nonexistent. She bonded with her father somewhat, but he traveled a lot and was sometimes unwell, and between those two reasons, he was often not available. The interaction between Marta and me was so infrequent that when she was away, I didn't notice much of a difference in the household. We hardly spoke, though I did try much harder from the time of the rocking chair reconciliation, for whatever that was worth.

Marta did not seem interested in having my attention like the other kids did.

More years passed. Marta grew up and became a miserable, sad, depressed, anxious, difficult teenager and then adult. She drank too much, starting at age fourteen. She began smoking marijuana. She put on weight. She cared very little about her appearance and was the only one of our six children to look sloppy all the time. She was diagnosed with all sorts of emotional problems, including acute anxiety disorder and OCD, but the diagnosis that fit her best was Aaron Lederer's: deficient maternal attachment. I learned from one of Aaron Lederer's workshops, the reading materials he gave me, and our subsequent telephone appointments that the nature of the attachment that a baby has with his/her mother is crucial. It is the most important attachment of his life, and it affects all future relationships, including those that a person has with his or her spouse, boss, colleagues, children, and self.

Though she was intellectually brilliant, Marta could not let herself succeed at anything, perhaps because she unconsciously believed that if her own mother could not love her, she was not lovable and deserved to fail. When asked how she felt about me, Marta was overheard to say, "I don't understand her. It's as if we speak two different languages, and neither of us can really hear what the other is saying." Marta found me, her mother, mystifying and annoying, and I found her distant and just as difficult to understand.

In her early twenties, Marta's mental disturbances grew to the extent that she was once arrested for running repeatedly up and down the stairs in an apartment

building. She was tormented by recurrent, worrisome thoughts and desperately sought relief, and soon she began taking prescription drugs to combat her OCD. The drugs did not work too well, but they anesthetized her enough that she thought they were working. Soon Marta had no life; she basically slept the days and nights away.

Our other children grew up, left home, built successful careers, got married, and started families. While they lived at home, they worked or furthered their educations, took care of themselves, and helped with the household chores. But not Marta. She failed at whatever she undertook. When Marta was twenty-three but less mature and less responsible than a five- year-old, Aaron Lederer offered to teach me new ways to communicate with Marta that he said may help cure her and help our relationship. He said it would be painless and uncomplicated and would probably only take a few months, and eventually Marta would stop "shooting herself in the foot," which is how I described how she lived her life. For example, she would get a job, then do something inappropriate and get fired. She would make a friend, then act gross and lose the friend. She would make the other people in our household (her best friends, really) angry at her by leaving messes all over the house. Absolutely no one ever wanted to share a room with her because of her sloppiness.

Things also got to a point where her siblings would not lend her money because they knew she would not pay it back. My husband and I also stopped giving Marta money because all her money went toward impulse buys like donuts and coffee, never to the legitimate needs for which they were intended, like a sweater or transportation.

If we bought her a new coat, for example, she was likely to lose it or forget it on the subway. She stole money from wherever she could, and when confronted, she casually admitted it. Caring for her was frustrating, to say the least.

Aaron Lederer and I began having weekly, half-hour-long telephone appointments with unlimited contact by e-mail between sessions. I told only my husband what I was doing, not Marta or anyone else in the house.

Aaron explained to me that the first step in our work would be to help Marta form the secure and affectionate attachment with me that she'd missed the first time around. He said that accomplishing this shouldn't take more than a few weeks and instructed me to simply stop giving Marta any orders or lectures whatsoever. We were always strict about chores and personal responsibility, but Marta was now exempt. In short, my first assignment was just this: do not tell her what to do. Do not rebuke her if she does something wrong. Unless there is actual physical danger, do not warn her of the consequences of her behavior/misbehavior. Just coexist. "You are bringing her back to the baby stage, when you expected nothing of her," Aaron said. In cases where it was necessary to get her to do something right away, he instructed me exactly how to do it.

The first week that I did this, my overwhelming reaction was one of vast relief. It was a relief not to feel obligated to correct Marta or to explain to her the error of her ways, even when she did blatantly stupid things like leaving the refrigerator door hanging open after taking something out. It was a relief not to have to work so hard to get through to her. With Aaron's clear instructions

echoing in my head (and in my computer, because I typed them up each time as we spoke), I just smiled to myself and casually closed the refrigerator door. I acted as if it were no problem, as if I hadn't even noticed who had left it open, as if closing fridge doors after other people was just something I did all the time.

I didn't say a word when she left her clothes in middle of the hallway steps. I didn't say a word when she spilled food on the floor and didn't clean it up. I just acted like one might if a small baby did that: I cleaned up after her without comment. I truly felt no anger, since I had not been haranguing her to be neater or more responsible. Her irresponsibility no longer made me feel ignored or disrespected because I was no longer asking anything of her.

After a few days of this, I noticed something rather fantastic start to happen.

Marta seemed to start liking me and finding me interesting and worthwhile to talk to. This alone made me happy.

And I was much happier, too, for another reason: I had been busy teaching and correcting Marta because I had felt this was my parental responsibility, but I was constantly upset because she never really listened to my advice at all. I had been doing a lot of talking to the walls. Now I wasn't doing any more of that. Ignoring wrongdoing felt much more useful and right to me than pointing it out to someone who was not listening and was not able to absorb what I said.

Marta was her usual, irresponsible self, but I didn't play the all-knowing, irate mother/guidance counselor anymore. Instead, I was all-accepting. Seeing how

positive and beneficial this was to our relationship, Aaron assigned us several more weeks of this.

I enjoyed these weeks more than I can describe.

Each week when we spoke and I told him about the changes in Marta, Aaron said, "Just continue doing what you have been doing. This is progress. You are starting all over again with a clean slate." And I truly felt the progress. The relationship between Marta and me was blossoming. Now that I was not correcting, not criticizing, not lecturing at all, Marta no longer avoided me. She would often sit down wherever I was just to talk with me. One time, my husband was out of town on business, and all the other kids were away. I got up my courage and asked Marta if she would like to go out to dinner with me. Why did this take courage? Because although I had been out to eat alone with all my other children countless times, I had never been out to a restaurant alone with Marta. It was unspoken but understood that we were from two different worlds; we wouldn't have anything to say to each other. I would no sooner have asked her out to dinner than I would have asked the postman in for breakfast. But now I asked, and Marta agreed.

As we drove out of the neighborhood, I asked her what kind of food she wanted to eat. She looked at me in surprise and asked, "You mean we're not picking up the other kids? We're not picking up—" and mentioned each one by name. Each time I said no, not this one, not that one, nobody, just you and me, she grew more surprised and a little bit uncomfortable, but as we drove, she seemed to get used to the idea. She had assumed I would want to take her somewhere close by, but I suggested that we drive a little, so we went to another neighborhood.

At the restaurant, conversation flowed easily between us. On the way home, there were some companionable silences when we ran out of topics, but there was no tension. Marta put on some music, and I let her change it as often as she wanted and control the volume. Aaron's words rang in my mind: no criticism.

In this first stage of therapy, the heat was off me to raise Marta into a responsible adult. Anyway, my way had not been working, so it was best dropped.

Even if this is as far as we get, it has still been a huge gift for both of us and for the whole family, as we definitely began to heal our strained relationship. With Aaron's continuing direction, with patience on my part, and with God's help, I hope this will be the first step toward a healthy future for this troubled young woman.

I have been following Aaron Lederer's instructions for about nine months now. When Aaron first told me to stop making demands on Marta so as to return her to infancy, so to speak, I was shocked, but I soon became grateful. After a few weeks of following his instructions, it became clear to me that this was the right thing to do. Marta and I were able to slowly construct a relationship. I do not say "reconstruct," because we never had one to begin with. Now we do.

When I first stopped making demands, Marta tested me, waiting for the other shoe to drop. But slowly, she saw that I was really, *really* not making demands. Even when there was truly a lot of work to do, she was exempt unless she wanted to help. Often, she would sit there and watch everyone else hustle and bustle but not help. Sometimes it took a lot of effort and restraint on my part not to demand her participation, but I passed these tests.

Sometimes I had to explain to the other kids (especially the one who particularly resented Marta's ongoing "vacation") that we are working on something special for Marta and that that was why the rules were different for her right then. Aaron taught me to acknowledge the complainer's feelings of unfairness even while explaining that things were different for Marta.

It was fascinating to note that slowly, even the things Marta did that were "wrong" according to house rules, such as leaving a wet coat on the couch, stopped irritating me. I guess that when you really love someone, her mistakes and even her deliberate wrongdoings don't bother you so much.

Then Aaron said that the time had come to gently move Marta into and through the "terrible twos" and help her leave them behind successfully. He explained that the terrible twos is a developmental stage during which a child learns to accept that he or she is no longer the center of the universe but is "just" an ordinary member of the family, hence becoming socialized. "We will give Marta the opportunity to decide to leave her position as an infant and begin maturing. But," he added, "only she can make that decision."

In our weekly sessions, Aaron gradually gave me instructions on how to speak with Marta to accomplish this transition. For example, I learned to make gentle, carefully phrased requests: "Marta, would you do me the favor of putting your coat into the closet every night when you come home for supper?" I didn't give orders; I asked for favors. And he told me how to respond when she messed up or "forgot."

I added favor requests very slowly.

Recently, my husband and I took Marta on a trip to the doctor. We talked and sang and laughed, mostly at Marta's jokes. How different this was from our earlier trips! On those earlier trips, my husband mostly talked with Marta in the front seat, while I sat in the back and cried, knowing that we were about to deal with The Marta Problem again and that I had little hope for success. I knew I would have to explain again about that nightmare infancy and childhood. But this trip was totally different. Marta was funny and interesting, and she was honest about her OCD-style anxieties about being taped (she would not open her mouth at tollbooths because there was video surveillance). And halfway there, my husband turned to me and said, not realizing how important it would be to me, "Honey, you know, Marta told me a few times that lately she has had a real relationship with you, that 'she and Mommy are like friends now'."

I wanted it confirmed, so I said, "You mean as of recently?" And my husband said, "She feels like it's been this way for the past few months, approximately since October."

I just calmly said, "Oh, that's good. I'm glad." Outwardly I was calm, but inside I was euphoric. I knew exactly what had made the difference: it was my telephone sessions with Aaron Lederer. My husband did not make the connection, but I did.

I looked up the dates just now. We began our weekly sessions on July 20. August didn't make a visible, measurable difference, but by October, even Marta had noticed the change in our relationship. The importance of the statement "Mommy and me are like friends now" coming from Marta cannot be overstated.

I wrote an e-mail to Aaron Lederer that said, "Ahaaa … (joyous, contented sigh)!"

The biggest regret of my whole life has always been the way I treated Marta when she was in utero and then when she was a baby. It feels unbelievable to me that I have finally been given the tools to "undo" or somehow rectify that.

We are very active in our church, and Sunday dinner is a big deal in our house. On Saturday, we clean the entire, huge house from top to bottom in preparation. We change the linens and prepare the guest rooms. There are always huge pots of food and cakes, and the tables are set with china and crystal. The fact that Marta had not been helping with any of this for the past few months was extremely strange, but I was "making no demands," as instructed! The big breakthrough came on Saturday, March 4, 2006. Marta came over to me and quietly asked, "Mom, how can I help for Sunday dinner?"

This was the first time I'd ever heard these words from her. The other kids asked very often, but Marta never had. And this meant that she had had enough of total freedom from responsibility, enough of infancy. At least, enough for that day.

Aaron had taught me the proper response for this sort of situation, which was, "Such-and-such needs to be done. Is that something you would like to do?" I swallowed hard, and said, "Mrs. Watkins needs a ride over; would you like to drive over and pick her up?" Marta took the car keys and went and got Mrs. Watkins for Sunday dinner as if it were the most natural thing in the world. I just stood there watching the car disappear; I could not believe what was happening.

There has been a slow sea change in this family. Suddenly, I have become Marta's defender; I am her ally. Several of the other children have noticed it. And my husband has commented several times that Marta has been telling him how good our (Marta's and my) relationship is.

Sometimes, when my husband makes a demand of Marta that I think is unfair ("Lose weight!"), Marta glances at me, waiting for me to rise to her defense, which I do. I even prepared my husband for the fact that sometimes I might contradict him in front of the children in defense of Marta; previously, this was a cardinal sin that we never, ever did.

The children were heard to comment, "Hey, look, Marta loves Mommy!" Interesting that they did not notice the changes I made; they saw only the changes in Marta!

Recently, my husband made a joke at Marta's expense. My younger son (who likes to give us a running commentary on what is going on in the family, as if it's a baseball game) immediately said, "Now Daddy is going to look at Mommy and see if he's in trouble with her for making fun of Marta."

The kids have been remarking among themselves that Marta is happier and more relaxed. I think she feels safer. I am going to e-mail them all and ask them to describe exactly what is different. Marta makes more jokes, and they're very funny; for example, she sings an OCD song that she made up while checking to see whether the windows were locked.

I had gotten myself into a bind. I started a huge housecleaning project late Saturday night—washing all

the curtains—and we were planning a big Sunday dinner for fifty people, which was to take place in the very room where the curtains were down. It was taking much longer than I expected to take them down, wash them, and put them back up. I was starting to sweat. I was panicky. My usual rescuers (the kids who always came to the rescue when there was a crisis) were not there or not available: they were at their places of employment, out of town, or busy with their babies. I was in tears, trying to hurry with the re-hanging of the wet curtains but seeing plain as day that with my skeleton crew, I would not finish without staying up all night—something I cannot do.

Suddenly, I realized that something was happening. Marta—*Marta*—was coming to the rescue. She set up an assembly line with two nephews, both not old enough to help on their own; one of them stuck the hooks into the curtains, and the other passed them up to Marta. Marta went up on a ladder and quickly started taking and re-hanging the curtains.

I tried not to stare. I could not believe my eyes. *Marta was saving the day.* She was working hard and doing it well, and it didn't look like she would leave this job halfway through, as had previously been her custom. As I started to realize that everything *would* get done before the guests arrived, my tears of frustration and fear and panic turned to tears of joy and relief and delight and gratitude to Aaron Lederer. "She is a different person," I told Aaron during our next telephone consultation. "She saw me suffering, and she responded. Marta saved me."

After the whole shebang was over, I decided to try verbalizing it, but Marta has never been comfortable with loving words from me. Quietly, I began by saying, "Marta,

you saved me." She immediately seemed uncomfortable, so I stopped. But then, when my husband walked in, I informed him loudly enough for Marta to hear, "You don't know what this place looked like last night. Look now, look how clean and beautiful all the curtains are! Marta saved the day today. She literally saved the day. There was no way...."

I came to understand that I could tell the story to many people, but I could not speak of it directly to Marta with too much emotion. Too much emotion from me makes her uncomfortable.

In our family, we have a few birthday customs. One of them is that at each person's birthday supper, we go around the table, and everyone says some nice things about the birthday girl/boy, tells some true stories. That Sunday, looking at the clean curtains, the thought struck me: finally, I had a personal story to tell at her birthdays. Lack of advance planning gets Mom into tight spot. Marta rescues Mom. It would have been nothing special for the other kids, but it was a milestone for this one.

My other daughters all had albums with their childhood pictures. But somehow, I had never made one for Marta. Here she was in her twenties already, and she did not have her own album. Suddenly, I had a burning desire to create one for her. And I did. Only I didn't make one for Marta that was the same as her sisters'. I custom-ordered a very high-quality one, bound in red cloth. On it were brass, embossed letters: *Marta's Life*. I got a calligrapher to write her name and the date of her birth inside the front cover. And then I found the negatives, printed the pictures, and put them in the album. I gave it to her. She didn't react too much (photo albums are not

her thing), but I felt very good about it because I knew it had been the right thing for me to do for her.

I think I did this because Aaron showed me that it doesn't matter how many years pass, you can fix your past mistakes. Marta passed the age for collecting pictures years ago, but so what? Give her the album now. I am so glad I did. One of my other daughters was more than a little jealous of Marta's album with the brass letters and the calligraphy, but I told her, "You got yours when you were four years old. Marta waited all these years for hers. She deserves something better." She understood.

Marta is physically an adult but is still emotionally immature. She still borrows money and doesn't repay it. My daughter Lynn is upset with her right now because she lent Marta her summer clothes–shopping money, Marta did not return it, and now Lynn has no new summer clothes. (I told all the children long ago not to come to me for Marta's loan repayments. Most of them don't lend to her anymore, but tenderhearted Lynn succumbed to her begging.)

Despite the progress we have made, Marta can still be so irresponsible at times that I want to cry. If the sheet comes off her bed, she just sleeps on the bare mattress until I notice it and put it back on. She does not put covers back on food containers, and the food gets ruined. The night before she left to go on a month-long trip, I asked her to collect all her dirty laundry from all over her room and put it all on the floor of the laundry room. I wanted to wash it and dry it and fold it for her so she could pack clean clothes. I did all that but saw that she still didn't have enough clothes. So I went up to her room and found that she had missed a few piles.

I had to start all over again with the laundry, and it was past midnight. I was upset and beyond exhausted, and I wondered whether this child would ever grow up. My other children did their own laundry before they had to pack for a trip. And here, this "grown woman" could not even manage to collect her dirty stuff that had been gathering in her room for heaven knows how long. (The thought of having Marta pack for her trip alone did not even enter my mind.)

Marta has emotional disorders, and she has a long way to go before she catches up with others in her age group. In our community, many others her age are married with two children or holding down responsible jobs. Marta is far from these things. She has impractical ideas and thinks very short-term. But one thing is well on the road to being fixed, and this is a major thing. The relationship we never had has finally been forming. I did not think it was possible. I thought I would take my pain and regret to my grave with me. Instead, a miracle is happening.

If the lack of a relationship with me was (at least partially) the cause of Marta's problems, then forming one now might help alleviate them, with God's help, of course. I also thank Aaron Lederer. I never would have followed the weekly instructions if I did not have full faith that he was an honorable, ethical human being who possessed real integrity and deep generosity. Many times, his instructions did not make sense to me. They flew in the face of everything I believed. Because I trusted him, I listened anyway. Now, I am so glad I did. I also appreciated his honesty even when he had to tell me painful truths about our daughter.

There is no question that Marta is becoming less self-centered. My other children, whose homes she visits, make comments to me that prove this is the objective truth. For example, they notice that she "is more chilled," "is better company and does not run away from social situations anymore," and "takes messages for me when I am out."

The most difficult task I was given by Aaron Lederer was to not ask her to help with things, and the end result is that she now offers help of her own accord. It is ironic that I was worried about following that instruction because I was afraid it would make her into a parasite and a taker, but the exact opposite has happened.

Possibly because he himself suffered as a child and was abandoned, Aaron has a sixth sense when dealing with children like Marta. Sometimes when we are talking on the phone, he gets an idea about Marta, something he just "knows," and he is often right. I have learned to trust his intuition. Sometimes he subscribes to a "tough love" philosophy. For example, he once told me to inform Marta, "From now on, I won't be doing your laundry." When she asked why, I was supposed to respond, "It is just too much for me. I have so much housework to do, plus I have my job. I need to unload some of the housework." I was not to give in and wash a single item of Marta's, even if it found its way into my laundry hamper. I collected the dirty clothes from all over the house and tossed them in front of Marta's bedroom door instead.

On the other hand, sometimes Aaron instructed me to be the exact opposite of a tough-love mom. For example, when Marta "forgot" her key repeatedly and rang the bell, I was forced to get up from sleep or from my work to open the door for her. I was sure Aaron

would tell me to say, "Marta, from now on, if you forget your key, you will have to borrow one from the neighbor to get inside the house." But no. Instead, he said, "Marta wants an affectionate greeting from you; that is why she summons you to the door when she arrives home. It's not to get into the house that she rings the bell, it's to get the big hello from you."

I was shocked to hear this; a big hello, at her age? But he reminded me that emotionally, Marta was a small child. So the next time she rang the bell, instead of an angry "Why don't you have your key?" I opened the door and said, "Hi, honey, how was your day?" Her response shocked me. Firstly, she told me about her day. And second, about an hour later, she walked over to my desk and said, "Mom, when Uncle Sal was visiting last week, I gave him my key, and he never gave it back. Sorry for ringing." I replied, "It's okay if you ring the bell." She gave me that startled look that often follows one of Aaron's "communications" that doesn't fit in with the way I have always acted and walked away.

Today was my last session with Aaron Lederer. Together, we have brought Marta as far as we can. Her relationship with me, which was once somewhere between bad and nonexistent, is close and secure. She seeks me out frequently for reassurance, and I gladly provide it. Although she often helps with household chores now, she still lacks initiative when it comes to taking on responsibilities and preparing for an independent future.

At this point, Aaron has suggested that I enroll Marta in a group residence for adults with emotional disorders. I am in the process of doing so, although many of our

relatives are against it. So is Marta, but she's getting used to the idea. Aaron gave me the "communication" to give Martha when I talked with her about it. I know for a fact that I would not have had the wisdom or the strength to do this if not for Aaron's encouragement and guidance throughout the process.

Interestingly to me, Aaron's whole philosophy is to counter the abandonment the child suffered with a secure maternal bond. He himself embodies this with the ways he relates to the mothers he counsels. The best example of this is our last e- mail conversation. I e-mailed him the following:

> I am slowly realizing something that I don't want to realize, but if there is anything you have taught me, it is to face painful truths head-on. It doesn't really make sense for me to call you weekly anymore. Under your guidance, a miracle happened: the bond between me and Marta has been created anew, and it is strong. I know what I have to do as far as the group residence goes. I know how to talk to her and how to react to the things she says. Possibly, there is not much more you can do for me or for Marta. I love talking with you, but I feel that our work with Marta is done. What do you think?

Aaron replied:

> Congratulations; I couldn't agree with you more. It is my usual practice to wait for the mother to signal when the time to stop is in sight. She usually knows, as you are beginning to.

Once Marta's move is complete, it will become up to her how far she is willing to go toward independent and successful living, of which I have no doubt she's fully capable. At this point, no one can make her make the decision to live as an adult. This is true for all two-year-olds; only they can decide to give up their wish to remain the entitled center of the universe in favor of becoming ordinary, cooperative members of their families and societies. What helps them decide that is their secure attachments with their mothers. Through your devotion to Marta's recovery, you've been able to help her attain such attachment. The rest is up to her now.

But there is no need to rush. I suggest that we nevertheless talk next week as planned and take it from there. What do you think?—A.L.

I think I was deeply blessed to find Aaron Lederer. I hope he continues in good health to do his work with children who did not form secure, positive attachments with their mothers in infancy for whatever reasons. I am happy he is having this book published because it will spread the word that there is real hope to those who need to hear it, and I am pleased that he has been training therapists to do what he does and carry on his work. However, even when his therapists are all over the world, numbering in the hundreds, doing what he trained them to do, I will know I was one of the lucky ones who got to work with the master himself.

14

Alex, 14

At twelve years old, Alex was adopted from Russia, where he had been institutionalized several times. He defied authority, lied, stole, and refused to abide by any limits or rules. He did not cooperate in his homeschooling and endlessly annoyed his eight siblings, one of whom suffered from nightmares as a result of the constant harassment. He "shut down" when confronted. He was uncontrollable at home but charming outside in the world. He ran away from home on occasion and was hospitalized after his last disappearance. He was variously diagnosed with attention deficit disorder, reactive attachment disorder, oppositional defiant disorder, and post-traumatic stress disorder. Bipolar disorder and borderline schizophrenia were also mentioned, and he was at various times prescribed Prozac, Risperdal, and Ritalin. Therapists were pessimistic about his chances to ever be normal.

In 2002, when he was twelve, we adopted our son Alex from Russia. He is now sixteen. Alex had been institutionalized several times in Russia, but we were told that it was just because he had ADD.

In the beginning, Alex was difficult, but we were able to handle him. But his behavior became

increasingly uncontrollable. We tried every type of parenting technique, took him to counseling, and even tried medication. He refused to do any schoolwork and threatened to kill himself if we put him in any kind of school; I homeschooled him from the time he came here from Russia. He smoked, stole, huffed, ran away, sometimes stayed out all night, and constantly lied. Nothing helped. He would not talk to a counselor and often refused to even go to the appointments. When Alex stole some of his sister's medication from her room and then ran away when we confronted him about it, we felt he needed more intervention, so we had him admitted to a children's psychiatric ward at a nearby hospital.

He loved the time there—it was like a summer camp for him. It did not help his issues, however, and actually made things much worse for us. The hospital referred us to a psychiatrist who had seen adopted children like Alex before. Alex was diagnosed with bipolar disorder, ODD, and borderline schizophrenia, but none of these diagnoses were definitive or exclusive. That he might have an attachment disorder was mentioned only briefly, despite the fact that he was adopted at age twelve.

As we were mulling all of this over and wondering which way to turn, a woman from our adoption agency mentioned RAD. We researched it and felt that this was Alex's true diagnosis. RAD, however, cannot be treated with medication, and the "traditional" therapists were very leery of RAD therapists.

But we were desperate. While Alex was in the hospital, we made calls to RAD specialists, trying to find a placement for him outside of our home. I knew I could not emotionally handle the stress of his out-of-control

behavior in our home anymore. At that time, I didn't want to ever bring my son home again—I was concerned about my other eight children. I checked with institutions that took RAD kids, but they charged astronomical prices—some were $1,000 per day!

It was during our online search for RAD resources that we found the RAD Consultancy and Aaron Lederer. When I had a free consultation with Aaron, I felt that he truly understood what we were dealing with. He told me about things that he thought were happening in our home, things that I hadn't told him. He just knew.

I had felt from the beginning that taking Alex to a therapist to work out his issues wasn't the key—somehow I knew that *I* was the key. I just had no idea how. Aaron Lederer worked with children without ever meeting them; he worked solely through the mother. This matched my instinct.

My husband is a pastor, and I only work part time giving music lessons. Aaron's relatively modest weekly fee seemed insurmountable, but I really felt I needed the insights and e-mail support that he would provide. Aaron said that most people see significant changes within six weeks.

The total for six weekly payments was not so insurmountable, and Aaron Lederer said that after six weeks we would *know* whether the therapy was working.

So before Alex even came home from the hospital, I began working with Aaron Lederer. I had been warned that RAD therapists could sometimes ask for strange things, so I decided to e-mail all of his suggestions to my friend who has a master's degree in social work and works with kids with attachment disorders. I just wanted

to make sure that Aaron didn't tell me to do any "off the wall" things. I thought I would recognize a crazy suggestion, but I felt better having someone else check.

And so I began speaking weekly with Aaron Lederer. He was very helpful with many of the situations we were dealing with, like the fact that Alex showed one face to us and another to the hospital staff. Because of the nature of RAD, the hospital personnel—with the exception of his psychiatrist—were convinced there was no problem with Alex. "He is so charming!" was the most common description of Alex that we heard from the hospital staff.

This part of RAD behavior was one of the hardest things for our family to live with. We were living a nightmare at home, and because of Alex's extremely charming and charismatic personality, people outside our home thought we were the ones with the problem. Even the receptionists at the psychiatric hospital kept telling us how great he was and insinuated that we were the ones who needed help.

Perhaps for this reason, things got worse instead of better while Alex was at the hospital. He lied about us during one of the hospital's group therapy sessions, after which we were reported to the Department of Social Services as abusive parents. This only added more misery to an already devastating situation.

One person I spoke with who sometimes took in RAD children said that we were definitely in a dangerous situation. If Alex had already started lying to the authorities, then things could go downhill fast for the entire family. Since seven of our nine children are adopted, we were treading on thin ice. Aaron Lederer walked us through that traumatic period in our lives. He helped

me learn how to handle the hospital personnel during each of the situations that arose. Personally, I wanted to scream at them. I was so angry. How could people who worked in a children's psych unit not understand the nature of RAD?

Because of Aaron's help and the significant support of our church, we were eventually able to successfully bring Alex home. Those were rocky times, but I can tell you for sure that Alex's behavior did change a great deal in the first six weeks he was back. Every time we had an issue, Aaron would tell me what to do. I would implement his suggestion, and it would completely change the situation.

Alex's counselor from before his hospitalization, with whom we were still working, said that Alex's positive response to Aaron's communications (all relayed through me) was nothing short of amazing. In fact, the last time I asked the counselor, who has twenty years of experience and a terrific reputation, for his input, he said that we should just do whatever it was that we'd been doing—as directed by Aaron—because it always seemed to bring the situation under control quickly.

The most difficult part for me was that Aaron's approach often required me to treat Alex in ways that contradicted some of my strongly held parenting principles. Often it was extremely difficult for me to follow his suggestions. It was also difficult because my husband and I worked as a team with our other children, but with Alex, I was the one bearing the entire burden. I had to do all the communicating with our son. But for the most part, when I said exactly what Aaron told me to

say and was able to effectively "disengage" and not take Alex's bait, things worked better.

At a few points during the therapy, I felt that I could not do what Aaron said. I was very honest and vocal about my disagreement, and I expressed my distress about what I was instructed to do. In fact, sometimes I would yell at him and challenge his suggestions, as I was not convinced they were the best things for my son. Then Alex would regress, I would start thinking about how tight our budget was, and I would have doubts about the whole method. But after a week or so, I would usually be ready to try whatever Aaron had suggested. It usually helped.

The work has definitely been worth it. It has helped to make our home a much more peaceful place. The unlimited e-mail privileges between weekly phone sessions were of great value to me as well. Before we connected with Aaron Lederer, I never knew what would help in a crisis and was often extremely stressed and frustrated. Knowing I could consult Aaron if and when a problem arose decreased my stress and frustration significantly.

After working with Aaron for thirty-six sessions, we could no longer afford to continue, and we had to stop.

Since we discontinued the therapy, Alex hasn't huffed or stolen from the neighbors. He hasn't run away. He is treating us all much better. He is making better choices on a daily basis. He is much more cooperative. He isn't stealing from us or lying. He seems open about telling us when he has done something wrong. Yes, he actually admits that he has done wrong sometimes and says that he is sorry! Before our work with Aaron, he would lie regularly, even if the lies were transparent.

Another significant change is that Alex has become more consistent in his behavior inside and outside the home. He is not always "charming" outside in the world. He is more like a regular person, showing all of the aspects of his personality. He still does not want to do any kind of work or chores around the house, and his life is often still all about what he wants, but he has truly attached to me. I see it daily in ways he communicates with me about hard issues.

We still have our ups and downs, but there are more ups than downs, and there is no question that Alex can continue to live at home. He still becomes angry sometimes, but he does not threaten or frighten family members anymore. He now chooses to spend time with the family sometimes. He treats his siblings with much more respect and kindness. Slowly, they are beginning to trust him. We rarely hear that they would rather he be gone from our home or that they wish we had never adopted him.

Originally, our psychiatrist, who treats a lot of kids like Alex, said that people like him are never able to hold down full-time jobs or be contributing members of society. I believe that because of the work Aaron Lederer does, there will be a lot more successful, contributing members of society.

The psychiatrist calls the change in Alex a "miracle." We are a people of prayer and believe that God works on our behalf, but we also believe He led us to Aaron Lederer as part of the healing process.

15

Michelle, 4

Michelle is 4 years old and was adopted. Although very bright, she was in a constant power struggle with her mother, bossy and challenging every step of the way. She talked back and had no respect for her mother's authority. Punishment had no effect because she would return to the same behavior immediately afterward. When she didn't get her way, she'd fly into uncontrollable rages, screaming and kicking walls and doors. She could be friendly one minute and mean the next. Her mother was exhausted and afraid of what the future would hold for Michelle if a solution could not be found.

Our family was in constant strife because of our daughter. She was disrespectful, insincere, manipulative and demanding. Her anger was so explosive that even though she was never violent, her emotions were so out of control that there was no way to calm her. We tailored our life to appease her and to avoid confrontations with her. When we were in public, we were her hostages because we would have to give in to her demands to prevent her from making a scene.

I saw her actions as those of an extremely active, strong- willed, intelligent child. She was never bad in

school or with her grandparents. She was sweet and charming to other adults. I thought that maybe I wasn't patient enough, maybe I expected too much of her, maybe she needed more physical activity. I thought that she would get better as she got older.

After she turned four, I compared her behavior to mine at the same age. I remember being afraid of displeasing my parents, being eager to make them happy, and being willing to follow instructions, at least most of the time. She never cared about any of this. It was all about what she wanted when she wanted it. Although she was affectionate with me, I often perceived her affection as insincere. Whenever I heard her wake up in the morning, I would secretly dread having to see her, and think, "I'm not ready to deal with her yet." I hated myself for feeling this way.

I was afraid of what the future held for my daughter. If I couldn't control her when she was four, what would happen at 14? I had tried punishing her by taking away toys, sending her to her room, giving her time-outs, and even yelling at her. No matter how consistent we were, absolutely nothing worked. While she hated the punishment, screamed and cried about it, it did nothing to change her conduct. All it did was turn our home into a war zone. I found my two-year-old younger daughter retreating into her own world to avoid conflict. This was not the kind of home life I wanted. I had become a harsh and critical mother. If I wasn't constantly policing my daughter, I felt that she would completely take over our family. In fact, she already had.

A friend told me about the RAD Consultancy and the work Aaron Lederer was doing there. I called, and

after spending no more than a few minutes speaking with him, he was able to describe my child to me in a way that no one but me understood. What sold me on his treatment is that our daughter never has to see a doctor, does not take medication, and does not even know that Aaron Lederer exists. All I had to do was change my interaction with her in order to change her behavior. I had heard about RAD but never thought that Michelle could suffer from this because she was adopted as an infant and had never been abused or neglected.

I realized during the first day of our treatment that my child was directing all of her behavior at me. While I knew that her actions were more annoying to me than to anyone else, I never realized that this is exactly what she intended. On the very first day of treatment, a power shift took place. She had been controlling me by pushing my buttons. Once I didn't react in my customary way, her power over me was gone; and we could work on learning how to have a normal relationship. I can honestly say that after a few days, I noticed that our lives were calmer. After a few weeks, there was a real change for the better in our home. I felt as if we could breathe again. After a few months, it was difficult to remember how life had been before.

While we targeted one bad behavior at a time, usually one every week or two, other bad behaviors that were on the list to be dealt with "later" seemed to melt away.

For example, one of the things that caused us tension was Michelle's refusal to stay seated during meals. She would get up dozens of times during a meal. When I followed Aaron Lederer's instructions, it worked right away. Within two weeks, she was able to stay seated at

a meal without getting up once. We then worked on having her stop screaming in the house, annoying her sister, speaking rudely to her father, not coming into the house when I asked her to, and not standing or jumping on the furniture. Each week or two, we were able to eliminate a behavior.

When I first started following Aaron Lederer's instructions, Michelle expressed anger and hostility, either by screaming or throwing a tantrum. Soon, she began to express her displeasure by calling me stupid instead. While I was shocked at first, Aaron Lederer explained that she was improving because she was becoming able to verbalize her anger instead of going into action; as he predicted, her name-calling soon stopped. Thereafter, when she didn't get her way, she would express sadness instead of anger, but in appropriate ways, such as by asking me whether I still loved her or asking for a hug. Eventually, she simply accepted not getting her way by simply acknowledging the reasons for my withholding. As we progressed, other things that caused us annoyance also stopped without our having to ask her. These included refusing to hold hands when crossing the street, interrupting adults, yelling at us when we refused her demands, refusing to leave a place she enjoyed, having a public meltdown at a social event that would force us to leave, and having a tantrum whenever I left the house without her.

We also learned methods of coping with her when she tried to argue with us. Aaron Lederer would give us statements that we would say to her that put an end to her debates with us. For example, when she would make a request that I would not comply with, she would keep

demanding an answer. Instead of having to keep telling her no or explain, I would say, "You already know all there is to know about it." In response to her repeatedly asking why I would not give her what she wanted, I would respond, "I don't know, I don't understand it myself." Miraculously, she would stop asking or whining.

Available throughout the process, Aaron Lederer was patient, kind, understanding, and calm. When I would present him with a new issue by e-mail in between our sessions, he would come up with a solution to keep me sane until our next session or advice that completely eliminated the problem. He completely understood what my child was doing and the effect it was having on me. He accurately predicted my daughter's reaction to each part of the treatment, which helped tremendously. Even when Michelle's reaction was negative, I was able to handle it better because I was prepared for it, and I knew that it meant the treatment was working.

Sometimes, I would have a week or two when I felt as if I had failed in the process. Instead of criticizing or judging me, Aaron was patient and would explain why I was having a difficult time. He would offer advice which helped me get back on track to continue our treatment. He would remind me that it is not possible to be perfect in this process and that the treatment can tolerate errors. This was a huge relief to me since I felt, when I wasn't perfectly following the treatment, that I was failing my child.

His treatment helped not only my daughter but my self-esteem as a mother. I had come to him feeling like a complete failure as a parent. With each week of improvement in my daughter, which she accomplished

with my help, I began to feel that I could successfully and lovingly mother her. The skills I have learned have helped me be a better parent with my younger daughter, as well.

Michelle is now the loving, cooperative, and kind person I knew she could be. I miss her when we're not together and can't wait to be home with her. She is still strong-willed, emotional and active, but completely within normal limits. These are now her positive traits instead of her negative ones. It's as if a weight has been lifted from her, and she is now free to be who she really is, rather than hiding behind her bad behavior to protect herself from the world. I am so grateful to Aaron Lederer. I believe that without his methods, my daughter would have continued to go through life unhappy, misunderstood, and unable to enjoy successful and loving relationships.

◆   ◆   ◆

It has been six months since I began working with Aaron Lederer, and I am amazed by the complete turnaround in Michelle. Even though I was optimistic that the treatment would bring about positive changes in her, I never expected the difference in my child to be so profound. As we neared the end of the treatment, I began noticing her willingness to cooperate with requests. A few weeks ago I asked not do something, and her response, to my complete shock, was simply and calmly, "OK, Mommy." Gone are the days when I would say "no" to her demands and then brace myself for the tantrum that was about to explode. She no longer makes demands but only polite requests. If the response is not what she wants,

there is no crying or screaming, not even whining, but just an acceptance that she cannot have what she wants at the moment, and we continue our day as if the request had never been made. She doesn't continue asking but instead accepts my authority as decision-maker in the house.

For a short time, while she accepted my role, she did challenge my husband's authority. I e-mailed Aaron Lederer with this problem, and he provided a very simple solution which began working immediately. When she would make a request of me, I told her to ask her father if it was all right. When she asked why, I explained that Mommy and Daddy are both in charge. She accepted what I told her, asked him for permission, and from then on, she respects his authority.

Our lives have been improved in other ways, as well. When it is time to leave a place she enjoys, such as a toy store, my saying that it is time to leave is met with complete and friendly compliance the first time I ask. She never gets up from the table during meals, and even when she has finished her meal, she doesn't get up before she first asks whether she may be excused from the table. She no longer runs away or hides from us in stores; she doesn't go into neighbors' homes unless we're invited in; she holds hands when we ask her to, greets us when we come home, and always takes time to tell us, sincerely, that she loves us. Friends and strangers alike remark on what a polite, sweet, and delightful child she is; and now, I completely agree with them.

While she is still a child and therefore occasionally makes mistakes, we now have a way of dealing with her mistakes in a way that actually works so that the behavior

is not repeated. It is unbelievable that I am able to cause her to behave the way that is appropriate without punishing her or even raising my voice. Had I read this sentence six months ago, I would never have believed that attaining this result was possible. With Aaron Lederer's help, Michelle has become the person I knew she could be, and we now finally have the calm and loving family that we had dreamed about.

16

Drew, 11

Drew's mother died when Drew was a baby, so he was raised by his father and, later, his stepmother. At home, everything was a struggle; he rejected affection, lied, stole, and infuriated his parents to no end. He would fly into a rage whenever he didn't get his way, defy his parents, and physically attack his younger brother. Drew refused to do any schoolwork and was failing. He was socially inadequate and aggressive with peers. At home he was clingy, wanting someone with him all the time, following his mother around so much that she felt as if she was being stalked. Diagnosed with ADHD, RAD, and general anxiety, Drew was placed on multiple medications and saw several therapists. By the time Drew's parents contacted the RAD Consultancy, they had reached their limit and were preparing to send him for residential treatment.

When I met my husband and his two small sons, they seemed to be the perfect family. We dated for a full year before getting married, but during that t ime   I began to be aware of problems with the older boy. He was only five years old at the time, and his brother, Jack,

was just three. During a visit with my husband's entire family, his parents and sisters told me my husband had been the one who changed his diapers, comforted him, and generally looked after his needs. I had no idea at that time of how important attachment to the mother was to a developing child, and I believed that whatever problems this child had could be fixed simply by providing him with a loving, stable family. I was hopeful and determined to be the mother that he so desperately needed, and I felt that if I gave him enough love, he would soon turn into the sweet, loving child that everyone had hoped he would be. I was unaware that the journey would take me to the edge of despair, change me forever, and show me the true meaning of love.

At first, daily life with two small boys was everything I had expected it to be. I had a very successful career, and my husband was a family physician, so work was a large part of both of our lives. Evenings and weekends were full of family outings and time spent with one another. The very first time I remember feeling that Drew's problems were more than just that of a normal five year old's way of behaving began with a "time out." The two brothers were playing with a large train set in the living room. Drew was taking all of the pieces for himself; and when his brother even touched a piece, Drew would quickly snatch it from him and shout, "I was playing with that!" The floor was scattered with train tracks, literally a hundred pieces; and each time the little brother picked up a piece, it was taken away, and the little brother began to cry. I stepped in and gently said, "Drew, you must share the train set; there are more than enough pieces for both of you to play with. If you do not share with your brother, you will have to

go to a time out." The little brother quietly picked up a train piece from the other corner of the room, and Drew screamed with rage, "I was using that piece!" Within seconds, pieces of the train were flying across the room at the little brother, who cowered with fear. I quickly picked Drew up and dragged him, kicking and screaming, to the corner. "Drew, you must stay here in time out for five minutes." Drew did not protest; instead he stared off into space with a horrible scowl, his hands clenched with rage. I turned away, tried to act unaffected, and went into the kitchen to prepare dinner. Drew yelled from the chair, "I can go back now, I'm done." "No," I said firmly, I will tell you when you're ready." More screaming and protests told me that he was indeed not ready to go back. Five minutes went by; still Drew screamed and yelled while I calmly said, "No!." He began to kick the wall with his feet and scream even louder than before. Finally, after I had ignored him for 20 minutes, he began to quiet down just a little. I came into the room and told him he could resume play but only if he would share. I went back into the kitchen, relieved. Feeling good about things, I walked back into the room several minutes later and asked, "How's the train building coming along?" To my horror I found Drew with his hands around his little brother's neck, the younger boy's face turning horribly blue! I pulled them apart and held Jack until his crying subsided. I turned around to see Drew quietly building his train tracks with a smug smile on his face. Enraged, I pulled him by the arm back to the time-out chair and roared, "You will not leave this chair until I tell you to!" I scooped up Jack and spent another 15 minutes consoling him in another room. When I returned, the rattan chair

seat was torn to shreds. I knew I could never leave them alone together again.

Knowing that this incident was not sibling rivalry, I searched the Internet for answers, scouring every medical website available. Drew's symptoms matched the clinical diagnosis for ADHD to the letter. He never looked at us directly in the eyes; his gaze was distant or just inches away. He was always moving and always talking. He never sat still or relaxed even when we were reading a book or watching a movie together. He was impulsive and disruptive in every social interaction. I thought I had found the answer and that medication could help him settle down and behave. We scheduled a visit with a doctor, and he prescribed Concerta (methylphenidate) right away. We saw changes the very day he started taking the medicine and felt relieved that we now could have a normal life. The medication did make him slow down, but he was still not behaving in a kind, caring way. If Drew did not get what he wanted or was told to do anything, he would have what we called "a meltdown." Like a tantrum in a two-year-old-child, Drew would first protest, then scream, then cry and throw his body on the floor and kick or pound with his fists. These meltdowns would occur over the smallest things, like what he would eat for breakfast or even who got breakfast first. Every day would start with loud banging or squeals or singing as if to announce, "I'm awake now." He never left you alone and would never, and I mean never, play alone or be by himself. He was constantly asking what time it was and what we were going to do that day. He demanded your constant attention by doing any annoying thing he could think of. If you were doing something that didn't

involve him directly, he made so much noise that you were forced to tell him to be quiet over and over again. As the weeks went by I secretly wished he would just go away.

My husband and I would walk a tightrope every day between granting his every wish so he would be quiet and tolerable or say no and deal with the meltdowns that followed if the day did not go as expected. Of course it was not humanly possible to never say no, but saying no had become our worst fear. Still, we tried to correct him, set boundaries, and back up our discipline with love and affection; but our approach never worked. His little brother's behavior was totally the opposite. We could disapprove of Jack's bad behavior with merely a glance, and Jack would apologize and stop. He would also show us genuine affection, while Drew did not. Giving Drew a hug was like being forced to squeeze a cactus. He would demand to sit in your lap, then squirm and wiggle until you were forced to put him down. He held up his arms to be hugged and whined for you after doing something bad or when he knew we were mad at him or he even if he felt we wanted to be away from him. We next tried behavior charts with stickers and prizes. He just would not respond to the positive and negative reinforcements that his brother so easily did. Instead of the goals and rewards giving him a sure sign of his success, they became a haunting reminder of his failures. His anxieties grew even worse as he worried about when he would attain the prize; and we knew that no matter how much we coaxed and tried to help him make good decisions or behave correctly, the prize was always outside his grasp. We tried making the goal be that of happiness instead of a toy or

a monetary prize, believing that his desire for the prize itself must be the problem. Telling him that being happy was what he really wanted; we had him put smiling faces and frowning faces on the charts to mark his success. The charts always ended up being frown after frown with just a few smiles here and there. He even would say, "I just want to be happy," but he and I both felt happiness would never be attainable. Why didn't the parenting skills that worked so well with his brother work with him? I read every book I could get my hands on about parenting a troubled child and followed their directions, to the letter, but things got worse.

Eventually we took him to a psychologist to be evaluated. The diagnosis was attachment disorder. Again we were relieved to have a name for our problem, and again we were hopeful that he could be fixed with professional help. We had tried psychiatrists, psychologists, psychotherapists—group therapy, one-to-one therapy, several mood-regulating medications; and still nothing we did, or they did, changed his behavior in any way. Finally, exhausted and beaten, I walked into the office of "the best" psychotherapist in town and asked her point blank, "Drew has been coming here for treatment for over a year; have you ever felt that you have connected with him or seen any sign of your therapy sessions working in any way?" "No," she said. "Do you think my money would be better spent on some other type of therapy?" "Yes," she replied. "What kind of therapy would you suggest that I try?" "I'm not sure," was her answer. I walked out of her office believing, as she did, that no therapy existed to help my son.

I could list hundreds of incidents that have occurred in my son's life to make you understand why we were so horrified with his behavior. Like the time he forged a check in kindergarten for $1,000 and tried to cash it at school. The dozens of times he stole money or our credit cards and tried to buy things he wanted. When he stole classmates' things at school and never brought home the "behavior reminders" from the principal or lied and said he forgot. The time he called a classmate a "dirty nigger" or "fat bastard." The time he took his only friend's birthday present and rewrapped the gift with an old toy of his so he could keep the new one. The time he went to the neighbor's house to use their phone to call 911 and report me to the police for child abuse. The millions of times he called me the worst mother in the world, asshole, motherfucker, or said simply, "I hate you" or "I'm going to kill you." We installed a lock on the outside of his bedroom door so he couldn't come after me and hit me anymore.

We could hear him scream and kick holes in the walls, but at least we were safe from his physical abuse. We not only disliked being around him but were afraid of him and hated him. He was a liar. He was mean and cruel. He was self-centered beyond belief. He was needy, annoying, and demanding. He made you hate him, and he didn't care that he did.

Every day, every minute with our son was horrible. My husband hated coming home after work. He hated seeing me beaten down and depressed. He felt guilty for having put me in this situation and having no way to help me out. I also hated coming home after work. It got so bad that I enrolled Drew in an after-school program

so I didn't have to be around him and could have at least two hours a day with my good son. Those few hours gave me the relief I needed so I could then deal with the few remaining hours of my always terrible day. It gave his brother a few precious hours of relief, as well. One day Drew came home from school on his own instead of going to his after-school program. I arrived home just minutes later and found that Jack had locked himself in the basement to escape his brother's wrath. Drew had pounded and kicked on the door yelling at Jack to "Open it now or I'll kill you!" I tried to pull Drew away from the door and told him to stop yelling, but he wouldn't. I thought maybe I'll just walk away and ignore him and he'll stop, but still he screamed profanities and pounded on the door. Then he got really quiet. "Jack," he sweetly said, "I'm sorry I yelled at you. I have some candy here for you if you just open the door." My heart jumped. "No, Jack," I yelled from the top of the stairs, "Don't open that door, no matter what you hear." Drew went into a fury that lasted for almost an hour, screaming, "I'm going to kill you," over and over again while shoving a screw driver into the keyhole to open the lock. Worried that the lock would finally break, I sweetly called to Drew, "Let's go see what Daddy is doing at work; maybe he will have some candy for you." Drew quietly put down the screwdriver and without skipping a beat said, "Let's go!," with a huge smile on his face. As I drove to my husband's office, terrible thoughts raced through my head. Drive for several miles and then just trick Drew and leave him. That would give me enough time to drive home to get Jack before Drew could walk back. Silently I drove to my husband's office, went in, and told Drew to play on the

computer until Daddy was done. When I got back to the house I discovered that Drew had indeed broken the lock and that Jack was locked in the basement. I crawled through a small basement window and pulled Jack out. My good son and I quietly drove to soccer practice.

I was hopeless and desperate and believed that I had failed. Was my son going to grow into an adult who had no conscience? Someone whom everyone would hate and who could possibly even kill someone? I was terrified. He was just 11 years old, and I knew that if I didn't find something that worked he would soon be a teenager, and teenage hormones could very well push him over the edge and into jail. I found a rehab hospital that was touted as the best place in the country for children suffering from attachment disorder. I contacted them and got all the necessary documents and information. It would last a year and cost $12,000 a month, but they assured us of their success rate and that he would come back to us a "normal" child. We would be able to visit him only on the weekends. My husband and I felt that, for the safety of our other child and our own sanity, it was the only thing left for us to do. They said they wouldn't have any rooms available for five months and suggested that we drive several hours a week to attend therapy sessions with Drew until that time. Four months of therapy sessions came and went, and no signs of change occurred. Then one night I found on the Internet the RAD Consultancy website. Of course the testimonials were just a recap of my current horrible life, but there was one statement that intrigued me: "Most people see changes in a few weeks." "Yeah, sure, the lucky few," I thought. "That would never be me." I e-mailed them anyway and waited to hear what

they had to say. What did I have to lose? If I saw no change in several sessions, I could just stop the program, and I would only be out several hundred dollars. I was already preparing to spend several thousand dollars for residential treatment and not see my son for a year.

Aaron Lederer called me the next day and assured me he could help. He briefly asked some questions about my situation and informed me that Drew was about five out of a possible ten on his reactive attachment assessment scale. A five! My mind couldn't imagine what a ten could be like! We set up a time, once a week, when I would call one of his associates and receive instructions on what to do. He said I would be the one who would work with Drew and help him recover. I would work with one of his personally trained therapists who would guide me through the process. "Why me?" I asked. Drew had screamed, yelled, and hit me more than anyone. Drew hated me the most, and my feelings were mutual. Why not the father?

"No," Aaron said. "It may not seem so, but he is the most attached to you; it is hostile attachment, but a strong one nevertheless, evident by his making you suffer the most." He then added, "And don't tell Drew of our work." I thought, how can I help my son if he is unaware that he is being helped? How could this possibly work? In desperation, I said, "Ok, I'll do it."

I called my assigned professional. She was gentle and understanding, easy to talk to, gave me directions, and patiently answered all my questions. The things she told me to do were not at all what I had expected and not at all what I had done in the past. I was worried that my son would see through me and notice my new ways of

dealing with him, but he didn't. Instead he was puzzled and almost unaware of what happened throughout the following weeks. At my first session I was given one simple directive: to temporarily free Drew from pressure to change. She then began to list the things I was *not* to do in order to accomplish that goal, and then gave me two simple things to do instead. I was very skeptical and, as the session was nearing its end, flooded her with questions which she calmly answered, then reminded me of being available for e-mail contact between sessions and encouraged me to write during the coming week as often as I'd need to.

Following her directions, I felt I was doing the wrong things and behaving like a bad parent when in fact her directions proved to be exactly what Drew needed. In the following weeks he became easier to be around, doing more good things than bad. He even started to do things on his own without having to be near me all the time. He stopped provoking me and started to ask my permission to do things. The veil of uncertainty slowly lifted. It was exciting; we had found a program that worked! No one was more amazed than I was. Slowly my hatred turned into empathy. I was actually worried about him and cared how he felt.

◆   ◆   ◆

The months that followed were filled with his personal successes as well as mine. At times when he stumbled or went backwards it was usually because I wasn't following the program. I talked with my counselor weekly and then towards the end bi-weekly, and always

she guided me back to the basics, getting me through any situation that arose. I finally said one day that I felt ready to move forward on my own without her help, and she graciously agreed. I had done it. Drew was on his own and able to make good choices about his life. His relationship with his father and me greatly improved and kept improving every day. His relationship with his little brother has also turned around; and, as I write this, they are quietly playing together downstairs—well, maybe not so quietly. They are boys, after all. It's been a month since my last session, and there have been no meltdowns. I've seen him do caring things for his little brother that I never would have believed he could do. Life's not perfect. We still have times when we get frustrated, scared, or upset; but I now feel like I can deal with them, and so can he. He now quietly says, "Okay" when he doesn't get what he wants. He still shows disappointment over it, he may even mumble a small profanity under his breath, but he's okay with the outcome. I find myself wanting to hug him, and he comes to me when he's sad, tired, or hungry. My feelings about him have changed with his progress. I face the fact that my behavior before the program was perfectly natural. Who would want to love anyone that acted in such terrible ways? Now because I opened the door and showed him a way out of those terrible behaviors, he chooses to do the right behaviors, on his own. Now I feel what love truly is. Love is not a responsibility that I have because he's my child. Love is now something I want to freely give to him. Isn't that what true love is?

17

Scott, 6

For his first six months, Scott suffered from a severe case of colic. When, at age six, his mother contacted the RAD Consultancy, Scott had been acting in ways typical to children with a combination of RAD, ODD, and HDAD, causing great suffering to the family as a whole and to his mother in particular, getting into major tantrums when not getting his way, and being hurtful to others with no regard for their feelings.

Right from the start, things were difficult with my son. I had had two miscarriages, so we were extremely excited when our little baby boy was born. Yet, as soon as we took him home from the hospital, things went sour. He developed colic; and if he wasn't eating or sleeping, he was crying. For four full long months he screamed and cried from the pain. We tried everything we knew, including nursing and eliminating things from my diet but nothing worked. The doctor said the colic was caused by an underdeveloped digestive system and would go away within a few months. He said, "I know it is hard now, but don't worry about it; he will be fine." Easy for

the doctor to say as the baby cried and cried and cried. We took turns comforting him while trying to stay sane at the same time. Finally the colic was gone. He gave us his first smile, and we breathed a sigh of relief. Just like the doctor said—everything would be fine now!

As he got older, he was always busy child, curious and into everything. Sixteen months later, he was joined by a brother and two years afterwards, a second brother. We were busy just keeping up with diapers and feeding schedules. Soon after our third son was born, we realized that Scott was abnormally active. We thought he might have ADHD, but we did not want to medicate him or give him a label. We prayed and came across some information on kids' reactions to sugar, food additives, and food colorings, so we decided we had nothing to lose and quickly took him off all these things and kept a record of his behavior. Immediately from the very first day he was much better, calmer, happier, and able to handle little things without crying over them. We were relieved and thought everything would be fine.

As Scott grew hoever, we observed that he refused comfort when he got hurt or upset. He would withdraw and curl up into a ball, simply enduring the pain. He also never gave affection and didn't want it, either. Scott would not climb up into your lap and ask you to read him a story; he preferred to sit on the floor by himself and look at the pictures. As Scott approached the age of six, we noticed some disturbing behavior patterns. He showed no remorse for hurting people emotionally or physically. At a zoo, he stomped on a snail and killed it, showing a complete emotional disconnection from the act. It was obvious that he was detached from his emotions. He

began to rebel against any correction and all authority. Scott was a loner and was finding it difficult to relate to other kids. Scott mostly kept to himself, and his few interactions were inappropriate. With younger kids he would only play if he was the boss and in control.

Then one Sunday morning when I picked up our son from the children's ministry, the teacher told me about an incident in class that day. It seems that Scott was having trouble with one of the other boys in the class, so Scott took a pair of scissors and stabbed them at the other boy. The other boy was fine, not even a scratch; but this behavior was very upsetting and put us in an awkward situation, as my husband is the founding pastor of the church. Things went downhill rapidly from there. We began having more and more trouble with our son at home and at church. It hit its pinnacle when my husband said, "I'm your father and you have to obey your father!" Scott's response was, "If I kill you, I won't have to obey you."

My tenderhearted husband was shaken and knew it was time to seek help. He stayed up much of the night praying, searching, and reading on the Internet for help. In the morning he said he thought he had found the answer and wanted me to read what was on a particular website. We set up a consultation with Aaron Lederer. A couple of days later, we spoke to him about our son, and Aaron described exactly what our son was like. He said that babies who have colic or other painful symptoms tend to associate maternal love with pain and then seek negative, painful attention instead of affection. He called this "negative attachment behavior." We realized that this description matched our son. Scott was constantly

prodding us for negative reactions. Aaron also said that our son was unable to complete his terrible twos successfully and was stuck developmentally at that stage. This observation also rang true. Aaron suggested we try the program for six weeks. If we thought we weren't progressing, then we could quit. Aaron also said that our son shouldn't know that anything was going on. All the appointments would be between me and Aaron. I would just begin to relate to Scott differently, and Scott would change. And so began his treatment.

During the first session, Aaron told me to relieve Scott from all pressure to change and dictated details of how to do this. Aaron warned us that just as we stop putting pressure on him to change, Scott will temporarily go to greater lengths to force us to continue doing so. And exactly as Aaron had predicted, things got crazy around our house, and it was an effort just to get through each day. As Scott's regular efforts to get us to correct him were no longer working, he seemed to go to greater and greater extents to upset us, from sawing on my bedroom door and beating on his brothers (I had to pull them to safety until Scott calmed down) to tipping things over, throwing things on the floor, and turning off the TV while we were watching it. But over the next couple of weeks, as he was no longer being corrected, he began to stop trying so hard for the reactions. Soon his efforts became less and less intense, and he began sitting next to me on the couch and then putting his head in my lap. He crawled up in my lap more and more often and wanted to be held and hugged. This behavior was amazing because he never liked hugs before and would always sit by himself. Aaron explained that Scott was responding well, as one of the purposes

of this first stage was for him to become baby-like in his relation to me—younger than the terrible-twos—and develop a baby-like positive attachment to me. It'd be the healthy, secure attachment he'd never experienced before. Aaron said the positive attachment would be the foundation on which the success in his treatment and in his life would be built. We were surprised at how quickly this attachment was developing.

As we began to enjoy little bits of positive interaction, Aaron pointed out that we needed to be careful because if Scott got too much positive attention, then we would notice him swing back the other way. It was a delicate balance between swinging back and forth until, to our amazement, he finally got to the place where he mostly wanted positive attention.

Aaron then began to work with me on the next phase. He said that, during the weeks of the first stage, Scott had attained all the goals of that stage. Besides successfully developing his baby-like attachment to me, Scott had changed his need from a negative contact to a positive one and was no longer provoking us to get furious with him. Aaron said that since these aims had been met, Scott would now get a second opportunity to go through the terrible twos, this time, we hoped, successfully. Aaron explained that we would gradually and gently put small demands on Scott and, using corrective communications, help him become willing to meet these demands even when he didn't feel like doing so.

Aaron would direct me on how to ask Scott to begin doing a task and what to say when he had failed to do it. There was to be no pressure, no punishment or reward. At first Scott became angry when I asked

him to perform the task, and I'd react to his anger as Aaron had instructed me to. Soon we started to see Scott beginning to do things that were asked of him, one at a time, without any struggle and without being reminded. It was truly amazing. Aaron instructed me not to praise him for doing what's expected of a child his age. He said that, now that Scott's attachment to me is strengthened, Scott is becoming willing to do what I've been asking him to for one reason only: to please me and maintain my love for him.

Scott began to do things like staying at the table at mealtime, keeping his toys off the floor at bedtime, going to bed on time and staying in bed at night, making his bed in the morning, brushing his teeth, showering and shampooing, hanging up the wet towel, and putting his dirty clothes in the hamper, dressing and getting ready for school on time, all without struggle and without even needing to be reminded!

◆　　　◆　　　◆

We are now 22 weeks into his treatment, and Scott is a totally different child. He has a sparkle in his eye, is happy and cooperative. Of course we have not "arrived" yet, and we still have some bad days. But his bad behavior is getting less intense and less frequent, and he gets over it sooner. Some days we can see that he just wants negative attention, just to see if he can still get it, and my husband and I will say, "He's trying hard today." There were so many issues to work through that changed over time as we went through the process, and Aaron helped us with each and every one. For example, I was having trouble with

Scott constantly saying he was hungry, even right after he had eaten. Aaron said these requests are not really for food but for attention. So when Scott says he is hungry, don't give him food; just say dinner will be in _____ minutes. Disengage if he persists; and if he helps himself to food, just ignore him. This approach worked; and, within a few days, Scott "got it" and quit this behavior. Another one that is my favorite is when Scott would come around and say, "I'm bored" in an irritating way and follow me around the house repeating himself. Aaron instructed me to say, "What are you going to do about it?" It was a brilliant response that quickly curbed his behavior. When Scott started school, Aaron told me to say, "Scott, from now on, getting up in the morning and getting ready to go to school and be on time to leave the house are all up to you to deal with. Let me know when you need my help." Sometimes he would wait until five minutes before the time to leave before he'd try to get dressed, find his stuff, eat breakfast, etc. But it was important for me to put Scott in charge of that routine. A few times he forgot to take his backpack to school, but the burden was now on him. Aaron said it was important for him to own both his successes and his failures. I was also to not say, "I'm proud of you" when he did well but rather, "I'm happy for you." Again Aaron said this response would give Scott the full ownership of his accomplishments. We also had had problems with Scott in a swimming class. After a long break, we put him back in. I shared my concerns with Aaron, and he said to ask Scott before the lesson if Scott thinks he will be able to behave well during the lesson. Aaron said Scott's response won't matter—just the communication itself –and, sure enough, he did

the best ever in swimming class. Another major part
of the work with Aaron, besides meeting weekly for our
scheduled phone sessions, was communicating any time
by e-mail with a problem, question, or even an update
(which he appreciated). Aaron's response was a lifeline
during the week. There were many times when we would
be confronted with a situation that we had no idea how
to handle, and being able to communicate with Aaron at
any point during the week was essential. Many nights
would end with a quick (or long) e-mail, depending
on the situation. These e-mails allowed Aaron to better
know what was going on every day and helped him make
adjustments. We never felt as if we were on our own, but
just an e-mail away from help. Aaron says that we are
now close to the end of our treatment for Scott.

After this stage we experienced a slight setback with
our son. He had been brought back (through treatment)
emotionally to being a baby and was now about a 2½ to
3 year old, but in the first grade. Suddenly he was not
able to handle being directed by the teacher (not that
he was great before, but can you imagine a 2½ or 3 year
old in school all day long?). "Scott, let's get in line."
"No, I'm not going to do it, and you can't make me!"
We almost had to pull him out of school altogether, and
Aaron led us through the process. I started taking him
home every time he was disruptive. I would get called
down to the school, and Scott would come home for
the rest of the day. On the way home, I was to say in a
friendly tone, "Scott, I heard you did this…", then ask,
"How do you feel about that?" Then I was simply to
empathize with his feeling. It got to where I had to go
down to the school often, and I was really getting upset.

Scott was almost expelled. We dealt with this threat through a series of communications. Aaron instructed me to say, "Scott, it looks like it is difficult for you to sit quietly in the classroom for too long, and it is difficult for your teacher to have you not sit quietly in the class. So we need to find a solution to this problem. Do you have any idea what can be done?" He said to reply to whatever Scott's response was with, "Thank you, I will think about it and let you know." Scott said that he did want to stay at school (he is a very bright child and eager to learn) but continued to be a disturbance (he would not stay in his seat, would yell in kids' faces, tip over desks, etc.). Aaron said Scott was not being "bad," that he was doing the best that he could. Then a few days later Aaron had me tell him, "It looks like sitting quietly in the classroom for too long is too hard for you. Should we have you stop going to school for now or go to school for shorter times until it becomes easier for you to sit quietly?" Scott still said that he wanted to go, and so I was to tell him," It will only be possible for you to go to school full time if you're able not to disturb anybody in class while you are there. Do you think that it would be possible for you to be in the classroom full time without disturbing anyone?" Scott said yes, and the very week I believed he would be expelled from school, he was able to control himself all day.

◆   ◆   ◆

Now it is 33 weeks, and we are at the final phase of treatment—the "consulting" phase. (The previous phase was called the "socializing" phase). Whatever the

problem was, I was to consult with Scott about it in a particular way. As with all the corrective communications I've given Scott previously, Aaron dictated to me the exact words to use in my consultations with Scott. He said it didn't matter what his response was, just that the communication was made. Scott usually had no answer, but he immediately began to respond to these communications.

We now completely enjoy this little boy. He is seven years old and can make friends at the park and at school. He interacts with other kids without getting that "look" that makes you know trouble is coming. We no longer "flee" situations because our son is out of control. I actually was able to take the kids to a birthday party, and he was extremely well behaved. He asks for things politely, says thank you when he gets them, says "I love you, Mom," which he would never say before, tells me how many more hugs and kisses I am "ahead of Dad"—he even voluntarily helps bring in the groceries after shopping! We shudder to think of what might have happened had we not been led by God to Aaron. Our son is now on the right track, headed in the right direction, and words cannot express our gratitude for the help of Aaron Lederer and the RAD Consultancy. I could take up this whole book with specifics of all the things Aaron has helped us through, but I hope I have shared enough for you to see one life truly changed, one transformed child. At the beginning of our work, Aaron asked me to make a list of things I wanted to change about Scott's behavior, and the list was quite long. Over time we worked on them one by one, and we went through them again at the consulting phase, and we have dealt with every one

of them! And, to top it all off, the best part is that Scott has no idea what happened to him. He never went to see anyone because of any problem; he just changed as I, his mother, began to relate differently to him through the direction and counsel of Aaron Lederer!

18

Patrick, 11

Patrick was adopted from Russia at the age of ten. He was severely abused by his biological mother until he ran away at age seven. He lived on the street and experienced more abuse. In the year since he was adopted, Patrick was diagnosed with RAD and post-traumatic stress disorder (PTSD) and was hospitalized four times for violence and threats of violence, including potentially suicidal behavior. In his new adoptive home on the west coast, Patrick fluctuated between being annoyingly clingy with his adoptive mother, following her everywhere, and becoming violent when he didn't get his way.

Six weeks ago, our lives began to change in ways we could not fully understand at first. We have an 11-year-old adopted son who was severely abused as a child and who has had four psychiatric hospitalizations for violence since he came to the United States last spring. We operated our household like a psychiatric ward, awarding daily privileges and rewards based on points earned for cooperation. This task left me exhausted and burned out. We were taught how to passively restrain our son when he

became violent, as he did periodically. The violence was so traumatic that we actually moved our older son out of our home briefly. A woman who had worked with Aaron Lederer told me about what he had done to transform the lives of her son and her family, and I was desperate for any possible help, so I began working with him as well.

The first week, I was to abstain from any attempt to control my son and was told what to do instead. I am a teacher by profession, and my life was a constant stream of directions and corrections; in fact, I was under the impression that those things made good parenting.

I missed the mark sometimes that first week, but Aaron Lederer told me it was like driving a car: aim and correct, aim and correct, aim and correct. His advice helped me not to become discouraged.

Two weeks after we began, I took my son out of State to visit friends. During the visit, he became angry and started hitting me repeatedly and threatening to run away. I used passive restraint until he calmed down.

My son was relentlessly demanding, imperiously requiring my attention during every waking moment and acted terrified if I was not in the room with him or just outside the door at all times. By the third week, I was carrying out Aaron Lederer's instructions more often than not, still occasionally slipping up and giving instructions or corrections but for the most part following the plan. I sometimes felt extremely frustrated by all the behaviors I was *not* supposed to exhibit. What was left? When I disengaged and walked away from his unpleasant, rude behavior, I felt like I was punishing my son with my withdrawal.

Soon, we began to see some small victories. Whereas in the past my son had become violent when one of his siblings left home, this time when a sibling went away, he stayed relatively calm.

One day when I announced that it was shower time, my son ignored me, and I calmly went outside to water plants. He soon came running out after me, demanding his shower.

I was working on a home project with Patrick at this time. When he was rude and saw me getting up to leave the table, he quickly and loudly responded, "I'm *sorry*." I then sat back down and continued working with him.

After several weeks, Aaron Lederer told me that it was time to start the socialization stage, since my son was now clearly well attached. We picked out one behavior to target, and I was given my first "corrective communication," something that I was to say to Patrick once and not repeat.

The first desirable behavior we agreed to target was giving me uninterrupted time for myself when I asked for it. If he interrupted in any way, I was to give him a scripted "corrective communication." After one temper tantrum during the first day, my son began to respect my requests for uninterrupted time alone. I kept my self-imposed time-outs brief and reasonable, of course.

Another change in my behavior is that I used to immediately say, "I forgive you" whenever my son apologized for bad behavior. Now I say, "I hear you." Aaron Lederer explained that forgiveness requires my processing the damage he has done or the hurt I had endured before it could be genuine. Forgiveness offered

too quickly constitutes permission for the offender to abuse again.

I learned that I should have no higher priority than my son's progress. I also learned that children are not entitled to all the information available, so it was not lying if I simply withheld information from my son when I needed to do so. And I learned not to put him in social situations for which he was not ready, as he was still behind his peers in his social development and had virtually no impulse control.

The second desirable behavior that Aaron and I agreed to target was to get Patrick to make his bed before breakfast each day. Now he makes his bed right away with no reminder. I have learned not to praise my son for basic good behavior that he should be doing anyway. Generally, I am learning to talk less, offer less, and leave the initiative for communication to my son. I still give him plenty of affection and contact. But Aaron explained that if I reminded my son to do what he needed to do each day, he would learn to believe that he was entitled to reminders instead of learning to think for himself, develop his own brain, and take responsibility for his own life.

At this point, six weeks after we began, our house is a much less tense and exhausting place to live in. My son still takes medication. Long range, beyond socialization, we are moving toward an independence for him that is appropriate to his age. There is a long way to go, but now we have hope.

◆   ◆   ◆

I have been working with Aaron Lederer for 18 weeks now. For the most part, my son functions beautifully in school. At Aaron Lederer's suggestion, I leave his attendance, homework, and behavior there strictly between him and the school personnel. At home, Patrick plays independently much more often. He has also started acting less fearful of going places by himself.

There is still the very rare upsetting episode at home in which Patrick threatens violence, but he always stops short of hitting me. These episodes usually happen when he doesn't immediately get something he wants. (Aaron Lederer said that although these episodes will continue occurring further and further apart, Patrick could not be trusted to abstain from violence until he permanently gave up the use of violence or threats of violence; and that aim can be achieved only at the end of our work.) He is still extremely self-centered and insensitive. On most days, however, my son makes his bed, brushes his teeth, takes a shower, sleeps through the night without disturbing my husband or me, respects my requests for time to myself, and asks permission before he touches me (he used to touch me inappropriately when hugging). He has become less rude in the way he speaks to me. I have used Aaron Lederer's corrective communications to address these behaviors one at a time, often waiting a week or two in between while we waited for the latest new behavior to become an established habit. My job has been to continue to apply the "basics" unless someone's safety is at stake. As a rule, I do not initiate communication between us aside from friendly greetings and pleasantries, giving him complete control of our interactions. This way, he doesn't feel as if I'm trying to control him.

There have been some very important support systems in place for me all along. First, I have been incredibly grateful for the unlimited e-mail contact that Aaron gave me between phone sessions because each week situations would arise in which I felt very unsure of how to respond. Aaron would send back brief messages with directions and encouragement, and I was able to keep going. Second, I have been able to grow toward acceptance of my own humanity, feelings, and fallibility. Aaron told me that when I slipped up, I needed to just climb back on the horse. He told me that I was not allowed to beat myself up when I made mistakes. He said that the process could survive imperfect application as long as the basic principles were not violated. I'm hopeful.

Each day, life contains a hundred small decisions to be made in a split second. The look on my face, the tone of my voice, the words I use, and the judgments I make all add up to my son's experience of me. I recognize that I cannot pay attention to everything at once, so I fumble through, doing the best I can. And the amazing reality is that by the grace of God, my imperfect efforts have been enough, and my son and I are both growing and healing.

It has been interesting to see that as Patrick's mother, I am his "change agent." I have been coming to accept that the process of my son's healing clearly corresponds to the process of my own growth and maturing. I am steadily learning to differentiate myself from him and his issues, to establish my own boundaries, to separate his feelings from my feelings, and to strengthen my ability to take action for his good despite his reactions.

Another aspect of this journey has been my husband's interaction with my son. My husband has seen our household transform into a vastly more peaceful place to live. Although Aaron told me that my husband could relate to Patrick in my husband's customary ways, for the most part my husband has wanted to support my efforts and all the methods Aaron has taught me. The day finally came when my son asked a favor of my husband, who answered, "Go ask Mom." This is what Aaron had said he should do. My husband's responses have been very uneven, however. That type of response does not come naturally to a dad. He has had to work at remembering. But he and I work together, and I give him a lot of support. I tell him how hard it is for me to be perfectly consistent and that I do not judge him when he forgets. It amazes both of us how hard it is to apply such simple instructions! But we keep working away at remembering, and we celebrate the progress.

◆   ◆   ◆

It has been 24 weeks now since we began, and two nights ago, I took my 26-year-old daughter and my son out to dinner. At the restaurant, I saw a miracle: I saw a healed human being looking out of my son's eyes. That's the only way I can describe it. I saw a distinct glimpse of the sane, intelligent, humorous, warm, affectionate personality that is Patrick as God knows him and made him to be. I asked my daughter later if she had noticed it, too. She told me she only noticed that she was enjoying being with him.

For me, this glimpse of Patrick's healed self was a monumental gift. I felt greatly encouraged. The journey may still be trying and stormy at times, but I have new hope for his healing and a new idea of what that may look like soon.

◆   ◆   ◆

Last June, our son was generally making good progress. He was functioning well overall at school, and he was cooperating in most key behaviors at home. But we had some incidents of his playing too roughly with school-aged children and sometimes breaking things. He was routinely roaming the town and bothering people by asking for work or asking to play with their children.

In my weekly conversations with Aaron, we agreed that there was still some work to be done with Patrick in giving up violence, but that communication was still a few weeks away. I did finally communicate to my son that I would call the police whenever he threatened me or destroyed property.

One day he played too roughly with some younger children and was told he could not come back. This rejection hit him hard. He had no real friends in the town and now he had lost the one house where he had been allowed to play occasionally.

A day or two later, my son got upset and threatened to harm another child with a weapon and was arrested. He was charged with many crimes. We went to court once a month while the authorities kept our son in juvenile detention. Finally our son pled guilty and was transferred to a therapeutic residential treatment center. Our son was

sentenced to treatment and probation. The entire ordeal was extremely traumatic and full of grief for our whole family.

◆   ◆   ◆

Six months later, our son is doing well in the treatment program. He is relating to us decently when we visit. In prison our son was so shut down emotionally that he was almost unable to relate to us at all. Now he dwells on the future and what we will do together on visits.

I still communicate regularly with Aaron to find out how to relate to my son so that he will continue to progress. There are no promises or guarantees. The decision to give up violence still rests with my son. If he chooses to give up violence, he could live at home sometime in the future. If he doesn't make this choice, I can still love him and visit him. I have had to accept these realities. We have every hope still.

Aaron's advice to me during the entire legal proceedings and prison and treatment phases has helped keep me sane when I felt as if I was coming unhinged. Once Patrick fell into the hands of the justice system and then the residential treatment system, Aaron counseled us to "let the wheels turn." He explained that each of these institutions has a life of its own. In the judicial system, parents have an extremely minor role while each character in the judicial system plays out his function. He told us we would do well to keep on relating in a supportive manner with our son as we were allowed to do so, but the process simply has to play itself out. This

proved to be not only very true but also key in helping us maintain our sanity.

In the residential treatment system as well, parents can keep on being supportive, but each professional person in the system has a certain perspective and part to play; the dynamics of institutional life, including the peer relationships of the patients, have a life of their own that is beyond professional or parental control. Aaron counseled us to let the system play itself out over time. Again, this advice has helped us keep our sanity.

We continue to work on the basics of attachment with our son inasmuch as we get to be with him. Blow by blow, as events unfolded and our son reacted, Aaron has taken my questions and guided me through one situation after another. Just the support of e-mail and phone contact has been incredibly important to my own emotional stability and mental health as we navigate the various "mine fields" of these systems and institutions. We are just much more grounded in the reality of what we can control. We still trust that God has the ultimate control and purpose for the life of our son and the rest of our family.

19

About the RAD Consultancy, LLC

When the demand for his services outstripped his availability, Aaron Lederer founded The RAD Consultancy, LLC, where he trained other therapists in the application of his corrective communication method and let them take on some of the new clients. The therapists were carefully selected for their educational credentials and for their professional licenses as well as for their maturity, experience, and in parenting their own children.

Intake

The mother of a problem child is almost always the first to make contact with The RAD Consultancy, as she is the one who is usually the most involved, who suffers the most from the child's behavior, and who is the most motivated to find a solution. When the mother gets in touch with the Consultancy (by e- mail, info@RadConsultancy.com or through the "Contact Us" page of the Consultancy's website, www.RadConsultancy.com), she receives an invitation for a free phone consultation with Aaron

Lederer. Before the consultation, she completes a short questionnaire with a brief description of the situation with her child and e-mails it back. During that initial interview, Aaron Lederer gives the mother his feedback regarding the child's problem, assesses whether the case might be suitable for the corrective communication method, explains to the mother how the work would be done, and schedules her first work phone session.

The process

The mother, as the child's sole agent for change, is assigned a counselor to call weekly for sessions that can run up to fifty minutes. The entire process is completed over the phone; there is no need for face-to-face meetings. During each session, the counselor and the mother discuss the events of the previous week, and the mother receives directions on what to do in the coming week and how to do it. Between the weekly sessions, the mother has unlimited access to her counselor by e- mail, to which the counselor generally responds within hours, except on weekends and holidays. The fee for each session is about double that typically charged for private face-to-face therapy, and includes the unlimited e-mail contact between the sessions. It is payable in advance of the session by check or on line payment.

Although the company doesn't take insurance, insurance reimbursement for the work is available from many insurance companies. The Consultancy sends all the mothers monthly statements suitable for submittal to their insurance companies.

A mother is never required to make any commitments. She can stop at any time, and she is never asked to pay for more than one session in advance.

In almost all cases, children improve significantly by the fourth to sixth session. Experience has shown that the presence of such improvement serves as a reliable indication that the case has an excellent prognosis. Conversely, a lack of improvement in this period of time indicates that the corrective communication method may not be suitable for a particular child. Therefore, during the sixth session, the counselor and mother discuss the child's progress and decide together whether to continue.

Overall, treatment averages about six months. Cases involving children up to age five average about three months; those involving grade-school-age children average about six months; and those involving high-school-age children can last up to a year.

The RAD Consultancy's team knows of no other method that is, overall, as economical, effective, fast, and convenient as the corrective communication process.

Termination

The treatment has three goals: to strengthen the child's attachment to the mother, to help the child finish the terrible twos and leave them behind, and to change negative attachment behaviors to positive ones. When these goals are met, the child becomes "socialized"— that is, he abides by rules, does what is necessary even when he doesn't feel like it, controls bad impulses, delays gratification for long-term goals, and takes others' feelings and needs into account. He becomes responsible and easy to live with.

It is usually left to the mother to signal when the time to stop is in sight; she usually knows. The mother and counselor then discuss the situation and may decide to spend several sessions tying up loose ends before discontinuing. There is always an understanding that a mother is welcome to call on her counselor for help in the future whenever she needs to do so.

20

Tale of Two Sallys

The wild child is stuck emotionally and socially in an early developmental stage. S/he cannot become unstuck without help and, if not helped, will remain self-centered, uncaring, impulsive, irresponsible, prone to rages, and lacking remorse. His/her prospects will remain poor throughout life. To succeed in relationships, family, and work, s/he must be helped to complete unfinished early development and so leave infancy behind—while still a child—as the window of opportunity will begin closing at adolescence. Two girls named Sally illustrate this truth rather graphically.

Sally was born to a 14-year-old mother who gave her up for adoption at birth. At six months she was adopted into a loving home. She was underweight when adopted, stiffened up when held, and would not make eye contact; but quickly gained weight and soon became a happy, responsive baby and a delightful toddler.

At the age of seven, however, Sally reported to her mom, Debra, that she didn't have any friends and didn't like school.

At the age of nine, Sally lost interest in her schoolwork completely.

At age ten, for the first time, Sally was caught shoplifting. Debra discovered that money was missing from her wallet and Sally denied any knowledge about the missing money, but afterwards more money kept disappearing.

At the age of eleven, she was found smoking pot with her fifteen-year-old boyfriend, a gang member and high school dropout.

At fourteen, expelled from school for possession of drugs on school grounds, she gave birth to an illegitimate child, who was given up for adoption.

When Sally was fifteen, a friend of Debra's tried to convince her that her daughter's problems were not her fault, but were due to Sally having gone the first six months of her life without a mother. "According to what I learned from Aaron Lederer, the help Sally needs can only be provided by the natural or adoptive mother," concluded Debra's friend hopefully.

Debra did not believe her friend; it just sounded too far-fetched. Something that happened so many years ago was affecting Sally now? After she had been such a happy baby?

By the time Sally turned 19, she had been arrested several times and was labeled "incorrigible" by the state. Her parents could no longer have her at home. She moved

in with her current boyfriend, and when she became pregnant, they got married.

At 22, she was divorced. At 30, she is an alcoholic single mother living with her child in a dirty apartment in public housing. She cannot keep any job she lands, and her relationships with men do not last. Her ten-year-old often spends the night at friends' homes, sometimes not seeing his mother for weeks at a time.

Contrast this tragic, all-too-common story with the story of another girl whose name is also Sally.

This Sally was also adopted when she was six months old. At her adoption, Sally was underweight and apathetic. She didn't smile, nor did she make eye contact.

A year later, Sally became difficult to manage; she talked incessantly and threw screaming tantrums whenever she didn't get her way.

At age two-and-a-half, Sally tried to control everything and all attempts to discipline her had failed. At day care, Sally was wild and hard to control, always doing the opposite of what she was told.

At age four, Sally was bossy, challenging her mother, Amber, into constant power struggles. Amber was exhausted by the constant struggle and afraid of what the future would hold for Sally.

By age seven, Sally, having been seen by several therapists and a psychiatrist, was variously diagnosed with ADHD, ODD, bipolar and dyslexia. At school she was disruptive

in class and shunned by her peers. At home she created a mess wherever she went, and, stuffing herself with food, she became overweight. Amber tried various parenting approaches she had learned, all in vain.

At age nine, Amber discontinued yet another therapist after a couple of months. Sally deteriorated further at school, both academically and socially. At home, Amber says, "The entire day, from the time I get up to the time I go to bed, is nothing but suggesting, begging, criticizing, and yelling." She felt bad about herself as a mother.

At 11, Amber discovered that Sally had used her mother's credit card, without permission, to buy things online.

The constant tension at home began to adversely affect Amber's relationship with her husband.

At 12, Sally's behavior became even more out of control both at home and at school. A friend told Amber about the RAD Consultancy and, realizing she had nothing to lose, Amber called and spoke to Aaron Lederer. After she described the problems she was having with Sally, Aaron said, "This is a classic case of attachment disorder combined with Sally being stuck in the terrible twos. We can probably help, but if you don't see improvement within six weeks, my diagnosis is incorrect and we will stop therapy."

Amber began phoning a counselor Aaron assigned to her every Tuesday morning at 9 a.m. Each week, the counselor gave Amber her instructions for the week. Amber followed the instructions the best she could—not

perfectly. After five months, the therapy was considered an unequivocal success by all who knew Sally and it was discontinued.

Sally dropped her bad friends. At school, her teachers were amazed by her improved attitude. Her grades began to climb and she began making friends with kids who had held her in disdain just a few months earlier. At home, Sally began to enjoy spending time with her parents. As Amber put it, "We went from 'F-you' to 'I love you.'"

Now 20, Sally is doing well at college away from home. She calls home regularly and talks enthusiastically about school and friends. She consults with Amber on problems she encounters and ends each call with, "I love you, Mom."

◆   ◆   ◆

The question is: Do we, as a society and as individual parents, want the first Sally story or the second? The first Sally story left society with one illegitimate, parentless child somewhere in the adoption mill, an unemployable woman dependent on social services, and an abandoned ten-year-old boy at risk of becoming as dysfunctional as his mother. The second Sally story puts an end to the cycle of dysfunction. Which Sally will your child be?

Today, we are facing an epidemic in the number of wild children, most likely caused by teen pregnancies, mothers needing to keep full-time jobs too soon after giving birth, and more and more overseas adoptions.

But there is hope. The corrective communication process taught by the RAD Consultancy actually turns these angry, emotionally damaged victims of early childhood deprivations into happy, well-adjusted children who grow to become affectionate and productive adults. Let's give them what they need.

25421 8BV00001B/2/P

26 January 2011
Breinigsville, PA USA

THE BLUE DEVILS OF NADA
A Contemporary American Approach to Aesthetic Statement

Informed on every page by its author's ardor, intelligence, and verbal fire, *The Blue Devils of Nada* inquires into the blues aesthetic, in arenas that range from music to painting, dismantling many a stereotype along the way. To Murray, the blues are neither a protest nor a lament, but a vibrant, complex, and playful expression of transcendence through sheer style. And style is what he illuminates in the work of such artists as Duke Ellington, Louis Armstrong, Romare Bearden, and Ernest Hemingway.

African American Studies/0-679-75859-3

THE HERO AND THE BLUES

In this visionary book, Murray takes an audacious new look at black music and, in the process, succeeds in changing the way we read all literature. His subject is the previously unacknowledged kinship between fiction and the blues. Both, he argues, are virtuoso performances that impart information, wisdom, and moral guidance to their audiences. Both place a high value on improvisation. And both create a delicate balance between the holy and the obscene, essential human values and cosmic absurdity.

Nonfiction/0-679-76220-5

SOUTH TO A VERY OLD PLACE

South to a Very Old Place is a classic African American memoir of growing up in Alabama during the 1920s and 1930s by the highly acclaimed novelist, biographer, music, social, and literary critic Albert Murray. Intermingling remembrances of youth with engaging conversation, African American folklore, and astute cultural criticism, it is at once an intimate personal journey and an incisive social history.

Autobiography/0-679-73695-6

VINTAGE INTERNATIONAL
Available at your local bookstore, or call toll-free to order:
1-800-793-2665 (credit cards only).

ALSO BY ALBERT MURRAY

TRAIN WHISTLE GUITAR

Train Whistle Guitar is a deceptively gentle coming-of-age novel, set in 1920s Gasoline Point, Alabama, which resounds with the whine of sawmills, the whistle of trains, and the pungent voices of its citizens. Scooter learns everything he needs to know in Miss Lexine Metcalf's classroom and Papa Gumbo Willie McWorthy's barbershop—and everything he's *not* supposed to know from older girls. But most of all, Scooter learns from Luzanna Cholly who carries a .32-20 in his shoulder-holster and plays guitar "as if he were also an engineer telling tall tales on a train whistle."

Fiction/0-375-70336-5

THE SPYGLASS TREE

The Spyglass Tree is a deeply affecting novel of elegant, lyrical reminiscence and profound sophistication about a young black man's advent into the world of academia—an imaginary Alabama college—in the 1930s. Amidst the excitement of the world of ideas and adventures with new friends, Scooter sallies into "the territory of the blues," where recollection becomes legend. Here he learns to deal with the vicissitudes of life—the complexities of family ties and camaraderie, his sexuality, pride of excellence in school, the darker realities of history and human passion—through confrontation and improvisation, and with style and courage.

Fiction/Literature/0-679-73085-0

THE SEVEN LEAGUE BOOTS

With *The Seven League Boots*, Murray gives us what is at once an African American coming-of-age novel and a pitch-perfect evocation of a touring jazz band at the height of the Swing era. Scooter graduates from an Alabama college and becomes a bass player in an ensemble headed by the legendary Bossman. As he criss-crosses the United States, Scooter and his bandmates find themselves retracing Sherman's march to the sea, the Underground Railroad, and the conquest of the West.

Fiction/0-679-75858-5